ONLY A
SACRIFICE CAN SAVE
THE LAND

THE DRAGON'S BRIDE

CHRISTIS CHRISTIE & ELLE BEAUMONT

Midnight Tide
PUBLISHING

GLOSSARY

PEOPLE. PLACES. PRONUNCIATIONS.

Brynjar (BRIN-yahr), meaning warrior in armor. The name of the country.

Ragnhild (ray-neal), meaning goddess or warrior. Ragnhild is the capital city of Brynjar.

Seidr (say-der) a Norse practice of magic, but in this book, they are much like elves and practice elemental magic.

Jord (yord), meaning earth

Hjemlstad (HE-yelm-stad)

Fafnir Jarvi (fahv-nir YAR-vee), meaning dragon lake

Fjellbrod (yell-brot), a whole wheat and rye flour bread with a variety of seeds and rolled oat

Risgrot (rees-gr-OT), a dish made from rice mixed with water or milk

Lajos (LYE-oh-sh), meaning famed warrior. Ronar's nickname amongst the people.

Skolleboller (scole-bawl-uh), a sweet, vanilla custard filled pastry

Kardemommeboller (KAR-de-mum-boo-lar), a pastry that is twisted and tied into a knot, sprinkled with sugar and cardamom seeds.

Eristyminen (AYR-es-ta-min-in), meaning isolation. An island occupied by Dragon Master Synda.

Cuyler (ki-el-er), meaning victory of the people. Cuyler is the High Mage.

Alfhild (AHLF-hilD), meaning battle of elves. The neighboring human village of Omdahl.

Mount Jotunn (Yo-Ton)

Jarl (Yarl)

For Papa, this one is for you.
Thank you for all of your tall tales, incessant teasing, and showing me what a truly stubborn person is like. I love you.
I miss you.
~Elle

For Natalie, who has shown what true strength in the face of great loss actually looks like. Just like Imara, I hope you always stand tall and hold your ground. Remember, you are fierce.
~Christis

IMARA

With a slight press of the blade tied to her belt, the stem of the witch hazel snapped between her fingers, coming away from the body of the plant to be placed in the small pile in her lap. Overhead, the sun shone down upon her shoulders with an almost blistering heat—unobscured by even the smallest of clouds. Imara couldn't remember the last time the noonday sun had been pleasant, rather than a sweltering force to abide, the days trying to hold on to the last dregs of a fading summer as fall approached.

"Oh, this won't do," she murmured to herself, examining the sprig, then the bush as a whole.

"What was that?" came a voice from over her shoulder.

Imara leaned back onto her heels and lifted her hand to brush the back of her wrist across her forehead, ending with a swipe of her fingers through the blond strands of hair at her temple, tucking them behind one delicately pointed ear. The grass-covered roof beneath her had seen better days. Where once thick, luscious green blades had grown, now yellow spiky strands fought to stay alive. What life was left in the soil had been driven toward the herbs and flowers Imara had planted several years ago, her father doing what he could to keep her garden alive.

"This witch hazel is dry as a bone. I don't know that I'll get much more than this harvest out of it," she stated, glancing over at her sister currently struggling to draw water from the soil around the house, sprinkling it over the rooftop garden once it had gathered upon her fingertips in small, perfectly formed spheres.

Words hardly free of Imara's lips, a spray of water splashed over her face and down the front of her. "Asta, the garden, not my face!"

Imara shot an irritated glare at her sister, who released a giggle of surprise before offering an apologetic smile.

"I'm sorry, that wasn't intentional, I promise. I wasn't paying enough attention to where I was pointing," Asta explained, reaching out to brush a few drops of water from Imara's face. Collecting them with a soft tickle of magic upon her skin, she turned to sprinkle them over the bush of witch hazel.

"Fortunately, it was rather refreshing." Imara cast an accusatory glance toward the sun. Whatever relief could be found from its rays was welcomed.

She brushed a trickle of water along her own temples, Asta turned and plopped down at the edge of the roof, her feet braced where the roof became actual ground. "When do you expect Birger today?"

Clipping one last branch from the bush, Imara turned to sit beside Asta, her eyes drifting over their lands. Situated just a stone's throw away from the village of Omdahl, their little farm was immersed in a breathtaking landscape of rolling hills dappled with tall, branchy trees and split below by a winding river that reflected the blue skies above. The seidr had chosen this valley to settle in many moons ago due to the snow-capped mountains that loomed on either side, majestic giants of protection that graciously supplied fresh spring water to the village and its inhabitants. The valley had also been a land of opportunity, its soil rich and fertile—the perfect place for a people known to cherish the earth and all that she supplied to take root themselves.

Their family plot had been the ideal location for raising sheep and growing cotton—the supply for Dagny Hjelmstad's beautiful woven fabrics and tapestries. Erlend had seen in these fields everything he had hoped to give his new wife: the home, the opportunity, the prospering family. It was everything—until the rains stopped coming, the river began to dry up, and the soil turned to dust beneath their feet.

"He usually arrives about midday, once he has passed through Omdahl proper and spoken to anyone who has dealings with him there." Imara glanced down at the small pile of witch hazel in her lap—not nearly the offering she had hoped to have once he arrived but the best that she had to give.

Asta peered up at the sun, gauging the time by its position in the sky. "It's half past two, but is there time for a quick drink before we need to bundle and prepare that?" she asked, eyes flicking quickly to indicate the witch hazel.

Nodding slightly, Imara pulled up the corners of the blue apron-skirt layered over her green shift, containing all of the branches she had cut, and rose to her feet. Having been outdoors for some time now, a break from the sunshine was more than warranted by both.

"Yes, let's fetch ourselves some water and perhaps run some down to Father. He's been working in the fields since early this morning." Keeping the corners of her apron-skirt swept up, Imara walked off the roof and down the small bank to the front of their home, the curved white frame set just inside the hillside as familiar to her as her own self.

Toeing the partially opened door all the way, she stepped into their home. Her mother, Dagny, stood before a loom, a finger tapping idly upon her lips as she contemplated it. Moving easily to her side, Imara pressed a soft kiss to her cheek.

"It looks beautiful, Mother, as all your pieces do. Jorunn will love it," she murmured in passing, slipping by to deposit her collection of branches onto the table.

"Thank you, Mari," was her mother's contemplative response.

Behind her, Asta came into the house with a flourish of cotton skirts and the scent of spring rain, her elemental affinity so strong she wore it like a mantle upon herself. As Imara brushed a few lost yellow petals off her skirt, her sister got busy pouring them glasses of water from the tap in the wall.

"Is Father down in the western field today?" Imara asked, reaching for the clay goblet Asta held out to her. The fresh mountain water was crisp and cold, sending a blessed chill through her body. A grateful sigh escaped her lips, shoulders relaxing as she soaked up the moment of relief.

"No, he took the sheep to the north pastures, so he

ventured to the southern field instead to see how it is faring," Dagny murmured in a distant tone, her attention remaining more on the tapestry before her than on the girls.

Her questions answered, Imara finished her goblet of water and placed it on the counter beneath the tap. Freeing a water flask from the cabinet below, she worked on filling it with water, the tap squeaking softly in her grip.

"I'll take Ishka down," she said to Asta, letting her know there would be no need to walk down with her. "Should I take him a bite to eat as well?"

Her sister plucked a ripened apple from the basket on the table and brought it over to her. Once upon a time, Magnhild's apples had been so large one needed almost to hold it up with two hands to take a bite. Now, the crisp fruit nestled easily in her palm as she accepted it and slid it into the pocket looped around her belt.

"If Birger arrives before I've returned, please ask him to wait. I will be but a moment," she asked of Asta, who nodded with understanding.

"Of course."

With a smile of thanks, Imara stepped out the door and back into the bright sunshine, the ground crunching beneath her soles with every step toward the paddock. Sensing her approach, Ishka wandered over, her snowy coat gleaming against the backdrop of hills, mountains, and sky. There was a brief moment of nuzzling as girl and horse greeted one another, and then Imara mounted the mare and they were off, down the lane leading to the cotton fields closest to the river.

Fingers twined lightly in the horse's mane, Imara

started her in the right direction, then left the rest to Ishka. This trek down to the lower fields had been made so many times in days past that both horse and rider could have made it in the dead of night without even the glow of the moon to light their way. While communication with animals was not an elemental strength, nor could she have tapped into it if it were, there was an unspeakable bond between them, a way of understanding each other that had been there since Ishka had been a foal and given into Imara's care.

It was a swift, and easy ride down to the southern field. Spotting her father kneeled down with his hands in the soil, Imara slid off the horse's back. Smoothing a soft touch down the side of her neck, she praised Ishka for a job well done.

"Stay here, girl." With her parting words, Imara pulled her skirts up above her ankles to keep them from sticking to the cotton as she went by and headed down the row her father was in.

Down on one knee in the brown soil, his palms on the earth itself, Erlend Hjelmstad was muttering softly beneath his breath. While she could not make out the words, Imara instinctively knew that they were words of summoning, and her father was trying desperately to pull nutrients and life from deep within the ground and up into the topsoil their crop was planted in. Sensing her behind him, Erlend stopped. His head lifted and he gazed back at her over his shoulder, blue eyes a mirror of her own, shining with love as he took her in.

"Imara, haven't you a trader to meet with this

afternoon?" he asked, running a soiled hand through short-cropped blond hair.

"It isn't quite time for that, and I thought you could do with some fresh water." Her hands were already upon the flask at her waist. Loosening it from her belt, she uncapped the top and held it out to him.

A look of gratefulness came over his features, and without further prodding, he stood, taking the water flask from her and tipping it back. As her father drank, Imara held a hand to her forehead, shielding her eyes from the sunlight so that she could survey the area around her. While the soil was meant to be brown, the cracked nature of it was worrisome. Both her mother and sister had been down here the day before, pulling what water there was left to the surface. It looked as if nothing had been done at all.

"It's not going so well, is it?" she asked, eyes returning to her father at last.

Erlend swiped a hand across his lips.

"No, it is not. I'm doing what I can, but there is simply nothing left in the ground to pull out of it." His hand motioned to the grounds around the cotton field. Just two months ago, they had borne green grasses and wildflowers; now they were withered, yellow, and barren.

"Is it even worth it anymore?" Imara questioned, taking in the sight of the cotton plants, perhaps only a third of them bearing anything worth gathering.

The decline had started gradually, beginning with hotter-than-typical days and a lack of fresh rain. With two water elementals in the family, fewer rainy days had never been an issue before. But then the grounds dried up faster than what had made sense. The grasses withered, flowers began dying, and everywhere one looked, the world was turning brown.

There had been difficult farming years in the past, but elemental abilities had always been able to combat it.

"To be honest, I'm not so certain. This won't be enough to supply what your mother needs for her fabrics . . . The yield simply isn't there this year." Erlend shook his head, his frustrations melting away into something resembling defeat.

It would have been nice to reach out a comforting hand and reassure him. However, reassurance wasn't something that Imara had to give. Not when, everywhere they looked, their neighbors were fighting the same effects. Each day seemed to bring new struggles, and with the lack of crops this harvest, people were beginning to question if they would have enough to get them through the winter, let alone hold over until next year for planting.

"Will there be enough wool to compensate?" They had not lost any numbers from the flock, the sheep hardy enough to withstand poorer grazing. Whether their coats had held up would be the next question.

"We'll see when we start shearing in a couple of weeks." The look in his eyes wasn't necessarily hopeful, which was difficult to see.

"What of our offerings for the Dragon Master? Do we need to lessen the amount we give?"

Each Fallfest, the residents of Omdahl welcomed Lord Lajos the Dragon Master to their celebrations. A powerful being who resided in the forests surrounding the mountains, he had centuries ago come to an agreement with the founding Elders of their village. At the commencement of the fall harvest, each household in Omdahl would provide a portion of their yearly produce, cattle, or craftmanship to him, and in return, he would keep the dragons in the woods from raining fire down upon them all.

It was a burden felt heavily by each citizen this year.

Erlend sighed. "We cannot, you know it. Each family offers up the same portion of their goods. We are not the only ones suffering this season. There can be no leniency for us if it is not offered also to them." His features were pinched with concern.

Imara's father had always been a lighthearted man. While he worked long, hard days to care for their crops and the flock, he had always upheld a cheerful countenance. Worry was a weighted cloak that had come only recently to rest on the Hjelmstad family's shoulders.

"Something will work out," Imara assured him, feigning confidence she did not feel. Pressing a soft kiss to his cheek, she left him to his work and returned to Ishka, who awaited her patiently.

As Imara came up the hill to the family house, she was welcomed by the sight of a small horse-drawn cart covered by a canvas tarp that hid several items beneath. It was a sight that brought a smile to her lips, and without thought, she urged Ishka on a little faster. The days of splurging were behind them, but her trade relationship with Birger was the one allowance Imara still afforded herself. It came at no cost to her family, her small rooftop garden supplying the barter items Birger required for their exchanges.

The cart's seat sat empty, his horses standing

unattended and unconcerned. Releasing Ishka back into the paddock, Imara was drawn toward the open door of their home, familiar voices sounding out from its depths.

Inside she found her mother and sister seated at the table with Birger, who was in the midst of sipping tea from a clay mug. Her presence did not go unnoticed, and all three turned to look her way, greeting her with three unique smiles.

"Miss Imara!" Birger called. Setting down his tea, he held his hand out to her, which she took as she approached. The rough fingers used to holding leather reins gave hers a fond squeeze. "As always, it is a pleasure to see you. I managed to find not two but three of the volumes you were seeking."

Smiling at the warm greeting, she pulled out the wooden chair beside him and took a seat, noticing that the witch hazel she had picked this morning was neatly bundled in cheesecloth and tied with twine—Asta had been kind in her absence.

As they began to speak, her mother left the table to fill their little teapot with more water from the tap. As she turned back toward the table, her hand rested upon its ceramic side until steam rose from the white spout. A mug with tea leaves nestled in the bottom was placed before Imara, and then her mother poured in the now steaming liquid, leaving the perfect amount of room for a dollop of cream to be added once she was ready. Imara waited for the leaves to settle at the bottom, then added a tiny portion of cream from the small jug on the table. Letting it all steep for the time being, she peered over at their guest.

"That is wonderful to hear, but I don't know that what

I have is worth three hard-sought-after books on mage medicines. Try as I might, I couldn't keep the witch hazel from drying out," she explained.

"Nonsense," he replied. "Our arrangement has always been my books for one bunch of witch hazel, and that is what you've offered up."

"Yes, but—"

"Imara." He reached out to rest his hand over the top of hers on the table. "I've seen the state of Omdahl." He shook his head before continuing. "I'm not looking for more than what you are able to give right now."

IMARA

Birger stayed until the end of tea, passing on tales of all the places he had visited within Brynjar as a whole but most specifically of his weeks in the capital. Imara always found the stories of Ragnhild to be the most fascinating, the lives of those living in and around the castle both similar to their own and yet so vastly different. It felt as if they lived on the other side of the continent rather than the kingdom.

Men and women vied for royal favor from the human king, and in the process, risked everything they had. Vendors bickered over whose stall was encroaching on whose territory. Knights in leather and armor encrusted with the king's seal marched through the streets, maintaining order. Citizens by the thousands went about their day-to-day business all amidst the crush of the city. The bustle of the capital was intriguing. So much so that Imara wished to experience it herself, so as to understand fully the picture Birger had painted for them, yet she had no wish to live where every waking moment was overseen by so many others.

A small collective of seidrs did live in the capital city,

acting as council for King Thorne when he had need of it and selling their abilities to the humans with enough coin to purchase it. While a giant village made of stone buildings and cobblestone streets sounded mesmerizing to witness, it was too far from the things of nature that made life worth living to their kind. Seidrs needed access to their elements to feel complete, and Imara wasn't sure how those in Ragnhild managed.

"Imara, can you please not read those at the table? I need to set it for the evening meal."

Before her were spread the three books Birger had brought her, in-depth looks at the procedures and medicines commonly used by the mages. While the seidr were capable of magic when they tapped into their specific element, medicinal magics were limited in their cultures and relied more heavily upon knowledge of herbs and potions or manipulating internal water or mineral levels. Imara was not a physician by trade, nor even considered a medicine woman, but she believed if she could focus her mind and her natural abilities on research and learning, perhaps she could bring to their village something useful, something that did not require an affinity to the elements.

"Sorry, Mother." Imara looked up, blinking in surprise at the time. The house had begun to grow dim as evening approached. She had been so engrossed in her study that she hadn't realized what time it was.

Standing, Imara closed up the books and stacked them one on top of the other, then moved them over to rest on the bottom of the steps so she would remember to take them up to her room.

"Turn the lights on, girls, would you please?" Dagny

requested, her back to them as she worked on finishing up their evening meal.

Behind Imara, Asta moved from one wall-mounted crystal to another, tapping them lightly in passing so that they began to glow from the inside, filling the room with a warm yellow light. Imara reached out to the one nearest her. Placing her hand over the globe, she took a deep breath and focused all her energy on reaching out to the depths of the crystal and finding that small part of herself that connected to it. With as much strength of will as she could muster, Imara lit hers. By this time, Asta had lit the rest.

It would be easy to be envious of the ease with which her family used their elemental magic from day to day, but Imara had long ago learned to contribute in her own way, without the aid of the elements.

"Father, dinner is being set," Imara called out into the yard. She spotted Erlend down by the gate, near the road, speaking with someone whose features she could not make out due to the encroaching dusk.

"Will Imara and I be going to market tomorrow morning, Mother?" Asta asked, moving around the kitchen.

"Yes, Magnhild's expecting her tapestry."

Imara waited until her father signaled with a wave of his hand that he had heard, then turned back to the kitchen. With the ease of two who had worked side by side for all of their lives, the girls prepared the table. Plates and goblets were set down, a pitcher of water and the basket of Imara's fresh bread loaves, made just the day before, finished off their work.

"Are we leaving for the market first thing in the morning?" Imara asked, glancing over at Asta as she placed a platter on the table. In the center, a steaming lamb roast sat, surrounded by what remained of the vegetables from last year's harvest.

"That's fine by me."

Soon enough, their father was coming in through the front door, tapping his toes on the doorframe before stepping inside. He looked worn and tired, his body showing signs of a man who had spent the entire day in a losing battle and was only just now deciding it had been for naught.

With Erlend inside the house, the family settled at the table. A quick word of thanks to Mother Earth for their bounty was murmured, and then each reached for the food before them. Picking off a small piece of lamb, Imara placed the savory meat on her tongue, chewing slowly. Around her were the soothing, familiar sounds of her family eating together, but rather than be lulled into a peaceful frame of mind, Imara found herself still curious.

"Who were you speaking to out at the gate?" she asked finally.

"It was Holger, asking if by chance we would like to purchase his hog," Erlend explained.

"But he always butchers in the fall. Why would he sell it now and not keep for himself?" her mother asked, confusion on her face as she carefully broke her small loaf in two.

"He and Selby have decided to pack up and head into Ragnhild to see if they mightn't have better fortune there."

There was a shocked silence around the table as the

rest of the family sought to process the information. This was the first time that Imara could remember one of the families in Omdahl selling off their livelihoods and moving away.

"They're leaving?" It was Asta who spoke, surprise evident in her tone.

"The fish have all but died off. What with all that washed up on the riverbanks last week, there's simply nothing left to catch. Holger relied on the fish to fill in for the loss of his corn and wheat fields."

There was further silence until at last, Dagny spoke. "Will we be taking the hog, then?"

"I told him we would. In exchange for one bolt of your blue wool. They ought to be able to fetch a good price for it in the capital."

Her mother nodded in agreement, and that was the end of the conversation for the moment as the family ate, their thoughts all on similar matters. How many more would eventually pack up and leave Omdahl, and would it come to that for them too?

Early the next morning, the crystal on the wall of their room, spelled to go off at dawn, woke Imara and Asta from their sleep. Slipping from bed with only minor grumbles of sleepiness, Imara lit the crystal to full brightness, feeling the weariness of the struggle to do so within herself.

Meanwhile, Asta swept her hand over the basin on their dressing table, filling it with water that she warmed with just a murmur under her breath. Their mornings were routine by now, each moving around the other with ease as they dressed for the day.

Downstairs, they were quick to have breakfast, cleaning up after themselves before they were off to hitch Ishka to the cart and load it with bolts of fabric and the tapestry for Magnhild.

Imara turned her head to the side as a guttural grunt sounded. Holger must have dropped the hog off already, which meant they planned to leave *soon*. Not that she could blame them, but this was *their* home and *their* land. It was only a matter of time before things turned for the better, right?

Asta quirked a brow in question as Imara sat next to her.

"The hog is here already," Imara said, gathering up the reins.

"Already? I didn't realize Holger meant to bring it today. I guess it's a good thing we're heading to the market."

Indeed, agreed Imara silently, and put an end to the thought. Their family now had food, and their friends would prosper in the capital. She clucked to Ishka, wiggling the reins, and off they headed toward the market.

A quarter of an hour later, they arrived in the bustling marketplace. Most of the vendors' faces were drawn, eyebrows narrowed, and lips thinned. These were not joyous times for anyone, and produce was becoming quite scarce, which drove up prices. The humans in the neighboring village had refused to barter with the seidr, encouraged by their town mages to keep for themselves what crops they had. The dislike between their kinds only grew stronger.

"It's strange. Just a fortnight ago, t'was fertile and green. Now the garden is ash," one of the vendors ranted.

Ishka wove through the narrow market until they came to a halt in front of Selby's stall. Staring off into the distance, a pleasant smile tugged at the woman's lips, but the tiredness and hollow look in her eyes didn't match it. The expression was becoming more and more frequent amongst the villagers as the months dragged on.

"Good morning, Selby," Imara said as she hopped from the cart. She nodded to Asta, who also slipped down and perused the vendors for the list of goods they came for.

Pulled from her thoughts, Selby's smile disappeared quickly at the sight of Imara before her. "Oh . . . Imara. Morning. Holger tells me you have some fabric to give me." She motioned toward the cart, then promptly put her fist on her hip.

Selby's words were curt, more so than usual. Though it was something Imara was used to, Selby typically made a better effort to hide it. Unlike others. Imara was, after all, considered a blight on their village and fairly useless in their eyes. There was more to life than magic, however, in spite of what the villagers thought.

"Yes, I do. You'll be able to make a good amount on this fabric in the capital." Imara pulled the bolt of fabric from the cart carefully and handed it to Selby. "This shade is popular right now." She smiled, lifting a hand to tuck one of her errant curls behind her ear.

"It'll do." Selby sighed and tucked the bolt into her belongings. She waved Imara off and went back to organizing her goods. "Be on your way now, girl."

It wasn't as if Imara wanted to linger around the woman, but she was curious as to why she and Holger were leaving so abruptly. "Have a good day, Selby." Despite the woman's sour attitude, Imara still offered her a smile—even if within, a tangent brewed. "Let's find Asta," she murmured to Ishka.

Climbing back up into her seat, she didn't bother to give the other woman another glance, for surely Selby had already put Imara far from her mind. Snapping the reins gently, Ishka pulled them forward, and Imara steered her down the main street of Omdahl, searching for her sister. Riotous energy typically reigned in the market. Voices would rise, tempers would flare over haggling, and bards would line up to play a tune in hopes of gaining extra coin. But lately, the markets weren't as lively, not with the lack of things to sell. Nevertheless, the lack of people in the marketplace made it easier for Imara to maneuver the horse and cart along.

A familiar laugh hung in the air, one that brought a smile to Imara's face. Pulling the cart to a halt, Imara hopped down, heading over to her sister. Asta possessed a lyrical laugh that suited her; while it was a touch loud, it wasn't bothersome, and it brought joy to those in her company. Not surprisingly, the cantankerous man Asta spoke with chuckled along with her—that was, until Imara stepped into his sight behind her. *Of course,* Imara thought bitterly.

The burly vendor smiled at Asta, then stroked his

cheek. "If you return in two days' time, I should be able to fulfill that order. The land isn't as it used to be. She's a touch slower these days, but have no fear, I will get this done for you."

Asta's eyes brightened, and she turned on her heel to face Imara. "What a nice man!"

The man lifted a hand to scrub the back of his neck, then his eyes darted to Imara. As if suddenly remembering himself, his face fell into a blank look. He waved to Asta and turned back to his work.

"What a nice man, indeed." Imara waved her sister on and continued down the way until a middle-aged woman approached them. Beauty amongst the seidrs wasn't uncommon, but this woman, although aged, was stunning. Silvery hair fell over her shoulder in several tidy braids, and though her skin was creased with a few wrinkles, she bore them well.

The woman drew in a breath then reached out and grabbed Asta's hand. "You're Dagny's girls, yes?" She posed the question to both of them, yet her eyes remained glued to Imara, who stood just behind Asta.

Beautiful or not, Imara wasn't going to allow someone to grab her sister. Stepping around Asta, Imara situated herself between the two and lifted a brow. "We are. Can I be of help?"

Imara's actions must have brought the woman back to the present, and she sighed. "Yes, sorry. It's only that . . . " She paused for a moment, glanced down, and chewed her bottom lip. "I was wondering if you might have some fabric. I'm low on funds, so perhaps you have something of lesser quality? Between my magic faltering and the orchards drying up . . . " The woman teared up and lifted a hand to her face. "Forgive me. I've never seen our soil this terrible before. It's . . . infertile. We'll be run out soon."

The ground itself was sick. Once-grassy knolls were swiftly becoming sandy dunes; trees were drying up and snapping. It wasn't just the flora that was crumbling but the fauna too. The livestock amongst the village was suffering, and as soon as winter came, many would die.

Shaking her head, Imara took the liberty of reaching out for the woman's hands. "No need to apologize. It's been a bad season. I have a bolt of fabric I think you'd like. What did you say your name was?" Imara walked to the cart and pulled out a piece of soft green fabric.

"Linnea. Thank you, girls, thank you."

"This will do." She handed the bolt over, and in turn received a small pouch of coins. "Be well, Linnea." Toying with the bag in her hands, Imara's mind mulled over everyone's words thus far. There had to be a solution to the problem, but trucking in more earth wasn't it. That had been done, and nothing had come from it, nor from fertilizing the land.

A squeal filled the air, causing Imara to jump. She twisted her lips and folded her arms as she watched Asta spin around with one of her foolish suitors. "Asta, we don't have time to play today," Imara said, in hopes the dark-haired male would take the hint. He didn't; it seemed he took it as an invitation to step into Imara's space.

"Maybe Asta does. There is always time to get to know your better half, don't you agree, Imara?" His eyes focused on her, and even though Asta swatted his arm, he continued to stare.

Blood rushed into Imara's cheeks. Never once had she been courted. Not that she was old, but no one had ever shown interest in her. They all knew her skills were quite limited, and wouldn't it have been horrible if her progeny had no magic at all? It was something all the villagers murmured about. "There is a time for play and a time for work. We cannot afford to dally. Come along, Asta." What his name was, Imara didn't know and certainly didn't care. He was a face among many who came looking for Asta.

"Anders meant nothing by it, Imara. It's just been a while since we saw each other!"

Imara's gaze flicked to her sister, and she shook her head. "We have a few more deliveries and a few things to pick up still. Once we're done, you can go see him." She laughed at the dramatic groan that followed.

After they were done delivering their goods, Asta began readying to leave the marketplace, until the sounds of shrieking and gasps filled the once quiet hum of the area.

What was that? Imara instinctively rushed forward and grabbed her sister's elbow, stopping her from running. "Stay with me," she demanded. "I don't know what's happening, but you're not leaving until we find out."

"He's bleeding!" a voice cried.

"Is he dead?" another shouted.

"He's alive, but barely. It was a mage—a mage did this to him."

A mage? Deep in Imara's bones, she knew this was the dawn of something terrible. Relations with the human village of Alfhild had never been the most peaceful. While the seidrs were tied to the earth through their elemental magic, the humans toiled with only their hands. The closest they came to magic was through crystals. Humans had discovered that channeling natural energy through precious stones such as quartz, agate, and amethyst dug from deep within the earth gave them the ability to cast spells, create elixirs, and do more than their human bodies would allow. Thus, the mages had been formed.

It had still not been enough.

Seidrs looked down on mages for toying with powers they did not feel humans understood. Mages looked upon seidrs with disgust for naturally possessing that which they craved.

Omdahl should have been able to turn to their neighbors in this time of need, as their animals starved and their crops failed, but tensions which were already high between the villages had only increased with the rise of the High Mage. Cuyler Hagen felt no love for the seidrs and made it quite clear that he felt their time had come and passed, and now was the time for the mages to rise and conquer. It had not made for peaceful dealings between Omdahl and Alfhild.

Imara squeezed Asta's hand and pulled her toward the cart. They had to get home. There was nothing either of them could do here.

The market erupted into further disorder the moment the wounded man collapsed to the ground. Much to Imara's dismay, she couldn't hear anything except for what was repeated or shrieked. Mages, for the most part, stayed away from Omdahl. Despite how they were seen by many here as heretics, harnessing Jörd's energy in ways it was not meant to be tapped into, there had never been violence between them and the seidrs before.

"I don't understand," Asta shouted over the noise. "Why hurt someone?" Panic creased Asta's brows, and her bottom lip trembled.

Imara didn't have an answer for that, and she didn't know the whole of the matter either. Curiosity itched and nagged her, but it was unwise to stay here. She couldn't peel her eyes from the gathering mob. "I can't say, but there is no place for us in the midst of this. Let's get home." Ishka squealed in annoyance as people backed into the path.

"He took only a blow to the head. He will be fine," a voice called. "Clear back!"

It was just as well that the two sisters were leaving, but

Imara took a moment to bow her head and send up a prayer to the gods, thanking them for protecting the villager. There would be no death today, but the uneasy feeling still unfurled within. Clucking to Ishka, she pushed the horse on and headed home.

The sisters were quiet on the trip back, neither finding the words to express their concerns over what had happened in the marketplace. It didn't sit well with Imara. Why would the mages choose to attack someone for simply traveling on the streets? The answer was hardly likely to bring any peace of mind.

When they arrived back at the farm, Dagny was mixing a batch of wool inside a wooden tub of dye outside of their home. The fiber drank the cornflower pigment in greedily, coloring the once-white wool a brilliant shade. Her head jerked up the moment the cart pulled down the dirt path, and she dropped the paddle she was using.

Hastily, Dagny clutched the fabric of her skirt and ran. "Girls! Oh, my girls. I'm glad you're all right. Your father caught wind of the mayhem on the road. He saw a carriage barreling toward the market. Did you see anything?"

Imara's eyes darted toward Asta and back toward her mother. "We did. The man the mages assaulted will live, but did Father say anything as to why he was attacked?"

"No, he left to speak with the Elders immediately. It's something they must know." Dagny leaned forward and placed a kiss on Imara's cheek and then Asta's. "Unload the goods and start on supper." She lifted her hand and brushed her thumb against Asta's cheek. "It'll be all right. We all will be all right."

Whether she spoke for her own benefit or for theirs,

Imara couldn't say. With a nod, she and Asta gathered up the supplies from the cart and brought them inside.

That evening, they waited on supper for as long as they could, the daylight outside having faded beyond the hills and their supper having been kept over the fire until it was nearly charred. At last, their mother decided that they should eat, and Erlend could be seen to once he returned. Though none of them spoke it aloud, the length of his absence concerned them.

A darkness overshadowed their village now, one that would only worsen as the days went by, and with it, Imara could feel a special type of dread building inside of her. Something was approaching, a change that would alter the course of all their lives.

Whether any of them were ready for it was yet to be seen.

When her father came through the door at last, they were seated near the fire, each with a basket of wool needing to be hand-pulled at their feet, their hands resting in their laps as they went through the motions of working without truly accomplishing anything. For the past hour, barely a word had been spoken between them, as if each was worried they may prolong his absence by breaking the silence.

Imara hadn't realized her ear had been trained toward

the door until the sound of his boots scraping at the step caused her shoulders to relax.

As he stepped through the door, all three dropped their work and moved about the kitchen. Dagny fussed over plating his meal while her daughters grabbed the bread and a goblet of wine, setting their offerings before him on the table as he claimed a seat with a weary sigh. His features were drawn, a crease of stress having made its way across his brow, and there was a darkness to his gaze that Imara had never seen before. Without saying anything, all three women pulled out a seat and sat down at the table with him, watching him as he took the first few ravenous bites of his dinner.

"There's to be a village meeting tonight. The Elders have called an emergency gathering. Everyone is to attend," he muttered around bites of rabbit stew.

"Tonight?" her mother questioned, confusion written upon her face. "What has happened, Erlend?"

"Oluf was not the only one attacked." This time he set his spoon down as he spoke, his eyes serious. "His young apprentice Sigurd was with him when they were ambushed on the road. The mages came from the forests banking the western valley, on the roads leading toward Vidar."

The dark foreboding swelled within her, making Imara's heart trip faster in her chest, as if something unavoidable loomed before them.

"Sigurd was slain there . . ." He seemed to have issues speaking these words, the sadness of a young life taken weighing down his voice. "Oluf barely escaped with his life. He says that there are more of them, an entire encampment of mages separating us from Vidar and any hope of help from Ragnhild." Alfhild was the only other nearby town, and it was filled with humans.

Asta gasped in distressed surprise, and without thought, Imara reached out to take her hand, squeezing it gently as they shared a look across the table.

"What can they possibly mean by this? Erlend . . . what is going on?" Dagny's fierce tone forced them all to look at her. Imara watched her father take her mother's hand in his, lifting it to his lips as their eyes met in a silent conversation between husband and wife.

"I am not certain, my dearest, but we will join our neighbors at the council hall tonight, and hopefully there will be answers for us all."

The council hall had been erected long after the village was well and truly established, so while the first homes had all been built into the hillside, their lovely, sculpted frames proudly protruding from under green rooftops of grass, the town council building was constructed of smooth, multi-colored stones from the riverbed. Its curling roof swept down over the sides and tipped up toward the sky at the edges, mimicking the breaking of a wave upon the shore. While a beautiful building, not even the welcoming light of the crystals glowing through the stained glass windows could lighten the mood of the villagers as they filed inside.

For once, the murmuring around Imara was not about her. Rather, hushed voices whispered words of suspicion, concern, and mounting dismay. Though their valley had always been a prosperous place that provided for its people, it was not the sort of place that evoked attacks from outside forces. And now that their soil had betrayed them, there was nothing anyone could hope to claim in raiding them.

Slipping through the crowds, Imara moved to take a seat upon the curved stone bench beside Asta, the elderly woman on the other side hurriedly moving her skirts to the side before Imara's hands could touch them by chance. The action made Imara's teeth clench, and a small muscle in her jaw tick, but a lifetime of sideways glances and barely veiled contempt had taught her to keep her silence. There was no changing the minds of a people centuries-old who had never seen one born with deficits before.

A hush fell over the villagers as the Council of Elders moved down the steps, heading into the center of the hall, which had been dug into the bedrock, the benches they sat upon curving around the center dais and creating a theater setting that amplified speech and gave everyone an equal opportunity to see and to speak.

The Elders were four of the oldest members of their village, grandchildren of the first seidr to move to the valley and found Omdahl. They had been chosen to act as a governing body, and used their centuries-old wisdom to help guide the village through major decisions, settle disputes, and pass judgment on dishonest or ill-intended actions on the rare occasion it was needed. There was an Elder to represent each of the four elements, a master in their class. While it need not be a position held for the duration of an Elder's lifespan, it had always been so in Omdahl. Renowned for his fire abilities, Elder Fridolf had been chosen to act as head of their council. Of the four, Elders Ranell, Ylva, and Jorunn had easily submitted to his lead, and done so for nigh on a century.

Tonight, they were here to hopefully explain what was happening on the outskirts of their village, and why it appeared they may be on the verge of being attacked by a horde of fanatical mages.

Elder Ranell lifted his arms to silence any of the remaining murmurs, capturing the attention of all within the building. "I am sure by now all have heard that Oluf Jorgenson was attacked on the roads leading to Vidar. That the attack came from a group of mages camped in the woods along that very road, and that his apprentice, Sigurd, was slain in the process of trying to escape."

For some, the announcement of Sigurd's death was a shock; several gasps and hushed conversations broke out among those seated. Imara found Sigurd's mother in the sea of faces. Seated across the room from them, her face was red and swollen from tears. She looked broken—faded —half the woman she used to be. It saddened Imara to see such sorrow in all its raw freshness. As if her thoughts were similar, Asta's hand slipped around Imara's, holding on firmly.

"This, however, was not the only act of aggression," Elder Jorunn said, raising her voice over the din of concerned voices. "The farms on the outskirts of town, closest to the roads leading into Vidar, were also attacked. The Karlssons and the Ibsens were run off their lands, and everything was burned. No one was slain, but everything they had has been destroyed."

This did nothing to calm the villagers. In all of the centuries they had resided in this valley, no one had ever brought violence to their doorstep.

Ranell held up a hand to silence them once more. "We have spoken in depth with Oluf, as well as the Karlssons and the Ibsens. Scouts of our own have also been sent out to survey the situation." His features were becoming graver as he spoke. "While we do not have reason to believe an attack on the village is imminent, we do believe this to be an act of war. High Mage Cuyler Hagen has gathered human and mage forces to cut off all access points toward Ragnhild. There will be no help coming from the capital."

This time the words were not whispered—the hall erupted into chaos as each man and woman attempted to be heard over the one beside them, thus filling the council hall with riotous sound.

"Why?"

"But we're not soldiers!"

"What are we to do?"

The chorus of concern rang out around them, and Imara felt their terror like a tangible presence in the room. Already frayed nerves were finding themselves now pulled taut, ready to snap at the first sign of more danger.

It was Elder Ylva who spoke next. Stepping apart from the others, she slowly turned, giving the impression that she was meeting each of their gazes. It was enough to dim the discord to a gentle rumble.

"Your fears are not ill-founded, and we mirror them within ourselves. This is why we've called you all together tonight instead of waiting for the morning light. We have found ourselves in a confusing and fearful time, but I beg of you, lend us your ears rather than your cries."

It was enough to soothe them for the moment, enough for Elder Fridolf to take her place at the center.

"Tomorrow night is the beginning of Fallfest." As they cried out in protest at the thought of celebrating at a time like this, he held his hand up to silence them before continuing. "The Dragon Master will be in attendance to receive his annual tributes from each household, and the council is in full agreement that we should offer him extra tribute in return for protection against the mages on our border."

Angry voices rang out once more at the idea. A chorus of frustrations trumpeted around them, echoing off the ceiling and acting as a battle cry. Fruitlessly, the Elders waved their arms, attempting to stem the tide of displeasure. Eventually, a tall dark-haired man stood. Imara recognized him as Magnhild's husband, an earth elemental who owned the local orchard.

"And what does the Council of Elders suggest we add to our tributes? My household has struggled to gather our portion owed, and we barely have enough to see us through the coming winter. What more are we to add?" He peered around him at his fellow villagers. "I know my neighbors find themselves in the same position. The waters are drying up, the soil turning to dust in the fields, and our crops dying by the acre. Why should this Dragon Master eat like a king upon the mountaintop, on what has taken our blood and tears to grow, while we starve?"

"Alfons is right. What good will his help do any of us if we are all to starve to death in the end?" another shouted.

"Stop speaking in such a manner, you'll bring his fury down upon all of us!" came a cry from the upper tier of benches. "What if he were to unleash his dragons?"

Imara's hand tightened around Asta's. The hostile energy in the room needed to be broken before a fight broke out.

"Brothers and sisters, please!" It was Ranell once more, shouting above all of them so as to be heard. "His Lordship has always offered his protection to us from the beasts of the mountains. He is the best suited to keeping the mages at bay, but it *will* require further tribute."

"A girl." Imara could not pinpoint where the voice had come from, or from whom, but it was followed by a series of shocked, abhorrent gasps and angry demands that he explain himself. "The one thing we have to spare, and the one thing the Dragon Master does not have for himself already, is a bride."

"We can't simply hand over one of our daughters!" cried another man.

"And who would do the choosing? Surely not you?" another spoke up in answer to the previous shout.

While the villagers argued amongst themselves, Imara watched as the council turned to each other, quietly discussing this new development. She was unable to hear what they were saying, but she could see upon their faces that they were taking this idea seriously. There must have been more to their fear of the mages than they were letting on.

"We would choose," Ranell spoke at last, having

broken away from the other Elders. "Brother Jarle has made a fair point. While none of you have extra to spare, a bride would be fitting of our request for further protection."

The volume of the angry shouts coming from the villagers increased, and Imara could feel Asta pressing into her side, seeking what reassurance she could from her sister. Whatever any of them had been expecting from this meeting, a bride for the Dragon Master was not it.

While each family provided a tithe to him each year, Lord Lajos was not a man that any of them took too kindly to. He was surly, distant, attending their Fallfest but remaining separate. He made it very clear that the only ties he felt to Omdahl were the offerings placed in the back of his cart each fall before he returned to his solitary existence in the mountains.

What woman would wish to find herself bound to such a man? One who snipped and snarled whenever he was forced to converse with the Elders during the celebrations. It chilled Imara to think it even a possibility they would consider this an option.

"I know this seems a harsh and unwarranted decision, but the humans find us in a weakened state. We don't have the strength or the defenses to protect ourselves presently —not against such magics as they will have. If the mages bring war upon our doorstep, we must have the help of the Dragon Master if we are to survive."

"We do not ask this of you lightly, and we will not seek to offer the hand of any maiden who is currently spoken for. But this may be the only hope for our village," Elder Ranell added.

The hall was still a riot of voices, some furthering their concerns, while the main tide of shouts had begun to turn in favor of this new suggestion. The fear of what an attack on the village could mean for them spurred them on to willingness for something they never would have considered otherwise.

Clutching Asta's hand tightly, Imara peered down at the dais to find Elder Fridolf staring intently back at her.

IMARA

The knock came at their door in the early morning hours, after the council had deliberated the night through and Imara found herself able to sleep for the first time since laying down the previous evening. While it was Erlend who went to answer the door, the women of the house were all drawn from their beds as well, making their way slowly down the curving steps to stand in a cluster at the base of them.

Imara felt a sickening tightness to her stomach as she recognized the forms of Elder Ranell and Elder Fridolf standing in the doorway, an apologetic air to their countenance.

"No," her father said, a tone of denial and resistance in the single word.

The two Elders looked past him, finding Imara there, flanked by her mother and sister, and understanding dawned on the women. Silently, Dagny slid her arm about Imara's waist, holding on to her as if she could ward off the words that were about to be spoken.

"We're sorry to wake you from your beds, but the

council has finally come to a decision." It was Elder Ranell speaking, doing so with a kind look upon his face that Imara guessed was meant to ease what was to come. "I want you to know that we spent a very long time considering all the options, and what was best for everyone . . ."

"And you've chosen me," Imara finished for him when his words seemed to lag, as if he weren't certain how to say them out loud now that he was faced with the girl he needed to send off to the Dragon Master.

To be the plaything of that egotistical man, who thought himself better than all of them simply because he had the ability to call dragons to do his bidding . . . What would he think of a powerless seidr, or would it even matter? Perhaps she would be nothing but an insect upon which to grind his shoe.

The angry part of herself that she usually kept buried hoped that Ranell was feeling guilty now that he had to look her in the eyes and admit that they were not asking her but ordering her to sacrifice her future.

"We have," Elder Fridolf responded.

Beside her, Asta whimpered, and from the corner of her eye, Imara could see her mother shaking her head while the arm about her waist tightened. Her family stood in shocked silence for a moment, until her father's voice barked out in refusal.

"No, Fridolf, you've made a mistake. My Imara is not the one you should be sending. You can't ask this of us." His voice trembled as he spoke, and Imara's heart ached hearing it.

Imara wanted to tell her father not to argue, that she

had been the choice from the beginning, and the wait to tell her was the only part she did not understand.

"We've thought a great deal—"

"No!" It was Asta this time, crying out in anger. "You can't simply tell my sister to hand herself off to the Dragon Master. Why?"

"Asta . . . " Imara reached to rest a hand on her arm, trying to calm her down. "It'll be okay."

"But *why?*"

Imara loved her for not understanding but also wished that she had been able to see what had always been going on around them. Before anyone could respond, her father had moved to stand before her, blocking her from the view of the Elders.

"I will not stand for this. We did not agree to the terms when they were announced, and we will not send our daughter off to be the bride of some monster in the mountains!"

Once again, her heart clenched tightly in her chest as her father spoke. There was such a depth of love behind his words. At her side, she could feel her mother trembling; the woman who had always been strong and capable now felt more delicate than a petal on the wind. Her family, who had always loved her no matter her failings, were at a loss as to how this could be happening. Why their family, of all families?

Both of the Elders stepped inside, moving closer to them in an attempt to calm the situation.

"I know this may be hard to understand, Erlend . . . but we all agreed this was the best thing for her," she heard Elder Fridolf murmur softly to her father, speaking as if she weren't standing right there, just behind him. "You know very well this could be her only chance for a mate. No one in the village will risk passing on her . . . deficiency."

Deficiency. By the moon . . . How many times had she heard that word uttered concerning herself since the day of her element ceremony when she failed entirely to draw any of the stones to her? More times than she could count. So many barbs piercing the tender flesh of her heart and mind, so many thoughts and opinions kept to herself. No more—if Imara was to be cast off and forced to lose whatever future she had planned for herself, let her at least have the peace of mind of saying what was on it.

"My only chance? Perhaps I was just fine with the prospect of my future! What makes you think I would even accept anyone from this feeble-minded town should they ask?" She pulled away from her mother's hold and stepped around her father to gaze directly up at Elder Fridolf, forcing him to look at her.

Happiness in a wedded union had never been a part of the future Imara had seen for herself. Aware of who she was, the males of courting age shied away from Imara, paying her little heed. It had hurt when she was younger, but now, she had grown to expect it. Imara had accepted that, as the decades passed and she drew nearer to the marrying age, she would be alone. But there was more to life than being wedded.

Now . . . now she would be forced to submit to the Dragon Master because she was the one maiden no one outside of her family would be dismayed to lose.

"Imara—" her father began, but she cut him off.

"No. He stands there speaking of me as if I am not right here to hear it all. As if I don't have thoughts of my own on the matter. Do not pretend that you are doing this as a favor to me, Elder Fridolf, for we all know that is not the case." A part of her knew better than to say it, but the rest was tired of not speaking the words aloud. "If this will save our people, and I have been tasked with the duty, then for our people, I will do it. Despite the fact that not a one of them will bat an eye at the loss of me.

"But not for one minute shall you placate your guilty conscience by pretending this was for my sake. No . . . It is because I am the expendable one. The girl no one wishes their son to be paired with for fear of how our children would come out. You've chosen me because handing me off to the Dragon Master is not a waste of a proper seidr and washes your hands of me once and for all."

Both of the Elders were silent after her outburst, not certain how to respond to the truth of her words. As Elder Ranell opened his mouth to speak at last, Imara held up her hand to silence him, looking to her father, who was already turning to her. Erlend cupped her face in his hands, his eyes bright with unshed tears.

"You do not have to do this, my daughter. It is not your duty to save us all." His voice was husky with emotion.

"I think I do," she rasped, throat tight. "If it's not me, then it's someone else's daughter."

This felt inevitable, and while Imara wished to fight this, the council had decided. Elder Ranell may be pained, but Elder Fridolf was determined, and she knew he would not sacrifice a healthy seidr girl when she was a viable option.

"I'll be okay, Papa." She hadn't called him that since she was a child, and her father broke down immediately, pulling her tight against his chest. With her ear pressed to it, she could hear his ragged breath, while his arms held her close—protected.

For a moment, Imara allowed her eyes to close, soaking in the feeling of her father's arms about her. All too soon, they drew apart, for the Elders were speaking once more. Breaking through the barriers they were erecting with their love to remind them that all too soon they would be parted.

"We will give you the morning as a family, but once the sun is at its peak, Elders Ylva and Jorunn will arrive to attend her. They will see to preparations and dress her in the proper attire. She should have only a small number of personal belongings packed to bring with her."

"We'll see to it that she is ready," Erlend said, his tone hollow.

Imara couldn't bring herself to argue with them for speaking about her without including her, not this time. The battle had already been lost, after all.

"We thank you, Imara," Elder Ranell murmured sincerely, turning to look at her once more. There was a kindness in his eyes as he gazed upon her. "It's a brave thing that you are doing."

"You haven't given her much of a choice," Dagny stated coldly, coming to wrap her arm around Imara once more, pulling her in close. "You should be ashamed of yourselves, choosing one so young. Imara is but twenty-three, a mere babe, and yet you demand this of her rather than those who are of marrying age."

For seidrs, who lived a lifespan of close to a thousand

years or more, marriage was not typically even considered until they had lived their first century. To offer one so young showed how truly desperate the Elders were to be rid of her.

With nothing further to say, Ranell nodded. Looking between them all, he finally stepped back. "We will leave you for now, to do the things you need to do as a family. Thank you." He said this last part to Erlend and then turned to head back into the early dawn, Fridolf following in his footsteps.

The door clicked shut behind them with a sound of finality that Imara felt to her core. Drawing in a sharp breath, she steadied herself for the onslaught of her family's emotions. Somehow, they had to be okay with what was to come.

They spent a long time standing there, in the circle of each other's arms, simply existing as a family. When at last they pulled apart, Imara could see the tears in their eyes and forced herself to stay firm. None of them would be able to let her go if she were to break down.

"I'll be okay," she whispered, and she kept repeating it to herself as the morning wore on. She thought the words while she and Asta packed a small bag to be taken with her, choosing from her favorite books what few she could allow herself to bring. Imara murmured, "I'll be okay," as her mother gave her what words of wisdom she had to offer, going into a lifetime with a man none of them knew. And the words repeated again as her father warred with his desire to protect her and what was expected of him.

Just before noon, Imara slipped away from them at last, excusing herself with the need of fetching a forgotten item from her room. She waited until she was within the safety of the bedroom before letting the walls fall. With her family safely behind the door, Imara released a sob, her chest desperately fighting to bring oxygen back into her lungs as the weight of the Elders' words crushed down upon her. In the solitude of her room, she allowed the facade of confidence to crumble. This. This was to be her fate, offered up to the demon lord whom the villagers feared, a sacrificial bride to a man who time had turned into more of a myth than a being.

She had known that her life would not be the same as anyone else's, that her differences set her apart. In her wildest dreams, she had not seen this coming. She had thought a lifetime of existing alone awaited her. Her palm curved over her lips to mask the sound of her cries, not wanting her family to know that she was anything but the calm and steady person they had seen thus far.

Squeezing her eyes shut, Imara allowed the last few strangled tears to slip out, then drew in a ragged breath to steel herself once more.

"No more," she declared shakily into the solitude of her room. From here on out, there would be no more tears —the Dragon Master wasn't bound to appreciate a weepy bride. Shuddering at the thought of it, Imara brushed her cheeks dry.

Distantly, she could hear the sounds of Elders Ylva and Jorunn arriving, and of preparations beginning. It was time.

"No more," she repeated more firmly.

Opening her bedroom door, Imara stepped out into the hall and made her way back downstairs.

A bath had been prepared for her, lavender petals and mint leaves floating upon its steaming surface. Without argument, Imara allowed herself to be stripped of her clothing, and she sunk into the depths of the hot water, letting the sting of it ground her in the moment rather than allowing worries and fears to sweep her away. Ylva supervised as her mother doused her blond locks and scrubbed at her scalp, cleansing away any hint of the farm girl that she was.

When every inch of her was deemed sufficiently cleaned, her alabaster skin pink from the brush and her cheeks flushed from heat, Imara was led from the tub and dried thoroughly.

All around her there was the bustle of activity and the chatter of the two female Elders delegating duties to her mother and sister, but Imara remained silent. It was easier to handle everything that was taking place if she remained a passive participant who went where she was directed. There were many things that she wanted to say to Asta, and to her mother, but now simply didn't seem the time.

In the end, the emerald gown they had her don was slim-fitting on her torso and hanging off her shoulders with long, sheer sleeves that flowed down to tease the floor. The skirt was heavy and full, the weight of it felt against her legs with every step that she took.

It was her sister who sat her down to do her hair. Combing the long, pale gold strands gently, each stroke of the bristles a tender farewell that dug deep into Imara's heart. When Asta was finished, it was braided down the right side of her head, then curled up and pinned at the nape of her neck. This did not contain the shorter strands, which had escaped to curl around her face.

"She must be brought to the council hall promptly at dusk and kept in the outer chamber until Elder Fridolf has announced the presenting of the fall offering. Her personal belongings can remain in your cart to be collected before she and Lord Lajos leave." Elder Jorunn was speaking to her mother, giving her instruction as Imara herself stood in the center of her bed chamber, gazing into the large mirror upon her wall.

She supposed that she had the appearance of a bride, what with the hand-embroidered hem of her dress, the satin slippers upon her feet, and the sprigs of red clover woven into her hair. Yes, she had the outward appearance, if you looked past the pale cast to her cheeks and the gaunt appearance of her eyes, which seemed far too round and large in her face presently.

"When you enter the hall, you will walk directly to the dais where he is seated, but do not look at him. While you will be his bride, you must show him respect. This is key if we wish to have his aid. Once you've descended to the dais, kneel before him, and Elders Fridolf or Ranell will take care of matters from there." Elder Jorunn had stepped up beside her, speaking directly to Imara now rather than her mother. "Understood?"

Imara nodded, understanding perfectly: she was to be a sweet, docile bridal offering, one who would cause no troubles for anyone during these proceedings.

"I hope you know this is not what any of us wanted." Elder Jorunn spoke softly, for Imara's ears only. "If there were any other way to protect our village . . . we would have chosen it."

There was pity in the older woman's eyes, but it was not enough to ease this newest bruise to Imara's soul.

"If only there had been." Imara didn't want her pity, and she didn't want her words of explanation. None of it would change the outcome of the night.

Once Imara was deemed fit, Elders Ylva and Jorunn took their leave of the Hjelmstad family. They should have felt some sense of peace in having this time together. However, now that Imara had been fully prepared, the fact that she was being gifted to the Dragon Master only hung over their heads all the more.

They tried, each of them, to speak the words weighing on their hearts with the Elders gone, yet there was a silence that held their tongues. Perhaps in remaining silent, they could hold off the sense of finality that followed each of Imara's movements in those last hours.

When at last the time came to make her way to the council hall, Erlend was there, offering his hand to help her up onto the wagon in all her flowing skirts. Asta took the back of the wagon without complaint, clutching Imara's small bag of possessions tightly in her lap. Dagny gazed up at Imara on the front seat of the wagon. Resting her hand upon her thigh, she squeezed it gently and then went to climb into the back to sit alongside Asta, holding her younger daughter's hand in solidarity.

They were halfway through town before her father spoke, his voice soft and meant only for Imara's ears.

"It is not too late," he murmured, peering at her from the corner of his eyes. "You have but to say the words, and I will turn this wagon about and head directly for the mountains."

Imara gazed over at him, her heart swelling with tenderness and love. He had no idea how tightly she would hold onto his unyielding love in the coming days.

"Thank you," she whispered back, her hand slipping around his nearest to her, feeling how desperately he clung to the reins in his hold. "But I meant what I said earlier. If it were not me, it would be someone else's daughter. I have no wish to be a martyr, but I also do not desire to send another young girl off to this future just for my sake."

The council hall was now within sight. Three of the five Elders awaited them on the stone steps. Imara would be lying if she were to say her body did not begin to tremble as they pulled up before those three stern looking seidrs. Fear was a tangible force within her, coiled deeply into the core of her being and freezing her limbs so that she had to force herself down and out of the wagon.

Like scavengers, they were upon her at once, adjusting her dress, tucking in wayward curls, and guiding her up the steps. Fearful that they would whisk her away without further word, her father leapt down out of the wagon and hurried over to them.

"Wait!" he cried out, pushing between the Elders to wrap frantic fingers around Imara's elbow. "Not yet."

Turning to him, Imara peered into eyes so like her own but which had seemed to age overnight. Their hands found each other in the space between, clasping tightly to each other.

"Say farewell to your family here," Elder Ylva

murmured softly, seemingly trying to show consideration with her tone of voice despite the command.

Imara understood what was behind her words though. Once she stepped inside the hall, she would no longer be a free member of this family. Once inside, she would belong to *him*.

"I love you, always," she said fiercely, moving quickly to hug her father, praying that the strength of her hold would convey more than her words. Her gratitude for his love, his life lessons, and his tender wisdom.

"Be strong, my girl, and never forget we love you," he whispered into her ear, returning her hug with a fierceness of his own.

Asta was there then, pushing him out of the way so that she could slip her arms around Imara's waist, tucking her head in against her shoulder just as she always had. "This isn't the last we'll see of each other, right?"

"Of course not," Imara replied, an edge to her tone as she wrapped her little sister up in her arms, holding her against her chest. "We will be together again, I swear. In the meantime . . . " She reached down to lift Asta's head up, taking in the smattering of freckles over her nose and cheeks, the flaming red hair that matched their mother's, and her tear-filled green eyes. "Be happy, sweet sister, and make those silly boys wait and grow up a little." She paused. "No, make certain they grow up a lot before you finally settle for one of them. Okay?"

Sniffling, Asta nodded, squeezing once more before giving way to their mother. Dagny Hjelmstad stood tall, pride there in the lines of her face as she gazed at Imara.

Her hands lifted to cup her daughter's cheeks tenderly, holding her in place while she kissed her forehead.

"The time for meekness is over, Mari Girl," she murmured. "He may be the Dragon Master, and to be your husband, but let him know you will settle for nothing but a true partnership, no matter his powers."

Eyes tearing, Imara threw herself at her mother's chest, soaking up what strength she could from her mother's frame. They stood for a moment, embracing each other, until one of the Elders cleared their throat, and Imara pulled away.

"I promise, Mama," she whispered. Then, gathering her skirts and her strength, she turned from her beloved family to face the doors, sensing the Elders slipping around her like a barrier.

Inside the council hall, voices boomed and called, and then the loud crack of a staff upon stone sounded. There was a hand upon her back, pressing her forward as the doors opened. Beyond, a sea of faces turned to look upon her, the bridal offering to their Dragon Master, unfit for their own but ripe for the sacrifice.

"Remember my instructions," Elder Jorunn spoke softly. "Eyes down, and kneel."

Imara merely nodded, finding that her throat had constricted with an unknown emotion, one that threatened to freeze her limbs and weaken her knees. Smoothing her hands down over her skirts, she drew in a tight breath, steeling herself for what was to come, then stepped through the doors. Let her descent into the abyss be one of strength and courage; she would not falter now with all eyes upon her.

Imara kept her body rigid as she walked through the council hall and down the stone steps—shoulders back, chin up, and eyes upon the foot of the chair seated on the dais. She would not appear as a wilted flower before them, though in their minds she was naught but a crumpled weed, unwanted and plucked from the garden to be cast away. She turned a deaf ear to the soft murmurs that followed her progress, years of practice coming to her aid now. Once her steps brought her to the center of the hall, Imara took the kneeling position and bowed her head before the throne.

Her head remained bowed for the length of time it took *him* to make himself known. Her eyes stayed upon the wooden floorboards, even as the heavy thud of boots crossed before her. She sensed him long before he spoke, a dark, heavy presence above her. Imara was meant to keep her head bowed, but there was only so much humility within her, and eventually, a rebellious curiosity took her over, and she glanced up.

He was attractive, in the harsh, daunting way that a mountain slope was. Majestic, beautiful, and looming but with the hard lines of dangerous stone and the threatening torrent of an approaching avalanche.

RONAR

onar had anticipated the evening would be dull as per usual, but the moment the Elders escorted a young seidr forward, he knew this time would be different.

What in the Mother's name are they thinking? he mused.

The Elders stood with their lips pursed and faces void of expression. No one spoke a word as the blond knelt before Ronar. No one said a damned thing as she bowed her head. Her sun-kissed hair was pinned back, exposing a smooth, elegant neck. Ronar's shrewd green eyes narrowed on the council as he stood from the carved wooden throne.

In all of his years, there had never been an offering like this. Why now? Their relationship was a mutual one—Ronar protected them, and they, for the most part, left him alone, supplying him with gifts from the fall harvest.

Moving across the dais, his boots fell heavily, and because the hall had grown silent, the sound was quite pronounced. The moment he bent over to inspect the beauty, a pair of brilliant blue eyes met his. Within them, he saw distress, which seeped into her overall expression.

Her porcelain skin creased between the brows as Ronar scrutinized her, poring over every detail, significant and minute.

He didn't need to delve into her mind to know her thoughts or feelings; he could feel them radiating from her. Whatever the seidr Elders had decided, it was more than likely not what this woman wanted. How could Ronar know? The Elders only did what they believed beneficial to their ways.

How does this benefit them as a whole? Ronar wondered.

A flicker of amusement passed in his gaze. His lips curved into the smallest of smiles. Reaching out, his thumb ran along the young woman's chin ever so lightly.

"What is your name?" he asked quietly. One of the Elders started to speak for her, but Ronar bared his teeth, which were a touch too sharp for them to be considered *normal*. "I didn't ask *you*. I asked the young beauty, and unless she is mute, she is capable of speaking. Is she not?" His tone brooked no argument.

Beyond the blond, a head bowed in supplication. Ronar turned his gaze to the kneeling woman and smiled. "What is your name?" he inquired again. His teeth remained bared, but he released her from his light hold.

"Imara Hjelmstad." She lowered her eyes again. The muscle in her jaw leaped violently.

"And why have you—Imara—been ushered in and forced to kneel before me?" Ronar's eyes slid shut as one of the Elders began to speak.

"We have brought you a bride—"

Ronar lifted a hand and placed a finger to his lips as he

stood upright. "Once more, I asked Imara. Once more, I tell you to remain silent until *she* answers." The same Elder bowed and said nothing more. If Imara Hjelmstad was his bride-to-be, she would speak for herself. "As you were, Imara."

Imara's cheeks reddened as she was addressed. "I am to be your bride, my lord. Our people have been attacked by the mages, and they press on, threatening to bring a war upon us we cannot fight."

Ronar's jaw shifted as he took a step backward. He glanced down at Imara and motioned for her to stand. Just as he had thought, the Elders had their own agenda. Instead of offerings of food, clothing, or livestock, they chose to gift him a bride. It seemed extreme, even for them, and it piqued his interest. "And in giving you to me, the hope is to . . . "

When she stood, she met Ronar's gaze. Anxiety furrowed her brow, and would have likely pinched her lips together had he not required her to speak. So, instead of closing her mouth, it hung open until she visibly gathered her wits. "To acquire your aid. To protect us as you *should*, as our lord." There was an unmistakable edge to her words, even though she kept them respectful.

Soft, barely audible whispers broke out in the hall, and it caused the hard lines in Ronar's face to relax. His mind reached out to the seidrs in the hall, sifting through their prone thoughts. He gathered intel as quickly as drawing in a deep breath. "Very well. I accept your offering, but I won't wed Imara tonight. I'd like my bride to warm up to the idea of marriage, rather than be thrown into it coldly. I will also put an end to these mages. You have my word."

Worthless. That word stood out amongst the seidrs' minds. *Impaired.* So, they thought to gift him some damaged flower?

Ronar's gaze drifted to Imara again, and he jerked his head to the minstrels. "I wish to dance with my bride." He extended his hand to Imara and waited for her to accept it.

The Elders released a collective sigh, bowing their heads repeatedly in thanks, but dared not utter a word, lest they found themselves on the receiving end of Ronar's fury.

There was little hesitation behind Imara's movement. She reached out and took his hand, her eyes wide with curiosity as she gazed up at him. "As you wish, my lord," she answered crisply.

As the minstrels played, the melancholic wail of the talharpa filled the once-silent room, and the beat of the skin drum set the rhythm for the dance. Ronar lifted his free hand, motioning for the beat to slow further, and once he was pleased with the tempo, he led Imara toward the center of the room.

"I'm afraid it's been a while since I've danced. You'll have to forgive my clumsiness." His lips tilted up at one corner.

Imara's eyes narrowed on him suspiciously, as if she didn't quite believe his words. "I am sure m'lord dances well enough." When her hand slid into his, her free hand took up the skirt of her dress.

Ronar lifted Imara's hand to his lips, brushing a tender kiss to the bare skin. He kept his eyes on hers, watching for the smallest hitch of her breath. After having lived for nearly two thousand years already, he took pleasure in ruffling feathers, and derived amusement in outlandish ways.

Color splashed into Imara's cheeks, brightening her already brilliant eyes. The battle between controlling her tongue and setting it free etched itself on her face, twisting her full lips and furrowing her eyebrows.

"Well enough for my bride not to need a healer, I pray." Ronar twirled Imara to the beat of the song, taking far more liberty with the physical aspect than the dance intended. His touches were prolonged, lingering on the small of her back, on her arm, her waist.

It was Imara that stumbled, not Ronar, but she didn't utter an apology. Amused with the glimmer of frustration in her gaze, he brushed his hand down her hip, but this time with the movement, he allowed his magic to sift through hers. The flow of magic in the room pulsed around him, but as Ronar allowed his magic to snake out toward Imara's, he was surprised to feel a barrier, a warning to not poke around. Of course he pushed beyond that, flexed his power, and surprisingly felt a deep well of magic.

Breathless, he withdrew his essence from her, nearly stumbling amidst their dance. These imbeciles. They believed her inept, but she was so much *more*. There was a strong pulse of magic beating beneath the barrier, unable to burst free. It lay dormant, in wait, and perhaps wishing to be free. Like a child locked away in a dark cellar, browbeaten into submission. It was strong, though a quiet energy. Ronar wasn't certain of why there was a barrier, nor did he understand why most thought her a leper amongst their kind, but it wasn't that she lacked magic.

Imara possessed more than enough. So what were these fools up to?

As the minstrel's song came to an end, Ronar's movements ceased, and he glanced down at his rigid partner. A possessive gleam entered in his gaze, then his arm tightened around her. "My lovely bride, I wouldn't want to be accused of not sharing you," Ronar whispered, his lips nearly against the tip of her ear. "Enjoy your evening. We will leave when the banquet is done, and should you need me, your people are rather fond of calling me *Lajos*." He withdrew from her, and as he did, the hall's inhabitants converged onto the floor, joining in the merriment as a new dance began.

Imara curtsied, bowing her head. "Of course, my lord." She turned her head, touching her ear as she walked away.

Ronar's gaze lingered on her figure as it wound through the throng of individuals. Perhaps the people had expected their Dragon Master to adhere himself to the young woman, but he wasn't in the hall to please them. Besides, Imara would soon reside in the manor in the mountains. She'd tire of seeing him soon enough.

"My lord, has your bride already run away?" Elder Ranell gave Ronar a knowing grin.

The seidr's voice alone grated on Ronar's nerves. "Elder Ranell, I'm not in the practice of *chasing off* women, let alone brides. But I can assure you, the soon-to-be Dragon Mistress will not run from me."

Instead of recoiling or reddening, the Elder smiled and lifted his brows. "Oh? And what is it she will do then? Imara is quite a lovely bauble to add to your collection."

A bauble? Every muscle in Ronar's jaw tightened. A

bride was the last gift he'd expected, let alone wanted. But he would never use such a degrading term for one who would sit by his side.

Ronar narrowed his eyes and leaned forward. "Make no mistake about it, Elder Ranell, any bride of mine will not simply sit on display for the village to gawk at."

The Elder, clearly feeling bold given the situation, prodded him again. "But you didn't say what she *would* do, my lord."

"What any Dragon Mistress is expected to do, Elder: stand by my side and order you around." A tight-lipped smile formed on Ronar's face, and he walked away from the Elder before he could drag him back into another dreaded conversation. One where Ranell would no doubt bait Ronar into delivering another cutting remark.

There would be more time to share barbs with the Elder. For now, the Dragon Master needed to eat, drink, and be merry with the villagers of Omdahl.

It was well into the early hours of the morning when the dancing stopped, the food disappeared, and the drink ran dry. It was a pity no dragon's mead had been served, but the seidrs hadn't disappointed with their stores of plum wine.

Ronar swept his hair back, knotting it at the nape of his neck with a leather tie. A long journey awaited him and Imara. She hadn't been forgotten as the night rolled on, but rather, he'd watched as she interacted with the villagers. None seemed too keen to speak with her, which raised a fair share of questions. It perplexed him and, had it not been so insulting to him, perhaps he'd find it amusing. After all, they were gifting one they deemed broken to him—a tribute in place of food, fabrics, and precious stones, and they had chosen the village's pariah.

"It is time we make the journey to the mountains, Imara." Ronar stood beside her, offering his elbow. "The carriage is waiting outside." He nodded to the window.

Imara glanced down at his offered arm, hesitating before she looped her own through his. Wisps of her hair had loosened from their groomed state, accenting her delicate features. "I have a few belongings that I wish to bring with me." Something in her gaze shifted—hardened, almost.

Ronar nodded. "Of course." He walked outside and motioned with his hand to a few of the villagers. "Have one of them retrieve it for you." A hint of mischief swirled in his gaze, but he turned his head away from Imara before she could catch a glimpse.

"What? It's not much at all. That seems—I mean—I can fetch them myself. There is no need for another to do it for me." Color rushed into her cheeks as she stumbled over her words.

No doubt frustration bubbled within her, but Ronar wasn't going to budge on the matter. "Choose which one you wish to grab your belongings," he repeated, slower this time. "I'm quite tired, and morning is almost upon us, darling." A slippered foot ground in the dirt behind him, nearly bringing forth a chuckle.

Imara hastily disappeared, and when she returned, it was with a young boy in tow. His clover-green eyes shone brightly as he delivered the items to the carriage, including a white mare, which he tethered to the back of the cart.

"For your troubles, young man." Ronar winked, dropping a few coins into his open hand. "Hurry back to your family. The sun is nearly up, and you're only going to get a few hours of sleep." Ronar jerked his thumb toward the sky. The warm glow of the sun already teased the horizon.

When the boy hopped away, Ronar moved to the front of the carriage. He waited for Imara to step closer, but she didn't. She stood mulishly where she had been since the boy left. "Very well." Ronar climbed up the small step and into the simple seat. Gathering up the reins, he stared ahead and only turned back when the stubborn woman moved.

Imara reached for the side of the carriage, the long dress hooking onto the tip of her toe so that when she pushed forward, it yanked the fabric of the dress down. Not only did it reveal more flesh, but it also knocked her off balance and caused her to slip down the step. Her cheeks flushed, but she climbed the steps on the second try without incident and glared straight ahead.

Ronar cleared his throat, disguising a chuckle in the process. Imara didn't want his aid, which she'd made quite clear, so he'd watch her fumble until she asked for it. "So glad you decided to join me on the journey, darling." He clucked his tongue, and the draft horse set off.

Beside him, Imara folded her arms and scooted as far away from him as she could. "At least you aren't attempting to hide the sort of man you are."

His eyebrows raised in question. Imara had scarcely said anything to him throughout the night unless prompted. He assumed, now that they were out of earshot of the villagers, she'd be hurling her verbal barbs. "Oh, please *do* tell me the sort of man I am." Ronar's green eyes flicked to her chest, her arms only bringing attention to the fact the fabric had been yanked down.

"The kind that would watch his *wife-to-be* stumble and fall," she hissed, tugging her dress into place again.

He hummed, pressing his lips together. "Normally I would have helped, but seeing as you refused my assistance when I offered it, I wasn't about to force help on a capable woman." Ronar twisted and reached around the back of the seat. Imara flinched, pressing herself into her corner all the more. Shaking his head, he tugged on a wool blanket and pushed it toward her. "We have a few hours' journey to the base of the mountain, and Dragon's Keep is beyond that. While I wouldn't dare tell you what to do, Imara, I *do* suggest catching some sleep." No doubt she needed to preserve some energy to glare at him later.

As he glanced over at her, he saw that some of the anger had faded, and in its place, something akin to dread had appeared. Imara had every right to be apprehensive, fearful, and angry. Ronar hadn't been expecting to have a wife riding home with him this morning, and he didn't suspect Imara had known for more than twenty-four hours that she'd be gifted to him to do as he pleased.

"When we arrive, I'll show you to your room, but I'm

afraid I wasn't expecting company. I can only hope the room will be to your liking." Ronar clucked to the draft horse, urging it toward another path, which would wind through Omdahl Village and up toward the mountain.

"We won't be sharing a room then." It wasn't a question but a statement.

This time, Ronar couldn't successfully stop himself from chuckling. "Not so hasty, my young bride. Some things cannot be rushed."

"I didn't mean that!" Imara bit out. She turned such a vibrant shade of red that her blue eyes seemed to glow.

Of course she didn't. Ronar let the argument drop and focused on the road before them. Hues of red, gold, and brown were steadily taking over the green foliage, heralding the arrival of autumn. The farther they traveled up the mountain, the more drastic the color change would become. This was Ronar's favorite time of the year, and it had nothing to do with the harvest banquet. It did, however, have everything to do with the tones of gold, and the crispness in the air. But this year was different. There was less beauty in the foliage and more death. Dead or dying trees ruined the once picturesque journey, and it was driving Ronar mad. *What is it?* These questions plagued his mind day in and day out.

Before long, the two of them fell into silence, and when Ronar checked on his companion, she was fast asleep. Leaning over, he tugged the blanket up farther over her and settled back. Soon they'd arrive in the labyrinthine forest, which meant they were more than halfway there.

Tall pine trees loomed over smaller oaks and even birch inside the forest. As soon as the carriage rolled through, the trees shifted, and the moss-covered ground rearranged itself. It was enchanted to confuse those who trespassed or dared to try to escape Dragon's Keep, but its master knew the way, knew the tricks. One more shift in the pathway, and a dirt road opened up in what once was a collection of trees.

Dragon's Keep, the home of the Dragon Master, sat atop a small knoll facing a crystalline lake. The sprawling home was crafted of whitewashed bricks and dark oak trim —a contrast to the villagers' homes. Behind the home was a stone stable with a few rows of fenced-in areas. A friendly bay horse rushed the fence line, trumpeting to his stable mate.

By some magic, Imara didn't rouse when the carriage halted, nor did she shift when the horse neighed. She must have been exhausted. As Ronar stood up, he hovered over her with the intent of lifting her into his arms. His arms slid beneath her, but that was as far as he got.

Imara flailed her arms, her closed fist connecting with Ronar's nose, resulting in a loud crack. She opened her eyes and yanked her arms to her chest immediately, gasping.

"That was my nose!" he bellowed.

Ronar immediately retracted his arms, one hand covering his nose from the abuse it had suffered. He groaned and shook his head. He should have known better, but that didn't stop him from at least trying to move her without waking her. Pain shot through his nose and into his skull, bringing forth a string of curses.

"We're here," he said, motioning to the house, his words muffled by his hand.

Imara wiped the sleep from her eyes, brow furrowing as she glanced up at him. For a moment, she almost looked sheepish, but as she sat forward, clutching the blanket to her figure, something akin to wonder filled her gaze. "This . . . this is Dragon's Keep?"

Blinking rapidly, Ronar shook his head, willing the sharp pain away. "That it is." His gaze fell on an approaching male figure. "Ah, Mikkel. The horses need tending."

Mikkel, a human closer to his forties than not, had been in Ronar's service as steward for around five years now. His sharp features gave him a severe appearance, but in truth, he was a solid and warm individual. No matter what the keep needed, the steward ensured it was there. And if Ronar ever wanted something, all he had to do was think it.

Mikkel's thin lips parted in surprise, his eyebrows disappearing into his hairline. "My lord, I wasn't aware that you'd be returning with a guest."

Ronar rubbed his nose, sighing. "Neither was I, but here we are. Imara?" He shot her a look, inclining his head.

She took the hint and nodded to the man. "Imara Hjelmstad."

"She will be staying with us for a while. I'll explain later, when we're not both travel weary." Ronar hopped down from the carriage and walked toward Imara's side. He offered his hand; this time she accepted the assistance and climbed down. His eyes locked onto hers, and he said, "There is little warmth left in this part of the valley. Lucky for you, Sylvi prefers a warm house to a chilled one." Ronar turned away, walking toward the entrance of the house.

"Oh. Sylvi?" Imara inquired, following after him.

"You'll meet her soon enough."

Inside, the house was warm, too warm for Ronar's liking, but he spent most of his days outside. Who was he to complain of the temperature when his staff were the ones who endured it? The tall ceilings and massive rooms were no easy task to heat, but with the aid of magic, it was easier.

"Before we venture to your room . . . " Ronar halted in the entrance hall, hovering over Imara. "I'll say this once and once only. Do not *ever* step foot in the forest without me or one of the staff with you. It has a mind of its own and wouldn't think twice about devouring you. Do you understand?"

"I understand," she said curtly. "Where did you say my room was?" Imara glanced past him.

Ronar nodded, leading her toward the stairs and up to the second floor. He couldn't remember the last time the rooms were occupied by anyone aside from himself and Sylvi. His staff had their own section of the house, except for Sylvi, who lived with Ronar.

"This will be your room. Your belongings will be delivered by Mikkel, and Sylvi will be attending to you." He pushed open the ornate door and stepped back.

"Although it pains me, I must bestow the honor of a tour to my help. I have things to attend to." He paused for a moment, then, "Are you hungry?"

Imara stared into the open room and shook her head. "Not right now. I'll be fine."

"Very well. I'll have something made up in the meantime, just in case you change your mind." Ronar bowed his head, then walked away.

Sylvi wasn't going to let him live this down. She was going to be unbearable.

6

IMARA

I accept your offering. Those words had sifted repeatedly through Imara's mind since the Dragon Lord had spoken them. During the dance, as her brand-new betrothed had spun her about the room, a spectacle for all to behold as his intimate touch branded her body unpleasantly, then afterward, while they made the long journey back up the mountain to his home. Even now, left alone in her own separate quarters—rather than being carted off to the Dragon Master's chambers to be unceremoniously bedded, as she had imagined he would want—the words were still repeating.

Perhaps a part of her hadn't thought it would happen, that once presented with his gift, he would refuse. A lifetime of refusal and living on the outside had taught her to expect this. In actuality, it had been such a simple exchange: the Elders had handed Imara over to him, and Lajos accepted her as a token for his aid without issue.

Hands ringing before her, Imara paced back and forth in the center of the very large, very ornate room, taking in none of the details surrounding her. Nothing about the feast last night had been as she thought it would be, which left her feeling more unsettled than she had anticipated. Although, how was one to prepare for such an evening in their life?

Imara ended up at one of the large, floor-to-ceiling windows, fingers pressed to the cool glass pane as she stared out at the manicured lawns below and an endless forest beyond. A fresh wave of homesickness swept over her, making her throat tighten as tears sprang to her eyes.

Her parents and sister had gone home from Fallfest without her, returning to their family home as a threesome for the first time since Asta's birth. It felt impossible that their lives would now continue on without her. Meanwhile, she would be here, in this large foreign manor, trying to avoid the attention of a man she did not know but who had taken her to be his wife.

Her ears rang as anxiety mounted. Would he visit her chambers later? Come to claim what had been given to him? The mere thought of allowing that man to touch her in an intimate way made Imara long to hurl herself out of the very window she stood at.

Imara clung to the final words her mother had spoken to her. The Elders had gifted Imara to Lord Lajos, but that did not mean she needed to be a subservient toy for him to do with as he pleased. Imara would demand the treatment she desired and would refuse to accept anything else.

She would, of course, have felt more confident in this if she knew what it was the Dragon Master planned for her.

There was a soft rap upon her door, causing Imara to jump and spin on her heel, startling her out of her frantic thoughts, before it opened and a head of chestnut-brown hair poked out from behind it. Imara relaxed slightly, realizing that, instead of the sardonic smirk of her new betrothed, it was a young human girl with a happy, friendly face. Offering her a soft smile, the maid tentatively stepped into the room, a silver tray in her hands.

"I don't mean to intrude, miss, but I thought after everything that's happened, your late evening, and the long journey up the mountain, that you may want a little tea to help settle in before dinner." Her eyes dropped to Imara's clenched hands ever so subtly, then she stepped across the room to place the tray on the small table near one large window.

Unclasping her hands, Imara inhaled deeply. Hysteria did no one any good, and working herself up into a state of high anxiety would not be beneficial. Instead, she made her way over to the small table where a brass pot of steaming tea awaited her. The idea of a hot, soothing cup appealed greatly to her.

"Thank you, this is very kind of you . . . " Imara smiled, lifting a brow as her tone implied she needed a name for the girl. While her own role here in Dragon's Keep was still a mystery, and she was finding it hard to pinpoint just what her affianced would do with her, the maid before her seemed friendly enough.

"Sylvi, ma'am, and you are most welcome," the girl responded, picking up the tea pot and pouring amber liquid into the delicate cup nestled in its matching saucer.

Gathering the folds of her now rumpled bridal gown in her hands, Imara moved to take a seat at the table, inhaling the fragrant steam drifting up toward her face. While she had napped for a good portion of the journey, there was a weariness within her which eased a fraction as her hands slid around the warmth of the cup.

"Enjoy your tea, m'lady. Master Lajos has ordered your dinner be prepared and served here in your chambers for tonight," the young woman explained, giving her a sympathetic look that Imara tried her best not to read pity in.

"Thank you," Imara murmured, wanting to ask if she were expected to stay confined to her rooms or if she were free to roam but biting her tongue in fear that releasing those first questions would open her to a flood of others.

With a slight curtsy, the maid was gone, and Imara was left alone once more, with a tray of tea and a head full of questions as her only companions.

The tea was a pleasant break from her frantic pacing, but as the heat spread through her body, so too did the weariness of two sleepless nights and a life-altering occurrence.

When her cup was empty, Imara eyed the large wooden bed, heavily laden with fur and guarded on either side by dragon heads carved into the curling headboard. It was looking more inviting as the seconds ticked by, and so she rose to her feet and struggled out of her gown. After only a moment of hesitation, she walked across her room, tossing the gown into the fireplace, feeling mild vindication as the red flames licked along the embroidered hem. Crawling at last into the bed, she succumbed to the peace of sleep beneath the watchful eyes of her dragon sentinels.

She woke the next morning, warm and nestled in the comfort of her blankets and a bed of down, her sleep-clouded mind telling her to remain where she was while her stomach rumbled hungrily—she'd slept through dinner the night before. Except there was someone moving about her room, making noises that, while hushed, were not conducive to sleeping.

Pushing herself up in the bed, Imara was greeted by the sight of an unfamiliar room, and a girl who was not her sister. Sylvi bustled about, laying out brushes, pins, and kohl on the surface of the golden dressing table. On the dressing screen near the table hung a clean shift and cerulean overdress—neither of which belonged to her. "Where did that gown come from?" she asked, drawing Syvli's attention over to her.

"Oh, good morning, m'lady. I'm sorry if my fussing woke you."

"It's quite all right," Imara responded, brushing loose curls from her eyes. "I've had more than enough sleep for one night." She could feel it in her bones.

"The dress is one of many that I've been instructed to prepare for you," Sylvi spoke as she picked up a tray from the table and carried it over to Imara, placing it upon her lap in the bed.

The silver-domed lid, when removed, revealed a small pot of tea and a piece of perfectly toasted bread with honey drizzled upon its top. "Just something to tide you over until breakfast with Lord Lajos," Sylvi murmured.

"The Dragon Master has a collection of gowns?" was her next avenue of thought, and her eyes drifted up to watch Sylvi, who had returned to preparing items for Imara's day. "Whose gown . . . was it?"

Had there been a series of other sacrificial brides given to him throughout the centuries? Was this bed one that another unfortunate girl had been forced to sleep in, torn away from her family, her friends, her life?

"The master has been given many interesting offerings over the years, several trunks of dresses amongst them." Sylvi offered her a comforting smile, perhaps guessing where her mind had traveled. "I chose this one, as it will bring out the color of your eyes."

"I brought a few gowns of my own," Imara informed her, lifting the toast to her lips and taking a grateful bite as her hungry belly grumbled in anticipation.

"Master Lajos wishes for you to be dressed in a way befitting the lady of the house."

Imara stiffened, a flare of anger slipping through her. The gowns she had brought, while not of the finest material or the most elegant of styles, had been made from the cotton grown on their own farm, the fabric woven by her mother's own hands, and between them, she and Asta had cut and stitched each garment together.

"I see," was her only response.

"He's only looking to make your stay as comfortable as possible and thought new gowns would be a pleasant gift of welcome." Sylvi was watching her, and when she did not respond, the maid continued. "You'll find him to be a thoughtful and kind man, if a bit reserved."

"Have you been here long?" she asked, because she could not fathom anything nice to say on the matter of the Dragon Master.

"Since I was thirteen, ma'am, or plainly, eleven years." Sylvi smiled, then returned to laying out the items they would need to prepare Imara for her first day at Dragon's Keep.

"So long?" Imara was surprised. "Your parents sent you to work for the Dragon Master at such a young age?" It would seem Imara was not the only maiden who had been gifted to Lord Lajos. "I'm sorry."

"No . . . Master Lajos took me in when I was in need of a home. My service here at the keep has always been of my own desire to pay back the great debt that I owe him. Master Lajos truly is a great man once you have the chance to see past his sometimes rough exterior."

Imara fought off a snort. All she had ever seen of the Dragon Master was a surly man who took the seidrs' offerings happily enough without ever trying to get to know them as a people.

"Well, I am glad you, at least, have been happy." The same could not be said for Imara.

While it felt strange allowing another person to help her prepare for the day, Imara realized that her bigger fight would be with Lord Lajos. So she sat before the dressing table and allowed Sylvi to brush and do her hair, listening while she filled her in on the other two servants making up the Dragon Master's staff. Fortunately, the maid was chipper and pleasant to be around, and Imara found it brought some comfort to her morning.

It turned out that the blue overdress was a touch too big for her slender form. Fortunately, the piece laced up in the front over the bust, and they were able to tighten it properly. It would seem that many of the dresses would need to be taken in or altered in some fashion. While the petticoat was also a touch too big, this only offered her a fraction more covering, which she appreciated, as the laces and boning at her waist from the overdress forced her breasts up and out more than she was used to. Her shoulders were also left bare except for the blue straps, with puffs of the cream petticoat circling lower on her arms.

It was pretty, and it did match her eyes wonderfully as Sylvi had suspected, but Imara hated it—one more reminder that she was no longer in control of her situation and about to join the man she had been given to for his morning meal.

Dressed, with her hair braided, the long blond tail left to trail over her shoulder, and her eyes lined with kohl, Imara was led down a large, sweeping staircase to the magnificent entrance of Dragon's Keep. There, looming, heavy-set doors taunted with the promise of the outside world and a freedom that could never be hers again. Rather than flee into the wilderness, Imara crossed the stone floor, the long hem of her skirts sweeping along with her, and stepped into the dining hall.

The table stretching nearly the full length of the entire room was grand enough to seat a small horde of people. It was dressed with tall golden candelabras resembling trees, twisting and stretching up toward the ceiling, glowing candles clutched in branch-like cups at the ends of each arm. As she made her way along the length of the table, Imara found Lord Lajos seated at the end, a great spread of food before him, and his plate already laden with his choices.

He stood as she neared, his eyes traveling the length of her gown before returning to her face in time to see the hint of red that had appeared in her cheeks—not from embarrassment but rather irritation. His own eyes sparkled with amusement as he took it in, moving to grasp the back of her chair and pull it out for her.

"Thank you," Imara stated stiffly, smoothing her skirts behind her as she took her seat.

"I trust that you were well taken care of last night, and you found your rooms and the bed to your liking?" Lajos asked, returning to his own seat and settling in to watch her with a keen eye.

"They were acceptable," she murmured, trying to find the words within her to hold a conversation with this man. Life had not equipped her for dealing with the circumstance she now found herself in. Instead of him, her eyes focused upon the food before her.

Honey-scented porridge steaming from a brass bowl, boiled eggs piled in offering upon a platter near slices of glistening ham and a mound of fresh fruit. Before her plate sat her own personal teapot, steeping happily in a sweet vessel painted with images of dragons twisted around flowers.

"Only acceptable? Well, I will have to thrash Sylvi for mediocre presentation and service," came his dry response.

Gasping, Imara jerked slightly, her hand hitting the knife beside it, causing it to rattle against her plate. "What —" she began, only to halt. Looking at him, she found that he was laughing at her, green eyes alight with mirth that caused her jaw and shoulders to clench.

"Sylvi was very sweet, both last night and this morning, despite us not having been formally introduced," Imara insisted. Was there a hint of scolding in her tone? Perhaps, but he had left her stranded in her rooms, knowing no one in his service and naught of the house she had come to reside in.

"I am pleased to hear it. Sylvi will be more than happy to help you come to know about Dragon's Keep and anything that may be of interest to you here." He watched her for a moment, seated stiffly at the table. "Please, help yourself. No need to wait on my account."

Imara eyed him for a moment, then decided that she was far too hungry to allow upset and annoyance to stop her from eating. Spooning the steaming porridge into her own small bowl, then adding a trickle of cream with a smattering of berries from the platter, she felt her shoulders relax. The warmth and sweetness were welcoming, reminding her of simpler times and simpler people.

"I find myself curious and in need of an answer." He was speaking again, and Imara froze in apprehension. "Why you?"

"Why . . . me?" Imara didn't know whether to be outraged or to weep.

"There must have been a reason, out of all the girls in

Omdahl, that Fridolf and his little band of Elders settled upon you as my beautiful bride-to-be."

It stung in so many ways, not because she had expected him to be beside himself with joy at having her but from the situation overall.

Imara wasn't certain where to begin, and suddenly, the porridge on her tongue wasn't tasting so sweet. Setting her spoon aside, she sat back against the high-backed chair and gazed over at him coolly. With a pragmatic air, she explained, seeing no reason to shield him from the truth that he had been duped.

"In simple words, I am a blight upon my people. I am . . . deficient, broken. I was born without any magic to speak of. Even the most menial of tasks is nearly impossible for me. Unlike the rest of my kind, I have no elemental calling." Her eyes remained on him while she spoke, curious to know what he would think once he realized he had been given not the best of their choosing but their most unwanted. "They gave me to you because, with me gone, there was no fear of passing on my impurity to children. I am afraid they do not fear tainting your bloodline as greatly as they do their own."

Lajos did not skip a beat, giving no sign of being upset at this deception. Instead, he calmly popped a berry into his mouth and chewed.

"I don't believe so," was his only response.

"Excuse me?" She could feel her brows knitting together. Did he think that she was lying in an attempt to make herself undesirable to him? If so, he was in for a great surprise later on.

Rather than responding, he withdrew something from

inside his jacket and reached over to place a small crystal beside her plate. It was not the sort her people used to store their elemental magic for lighting and sound but one of the roughhewn quartz that mages required to channel earthen magic. Imara looked from the stone to Lajos, confusion pinching her pale features.

"Take the stone in your hand, and while focusing on the quartz, reach out. See what you can find with the stone to amplify your pull."

She wanted to tell him that the Elders had forced her through many tests over the years, and what they had not attempted, her own parents had tried. Nothing had been successful; nothing had sparked within her the pull toward any of the elements. She simply did not have it. However, seeing as how the Dragon Master thought himself more knowledgeable than those of her people who practiced the magic, Imara took up the quartz, showing him the stone nestled in her palm, then closed her fingers around it.

Huffing in frustration at the entire situation she found herself in, Imara closed her eyes and focused on the texture of the quartz in her hand, feeling the way the rough edges bit into her flesh. *This is ridiculous and embarrassing. Haven't I suffered through enough at the hands of my people already? All the years of their dropping my name into hushed conversations or pulling just out of my reach to avoid contact. Now I must suffer through the trials of my betrothed just to make him understand what he has been given.*

A turbulent storm of emotions swelled inside Imara, like a cyclone of water capturing everything else in its wake, pulling them down, down into the depths, while the waves around grew more violent. Her hand tightened upon the quartz. *How long must I do this?*

Her eyes flew open, and a gasp was rung from her lips as the pitcher before her exploded, sending a cascade of water and clay shards over the table and dousing her in a wave of it. Breathless from shock, and with lashes dripping, Imara whirled on Lajos, who stared at her with a mixture of surprise and laughter.

"Why?!" she cried out, her curls clinging to the sides of her face as droplets streamed down to further dampen the petticoat clinging to breasts heaving with angry breaths. "Why would you do that? Haven't I suffered enough without your taunts and trickery?"

Unable to fathom his reasons for torturing her in this manner, Imara pushed back from the table. Quickly swiping her cotton napkin from the table, she spun on her heel and stormed from the dining hall. Without hesitation, she forced open the large wooden doors and escaped out into the morning sunshine, wanting—needing—to be anywhere but where the Master of Dragons was.

RONAR

R onar lifted a hand and swiped a droplet of water from beneath his eye. Imara had left in a fit of fury and, he surmised, embarrassment as well. She had wrongfully assumed it was *him* toying with her. In fact, that had been entirely *her* doing. The notion amused him because the villagers assumed her unable to perform simple magic, and he had proven she could in one morning. She could *clearly* perform—if perhaps in a manner a little unrestrained. However, there was nothing simple about Imara's magic, and nothing the Elders would have been able to prod either. Not that *he* could. It was a rather peculiar magic, one that he'd never felt before.

Ronar plucked up another piece of fruit and mulled over the steady hum, then the electric wave that had pulsed in the room when Imara's magic erupted. It was more than what he'd felt at the hall when they danced. This was no teasing energy; it was something great. But *what?*

Ronar missed the arrival of Sylvi as she entered the dining hall, but he didn't miss a berry being lobbed at his head. His nose twitched as he grabbed the discarded berry from his lap and proceeded to eat it. "Can I help you?"

"What did you do? Imara is outside and soaked. It's cold, and she'll catch a chill. Go fix this." She put one hand on her hip and motioned to the archway with the other. "Well? Go on. Whatever it is you did or said, go apologize."

Ronar curled his lip at Sylvi's antics. She'd been a girl when he'd brought her to the keep. He'd plucked her from a life of abuse and taken her in as if she were of his blood. She'd never forgotten it, but as her affection for him grew, so did her courage. Lazily, he picked up another piece of fruit. "I did nothing. I asked her to perform a simple task. That was all her." A grin replaced the small snarl, and he chuckled. "I don't know what she is, Sylvi, but she isn't the defect the villagers thought her to be."

"Ronar, what are you talking about? Speak plainly, I don't have time for your riddles." Sylvi leaned against the table, her brown eyes focusing on his face.

He leaned back in the chair, peering at the girl, dismissing her brazen attitude. "When they presented Imara to me, I was able to scan the thoughts in the room. None thought too keenly of her, and many fully believed her to be a blight due to her inability to perform the most simple of elemental magic. They believed they were parting with the lesser of their village—which is a grave insult to me but not the point." Rolling a berry between his fingers, he snorted. "Imara proved this morning that isn't true."

Confusion knit her eyebrows together. "What? There *is* only elemental and the defected mages. Well, aside from you."

"Or is there? If there is an answer, it'd be in the library. At least, I think so." He sounded half-mad as he rambled to himself. The idea of a riddle both excited him and also frustrated him. Ronar didn't need another puzzle to dissect, and he certainly didn't need one that was so unpredictable. However, it was in his nature to seek knowledge and to find answers to riddles and put the pieces together.

Sylvi nodded, chewing on her bottom lip. "Which means you're just going to sit there pondering this while your bride is outside freezing?" She leaned forward and grabbed the sleeve of his shirt. "Get out there, *Dragon Master*, and fix this."

Ronar's gaze shifted, and he took in the maid's freckled visage. Sylvi was the closest thing Ronar had to family. She was also the only one who knew *everything* about him. So when she assessed him with those fox-brown eyes, he knew exactly what she was thinking. He could dream she'd let it be, but it was just that: a dream.

"Let go of my arm," he barked. "My *bride* can sulk outside and believe I'm one of the underworld's harbingers of misfortune for all I care." Ronar grabbed for another handful of berries, but Sylvi took the bowl away. "Imara has been here for less than a day, and already you're favoring her side. Out of everyone, I thought you'd be the one loyal to me." His words held no bite to them. Ronar sighed and shook his head.

Sylvi didn't miss a beat as she continued to lecture him. "She has been torn from everything she knows and loves. Dig a little deeper for that compassion I know you have and remember that. Especially if, as you say, she was the pariah in the village. Imagine what she has lived through, and then imagine being dumped at *your* feet."

When someone lived for centuries, rather than a human's lifespan of eighty or so, compassion dwindled. Humanity, if it ever existed inside of a being, crumbled. But Ronar had always been different, and his peers often protested his differences. To say the Dragon Master was compassionate likely would have been pushing it, but he wasn't malevolent.

"Sylvi, you know as well as I do—"

"Please. I *know* you. I know there is a heart inside, no matter how well guarded it is. Whether you believe this is a temporary situation or a lifetime, she is owed compassion." Sylvi tilted her head to the side, bottom lip jutting out.

Ronar's brows pinched together, his lips thinning as he listened to the girl speak. Although he didn't pry into her thoughts, Ronar knew she was thinking of her prior life. The mere thought of Sylvi's predicament caused his blood to boil, while Imara's situation was different—she was a throwaway in the village's eyes. Amidst his frustration, Ronar found humor too, because Sylvi seemed to know he was already trying to find a way to return Imara back home. Where she belonged.

Dragon's Keep maintained a minimal staff, primarily because Ronar preferred solitude. A new bride in the mix only added a complication he had no desire to entertain. Nevertheless, Imara would have a home until he discovered a way she could return to the village without further harm to her reputation. They already viewed her as a pariah, so what would happen should he return her, untouched and unwed?

"Oh, all right. Quit your harping. Prepare some tea, and perhaps some bandages. I expect her to gouge my eyes out the moment I step outside."

"Maybe you deserve it." Sylvi laughed as she left the room.

"Traitorous girl!" Ronar yelled after her.

Before Ronar left the confines of the keep, he delved into his magic and summoned a large volume: *Olde Magicks*. It was bound in leather, smelled of dust possibly older than him, and inspired fear in anyone's heart that dared to open it. The volume had withstood the tests of time and, with a hint of magic encasing it, it seemed to be in fair condition.

As he stepped outside, he scanned the immediate area for Imara, but she wasn't in sight. *Where in the ancient spheres has that devilish woman gone?* he mused as he stepped around a gold-leafed bush. On the wooden bench that faced the crystalline lake, Imara sat with crossed arms and a face wrought with frustration.

"Do you carry a personal rain cloud with you?" Ronar teased, but when he received a scowl and a glare chillier than glacial waters in the mountains, he eased off. "I come with a peace offering." He extended a hand in good faith, and the warmth of magic pulsed through him, heating up the space between them. In a moment, Imara's dress was dry, as was her hair.

Imara blinked, her hand smoothing over the fabric of her dress. "I'm not going to say thank you. If you've only come out here to trick me or belittle me, you can leave now. I've had enough of that to last me a lifetime." Her arms remained crossed and pressed tightly against her chest.

Ronar leaned back, as if he were the offended one. "I wasn't expecting a thanks from you but have no fear. Much to my dismay, I'm not here to tease you." Ronar chuckled and moved the old volume in front of him. "Drying you off was a courtesy, but not what I came to offer. This is—" His fingers rapped on the cover before he moved it toward Imara. "I thought you'd find some use for it. It's a—"

"Why would I find that book of any use?" she asked petulantly, staring at the offering as she grudgingly gave it a once over. "It's a book on *magic*, and as you saw yourself, I have so little that it's laughable." She bit out her last words, eyeing him as if she were waiting for him to open the floor to mocking her.

When Imara didn't take the book, he pulled it against his chest. Ronar sighed and leaned on one foot, cocking the other. "It holds the secrets of old magic, prior to the foundation of your Elder Council as you know it." He paused, brows furrowing in thought. "There is an old magic that surrounds you still. I gain nothing by lying to you, Imara. I only offer the truth. You do possess magic, but a magic that cannot be explained. Take mine for example: I am not bound by elements." He held out a hand, summoning a bowl of fresh berries, which he in turn offered to Imara.

She recoiled, mistrust blazing in her eyes. "I can assure you, it doesn't matter how hard I study or how many different books I read. No magic will come from me— nothing useful, anyway." Like the book, she eyed the berries suspiciously and huffed. "I lost my appetite after your trickery, *my lord*."

"Don't starve yourself on my account." Ronar curled his lip and shrugged. "That wasn't my trickery. If it was, you'd be drenched from head to toe, not showered on. That was *you*, whether you want to believe me or not. It's neither here nor there. The fact is, you *do* have magic." He bent down and placed the book as well as berries on the bench beside her. Imara kept a watchful gaze trained on him; she looked like a hawk keeping tabs on a would-be captor.

Patience was a virtue Ronar had learned through the centuries, but everyone had their limits. He also knew when to withdraw from a situation. "Imara, just because you can't do what your kin are able to doesn't mean that you're impotent. It means they're too blinded and too foolish to realize something is blocking you, tamping down your abilities." His voice took on the soft quality one typically took with a frightened child or injured animal, but when he saw she was staring at him with a hardening expression, he rolled his eyes.

"Oh yes, because *you*, mighty *Dragon Master*, are so far superior to all of us that you know more about me than I know of myself . . . And only *you* can magically pull this untapped ability out of me." She flailed her hands in the air, cheeks reddening and eyes filling with tears. "One I have not felt in all my years." She had no need to add how hard she had tried to do just that.

Ronar's eyes narrowed, but he didn't bite back. "Why, in fact, I know I am. I also believe I'm one of few that can crack whatever barrier or shield is dulling your magic. You may call it a flaw, but I call it tenacity. I rarely ever give up once I'm focused on a task." He shifted his weight onto both feet and pressed his lips into a thin line. "If you would like more information, find me in the library. And if not—" He turned to take in the lake, the warmth of the autumn sun, and nodded. "Enjoy what Dragon's Keep has to offer. There are bushes full of elderberries waiting to be harvested, and our garden is still offering the cold weather crops." Without another word, he left Imara to sulk outside and perhaps mull over what he had said.

As soon as he stepped back inside the warm home, Sylvi clucked her tongue like a nagging grandmother.

"I don't want to hear it. Just give me the tea and bring some breakfast into the library." Ronar disappeared down the hallway. If Imara didn't join him, so be it, but that didn't mean he had to implore her to cease pouting.

Dragon's Keep's library was no small thing: shelf upon shelf lined the brightly lit room, and where there wasn't a wall of books, there were windows that stretched from floor to ceiling. Volumes, new and old, filled the dusty shelves, lending the room that distinct *library* smell.

Imara perplexed Ronar, but not because of the barbs hidden in her tongue or the tears that gleamed in her eyes. Rather, it was the erratic nature of what dwelled so deep within that it was as if it was almost forgotten, buried beneath layers of protection. He wondered what had happened to her, if perhaps someone else had drawn up the shield, or if she had done it unwittingly when she was a child. There was no mistaking the thrum he'd felt at breakfast, or even back in the council hall. It was there, lying in wait.

While Ronar waited for Imara to decide whether to join him or not, he browsed useful volumes, pulling them out and laying them down on the massive table in the center of the room.

A half hour went by. Ronar now waited outside of the library, sipped his tea, and arched an eyebrow when he caught sight of Imara, red-faced and flustered.

"You could have told me where the library was instead of letting me wander this . . . this maze of a keep!" She waved one of her hands around, clutching the book against her chest with the other.

He grinned over the rim of his cup. "I could have, but then I would have missed this." Ronar motioned with his free hand to her frazzled appearance. Sun-kissed blond hair frizzed around her face, curling and tickling the pale skin of her cheeks. She didn't look as if she had simply walked into the house—she looked as if she had run from a travesty down in the valley and happened upon his doorstep.

Imara's mouth fell open, and her eyes narrowed. The muscles in her face were tightening as though she were readying to breathe fire. "You . . . "

He sighed and moved into the doorway, motioning her inward. "Have been waiting for you, my lovely bride. It's given me time to reflect on our upcoming nuptials." Ronar shifted against the wall and glanced down at the steam rising and writhing from his tea.

She scowled at him, stomping her way into the library. "Reflect away, because you'll receive no input from me."

RONAR

Ronar spun on his heel and entered the library. He halted immediately, stopping himself from colliding with Imara. She stood at the opening to the stairwell's balcony, peering down over the vast array of books. He nearly bumped into her, and as it was, his chest was scarcely touching her shoulders. Imara appeared so lost in her thoughts, or in assessment of his library, she didn't seem to notice their proximity as she took in the collection of books.

"This isn't a library," Imara whispered, almost breathless. "This is an archive." When she finally took notice of his closeness, she pressed herself against the railing, retreating from him.

Ronar chuckled, stepping aside so he could descend the stairs. "One and the same, isn't it? What is a library if it doesn't hold a bit of history in it?" He glanced over his shoulder, peering up at her.

"This isn't a *bit* of history, my lord." Imara's eyes flicked over the shelves as she too walked down the stairs. Awe transformed her previously bitter expression into one of wonder. She spun in a circle, visibly marveling over the library.

Ronar dragged a hand along his narrow chin. "Well, it isn't all of it either, is it?" His eyebrows furrowed as he scanned the rows of books. There was another that possessed far more history than what he had here. Ancient scrolls that put his collections to shame.

Waving his hand, Ronar motioned to the table where breakfast had been moved. There was also a pot of tea and another cup waiting for Imara. "Over the years, I've collected much of what was nearly lost in some god-forsaken war or another. Anything that was written down and accounted for I've tried my best to save. Aside from what was never written or burned in battle."

Imara's mouth fell open. Her arms, which held the volume, tightened over it. "What?"

He arched his brow as he sipped at the tea. "Someone had to save the records. It might as well have been me." That was as close as he would allow himself to get to admitting how old he was. The less people knew about him, the better for all. What did it matter, anyway? Imara would soon return home to be amongst her people. "Let's try breakfast again, and this time, actually eat. But please try not to sully the goods." Ronar pointed at the book she held and sat down.

"Oh." Imara placed the book down hurriedly and slid it out of harm's way before she sat down too. "I read some of it while I was outside." The bite in her words had vanished, but the color still showed in her cheeks—the only evidence that she'd been upset not an hour ago.

Ronar drummed his fingers on the table, cocking an eyebrow. "And? Did you discover anything of import?"

The question came just as Imara was sinking her teeth into half of her skolleboller. Her eyes rounded as she chewed quickly. "I didn't have that much time." She wiped crumbs from her lips and glanced down at the book. "It's quite old."

"The book is likely older than your grandparents, or at the very least, the same age." Ronar paused for a moment before continuing. "Of what you did read, did you notice anything?" he inquired, watching the young seidr carefully.

A nervous or rather excited energy seemed to pour from Imara. "I noticed it didn't speak of elementals, but it went on about broader magic. Those who don't rely on an element at all."

Ronar opened his hands, waiting expectantly, and the book floated from the table into his waiting palms. "There is more than that too." He flicked through several chunks of the book until he landed on a particular page. Standing, he moved beside Imara and placed the volume off to the side in front of her. The scent of jasmine and sunshine wafted toward him, along with a distinct fragrance that was wholly her own. "They have been called more than one thing since the beginning of time. Supreme Elemental, Ambients, the list goes on. But whatever the world decided to call them, they were all the same thing."

Imara shifted, her head tilting to the side so she could look up at him. "What? I don't understand. I know elementals have been around since—"

"Yes, since the beginning, but here is the crux of it:

Elementals are limited creatures. Ambients, the *Supreme* Elementals, are not bound by one element." Ronar altered his position, allowing himself to half sit on the table. "Rather, they can tap into them all with equal power. A water elemental is bound to their element, and perhaps she can use a hint of fire, but it pales in comparison to her usage of water. But an Ambient . . . It doesn't matter what the element is, they are tied to them *all*." His brows lifted as he watched the expression on Imara's face shift from curiosity to confusion to absolute disbelief.

"Are you implying that *I* am an Ambient? My lord, they are a myth if anything at all. I have never heard of such a being existing. Ever." She jutted her chin out, pale eyebrows furrowing.

Ronar chuckled, draping his arms against his knees. He peered down at her with a sardonic smile. "Of course . . . I have forgotten that you, Imara Hjelmstad, know all. I don't know what you are, and we've seen you only react with water, but you are not what they think. I merely wish for you to realize that more magic exists out there than what is possessed by your contemptuous villagers." He reached out and tapped her on the nose like one would a rascally kitten. "I'll also have you know you are quite wrong. Ambients were once born quite frequently, but over time, through the loss of bloodlines, murders, and the like, they became an infrequent occurrence."

Imara's eyes narrowed at the touch to her nose, and she scoffed. "And I just happen to be that one in a thousand or more years." It wasn't a question; she was close to mocking him.

"Maybe. But who can say? There is one way to find

out . . . " He dismissed her lack of faith in his knowledge. There was an important history lesson to be taught here, and so he continued. "I want to begin our . . . journey with honesty. In the hall, while we danced, I performed a test of my own. I reached out to your well of magic, but rather than finding emptiness, I found a wall. Something is blocking your use of magic, a barrier of some sort. When you soaked yourself, I felt the thrum of magic, so I don't for one moment believe you are without it."

Imara's cheeks flushed at the mention of earlier. Her teeth pinched her full bottom lip as she visibly warred with the information. "I'm listening," she said softly.

As much as Ronar yearned to read her thoughts, he allowed her the privacy of them. But it wasn't his imagination. Imara appeared open to the idea that she wasn't as useless as her village pegged her. Ronar smiled, reaching out to flip the page to the illustrated side of Ambients. "Are you truly going to listen to me?" he teased, lowering his head so his lips nearly tickled the tip of her ear. "While I have your ear, perhaps we can discuss—"

"No." Imara quickly ended his words.

"Very well." He chuckled, motioning toward the circle of elements.

Her cheeks burned a lovely shade of red. "If what you say is true, how do we break through the barrier?"

Ronar squinted, truly stumped. "I don't know, but I aim to find out. In the meantime, all we can do is try to provoke your magic."

Imara snorted, flicking errant curls from her face. "My magic or me?"

A devilish smile tugged the corners of Ronar's lips, and

his green eyes danced with mirth. "I'll take pleasure in both, darling." He watched as her eyes glanced at him from the corners, and all he could do was chuckle. Imara turned toward him, their faces only a hair's breadth apart, and he saw then what he had seen in the hall: strength, intelligence, and obstinance—all traits that no doubt enabled her to strive where others likely would have succumbed. "You, however, are not the only thing I found curious this Fallfest."

Imara gazed back at him, questioning.

Typically, Ronar would have brushed off the glance and allowed his words to remain a mystery, but Imara's eyes implored him to reveal what else he'd found intriguing. "There are secrets buried deep within your Elders. I can't imagine why, but they're not as they seem to be." He paused, chuckling as Imara's features wrinkled into an expression of doubt. "Would it be such a leap to learn they were hiding something? They're hardly straightforward with me, let alone those beneath them." Ronar ran a hand down his jaw, laughing mirthlessly. "I've never been keen on them, but I didn't like the whispers I heard in the hall."

It wouldn't surprise Ronar one bit. Although he didn't believe they had any knowledge of how or why the land was dying. If only the village had come to him sooner, but he believed that was the doing of the Elders. They must have assumed it was something they could handle, though it clearly wasn't.

The state of the valley bothered him. It had been a few weeks since he'd taken the time to visit, inspect the lands, and check in with the inhabitants, but there were other tasks that warred for his attention. For starters, the king of Brynjar had kept him occupied with matters of the kingdom. In fact, he'd only just returned home in time for the banquet.

Now that Ronar knew the current state of the valley, he'd have to contact King Thorne sooner rather than later.

What sort of sickness could have caused such devastation, and so quickly, upon a highly fertile land? In all his years, he had never seen something of its sort. It occurred to him in that moment that someone or something could have placed an unnatural sickness on the land. Something blocking it from all sources of renewal, even the seidrs. Quickly, he flicked through the pages of the volume in his grasp, searching for an answer he wasn't sure was even in the book.

"What is it?" Imara stood from the chair. "My lord?" she asked softly, and when he didn't respond, "Lajos!" Her hand darted out to rest on his wrist.

Ronar's movements ceased when her hand gently touched him. "Tell me, Imara, have you or others tried to heal your sick land?" His eyes locked with hers, a new intensity burning within them. "Have you tried to heal your crops, replenish the water beds? I assume I saw little of what is actually taking place in the villages." He pulled his hand away from hers and with his other, ensnared her wrist instead.

Imara stuttered. "Of course we have, we aren't dullards!" She pulled her hand free and clutched it to her chest as if he had wounded her.

"How?" he asked patiently.

She looked at him as if *he* were a dullard. "What do

you mean *how*? Those with an affinity to earth tried healing the land, those with water tried replenishing the riverbeds."

"And there was nothing?"

"No." She slid away from the chair and put space between them, eyeing Ronar as if he'd lost his mind.

Maybe he had lost his mind. Maybe it was madness to believe that the earth also had a barrier—that something was stopping the magic from penetrating the elements. "I think . . . I think you share something in common with the land right now." He licked his lips and chuckled, threading his fingers through his hair. "Wouldn't that be something?"

"You realize you are making very little sense right now?" Imara's eyes narrowed on him.

Ronar's gaze focused, and he winked at her. "I know, my darling. What if the earth possessed a barrier of its own?" He mused out loud and began to pace around the library. Out of all of the books in here, there had to have been some record that could explain what was happening. That is, as long as it hadn't been destroyed.

"That is madness," Imara muttered.

Ronar spun on his heel and placed a hand on the table. An odd little smile turned the corner of his lips up as he looked at her through a fringe of dark lashes. "Is it, though? What is stranger: to think there is no barrier, or to think *everyone's* magic has been rendered useless? Everyone's, Imara."

She toyed with a few errant curls around her face. A nervous tick, Ronar was beginning to realize. Imara opened her mouth but halted herself as if she were expecting to be silenced. When Ronar lifted his brows expectantly, she spoke. "But why now? Why not ten years ago? And why so rapidly? What has changed as of late to make it spread so quickly?"

Ronar strode forward, his arms stretched out so he could rest his hands on Imara's shoulders. "Those are the right questions, and although I don't have the answers, together, we will find them." He dropped his hands when she balked, his lips twisting. "Oh, don't worry. I don't plan on biting, not until after we're wed." He purred his words lowly. Above him, the sound of feet shuffling on the landing caught his attention. He lifted his head and looked up at the balcony. Sylvi stood with her lips puckered and eyebrows arched. *Damnable girl*, he thought, *impeccable timing.*

"I wasn't certain if you needed anything, m'lord? Or you, m'lady?" Sylvi inclined her head.

"We are all set, Sylvi. You can go *now*." He emphasized the last word, baring his teeth in a predator's smile.

Sylvi didn't flinch, her eyes flicked toward Imara. "And m'lady?"

Ronar felt Imara's gaze on the side of his face, and he could have sworn he saw her smile, but his eyes were trained on Sylvi, who was now grinning from ear to ear.

"Actually, do you have any risgrøt? Just a little. But if you have to make it for me, please don't trouble yourself. It's usually what I have for breakfast at home."

"I will see what I can do for you, m'lady." Sylvi bowed her head and left without saying a word to Ronar.

The muscle in his jaw leaped violently, but when he turned to take a glimpse at Imara, he saw a flash of vulnerability. Of course Imara missed home, and to be housed with him and his staff must be a miserable thing. Perhaps it was within Sylvi's right to check on him. It wasn't as if he was known for being sensitive—or attentive, for that matter.

"In other news, I'll be leaving tomorrow. In accordance with the bargain." He motioned to Imara, his eyes shuttering whatever feverish expression they'd had moments ago. "I'll be off to deal with the mages that attacked your villagers. I plan to inspect some land while I'm gone too. I'll be sending word to the king as well. He should know what is transpiring here." Ronar walked away from Imara and sat in the chair at the head of the table again. With his attention focused wholly on the skolleboller in front of him, he bit into the pastry, ignoring the cream oozing outward.

"And what am I supposed to do while you're gone, Lord Lajos? Pine for you? Take up some sewing?" Imara's face pinched with disdain. Whatever silent truce they had moments ago was now over.

Ronar lifted his finger and swiped cream from his lips. "If it'd suit you, but I'd rather return to you not maimed. So perhaps no sewing. But if you're intending to pine for me, at least spare no expense telling me about it." The look on her face said it all: red-faced, eyes willing him to dissolve into a pile of ashes, hand clutching the napkin on the table. She was furious with him again, and maybe that was best. "Even though I'd *love* to hear about it, I have something else in mind. While I'm gone, I'm going to give you some tasks to perform. It'll tap into earth, wind, fire, and water."

Imara's hand clenched on the napkin again. The anger subsided and was replaced with trepidation. "What tasks?"

As he finished up the pastry in front of him, Ronar stood and fetched a small vase. Inside it was a piece of purple heather that had long since expired. It was without roots, and the stem was rotting. "Bring back the blooms. To do this, you'll need to remove the bacteria from the roots, replenish them, and lastly, bring the blooms back to the flowers." In an open hand, he replicated the dead twig of heather. In a show of what he meant, his magic washed over the wilted piece and slowly brought it back to life, or so it appeared.

Imara's mouth parted, but Ronar lifted a finger to silence her. "What you see isn't as it truly is. As much as I wish I could, I can't bring things back. My magic doesn't work that way. What you see is an illusion." He dropped the sprig, and it fell onto the table, instantly returning to the dried, dead branch it once had been.

Ronar reached for a candlestick on the table and pushed it toward her. His next task would be easier, he thought. "You may use a flint to aid you, which Sylvi can fetch, but I want you to use the spark from the flint so you can light the wick with *your* magic. I expect you to have these two done by the time I return."

As if summoned by the change of mood, Sylvi returned with the risgrøt and placed it in front of Imara. "Anything else, m'lady?"

"That will be all, thank you." Imara smiled at her and lifted the spoon to begin eating. "Are you to teach me anything today, Lord Lajos?"

Ronar's lips pinched as he looked at Sylvi. "I thought

instead of teachings, which you've no doubt sat through countless times, we'd instead read in companionable silence. Or at least I'd read in silence whilst you plot my demise. Nevertheless, my darling bride—"

"Stop calling me your bride. I may have been gifted to you, but I am not *yours* and I am not your darling. I am still me, Imara Hjelmstad."

He understood, of course, on some level how difficult this must have been for her. But Ronar hadn't a choice in the matter either. Not when his refusal of Imara would've been far worse for her than just being a pariah. Did she understand that? He snorted. "Very well, Imara Hjelmstad, as you said. You're not my anything and, yes, you were gifted to me by your village, which chose to give you away. But consider this too: you were thrust on *me*. I could have refused you, and then what?" His voice chilled as he stared at her. "You may choose to hate me, but it wasn't *me* who made that decision." Every part of him wanted to run off, to stew and storm in his room, but that would give Imara the satisfaction of winning, or at least he assumed it would. His presence rankled her, and so he opted to simmer in her company.

Ronar wasn't hungry any longer, but this wasn't a dining hall, it was a library, and he was surrounded by several volumes that could pass the time. Whoever left the room first would surely be the loser, and he was nothing if not patient. He summoned a book on diseases and settled in for the long haul.

IMARA

Having finally been able to eat to her heart's content, Imara finished her breakfast, ignoring the man in the room who seemed capable of setting her blood to boiling without so much as even trying. Fortunately, the library was large and stacked to the ceiling with books and scrolls, so there was no need to speak to each other unless absolutely necessary.

Full and content from breakfast, Imara filled her cup with a fresh bit of hot, floral-scented tea, plucked up the book Lajos had gifted her, and withdrew a great deal away from him. Settling herself down into a soft, tufted chair close to the fire—the library was cavernous and cool—she slipped her feet out of her silk slippers and tucked them into the chair with her. Folded up comfortably, with her teacup in hand and the book spread on her lap, open to the section about elemental magics, Imara stared down at the words before her.

While her fingers itched to leaf through the pages, and her curiosity niggled at the back of her mind to learn everything she could about this newly discovered seidr history, she couldn't focus. The last thirty-six hours had left her reeling, and the fact that the Master of Dragons thought her to possess any form of magic when she'd been told otherwise all her life . . . it felt beyond comprehension.

The library was silent except for the soft sounds of the flames crackling over wood in the fireplace and the occasional stirring of His Lordship as he flipped to a new page or shifted in his own seat. It wasn't a taut atmosphere between them, nor was it a companionable silence. Both parties were far too aware of the other in the room to be entirely off their guard.

Lowering her head over her tea, Imara peered at Lajos from beneath her lashes, studying him as he sat stooped over his own book, strong features tight with concentration. His dark hair, which was long enough to curl slightly at the ends, fell down around his face, tickling at the edge of his angular jaw and teasing at his dark brows. His green eyes— which had an unnerving way of looking more deeply into her than she cared to admit—peered down at the pages before him, intent for once on their words rather than on watching her become flustered at his behavior.

While she wanted nothing of this potential marriage, Imara was still a young woman with little experience in the attention of men, and Lajos, Master of Dragons, was an intense, enigmatic man with stormy good looks that the women of her village often twittered about upon the conclusion of each Fallfest. He was a lot to comprehend for a girl looking down the long path of a long life joined with his.

Could he be correct in his assumptions that there was more to her than even she was aware? Her eyes fell to stare at the hands holding her teacup, wondering if it were possible that they held the ability to control essentially all that was around her. Imara wanted so very intensely for him to be right, not because she wanted to go back to the village and prove they'd been wrong the whole time but because she wanted so badly to have a connection to the world all around her. To know what the others felt when they were joined blissfully with their magic and their element.

Yet, even though his eyes had held no sign of doubt, and his words had sounded with firm assurance, Imara could not bring herself to believe. Seated here with the tea in her cup and the flame brightly glowing at her side, Imara could neither sense nor affect either water or fire. No part of her was yearning to be set free, nor were any of the elements surrounding her calling out. Imara felt truly and entirely alone here, cut off from everyone and everything she had ever known and loved.

"Is this the only book you have on ancient seidr magic?" she asked, breaking the silence that had settled between them.

Lajos barely lifted his head from his book, pointing instead with one hand toward one of the walls lined with shelves. "You will find some on that shelf, but they are more life recountings rather than historical tomes."

While historical texts were useful and fascinating, the idea of an actual recounting of someone's life during the times she was investigating had her sliding her feet back into the silk slippers and wandering over to the wall he had pointed at. His directions had been less than helpful, but after scouring the shelves for some time, Imara found a book that seemed to leap out at her. Plucking it from its tight spot clutched between two other imposing bindings, Imara spread it open, fingers brushing reverently over the hand-scripted pages. Eyes falling to the opening lines a few pages in, she began to read:

Jarl Sarol visited today. He is to take Asger and myself under his instruction. It is a great honor for both he and I to be guided by one so wise and powerful. The village was filled with music and celebration until dawn after the announcement that both Asger and I had tested as Ambients. To have not one but two options for future Jarl is more than anyone could have asked for. I will train alongside Asger, and when the time is right, Jarl Sarol will decide who of us is best to succeed him when he steps down. This still feels so strange and so new, but Mother Earth guides her children, and I feel her all about me.

Taking a deep breath, Imara felt her heart hammering in her chest. There was something about these words that felt right, as if at last some unknown part of her people's history was being unveiled.

Stepping over to her chair, Imara gathered up the ancient text Lajos had given her, and without another word, headed for the door. She supposed she should ask if he were fine with her leaving the library with his books, but she simply couldn't be bothered—nor did she care at this time. Something about the writings in the book she had just found felt personal, and Imara had no desire to be around her infuriatingly perceptive betrothed as she read it.

Reaching the door, she could feel his eyes upon her, something unsaid in the air between them. Rather than look back and acknowledge Lajos, she opened the door and stepped out. A deep breath rushed out of her on the other side: relief at being alone for the moment. Lajos was not someone she knew quite how to handle or what to expect. At moments, he was baiting her temper, then in the blink of an eye, could be entirely serious as he offered her hope of escaping her defective lot in life.

Not knowing Dragon's Keep yet, Imara wandered the halls until she found what seemed to be a small sitting room. The fire wasn't yet going, but she was no stranger to taking care of herself, and she curled up once more in a chair, tucking her feet beneath her heavy skirts. Sylvi, it would seem, had been aware of her movements around the keep, and arrived very soon after with a tray of tea, biscuits, and fruit. This she set on the table nearest Imara, just within comfortable arm's reach, and then set about lighting a fire for her.

"Thank you," Imara spoke softly, watching the young woman kneeling upon the hearth.

"Of course, m'lady," she responded. "I know this must be so very strange and foreign to you . . . I know how it can be to be swept up from what you've known and deposited here at the keep. We're all here to help you settle in as best we can, even Master Lajos."

At this, Imara snorted, her eyes falling to the pages of the book in her hands, thumb brushing lightly upon their edges. "He has a strange way of showing it."

"He's a solitary creature . . . which means he doesn't always remember what others require to feel comfortable. But he does mean well, m'lady."

"Imara."

"Hm?" Sylvi's head perked up in question, and the two locked eyes across the room.

"Please, call me Imara. I may have been offered up as Lord Lajos's bride, but I am not the lady of this house. I would rather we simply be friends." She offered Sylvi a shy smile, desiring so very much to have at least one compatriot in this strange new life.

"I would like that very much too, m'lady . . . Imara," she corrected herself, a happy smile upon her own lips.

Imara smiled back at her, happy to have one ally here at Dragon's Keep. "Thank you."

"I will leave you to your reading now, but do let me know if there is anything I can help you with." Sylvi stood from the fireplace, wiping her hand on her apron, and moved to the doorway.

Nodding first to Sylvi's words, Imara dipped her head back to the book before her, falling once more into the written words of the young Ambient. The writer went on to tell of the beginning of her lessons with Jarl Sarol and young Asger, of the hours spent sitting in the soil, learning to listen to the essence of Jörd and all that she would direct. Imara poured herself cup after cup of tea as she read about months of training where Jarl Sarol seemed hesitant to take the young Ambients deeper into the knowledge of their power, until tragedy struck.

I became wroth with Jarl Sarol today . . . accusing him of withholding our training because he was jealous of our futures and loath to let us take his place when the time would come. I've not seen him so furious as he was with me at that time. He said, "Embla, you are a foolish girl who knows not of what she speaks," and then he excluded me from training today, instead taking Asger only. They left at noon for the forests of Hymir around the base of Mount Jotunn. I am meant to feel contrite and ashamed of my behavior, but I am not. I still feel valid in my words to Sarol. I simply handled the accusations in an inappropriate manner.

It had ended there, but the next page held a frantic energy to them, the pen strokes harsh and quickly scribbled. In places, it was hard for Imara to make out what had been written. Yet she found herself drawn into the desperate words.

Asger did not come back from the mount! Sarol claims they were separated in the woods, and after doing all he could to locate Asger, he was left with no choice but to return alone. I am not sure what it is, but my body is humming with an odd energy. I am distraught, but I do not believe it is the fear causing this strange sensation in me. I feel drawn to the Hymir woods. Something is pulling me there.

I went to the woods.

Father tried to keep me back, but I couldn't listen. The electric humming inside of me intensified to the point where I could no longer take it. Jörd was speaking to me. It sounds impossible even to mine own mind, but she was. Mother Earth pulled me through that forest as surely as a hand guiding me, and I found him.

Here there was a splash of ink that looked suspiciously like it had been caused by a droplet of water on the page, or a tear.

Asger is dead. His body crushed and twisted in a way that was by no animal. I do not want to think it, and know no one will believe me . . . but I am certain it was Jarl Sarol. He does not want to give up his position of power. We are threats to this. I have no doubt that I am next. If I am to survive, I may have to kill him first.

The words before her left Imara's heart pattering faster. Lajos had spoken of killings of Ambients, but she hadn't thought it would be at the hands of others of their kind. While she was saddened by this realization, there was something else staying more forefront in her thoughts. The earth . . . or Jörd, had spoken to the writer. Imara was certain that what she had read about were the forces and energies of the world coursing through the young woman to such an extent that it had led her straight to her fallen comrade.

Without thinking, Imara was on her feet, forgetting her slippers and instead hurrying down along the hallways back toward the library. She had to speak to Lajos of this. They did not have an Ambient to call upon, but perhaps there could be a way to use his own powers and that of the seidrs in Omdahl to speak with Mother Earth herself. The villagers had attempted to heal the land, but none had ever sought to commune with it instead.

Her hand upon the library door, beginning to push it open, Imara paused at the sound of voices. Lajos was speaking to someone.

"Yes, I leave at dawn. I will be gone a day at the very least. I don't anticipate much struggle from the mages, but I do wish to take a look at the lands and see how far the damage has spread. I've also written a letter for Thorne. Can you ensure it's sent by fowl? He needs to know what is going on."

"And what of Imara during this time?" It was Sylvi.

A heavy sigh sounded from Lajos before he responded. "Keep an eye on the girl, and make sure she doesn't destroy something in her path or make an outright nuisance of herself."

"M'lord . . . " There was a scolding tone in Sylvi's voice.

"I've left her tasks to do, if the hotheaded creature will get down off her seat of fury long enough to attempt them.

After what she did to the breakfast table . . . Just make sure she doesn't do that to the rest of our home in my absence."

Imara had heard enough. Stepping back from the library door, she turned, angry tears in her eyes. It was bad enough to be spoken to in such a manner, but to hear it secondhand . . . it was like being transported back to the village and overhearing the whispers. No matter where she went, she was never what anyone anticipated or expected; she was always faulty. Sucking in a harsh breath to force away the tears, she stiffened her shoulders. If she spent the rest of the day and evening in her chambers, she wouldn't have to see him again for several days, and perhaps then she wouldn't feel so much like stomping on his foot when she did.

IMARA

While the morning air held a chill to it, announcing that fall was upon them, the sun still beat down on Imara, warming her skin. Her head tilted upward, reveling in the feeling as she sat with her toes buried in the soil and her fingers threaded in strands of grass to either side of her.

It had been three days since Lajos had left. Imara had managed to avoid seeing him the evening before his departure, choosing to take dinner in her chambers so that she wouldn't have to sit at the table with him pretending that she wouldn't rather stab him with her fork.

Lajos had made the argument that he hadn't been the one to offer her up, that it had been the Elders and her village—which was true. Yet it had been Lord Lajos who had accepted her. The power had been his to refuse the need for further payment, and instead offer his help from a place of concern as their proclaimed protector. Instead, he had taken Imara without any real hesitation, like one might take a crisp apple offered in passing.

Sighing in frustration, Imara cleared her throat and tried forcing her mind to empty of all thoughts, searching for any kind of connection to the world around her. In the days that had passed, she had spent many hours wandering the large keep, getting to know her way around it and exploring all the hidden nooks and crannies. Her meals had been shared with the three staff that Lajos kept, Imara refusing to stand on some nonexistent ceremony when the master of the house was not around. Without those sardonic green eyes watching her, Imara had found herself befriending Sylvi and enjoying the motherly affection that Thyr, the cook, offered her. Even Mikkel's dry personality could be called almost humorous at times—almost.

"Focus, Imara," she berated herself, her toes shifting in the soil, digging just a little deeper.

Exploring hadn't been the only thing she had done. Burning the candles low, Imara had been up late each night, reading through the ancient text Lajos had given her, along with finishing the written journal of Embla. The two works had given her a semblance of understanding, a deeper insight into what the magic of the seidrs truly was and where it had come from. It wasn't simply the elements but the energy of the earth—of Jörd—speaking to them. Some were able to tap into the energy flow of their particular element and draw from it. In many ways, they were born of that energy, and it infused their bodies, giving them a direct link. An Ambient, however, was linked to all of the lines of energy within Jörd, and as Embla had written it, could use those lines to commune with her.

"By the sun and stars, Imara, you can *do* this!" Her hands tightened on the sprigs of grass, pulling a little. Each day, she had come to sit in the sunshine, amidst all of the elements, trying her best to imitate the meditations Embla and Asger had so studiously practiced. The difference was, both of those young seidrs had been in touch with their abilities already, whereas Imara still felt entirely blocked to whatever magic resided within her—if there even was any.

Each day she had tried to connect to the earth, to empty her mind of all thoughts and simply feel the buzz of energy around her, *through* her. There was nothing. Opening her eyes in frustration, Imara gazed up at the sun, tracking its location in the sky and realizing that she'd been out here for an hour already. Shoulders slumping in defeat, she shifted, folding her legs before her and reaching for the stem of dried heather Lajos had given her to work with.

"This is ridiculous. I don't know what he believes I will be able to do with you. You're not even in soil any longer." Her fingertips gently rolled the stem between them, watching the faded purple blooms as they spun in the air before her.

Taking in a deep breath and then slowly releasing it, Imara focused all her will and intent on the sprig, willing it to find life again, to be reborn. "Just grow!" she growled under her breath, searching herself for some sign of life, of energy, of anything that would help this plant.

As always, her body was silent, offering no sign of having anything it could give. Sadness and disappointment coursed through her, all the more vicious for the hope that had begun to dawn inside her due to Lajos' belief that she was more than what she appeared. It was hopeless though; there was nothing within her.

"Why can't you just do *something!*" she shouted angrily at the heather, her voice breaking into a sob as she unleashed her frustration and hurt at what life had doled out thus far. It was as her voice broke that she felt a zap of energy course through her, and a small leaf on the stem of the heather greened and came back to life.

Trembling, Imara stared at the small sign of life, finally having felt the magic come from somewhere within her. Biting her lip, she tried to tug on that little flow of energy, to push it further into the heather. There didn't seem to be any budging it, but instead of slumping in defeat, Imara smiled. She could feel it, simmering there below the surface, a tingle of something *other*, something beyond herself.

Laughing outright, Imara flung herself back onto the grass, staring up at the sky, feeling lighter and more full of life than perhaps she ever had. It was *there*. She couldn't control it yet, or draw on it at will, but there was no denying it any longer. Magic resided within her. She simply had to figure out how to tap into it. Anxiousness fluttered in Imara's belly, mingling with doubt. What if it was still laughable? What if it was still weak in comparison to the other villagers?

Rolling to her feet, Imara gathered up her things, clutching them happily to her bosom as she turned to head back to the keep, feeling rather hungry. Cheeks a little red from the cool breeze, and wisps of hair curling about her face, she made her way inside, a pleased smile upon her face. Abandoning the heather and candle on a table in the entry, the young seidr made her way down the hall to the back of the keep where the kitchen was tucked away.

What Imara had quickly learned was that Thyr was not a woman to remain idle, and so there was always something delicious brewing or baking. Sticking her head in through the door, Imara sniffed at the air, smelling a hint of sugary goodness.

"Oh! Imara, my dear, come in! You're just in time to test out these raspberry quark pastries. Come, come." Thyr waved her in with a quick motion of her hand, slipping a heavenly looking pastry mounded with glazed raspberries and custard toward her. She was a plump woman, whose upswept hair was graying in patches and always seemed to be escaping the bun she'd knotted it into.

Unable to resist, Imara moved further into the kitchen and took up the quark. "This looks amazing. How did you know I was craving something sweet and flaky?" she asked with a smile before taking a bite of the treat. "Mmm, even better than it looks."

Thyr offered a robust chuckle and continued to bustle about, cleaning up after her baking in preparation of starting something else, Imara was sure.

"You look like you could use plenty more sweets than that. So slender," she tutted with a shake of her head.

"Well, I appreciate all the delicious snacks. It reminds me of home." Imara smiled a little sadly.

Thyr glanced over at her, giving her an understanding look that wasn't entirely pitying. The older woman reached out her hand to cup Imara's cheek gently. "You feel welcome to come in here and make yourself at home any time you please. Even if you just want to sit and watch this old lady bumble her way around the dinner meal or sneak a biscuit from the jar."

"Thank you." She smiled at the older woman, feeling comfortable in her presence. "This is wonderful." She held the quark aloft, then spotted a small sack that had just recently been emptied of onions. Grabbing it up, she showed it to Thyr. "Would you mind too much if I borrowed this for a little while? I promise I'll return with it later today."

Thyr barely cast it a glance, busy washing up a large mixing bowl. "Of course, dear, whatever you please."

"Thank you," she repeated, grateful for the kindness of the cook. Offering her a little wave of her fingers, Imara slipped out of the kitchen with the quark and sack in hand.

In her haste to pack up her belongings, Imara had forgotten a few of her essential items, and there was an antiseptic ointment from one of her new medical books that she wanted to try. However, that meant going into the woods to gather a few needed ingredients. Lajos had forbidden her to enter them, but she had spent her entire life wandering the hills and woods around Omdahl; heading into the tree line a little way hardly seemed to be a dangerous thing to do.

Finishing the quark pastry on her way back up to her chambers, Imara went to fetch her medical text and a few other needed tools.

The woods were cool as she wandered through the underbrush, examining the leaves of plants and gazing at the underside of petals to ensure that she was picking the correct ones. It was pleasant though, the scent of damp moss and soil familiar and comforting. The little sack that she had fastened at her hip with a brooch was beginning to fill with the different herbs and flowers she had harvested, and it thrilled Imara to think of all she had access to right here in these woods. As she wandered, she sang softly, enjoying this moment when she felt like herself again and life felt a little normal.

At last, she found the final plant she'd been searching for. Imara stooped down to begin breaking pieces off, collecting the buds, which were still filled with ample amounts of seed that would later be crushed by her mortar and pestle. The forest was shaded, the branches hanging overhead thick with leaves and grown close together, but there was just enough sunlight drifting down to keep her warm. She had always felt at home when surrounded by greenery and life, and she was glad that she had ventured into the trees today.

Once the final piece of what she needed was picked and safely tucked away in her sack, Imara stood, brushing her hands off on the front of her apron skirt. Turning on her heel to head back, she felt her entire world shift, and the forest around her became blurred. Closing her eyes, Imara took a deep breath to steady herself, then opened her eyes to begin walking once more. But now the path back out to the keep seemed to be on her left rather than before her. Imara turned to face the path, only to find that the forest was spinning and shifting all around her yet again.

"Sylvi?!" Imara brought her hands to her mouth, shouting out the name of the young maid in hopes that she had stepped outside and was within earshot to help guide her. But Imara's voice seemed to only echo back at her, as if hitting a stone wall. "Sylvi! Thyr . . . Mikkel?!"

Each name was a futile attempt as her words became lost in the dense foliage of the forest around her. Knowing that she had only herself to depend on, Imara dipped her head down and began to walk in the direction she best thought Dragon's Keep lay. Keeping her eyes down, Imara focused on walking through the underbrush rather than looking up at the trees around her, hoping to prevent whatever disorientation was taking her over each time she did.

At the back of her mind, Lajos' warning of staying out of the woods circled through her memory, and Imara griped at herself for bringing it up. Lajos' *I told you so* would be of no good to her at this time.

Imara continued to walk, trying to keep her ears open for the sound of anything that felt like house noises, and every now and then shouting out for Sylvi or Mikkel. It was the snapping of a branch and the slight unfurling of breath in the form of a growl that brought Imara's head up at last. She found herself just on the edge of a clearing, and inside the clearing sat a hulking gold dragon, smoke coiling from its nostrils. Imara felt her breath leave her in shock as she stared up at the beast, whose sheer size made the trees seem like mere sticks.

From the top of its head protruded two proud, long horns, which were joined by smaller spikes that lined its fierce eyes, jutting also from the back edge of its jaw and the tip of its chin. The beast's gold scales gleamed in the sunlight like liquid fire, and its large taloned paws clenched at the earth beneath them.

Nothing in life had prepared her for this moment. While she knew of dragons, no one in her village had ever seen them, and so she had no knowledge of what to do. Her hand raised before her as she fought for the words to speak, something that would let the creature know she meant no harm by being here.

It was as if her movement set it off, for the dragon's head lowered toward the ground, its shoulders and body hunching as if preparing to attack. With a great roar that sent birds flying away in protest and forced Imara to reach out for a branch to steady herself, the dragon made its dissatisfaction known.

"Why are you in my woods?" the ancient beast roared, its voice a deep and gravelly rumble. It punctuated its words with a swift swipe of its tail that sent several trees crashing to the ground. Unfurling its wings, the dragon arched its head up into the sky, releasing a stream of fire that was hot enough to make Imara's cheeks burn.

Crying out in fear, Imara dropped down to her knees, her head bowing as her hands came out to rest together imploringly on the grass before her. "I'm s-sorry . . . I didn't mean . . . " Her voice trembled more than she wished it would, but it was difficult to face the potential of one's own death with a steady frame.

Head still bowed, Imara sensed the dragon shift in its form and, daring to peer up through her lashes, she found it was seated back on its haunches, wings drawn back in and its large tail wrapped in around its feet. The dragon was gazing down at her with a keen, knowing glance that burned with unbridled fury.

"Speak, little seidr, and explain what brings you into my forbidden realm," it rumbled once more.

Gingerly, Imara pulled herself up, sitting back on her heels so that she remained in a form of supplication. While she knew little about dragons, she did know that they were a proud lot, and it was best to treat them with as much reverence as possible.

"I came to the woods to gather herbs. I had not wandered in very deeply and was meaning to leave . . . but the world shifted around me, and each time I attempted to head back to Dragon's Keep, the forest moved once more." She watched as the dragon's eyes narrowed a little upon her, and smoke drifted from its nostrils as if in irritation.

"Dragon's Keep . . . Then you are aware these woods are forbidden to trespassers?" it questioned, watching her closely.

"No." She shrank back a little at the snarl that came from its curled lips, sharp teeth gleaming at her. "I was told not to come into the woods," she explained carefully. "Not that they were forbidden . . . " Imara pulled her hands into her lap, clutching them tightly together as she fought to cease their trembling.

"The woods have been enchanted against intruders, to keep them from me for their own sakes. And yet . . . "

Something had led her here, directly to it.

"Here you are nonetheless, in a place you do not belong," it snarled, shaking its great, horned head.

"Forgive me," Imara stated, bowing her head. "I truly do just wish to return to the keep, though I cannot find the way."

The beast huffed, agitated, and with its tail, pointed

toward a path through the trees on the opposite side of the clearing.

"Pass through that way. I will tell the woods to allow your passing . . . this time." There was a finality to the dragon's words that said it would not be so kind should this happen again. "Now, *go!*"

The dragon's roar had Imara jumping to her feet, fumbling a little with her skirts as she did so. "Th-thank you, m'lord," she mumbled, bowing her head before scurrying quickly across the clearing, keeping as far from its dangerous looking claws and tail as she could. Even in her terror, she couldn't help casting the dragon a searching look as she ran past, taking in the details of its form as well as she could in her hurry.

With a final curtsy, Imara darted down the path it had shown her, skirts hiked up in her hands as she ran, not entirely trusting that the woods wouldn't suddenly shift on her once more, or that the dragon wouldn't change its mind and decide to gobble her up instead.

She was panting harshly from her terror-induced run through the forest when at last she broke through the tree line out into the back gardens of Dragon's Keep. Safe, but for only a moment, for there on the stone steps of the keep stood Lajos, his hands on his hips and his glare so fierce that Imara was of half a mind to return to the dragon and take her chances there.

RONAR

A soft breeze caught the curls at Ronar's chin, the tendrils whispering against his lips as he glared at the infuriating woman rushing from the woods. He'd warned Imara against it, that much he recalled, but why on Mother's green earth *would* the stubborn seidr listen to him? The warning wasn't unfounded, for the land's enchantment was designed to disorient its trespassers, and even though Imara was to be the Lady of the Keep, she wasn't permitted to walk through the woods.

Ronar's hands hung at his side. The tension eased as he breathed slowly. Naturally, Imara would venture where she didn't belong. She was, after all, a curious creature. He saw it in the way she devoured the pages in his library, and in every quirk of a brow, every pursing of her lips. All that mattered was that she was safe, he reminded himself.

"I explicitly recall forbidding you from entering the woods, Imara," he spat in a seething tone.

Imara's pale brows furrowed as she skulked up to him, much like a chagrined child would. She gulped for air and then spewed her next words. "But . . . you didn't tell me there was a dragon!" She half turned to face where she'd come from, as if she expected the great beast to come lumbering out from where it hid.

Ronar rolled his eyes and ran his hand along his chin. "Say that I did. Would it have discouraged you any less from venturing into the woods?" He lifted his brows expectantly, but when no answer came, he nodded. "As I thought. I suspect you would have galloped even faster into the woods knowing the truth of it."

Imara's face scrunched, but whether it was from the exertion of running or knowing not to argue the truth, she said nothing in response.

Did she wait an hour, perhaps less, before she decided to go gallivanting in the forest? What did it matter now that she was back and stood beside him, looking shaken to the core? Ronar sighed and lifted a hand, motioning for her to come closer. His nerves were also on the edge, for his time away from the keep hadn't been a joyful one. The mages, as expected, had rallied against him. They weren't as small of a company as he'd thought, and it took a little more doing than he'd anticipated. A full day of battle had been the result, and in turn, Ronar's ribs ached, and his body longed for a deep slumber. But what upset him most was the condition of the land. Death, it seemed, was a contagious thing, and it was spreading through the land at an alarming rate.

Every ounce of tiredness he felt, he allowed his visage to reflect. "Come. I should have told you the truth of the woods the first day you arrived." Ronar wiggled his fingers to motion to her again, and when she reached him, he headed inside the keep. The scent of rich spices tickled his nose the moment he stepped indoors. Thyr was no doubt amidst one of her baking frenzies. As tired as he was, Ronar couldn't pass up the opportunity to eat.

"I'm sorry," Imara finally said. "If I had known—"

"Don't finish that." He chuckled at her. "I doubt it, but that's what sets you apart, isn't it? The curiosity and needing to know the truth. I can respect that. I'm not so different." Ronar shot her a sideward glance.

As if she would have remained out of the woods if she *knew* a dragon lurked in its depths. He clucked his tongue, continuing through the entrance hall.

"Aside from the dragon, there is the enchantment, and I know you'd find it surprising that there are those who wish to kill me. The enchantment is in place for the safety of myself and, yes, the dragon. There you have it, the reason you are *forbidden*, and now we can move on." He sounded annoyed, but the annoyance was wrapped in a distinct tone of exhaustion. Dark circles painted the pale skin beneath his eyes purple, and the typical tilt of his lips was replaced with a flat line. "Dispose of that," he said, motioning to the bag she held. "Once you have, find me in the library to discuss your homework."

Imara visibly bristled, her back stiffening as she clutched at the bag against her person. "Now I know," she retorted, but at the mention of the homework, her mood shifted. "Oh! Yes, of course. I have much to discuss with you about that. It was a success!" Imara unclipped the bag from her hip and disappeared down the hall.

Ronar shook his head, finding the smallest reason to offer a hint of a smile to no one. If indeed her homework had been a success, then he had been right, and there was much to uncover.

Once inside the library, Ronar took it upon himself to fetch a quill and paper so that he could take notes on their practices too. By the time he heard the telltale footfalls of Imara approaching, he'd calmed considerably. Glancing up from the table, he saw Imara at the balcony of the stairwell; sunlight streamed in from the floor-to-ceiling windows, bathing her hair in a golden halo, which granted her a heavenly beauty. As much as he wished he could ignore it, she was breathtakingly beautiful. Seidrs were renowned for their beauty, and amongst her kind, perhaps hers was lost on them. But Ronar took note of it like he would anything: deeply and studiously.

Imara smiled brightly as she hurried into the library and rushed down the stairs to the table. "I read a lot while you were gone, so I wasn't able to finish *all* of the tasks, but I was able to produce a leaf!" She laughed, shoving the container with the mostly dead heather onto the table. One green leaf stood out against the dead and browned branches.

One green leaf. Ronar stared at the dead clutch of heather, gritting his teeth as whatever good humor he'd gained died at the ghastly sight. "Imara, where is the rest of the heather?" he asked slowly and carefully.

Imara's confidence visibly waned, causing her smile to falter along with her excitement, but she continued. "What? I produced a green leaf . . . a full, healthy leaf! I've never done that before."

Standing from the chair, Ronar pressed his palms on

the table. "You've had days! Three days to complete all of the tasks, and all you present is a leaf?" He laughed without humor. Why had he expected more from her when she'd told him several times she was unable to conjure her magic? Perhaps he should have curbed his tongue, perhaps he should have praised her for the menial task, but Ronar had seen the explosion of water and knew her magic was stronger than that. A pitiful leaf didn't please him in the least. "You didn't try hard enough." He scoffed, looking away before he rounded the table and stood next to her.

Imara recoiled as if she'd been slapped. Her emotions flickered within her gaze, shifting from hurt to fury in a blink. "I told you," she said in a low tone. "I told you not to expect anything from me. Me—useless, broken Imara with little to no magic. I don't know what you want from me, *Lord Lajos*, but this is all I can give you!" she spat her words, glaring at him as she motioned to the heather.

Even though Imara's words should have tugged at his heart strings, should have implored him to subdue his growing ire, they did nothing but add fuel to the fire. Ronar had had enough of her reluctance. He didn't want to hear what she couldn't do, he wanted to see what she *could*, and the lone leaf wasn't it. "That is not good enough, Imara!" His green eyes watched as she turned away, and Ronar knew she was about to storm out of the library. "Don't you dare leave this room. Put your hands on that bloody vase and try it again." When Imara turned around but made no motion toward the table or vase, Ronar picked it up and shoved it at her. "Take it!"

Imara hastily reached out, her hands resting on the vase as she shot him an icy glare. "Why? So you can mock me again? No!" As she shouted, an electric hum filled the air, causing hair to rise along Ronar's arms and on the back of his neck. In the next instant, the vase shattered, spraying the both of them with water, and the heather grew to three times its size. Instead of a cluster of branches, the heather had transformed into a thriving bush with exposed roots, green leaves, and purple fragrant flowers. In the bush's transformed state, it slid through Ronar's fingers as well as Imara's and hit the floor with a thud.

Ronar cleared his throat, combing his fingers through his hair. "I assure you, I won't mock you." His gaze drifted down to the bush between them. It wasn't lost on him that this was the second time now that she'd lost her temper and her magic had flared to life.

Imara, still huffing with barely restrained anger, lifted her hands and motioned wildly. "As I was going to say, you tyrannical ass, I can feel it now. Where the magic comes from. I can feel beyond the barrier, and I've been probing the crack in it."

His brows lifted as she hurled the insult his way. Even Ronar knew it was a well-deserved one, and instead of retorting, he listened to her. "Perhaps next time, lead with *that* instead of a withered plant," he drawled, crouching to examine the bush. He pinched a branch in half; inside, it was a healthy shade of green, full of moisture. Ronar continued along the length of it, pulling off a green leaf and then purple blossom. "By the sun," he murmured, "you did it." Ronar stood up again, his eyes full of wonder, and faced a rather displeased Imara. If he were of a lesser disposition, he would have recoiled, but instead, he waited for the torrent of words that was surely heading his way.

"I know I did," she ground out. "If you had let me finish, there wouldn't be a—" She huffed, shoving at the branches of the heather bush that poked her. "A giant pain of a bush!"

Ronar cocked his head to the side, toying with a branch. "Oh, come now. It's a rather beautiful bush, and I'm sure Mikkel will find a lovely spot for it." He stepped around the thriving plant and, against his better judgment, Ronar lifted a hand to brush his fingers against her red cheek—or he would have, if Imara hadn't slapped his hand away. She shot him an accusatory look, her muscles coiling like a cornered creature of prey.

"Don't touch me," she snapped.

"As you wish." Ronar lowered his hand and nodded, shuttering his expression once more. He deserved her contempt and then some. "I am pleased with this, Imara. You did well." He motioned to the bush. Turning away, he rounded the table and sat down again, his fingers gathering the quill to twist and roll in his grasp.

With the distance put between them, Imara settled but didn't sit at the library's table with him. "What I wanted to say was that I believe you now, and that I want to learn more about how to control and wield my magic."

Ronar peeled his gaze from his paper and glanced over at her. "I will teach you what I can, I promise you that. Now that we know you have more than enough magic dwelling inside." He sighed, dropping the pen as he reclined in the chair. Before he'd returned home, Ronar knew that he'd have to divulge what he'd seen in the valley, where the mages had claimed the land. It was back in the hands of the seidrs, but what it was worth, he didn't know.

"I must tell you what I saw when I dealt with the mages, Imara." He inclined his head toward the chair next to him, and whether it was the small truce called between them or the mention of the mages, Imara sat across from him.

"What is it?" she whispered.

Ronar leaned forward, his chin resting in his open palm. "The land is worse than I thought. The valley is rapidly dying; trees not just brown but *dead*, streams dried up, the grass turned to mere dust. I've never, not in all my years, seen anything like this. I've witnessed plagues of ravenous insects. I've seen livestock fall dead from illness. But never this." The unknown wasn't something Ronar relished. He loathed not knowing something, and what was worse was that he wasn't sure how to fix it—if it even could be fixed.

Imara covered her mouth, shaking her head. "What are we supposed to do? How do we stop it or heal it? Those in the village have already tried healing the land, but nothing works."

"I don't know," he offered in a tired tone. "But I won't rest until I figure it out, I can assure you of that." Was there anything they could do? Or was this the course the land was taking on its own? "With that being said . . . " He paused, lifting his hand as he sat upright. Ronar summoned the volumes Imara had stored away in her room, and when they appeared in his waiting hands, he slid them across the table to her. "I believe it's time we begin."

IMARA

Imara felt the tickle in her nose as she gathered the stack of books into her arms, the ancient dust from one of the tomes wafting up from the movement. Halfway between the bookshelf and her table, the sneeze overtook her, echoing through the cavernous library and causing her to drop one of the books she carried. From across the room, surrounded by his own sea of books, Lajos looked up.

"If you wished to break the silence, all you had to do was speak. There are less alarming ways to go about it, and far more sanitary ones at that," he drawled, his eyes falling to the book sprawled open at her feet.

Imara didn't bother dignifying his comment with a response. She merely dipped down to pick the book back up, sniffing a little at the faint traces of dust.

"Oh, don't ignore me now, my darling, not once you've gained my attention."

Releasing a long-suffering sigh of irritation, Imara gazed over at him. "You know very well that I did not conjure a sneeze merely to broker a conversation with you."

One of his dark brows lifted, mocking her, even as a smirk settled upon his taunting lips. "But do I?"

"Yes," she replied shortly, dropping her books down on the table before her own form followed suit upon the chair. That brow of his and the matching smirk were enough to raise her hackles every time. She didn't know whether to smack him when she saw it or scream.

"Also . . . aren't you meant to be working on your tasks, not shuffling through more of my books?" There was a light to his eyes that Imara was beginning to understand: it meant that he was specifically choosing words that would rile her up, for no other reason than it amused him, she was sure.

"I have been working on it all afternoon, yet I am floundering today. I need but a moment of peace to center myself, which requires forgetting that damnable heather for the time being and focusing on something I enjoy," Imara stated, keeping her tone civil.

"Damnable heather? And here I had hoped it would be the symbol of our love and be used for the wedding."

Imara shot him a withering glare, unable to stop herself. Four days—that was the amount of time that had passed since his return and their heated argument here in this very space. While the heather bush she'd produced had since been removed by Mikkel and planted outdoors, Imara had been working on small sprigs from her bush in an effort to purposefully create more.

"Try it, and I will burn it all to the ground," she muttered under her breath, opening the book on top of her pile and beginning to leaf through. It wasn't an entirely unrelated work but a book on farming in the ways of the humans. She wanted to understand the process of growth from their point of view, to see if understanding more of how it worked would actually aid in willing the plant to grow herself.

What her magic could do didn't make sense. Her father had always used his affinity for earth to draw nutrients and other items out of the soil and into the plants that he was growing, but never had he brought a dead plant back to life. Especially one that was without soil. Foliage was not an element of its own. Even if somehow her abilities were connected to plants, what she had done to the water jug at the breakfast table her first morning here did not coincide with that. With a frustrated sigh, Imara tugged on the long length of her braid, searching for something that might spark an idea.

Imara didn't look up as she heard the scrape of Lajos' chair and his subsequent footsteps bringing him closer to her. Fortunately, things had settled between them since their mutual outburst, and once they had come to the agreement that she wished to learn and Lajos was willing to teach her, they had found their rhythm. Imara often spent her mornings out in the garden, doing her best to commune with nature in the manner of the young Ambient, Embla, hoping that by mimicking her behavior, a new pattern would present itself. Centering herself first seemed to make her afternoons spent in the library with the Dragon Master much easier to handle.

Her scanning of the text before her was interrupted as a shadow fell over the pages, and she could sense more than see Lajos behind her. He bent over her shoulder to read what she was looking up, his hand upon the back of her shoulder while the other reached out to flip a page. Lajos was everywhere, his presence invading her senses: the heat radiating off him, the masculine scent of spice and woods tickling at her nose, and the ever-looming feel of his body arching over her.

"Why are you researching farming methods?" he questioned, flipping a few more pages before his chin dipped down to peer at her features.

Imara kept her eyes downcast so that he wasn't able to read her expression, their current situation making her tense and unsure.

"I thought perhaps a better understanding would aid in my endeavors," she murmured softly.

Suddenly his fingers were slipping around her left wrist, his thumb pressing to the pulse on the sensitive underside of her arm. Swallowing, and feeling as though she should snatch her arm back, Imara looked up at him, ready to tell him to unhand her. However, he was not looking at her face but at her hand.

"What have your tasks been telling you, Imara?" he asked, voice soft but steely. His eyes drifted to her face, the look within them intent and frustrated. "While your curious brain is commendable, all the knowledge in the world will not help you perform magic. It is not in the understanding of words but in the understanding of yourself. It is here." His thumb brushed over her pulse, and Imara gave a little tug against his iron grip, seeking to escape the tingle over her flesh. "Here, in the very blood of you, coursing through you with every pulse and surge. We've seen how connected to your emotions your magic is. Stop *fighting* it so much."

This time, Imara managed to yank her wrist free and spin in the opposite direction from him, up and out of her chair, placing some distance between them. She did not enjoy feeling overwhelmed and cornered by him.

"I'm not fighting it," she denied.

"You are."

"No—"

"You *are*," he insisted. "What do you fear?" Lajos stepped closer to her, and Imara had to fight the desire to take a step back, keeping her chin up.

"I don't fear it," she argued.

"Then why the *resistance?*" he persisted, forcing her hands to clench a little as her frustrations mounted.

"I don't know!" she growled, her irritation shining through at last. It was difficult not to lash out at him. While they had come to a silent truce, Lajos' techniques on teaching her also consisted of a great deal of taunting her until some form of response was garnered. Imara understood the reason why—the use of her abilities seemed entirely wrapped up in her emotions—but it was an exhausting method.

Unaffected, Lajos picked up the sprig of heather Imara had been fiddling with all afternoon. Lazily, he brushed it beneath his nose, inhaling the soft scent of the blooms, his piercing eyes peering over at her in a way that made her fidget a little.

"Then perhaps you should be searching for those answers rather than farming techniques." His brow lifted.

Imara knew he was correct, but admitting that out loud was an entirely different story. So instead, she bit her tongue on a snappy retort, crossing her arms and looking away from his intent gaze. Lajos, of course, did not stand for this, and Imara found the sprig of heather suddenly in her face. Rolling her eyes, she snatched it from him.

"Fine! I will focus on searching myself rather than books. Happy?"

"Immeasurably," he murmured, eyes sparking with amusement that made her teeth grind. "And do rethink your stance on the heather. It goes remarkably well with your complexion."

Imara simply shot him a look of annoyance before brushing past him. Or at least that had been her intent. Lajos stopped her though, reaching out to gently grasp her elbow. When she looked at him quizzically, he merely offered that trying smile of his.

"Why don't we try moving this outside for a little bit?"

"I already spent time outdoors this morning," she argued.

"Imara . . . " He gave her an exasperated look, and for once, she took pity on him.

"Very well, let's go outdoors."

Giving her no time to change her mind, Lajos pressed a firm hand to her lower back and began to escort her out of the library. She wasn't sure what the rush was, but she allowed him to guide her through the vast house and outdoors. Fortunately, the sun was still shining brightly in the sky, making it a pleasant day to be outside.

Imara looked to Lajos for further explanation of what he wished to do now that they had left the library but found that he was looking at her expectantly. "What?" she questioned.

"We're out here to explore you, remember? Where would you like to go?"

She huffed a little, crossing her arms as she peered out over the vast property that belonged to the man at her side. Imara loved being out in the fresh air beneath the sunshine perhaps more than anyone, but this exercise he wished to enforce upon her felt contrived. They were not going to find the source of her magical blockage in one afternoon stroll.

He was still looking at her, waiting, so Imara moved down the steps and out onto the lawns of the keep, no plan of action in mind, letting her feet take her where they would. If he wished to explore, then that is just what they would do. Aimlessly.

It was almost nice enough to forget the annoyance of her companion, whom she was surprised to find remained at her side as she meandered over the lawns. Taking in the scenery, Imara took a deep breath and allowed the fresh mountain air to fill her lungs.

"See, you're already feeling better."

Imara shot him a look.

"What? Do not act as if I am the devil. You're freer out here. More open."

She hated that he was right. Nature had always brought a peacefulness to Imara's mind. Perhaps because nature did not require anything from her but her appreciation and knowledge.

"I grew up in the open fields. My father grows cotton and raises sheep. My sister Asta and I spent our childhoods helping him in any manner that we could."

"He must be suffering then, with what is happening down in the valley," Lajos acknowledged softly.

"Yes, he is. My mother too. Father grows the cotton and sheers the wool so that my mother can weave beautiful fabrics that she then sells at the market." Her hands went subconsciously to the gown she was wearing. Yet another of Lajos' gifts rather than one of her own.

A sudden wash of homesickness spread over her. Imara longed for nothing more than to be at home, sitting in the rooftop garden with Asta, or walking the fields with her father. How was her little family fairing now that they were only three?

Seeming to sense her mood, Lajos remained silent, giving her a moment alone with her thoughts.

They found themselves coming upon the lake, one that Imara loved the sight of. It was beautiful, reflecting the blue sky above, with only the faintest of ripples along its surface to disturb the calm. There was something so perfectly peaceful about this spot. Imara couldn't help but find a rock along its edge to sit down upon.

"Wow . . ." she breathed out in awe.

"She is called Fafnir Jarvi," Lajos murmured from behind her.

"And she is beautiful."

Lajos moved then to wander down along the rocky shore. Imara found herself watching him as he stooped to remove his boots, rolling his breeches up to his calves so that he could walk barefoot along the waterline. There was a calming quality to his presence when he wasn't mocking her, and watching him here, in this setting, she knew that he was also a part of this land.

Taking another deep, settling breath, Imara smiled a little as Lajos stooped down to pick up a flat stone and whipped it across the water so that it skipped a couple times before sinking below the surface.

"I bet I can beat you!" Imara found herself calling out, suddenly feeling playful. Lajos turned to peer up at her, a smirk on his lips.

"That does sound like a challenge, and I accept."

Hopping down off the stone, Imara kicked off her own shoes and carefully made her way over pebbles to the sandy area where he stood. Looking around her, she found the perfect flat stone for skipping and picked it up.

"What do I win once I've beaten you?" he asked, a grin in his voice.

"You will be winning absolutely nothing. However, *you* will be apologizing to me for being such a tyrant all the time."

"A tyrant? I will have you know most find me perfectly charming and amenable."

Imara snorted. "Perhaps the men." With that, she positioned herself properly and then let loose with her stone, triumphantly watching as it skipped not five but six times before sinking. Proudly, she placed her hands on her hips and looked over at him. "Your turn, my lord."

Lajos seemed unconcerned as he found another stone. "When I win, you will admit that heather is a perfect choice for a wedding floral, and that you want nothing more than to wear it in your hair."

Imara sent him a withering look, not rising to the bait.

Lajos drew back his arm and tossed the stone. Imara

watched as it hit five times, and then kept on skipping clear across the lake.

"What . . . ?" she asked, confused until she looked at that overly pleased smirk on his face. "You cheated!" Without thought, her hands rushed out to give him a shove, and she watched as he stumbled into the lake, caught unawares by her reaction.

Lajos nearly righted himself, but he must have hit a steep decline in the lake bottom, for suddenly, he was toppling further over. The last thing Imara saw before he went below the surface was his shocked face.

Gasping, Imara covered her mouth with her hands, staring in shock and a little horror at the location where Lajos had fallen. However, her horror was short lived as he broke the surface, hair plastered to his face and soaking wet. Now her fingers covered her lips to try and contain the peals of laughter. To see this usually well-contained man so out of sorts was a far better prize than him admitting he purposefully annoyed her on the daily.

Wading back out of the lake, Lajos eyed her with enough intensity that Imara began to think it was best she fled. Turning on her heel, she had almost made it to the incline back onto the grass when an arm snaked around her waist, pulling her back and flush with a solid chest. His lips were at her ear, hair dripping water onto her neck and shoulder.

"I may be a tyrant, but you are a devil of a woman." His growl was soft and low, sending flutters through her abdomen.

"And you are getting me wet!" She pulled free of his hold and turned to glare at him but found the drenched sight of him once more highly amusing, and it unleashed a fresh torrent of laughter she was unable to contain.

Realizing that she was a lost cause, Lajos shook his head and stepped back. "You wound me."

"I am . . . so very sorry. I didn't mean to push you in."

"Yes. Your laughter speaks very highly of how truly sorry you are." His gaze was unamused.

"I am! That being said, you *were* cheating by using magic to skip your stone across the lake, so I can't say you didn't deserve it." With those words, Imara bent to retrieve her shoes, then traipsed happily across the grass in the direction of Dragon's Keep, feeling light and free for the first time in days.

Lajos was still grumbling behind her about how lucky it was for her that he could dry himself with magic as they made their way back inside. As for Imara, she returned to the library with a smile upon her lips and fresh resolve to tackle her magical dilemma.

Instead of returning to her spot at the table, Imara plucked up the small branch of heather and moved to sit facing the fire, her legs folded crossways beneath her skirts. Unlike earlier, when the weight of all this uncertainty had been like a stone tying her down, Imara now felt a sense of peace inside. She thought of the fresh air in her lungs and the smooth surface of Fafnir Jarvi. While she would not admit it out loud, Lajos had been correct in his assessment. She was more open in natural settings than she was cooped up inside.

Taking a deep breath, Imara held the heather cupped lightly in her hands, her eyes on the fireplace before her rather than the bloom. With her next deep breath, Imara emptied her mind of all thoughts and worries as best she could and stared down at the fire. Concentrating on the heat of it on her cheeks, thinking of the flames and the similar heat that flooded her form when angry. Shutting her eyes, Imara thought of that anger, of the all-consuming nature of that feeling. She felt the tingle in her toes, the rush of something powerful welling up inside of her, too powerful to control.

It frightened her, and her body began to tense up, her heart beating rapidly in her chest. Something distant and forgotten tickled at the back of her mind, making her fear the swell rising up within her. What if she could not contain it? What if it were to consume her and everyone else? Letting out a shaky breath, Imara pushed on, fighting against the sense of foreboding that filled her, trying to picture the calm lake before her. Inhaling a sharp breath that felt charged with static, Imara focused all of that feeling—her fear, her apprehension, even the residual annoyance from Lajos—upon the heather in her hands.

Her eyes shot open as, with a gasp, Imara realized she could feel the plant in her hand beyond the physical sense of touch. There was a zing of energy residing within the stem, one that she felt attached to deep down in her core. Yet another deep breath was drawn, and then she pushed forward with that energy, with her entire will, all the fear and emotion inside of her urging the heather to grow.

It was too much, just as she feared. Instead of transforming it into a bush as she had done days before, the heather stretched out, growing larger and more tree-like, shooting straight into the fireplace. With a soft shriek of alarm, she was quickly on her feet, yanking the stick-sized heather out of the fire, flames already licking along its branches. With a quick swipe of her hand and a rush of magic, the fire was extinguished. Coughing from the smoke, feeling both mortified and furious with herself, Imara peered cautiously over at Lajos.

He stared at her, a blank look upon his face, before erupting into laughter that was full-bodied and loud. Imara's mortification grew, staining her cheeks red. Could she not do just one thing properly without causing some sort of scene? Containing himself at last, Lajos cleared his throat, a twitch still upon his lips as he gazed across the room at her.

"Great Mother . . . If you despise the idea of heather in your hair so greatly, you should have said. There's no need to burn the keep down around us. Though I do say, I feel vindicated for the lake."

As she opened her lips to retort, Lajos continued, his face now serious as he brushed off his laughter. "Imara, you put out the fire as well . . . " His words trailed off, puzzlement, and perhaps something more, in his gaze.

"Well, I didn't actually wish to burn the keep down."

"But you used magic." He paused, thinking. "Both water and fire . . . interesting." These words were for himself, musings out loud, rather than for her benefit.

Before she was able to ask him to further explain himself, Imara was halted by the sound of the library door opening. Sylvi stepped out onto the upper landing. Settling for shooting him a perturbed glance, Imara turned her focus on the young maid.

"I thought I would bring you something to eat, as

you've been busy for hours." Sylvi glanced between the two of them. "Am I interrupting?"

"Not at all. We could do with some refreshments. Imara just finished expelling a great deal of energy," Lajos spoke, standing to clear a space on the table for the tray.

Staring down at the large heather branch at her feet, Imara sighed deeply. Why was it that every time she managed to tap into the power inside of her, disaster struck? She had thought finding calmness within would help, but what if she were too old, and her opportunity to learn to control it had passed? Seidrs began training when they were around five years old. Once each child had made it through their test, they would begin learning magic specific to their elements from their parents and tutors. They had a lifetime to learn and grow with their abilities, to develop together. Perhaps hers, having grown untapped and unrestrained, was now a beast of its own.

"Imara." Sylvi's voice pulled her from her dark musings.

Glancing up, she found the young woman holding out a cup and saucer. Moving to her, Imara took the offering gratefully, smiling in thanks. Sylvi always seemed to have an innate ability to know when they might need a break—not from their work but from each other. Sipping the tea, Imara hummed at the fragrance and heat teasing her face, and the floral flavor upon her tongue. Taking a seat at the table, she found a plate set before her as Sylvi prepared their afternoon snack.

"Thank you," she murmured, sitting back wearily in her chair, the tea held between two hands as she relaxed.

"Of course. Now, both of you have a bite, and converse

nicely." A pointed look was sent in Lajos' direction at this; it was received with a snort from her master.

Soon enough, Sylvi was gone, and Imara and Lajos were left once more alone in the large library. Wordlessly, each reached for a pastry from the platter. Imara placed hers on the small plate before her, thinking of how wonderfully crafted it was.

"Has Thyr been with you long?" she asked softly, glancing over at him through her lashes.

Lajos thought for a moment before responding, "About twenty-five . . . twenty-six years now."

"That makes sense. She seems at home in the kitchen." In fact, one would think that there had never been a time when Thyr was *not* in the kitchen of Dragon's Keep, though Imara knew that there had to have been others. Lajos had lived here on the mountain for many generations. Her eyes drifted over to him, contemplating this fact, wondering who, and what, this man was. He was not seidr, that could be plainly seen by his lack of pointed ears. But no one had ever spoken of where his abilities came from, or how he had become Dragon Master.

He caught her looking, an amused expression on his face which she was sure was bound to lead to mocking her in some manner.

"Do I have jelly on my face?" he asked at last. "Or were you debating which floral would match *my* skin tone the best?"

Choosing to ignore this, Imara responded, "No, I was just curious. What brought you to this mountain? Why our valley? And why the pact between yourself and the seidrs in Omdahl?" She thought for a moment longer, then added, "Have you always been the Dragon Master, or were there others before you?"

He took his time, eating another bite and then sipping some of his own tea, before finally responding.

"Those are a lot of questions for being just curious." However, his eyes showed that he was not surprised. "I have always been the Dragon Master overseeing Omdahl and its villagers. Watching the growth and change, the marriages and deaths. The gradual change of young ones to Elders." Lajos brushed his hands upon the napkin plucked from the table. "For as long as there have been dragons and seidrs, there has been war and death. Seidrs feared the power and might of dragons, and so they hunted them. Dragons did not wish to die, and so they fought back and sometimes lashed out preemptively.

"When I first came to this valley and decided to settle upon the mount, these lands were home to many dragons. It was peaceful for a time. But then the first Elders arrived, seeking new farming lands for a small colony of seidr sent from Ragnhild. I had no desire for my beautiful new home to become a land of turmoil, so I sought out the dragons, vowing to bridge the distance between the two and prevent any attacks. What began as me acting as an emissary eventually transformed into an offer of protection and guardianship once the original Elders passed and the new generation arose."

Imara felt a great well of sadness for the dragons—not an emotion she had anticipated—who had been hunted simply out of fear for what *might* be rather than because of any true danger. The tendency for judgement and prejudice ran deep in the seidrs, their own beauty and power leaving little place for others who either threatened, or simply didn't meet their standards.

"So, you were here before my Elders—"

"Were even born, yes."

I must seem to be such a fledgling in his eyes, Imara thought. Her clumsy inexperience was a constant reminder that the Elders had gifted him not only a broken vessel for a wife but also a mere child in all of their aged eyes.

"Thank you for what you've done to create the village I grew up in. I know it can't have been easy. My people are not known for their leniency toward other beings."

Something unfamiliar flickered across his gaze as Lajos peered over at her. Imara wasn't sure, but it may have been surprise.

"I didn't do it for the seidrs. I did it for the dragons."

RONAR

The soft crackling from the hearth threatened to lull Ronar into a light sleep, and he would have succumbed if it hadn't been for the soft flick of a page, followed by laughter. He closed the book before him and stood up.

Imara's lips pressed together as she regarded him. "It's barely midday and you're already dozing off?" She clucked her tongue and folded her hands across the book in front of her. "Your age is showing, Lord Lajos."

Ronar's hands kneaded the muscles in his back, pausing at her teasing words. In the past two weeks, Imara had progressed in her magic, but more than that, *they'd* progressed in whatever one would call this budding relationship or mentorship. They still quarreled regularly, but it often remained playful. He hadn't forgotten the words she uttered to him not long ago. *Thank you for what you've done to create the village I grew up in. I know it can't have been easy.* Ronar hadn't expected thanks from anyone at this point, especially not Imara.

Years passed much like a day to him, and some memories felt as though they had happened yesterday, while others seemed so very long ago, like the building of the keep and establishing the mutual relationship between himself and the villagers. But the memory still freshest in his mind was the first time a young King Thorne had required his services. Thorne had been a boy of thirteen, frozen amidst an erupting battlefield, when Ronar saved him from an incoming spear. That day, Thorne became king when his father was slain, and in turn, Ronar had established himself in the king's court.

Thorne had thanked him then too, just as unexpectedly as Imara had.

His lip curled at her words. "Unlike a certain snoring someone, I didn't sleep well last night—"

"I don't snore." Imara's brows drew together, painting a serious expression on her face.

"You do." He brushed the comment off and dragged a finger across the library table. "I want to see you perform a few tasks. You've done well the past few weeks, and I want to see how far I can push you."

Imara leaned back into the chair and shook her head. "How would you know if I snore?" She lifted her eyebrows expectantly, seemingly not hearing the request.

Ronar chuckled as he walked around the table and sat next to her book. "It appears you have forgotten you've fallen asleep on me." He paused, pressing his lips together in a thin line before continuing. "It's not as if you sound like a grotesque pig. The noise is almost endearing, like a soft gasp of breath." He caught her wrist as she attempted to swat at him. His fingers gently probed her skin as he locked eyes with her. "About those tasks, wife."

Imara pulled her hand back, flexing her fingers as she

glanced down at the book. "I'm relieved I don't sound like a pig," she replied, hesitating before continuing. "I didn't forget about falling asleep on the way to the keep. And those tasks . . . Are you certain it's a good idea to push?"

"Now or never, Imara. If we don't push you, we won't ever know the truth of what you are. Besides, pushing you seems to produce results." Ronar commandeered the book she was reading and flipped it open to a well-worn page. A collection of glyphs stared up at him, begging for someone to speak them and bring them to life. Ronar didn't need to speak to tap into his magic, nor did he need to pull the strings of an element to wield it. Instead, it was there in an instant.

Imara fanned her fingers out on the table, then sighed in resignation. "Which *tasks* am I to perform?"

He laid the book down and pointed at the glyphs Imara had been practicing day and night. She'd successfully pushed the barrier open a fraction more, allowing another flood of magic to escape. Still, something blocked her, and all Ronar could do was push her time and time again, hoping with each flood that eventually the entire wall would collapse.

"This won't be easy." Ronar slid from the table and retrieved a withered potted plant. Unceremoniously, he plucked the dead plant out and sat the pot down before her. "I want you to search for life and make it grow. Blades of grass, an unseen flower, whatever lurks in the soil, bring it forth." With each task they attempted, her abilities were proving to be beyond a single element, something more. If Imara could perform this latest one, then perhaps there was hope for the failing land.

Her focus landed on the pot. Doubt flickered in the depths of her eyes, but as she exhaled, the doubt faded, and in its place shone determination. Imara's lips parted as she hummed, then she chanted the spell she'd learned with Ronar.

There was no mistaking the crackle of magical energy surrounding them. Even the fine hairs on Ronar's arms rose. He knew better than to praise her, but it didn't stop him from doing so internally.

Little by little, tiny sprouts from the soil formed. Imara's skin glowed with perspiration, but she didn't stop until the blades of grass grew, and tiny flowers shot up into fully bloomed plants.

"That's enough, Imara. You did far more than I expected you to." When she didn't acknowledge him, he placed his hand on her shoulder, but still her concentration didn't break. The blades of grass grew into a shaggy carpet, the blooms multiplied on the flower. "Imara!" he shouted, slipping his hand from her shoulder to cup her chin. He peered into her unfocused eyes and squeezed her chin. "Let go. Now." His words rumbled out, sounding more like a growl than anything.

Imara blinked, her eyes refocusing, and a blush painted her cheeks a vibrant red as she noted how close they were. "I did it. Why do you look so cross?" She didn't pull away from his touch, not until his fingers moved from her chin and Ronar attempted to tuck her errant curls back into place.

Ronar loosed a breath, his shoulders dropping as tension fled from him. "Because you were losing yourself to the spell. You did well, and I'd rather you not burn yourself out. You should be proud of yourself and what you've accomplished." He drew his hand toward his side, considering her appearance. She was flushed, winded, and coated in a fine sheen of sweat. As much as he didn't want to admit it, seeing her in such a state made a part of him ache. *For what?* He wasn't certain.

Ronar frowned as he looked away from her. "You're dismissed until this evening. I don't want to overtax you, so you're free to do as you please." He waved her off.

"What?" A loud scrape sounded as she stood abruptly. "Fine, have your moment, whatever it's about. It's beautiful outside, and I have herbs to collect anyway." She closed the book, picked it up, and turned on her heel.

Distractedly, Ronar watched her walk away. "Stay out of the woods," he mumbled.

"Mm-hmm," Imara hummed as she left the library.

"Damnable woman," Ronar said to the empty room. What he didn't want to voice was the fact it'd worried him seeing her dive so deeply into herself. On some level, he'd expected it, but what would happen if she couldn't pull herself out? Perhaps there had been a reason behind the barrier in the first place.

Ronar struck his closed fist against the table and sighed. "What are you doing, Ronar? She is not meant to stay. She is a pupil and no more." He spoke softly, reprimanding himself as he caught the way his emotions started to run away from him. It would do no good to grow attached to Imara. He frowned and sank into a leather chair, cupping his face.

Sylvi possessed the innate ability to find Ronar when he wanted to be left alone. More than that, she knew what to say to dig beneath his skin. At least this time she had the good grace to bring a morsel with her.

Ronar sat in the solarium, his face rumpled in concentration until he heard the footsteps coming toward him.

"Oh good, food to shove in my mouth so I don't *have* to speak to you." He took the fjellbrød from her. A layer of fresh butter gleamed on top of the bread, enticing him to shove the entire thing in his mouth. However, Sylvi stood rooted in her spot, which meant he had to savor the food, lest he be forced to speak longer than he wanted.

"You're ridiculous." Sylvi rolled her eyes. "Imara is outside, I thought I'd let you know. I also noticed she appeared out of sorts. She didn't say a word to me in passing, which I thought was strange."

Ronar rubbed his fingers together, ridding his fingers of crumbs. "That's it? You're put out because she didn't say *hello*? She is free to go outside and garden or scream at the giant bush of heather." His brows furrowed in growing frustration. "But what does it matter to you if she chooses to be outside, where she . . . I don't know, possibly *wants* to be?"

"You're truly an ass." She rolled her eyes again. "No. It was the look on her face."

He considered her words for a moment, then shrugged

his shoulders. "We've been studying, practicing, and working nearly around the clock. Imara is tired. I'm tired."

Sylvi twisted her lips. "Ronar, I've known you for many years now." She lowered her voice. "What is your plan with Imara? After your studies, after whatever *this* is?" She motioned to the table, to him, and then outside.

He wasn't certain what she was insinuating, but he wasn't keen on the vague idea Sylvi presented. "If you think I'm playing any games . . . I'm not. Once I figure out what is happening to the land and what we are to do, Imara is leaving. I don't know where she'll go, but Dragon's Keep isn't the proper place for her. She deserves far more than what it has to offer, and Omdahl doesn't deserve her."

"I'm curious, Ronar. Who and where deserves one such as Imara, if not you and if not Dragon's Keep?" When he didn't reply, she continued. "Have you ever considered that she is right where she belongs? Or at the very least, have you considered giving her the right to decide? Imara has had very little choice ever since Omdahl bestowed her upon you. I suggest that when the dust settles, you let her decide her fate. You have no right deciding it for Imara."

"Need I remind you that neither one of us had a choice? To deny her in front of the Elders would have branded her a leper!" he snarled, stepping forward as he glared down at Sylvi. "Little girl, you are not my nursemaid. You would do well to keep your nose out of my business."

She didn't flinch. She stared up at him and shrugged her shoulders. "As I said: perhaps she is where she belongs. You are so wise, and yet so foolish."

Anger rushed through his veins, spreading like

wildfire. Sylvi was stoking the fire, not allowing it to calm before unleashing another comment that sparked more rage. He'd heard enough. Ronar didn't need a lecture from a little girl, especially one he'd saved and raised as his own.

"Leave now, Sylvi Teig. You are treading dangerous waters." His emerald eyes flashed a brilliant hue.

Sylvi sighed. "Enjoy your bread, Ronar." Turning, she left without another word.

Ronar eyed the bread in his grasp, then let it roll from his hand into a wastebasket. He took a deep breath, exhaled, and lashed out at the nearest potted plant. A spindly tree that had been stretching toward the ceiling now fell to the floor, shattering the porcelain pot it sat in. Dirt sprayed toward him and peppered the ground.

"I liked that pot," he grumbled.

Ronar didn't believe in fate, didn't believe that the ancients pulled the life strings of every living being, but he wondered, *Why is Imara here, and why now? After all his time alone. Why now?*

After Ronar soothed his temper, he ventured outside. The cool, crisp air of autumn tickled his skin, as did the scent of fallen leaves. There wasn't a hint of death from his land, but that could change any day, and the thought terrified him. Dragon's Keep belonged to him. It was where he'd lived for centuries, and as possessive as he could be, he refused to relinquish it, especially to some wretched blight.

Not far from where he stood, Imara foraged on a knoll next to the lake. His lips twitched as he recalled his tumble in the water. Ronar surmised she was collecting the lemon balm that grew rampantly. Crossing the distance, he silently watched her pluck the leaves from the bush.

"Are you enjoying the view, my lord?" Imara paused long enough to shoot him a playful look.

Surprise flickered in Ronar's gaze, but he quickly shuttered it. "I always enjoy the view of my lake. It's rather breathtaking, wouldn't you agree?"

Imara huffed. "Did you seek me out simply for your sordid entertainment?"

Ronar sat down on the hill, shaking his head. "If you consider *this* sordid, wait until our wedding night." His words hit their mark. Imara flushed instantly, looking away as she resumed plucking the lemon balm, this time more furiously.

"Honestly . . . " Her words trailed, but a shrewdness entered her gaze. "Why do you do that? You deflect with those comments."

Ronar's jaw shifted. He hadn't come outside to be scrutinized by another female. He opted to ignore the question. "No. That isn't why I came." He sighed. Reclining against the hill, he propped his head up with his arms and stared at the clouds above. Puffs of white crawled across the clear blue sky, and he knew that soon the sun would fade, soon the gray sky would take over until spring. "I sought you out because . . . I'm going to be leaving for the valley."

"What?" Imara's voice cracked as she spun to face him.

"Inside, with your lesson, it brought something to mind. I tested you because I wanted to see if you could pull forth the tiniest of cells from the dead soil. Which you did—with relative ease, mind you."

She snorted. "Says you."

"Says me." He rolled his eyes and sat up. In his

peripheral, he could see blades of dead grass clinging to his hair. Some also littered his shoulders, but didn't bother him enough to remove it. "I want to know if you can do that to the soil from the valley, because if you can, there is a chance you can heal it." Ronar paused, toying with tufts of grass. "I want to bring back a sample for you to test."

"No one has been able to heal it, Lajos." Imara's shoulders slumped, then her eyes fell to his shoulders. She reached forward and brushed the grass from him.

Reaching up, he wrapped his fingers around her hand, squeezing it. He grinned. "No one is you, Imara. Besides, I'm not talking about what anyone else has attempted. I'm talking about what we are trying. I want to take my own notes. Also, I wonder what your magic could do for the dead earth." Ronar released her hand, but she didn't draw away. Instead, she sat beside him and stared out at the glittering lake.

"Do you think I can really heal it?"

A long silence spread between them, then Ronar replied, "I don't know. But we won't know until we try, will we? That seems to be our running theme." He turned his head, chancing a look at her. Imara remained gazing at the lake and oblivious to his attention. Somehow, she'd grown more beautiful during her stay. Perhaps it was the growing confidence in herself and her abilities, but whatever it was shined outwardly.

His fingers itched to stroke the porcelain skin of her cheek, and as invasive as that urge was, his thoughts were even more so. Ronar, in that moment, longed to taste her rosebud lips. He despised the part of him that longed for more moments like this, where they sat in true companionable silence, and neither one tore the other down. Ronar knew he shouldn't want anything remotely close to this, but he'd be lying if he said it wasn't difficult. If Sylvi ever asked, he knew he'd roar his denial, but that was all it was: denial.

"When do you leave?" Imara broke the quiet.

"At dawn. It's best if I leave soon, and early, so if it doesn't work, we can try something else. I also need to see if I can learn any more about the mages. They've always been a prickly lot, but this seems extreme, even for their standards. If I can help avoid a war, then I will. But if not . . . I'm still waiting for Thorne to send a letter in return."

Imara nodded. "And when will you return?"

"Two days or so." He paused, quirking a black brow. "Are you asking because you need to know how long you'll have in the woods? In that case, I'll be home in a blink." When she said nothing to deny it, he rolled his eyes and threaded his fingers through his hair. "Imara," he groaned, shaking his head.

What was he going to do with this impish seidr? Ronar tried not to think of it, which only led to him further pondering what he *wanted* to do.

In the morning, Ronar left Dragon's Keep before the sun rose. He packed lightly, neglecting to check in with Thyr prior to leaving, knowing that the woman would only force a ridiculous amount of food on him. By the time Ronar reached the base of the mountain, the sun was at its peak, and the shadows cast by the trees disappeared. In the shade, it was refreshingly chilly against his heated flesh. Beside him, his winded horse bobbed his head in discontent. The gelding had been ridden as if hellfire nipped at their heels, and it left both he and his rider exhausted. The pair of them needed to cool down and simply breathe.

"I know, boy, but we must see if the mages are still lurking." He patted the horse's lathered neck, grimacing as foam came away from it. "I don't need you collapsing beneath me." Ronar urged the horse forward, hoping to cool him off gradually.

When the horse no longer sucked in air in desperation, Ronar slid from his back and onto the ground. Dust kicked up beneath his boots, bringing a frown to his lips. He crouched down, scooped up a portion of the ruined soil, and watched only a fraction sift through his hands. The rest blew away on the light breeze.

He stood up and immediately pulled a satchel loose from his saddlebag. Ronar scooped as much of the dirt as he could. Perhaps Imara could test her ability on the dried earth. If there was any hope in saving the dying land, she'd be able to feel some form of life in the dirt—at least Ronar assumed she would. It was a theory he was willing to test.

For a half hour, Ronar walked down the path to the village but stopped abruptly when he noticed a cart on the side of the road. Beside it, a seidr knelt at the hooves of his horse, muttering to himself.

"Greetings! Can I be of assistance?" Ronar approached cautiously, leaving his horse behind him.

The male seidr flinched, then looked up at him. His slender, golden face was streaked with dirt and sweat, his clothing coated in the same ash-colored dirt that was in Ronar's satchel. It was difficult to discern if he was older or just graced with the seidrs' beauty. Silvery blond hair tumbled over his shoulders freely rather than be held back in braids. "Maybe. Can you make my horse young again?" He sneered, more at his situation than at Ronar.

"Unfortunately not." Ronar held his hand out and stroked along the tired horse's neck.

As the seidr stood, his amber eyes widened in horror. At once, he bowed at the waist and fumbled over his words. "M-my lord. I didn't know . . ."

In that moment, Ronar decided he was young. Seidrs possessed an ageless beauty, but the truly young ones lacked a certain hardness in their gaze. Ronar assessed the youngling, then proceeded to run his hands over the horse. "No apology necessary. Let's see what I can do for you." After a thorough going-over, Ronar found the horse was just sore and likely overworked. With a simple touch, he allowed for the warm, healing heat of his magic to flood into the horse.

At once, the equine perked up, his ears swiveling and dark eyes bright once more.

"Oh . . . Thank you, whatever you did . . . thank you." The seidr bowed again, smiling. "How can I repay you?"

Ronar's lips parted as if he were about to brush off the offer, but it occurred to him that while he had someone of Omdahl here, he should ask about the mages. "Oh, think nothing of it. Although, I do have a question I need answering."

"That is all?" The seidr blinked. "Go on, my lord."

"Have there been any mage sightings, threats, or disturbances of late?" Ronar lifted his hand from the horse and focused on the young seidr.

The male's eyebrows knit together. "Why, no. It's been quiet since you made good on your promise to aid us."

Ronar nodded. "Good." And it *was* good. Whether or not they'd remain at bay, he wasn't certain, but it would allow for him and Imara to learn more about the land in the meantime. "What about the land. Is it worse than this anywhere else?"

"Beyond the lake, it's the worst there. But I warn you, my lord . . . be careful there. Some say the earth will swallow you whole if you step in the wrong spot. I didn't believe them, but I have seen it with my own eyes. It's far worse than a forest after a wildfire . . . It's the smell, I think."

"The smell?" Ronar questioned.

"It smells like death."

Ronar's features pinched as he mused over this news. "Thank you. Be well." Turning away from him, Ronar whistled for his horse, who promptly trotted up to him. Dread unfurled within him. Although he knew something was wrong with the land, he hadn't expected it to change so rapidly.

Beyond the lake was his next venture, then he'd return home and deliver the news to Imara.

IMARA

Something was missing. The library had an empty quality to it that Imara had never experienced before when surrounded by her favorite things in the world. Yet, as she sat within its hallowed walls, the young seidr came to realize that the absence of Lajos was leaving her feeling lonely and a little distracted. While they were now getting along much better than they had in the beginning, she did not understand it. His lordship tended to be a distraction more than anything else when he was around, taunting and teasing her until she did what he wanted. With him gone, she should have been able to lose herself to her studies.

Instead, Imara found herself thinking about him, and wondering how he was faring. Had he reached the valley yet? What was he finding? Was it worse? Would she be able to actually do something with the sample he returned with?

Inevitably, far more intrusive thoughts plagued her too. What if something happened to him whilst he was in the valley? The idea twisted her gut more than she'd like to admit. Whether or not she was willing to accept it, she'd grown fond of him on some level. They'd spent hours in one another's company, and his taunts had become somewhat endearing to Imara.

In need of a distraction from her own thoughts, she went in search of books on dragons, wanting to learn a little bit more about the creature she had met in the woods. The fortunate thing about Lajos' particular personality was that he kept a remarkably well-organized library. Each section had a sequential placement that was easy to follow. With little effort, Imara found the books on dragons, fingertips brushing over spines in an itching desire to read all of them. In the end, she chose a couple of volumes and took a seat curled up in her favorite chair near the fire. The land around Dragon's Keep was much cooler than it had been down in the valley, and even after all these weeks, she was not used to it.

Around midday, Sylvi entered the library, bringing with her the typical slew of treats for Imara to feast upon. Gazing up from her readings as the young woman placed the tray on the small table before her, she couldn't help but smile.

"If you continue to feed me like this, I'm going to be in need of letting out all my gowns," Imara stated, laughter in her tone.

Sylvi tutted away her concerns and held out an empty plate to her. "Nonsense. All I am doing is sustaining you through your many hours of rigorous research."

Smiling, Imara took the plate and reached over to select a small biscuit from the tray. Imara had come to realize that Thyr's baked goods were some of the most delicious things she had ever eaten and impossible to resist. True to form, the flaky delight melted on her tongue.

"What are you reading about today?" Sylvi asked, casting a casual glance at the books momentarily discarded on the cushions beside her.

"Dragons." Imara offered her a sheepish look. "I know I am meant to stay away from the creature in the woods, but I find myself fascinated. I can't help but wish to learn more about it."

"Well, there's nothing wrong with feeding your curiosity, so long as you—"

"Stay out of the woods. I know," Imara cut in.

Sylvi smiled gently and sat on the low table before her, hands resting in her lap as she peered over at Imara. "I was going to say, as long as you do it smartly. You have to remember dragons are territorial creatures who have learned over centuries of being hunted to always suspect anyone encroaching upon their space."

Imara nodded, placing the small plate upon her thighs as she sighed softly. It was hard not to want to venture into the woods once more now that she knew what was there. Though her moment with the dragon had terrified her, and she felt she had been lucky to escape with her life, a part of her also wondered if the beast was lonely.

"It did not appreciate me being there."

"No, he wouldn't. So, whatever your curiosities, use that clever head of yours." Sylvi eyed her. "Understand?"

A part of her wanted to laugh over being scolded by someone only a year older than her. Instead, Imara nodded.

Satisfied, Sylvi stood up. Arranging her skirts, she cast another glance at the book on the cushion.

"I've seen Master Lajos take honey apple tarts into the woods," she mentioned off-handedly, motioning to the book, which was open to a section on how dragons preferred special offerings when approaching them for the purpose of conversation.

Without another word, Sylvi left the room, leaving Imara's mind whirling with sudden inspiration.

Thyr was more than happy to bake a batch of tarts for her first thing the following morning and agreed to fetch a good-sized perch during her early trip to the market—though she had been confused when told to keep it whole and uncooked. The fish was a heavy burden in Imara's satchel, but it also made her feel more secure going back into the woods. Lajos would be furious were he to find out, but Imara found it impossible to sit within the confines of the keep and practice her abilities while she waited for him.

Too many were counting on what she would be able to do upon his return.

Making her way from the kitchen to the front door, Imara suddenly found Mikkel heading her way, a concerned look upon his face as he took in the satchel hanging over her shoulder.

"My lady . . . May I speak with you for a moment?" While a scolding from Lajos made her blood burn and her hackles rise, Mikkel gave off a sense of fatherly disapproval despite only being ten or so years her senior.

"Of course, Mikkel." Imara paused, her hands moving to the band of her satchel, trying her best to seem unconcerned and not up to anything secretive.

"Heading off into the gardens?" he questioned.

While the keep was large, the staff was small. Everyone knew that Imara had wandered into the forest during the last trip Lajos had taken, and that during her wanderings, she had become lost and stumbled upon the dragon that lived there. Everyone was also aware that she was not meant to be returning to the woods.

"The garden, among other things." She found herself hesitant to lie to the man, knowing he was only seeking to uphold his master's rules and protect the would-be mistress of the keep.

"Thyr mentioned you had her pick you up a perch from the market. Might I ask my lady what she means to do with the fish?" His broad brow was furrowed, his tone smooth yet conveying a quality of sternness.

Imara knew why Sylvi always stated he looked like a man afraid to have any fun. Looking upon him now, Imara felt like a naughty child who had just been found with her hand in the pastry jar.

"You are free to ask, Mikkel, but for your own sake and you being able to deny any knowledge, I cannot tell you." He wasn't going to stop her, so if she could spare him a yelling from Lajos, she would.

"Mistress . . . " Mikkel began.

"I am not your mistress, Mikkel, and you needn't worry. I know what I am doing." Imara offered him a gentle smile, reaching out to squeeze his arm reassuringly. "I promise."

He did not look convinced, his brow still furrowed with unhappiness. How long would Lajos need to be home before Mikkel tattled on her, she wondered? Sylvi would not breathe a word for fear of being found out for her part in this, and Thyr seemed blissfully unaware of what Imara was up to.

"Perhaps I should . . . wait outdoors . . . in case you are in need of assistance?"

Imara laughed, appreciating his desire to help, even in his disapproval. "If that is what you wish to do. But I believe you have more important duties to attend to today than waiting on my meanderings to finish." She turned from him then, continuing on her way to the front door. "Be of good cheer, Mikkel! The day is far too beautiful to fret."

Stepping outside into the sunshine, Imara breathed a sigh of relief and released another soft chuckle. She hoped that she hadn't placed Mikkel into too much of a conundrum.

The woods were cheerful as she stepped into them, carefully following the path the dragon had pointed her down as she'd fled. She couldn't be certain the woods wouldn't lead her astray, but she would use whatever abilities she possessed to get her to her destination.

As if on cue, the moment the forest had truly swallowed her up, the path before her became overgrown with grass and roots, dusted with the disguising qualities of freshly fallen leaves. It was a scary sensation, how quickly things went from a lovely wood to a nightmare of mind-altering confusion.

Imara felt her breath pick up as the magic began to affect her, and in response, she shut her eyes against the assault. When she did, she found that she could feel the spirit of the forest all around her, the lines of energy that ran between every living thing and directly to her. Inhaling deeply and slowly, clearing away the haze of magic fighting to disorient her, Imara sought for a sense of the clearing that bore the stamp of the dragon's magic the most. Each step that she took was a battle, fighting off the confusing tendrils that were meant to keep her at bay.

When at last she felt herself at the edge of the clearing, she was feeling drained. It had taken a lot out of her to tap into her ability and through that internal barrier. Now she only had to hope that the dragon wouldn't be furious she had returned. Slowly, she opened her eyes, finding that she had indeed made it to the same clearing as before, except the dragon did not appear to be present.

Carefully, Imara stepped over an exposed root and through the last of the trees into the bright sunlight. The heavy bag on her shoulder was finally allowed to fall to the ground, and she took a moment to assess the place she found herself in. Perhaps the dragon was off flying or hunting. There was no true reason for him to always be in this clearing. She felt her shoulders sag with disappointment and possibly a little relief.

Of course, this left the question of how she was going to make it back through the forest without a decent rest beforehand.

"Why?" came the deep growl from behind her.

Whirling around, Imara found herself staring directly into a pair of large green eyes. The dragon released a breath of air, which ruffled the wayward blond curls surrounding her face. A quiver of fear went through her. He was close enough that, should he snap out to devour her, she wouldn't even have enough time to lift her hands to shield herself.

"Why have you returned?" questioned his deep vibrato.

Imara stood her ground, though every fiber of her being was screaming to retreat. She had made the wrong choice in coming out here, no matter what she thought Sylvi was slyly telling her. *Why can I never just listen to Lajos?*

"I—" Her words seemed to be stuck in her throat, trapped by her own foolishness.

"I?" the dragon rumbled, his eyes both glaring and sparking with something that seemed like mischief. Was the dragon mocking her?

"I brought you gifts," she rushed, moving only to stoop down and pluck up her discarded bag. Holding it out toward him, she watched as the great beast took a moment to assess the sack in her hands. Then, with a shake of his large head and a tuck of his wings, he moved past her and into the clearing. Despite his size, his movements were sleek and stealthy, like a housecat.

The dragon sat back on his haunches, his head now so high in the air that she was forced to tip her own back in order to meet his gaze. "Well? Show me."

With these words, Imara found herself scrambling. Setting the bag on the ground, she quickly opened it up, her heartbeat assaulting her eardrums and her hands trembling. Fishing out the batch of baked goods, she brought them over to him, set the bundle on the grass before him, and untied it.

"Honey apple tarts. I had it on good authority that you've been brought them before." She stepped back beneath his suspicious gaze and returned to her bag. From its depths she pulled the perch, the fish also wrapped in cloth, mostly to protect the tarts and the inside of her satchel from its slippery scales.

The fish was also laid before him, and then Imara removed herself several feet away. No amount of distance would keep her safe, but it felt better to place enough space between them that she could pretend she had a chance.

The fish was the first to go, after a quick blast of fire to singe its outer flesh. The dragon then dipped his head down and gobbled up the perch with a few quick snaps of his jaw. Imara watched, wide-eyed and a little amazed that this was possibly working. Once the fish was gone, the dragon settled down onto his belly and began to stick a single claw into one tart at a time to bring to his mouth. She would have found it comical if not for the consistent fear she had overstepped her boundaries once more.

"Why did you truly come?" the dragon asked at last, his attention still primarily on the baked goods before him.

"I was curious and . . . I wondered if you might be lonely." She found herself being entirely honest.

"Lonely?" Scoffed the dragon incredulously, his eyes drifting up to her.

"Yes. I know what it is to be lonely. Even when you're

surrounded by an entire sea of people . . . to have no one to turn to other than your sister, and even then, dismay that the mere association with you will be her undoing." The dragon was still staring at her with that incredulous look in his ancient eyes. "You are all alone. I thought perhaps . . ."

"I could use a friend?" A puff of smoke released from his nostrils, more disbelief showing.

"Yes," Imara stated firmly. "You are a clever being who seems to have no one here in the woods, and Lord Lajos spends most of his days in the library with me . . . Who is here for an intelligent being such as yourself to interact with?"

"So you thought you would be the one to come and offer companionship." There was amusement in the beast's gaze now as he released a sound that sounded somewhat like a chuckle. Imara felt a little affronted.

"Perhaps I am not the most obvious choice," she began, her shoulders stiffening. "In fact, I am never anyone's choice, but I am the only one who cared enough to come out here and offer."

One of these days, her stubbornness would get her killed.

The dragon gazed at her with a softening expression and, nodding his horned head, he motioned to the space before him. "Come, sit."

Imara was surprised by the invitation, and perhaps a little suspicious herself. She *would* be just as easy to snap up as the perch had been once she was seated where he had indicated. However, not one to look a gift dragon in the mouth, Imara stepped forward and lowered herself down into the spot he had indicated. Arranging her skirts, she plucked a wayward leaf stuck to the fabric and soothed herself by brushing her thumb over its spine and reaching out for what life was left in it.

"Tell me, how did you come to be at Dragon's Keep?" he asked.

Perhaps it was finally being asked by someone not in a position to judge, but Imara began to speak, and did not stop until she had laid out the whole sordid story. Her apparent lack of abilities, her stance as pariah in the village, and how, when their land became wrought with turmoil and death, it was her life the Elders chose to sacrifice in order to save the rest of them.

"That is quite the tale." His voice was soft, and almost soothing. "I am sorry the seidrs did not value your life."

"It's okay," she whispered. Shrugging gently, Imara brushed off the cloud of hurt and gazed up at the dragon. She did feel a little lighter, having borne it all. "In truth . . . I had accepted my life in Omdahl. I knew I would never find a life partner, but I had my herbs, my medicines. I had a life of my own planned out, where I would make myself useful outside of magic I did not possess.

"The hardest part has always been the loneliness. I had no friendships there, only my sister Asta. But she is a beautiful, wonderful girl who already has more suitors than she knows what to do with. I knew that soon enough one of them would capture her heart, and she would be busy with her own life."

"It doesn't sound like such a terrible life to have had to leave behind," the dragon commented, his honey apple tarts for the moment forgotten.

"Perhaps not, but there I knew my place. I had a plan

for my future, one that I knew I could find happiness with. Here . . . " Her eyes drifted off in the direction of Dragon's Keep. "I feel more lost than I did there. While I have been given the gift of my abilities, I do not know what my place in the world truly is anymore."

"Did the Elders not send you to become the bride of the Dragon Master?" he questioned.

"They did . . . and he accepted me. But he hasn't truly spoken his intentions beyond taunting me with a wedding I'm not certain he ever intends to happen."

"And what do you wish for, little seidr?"

"That is the greatest question of all." They both fell silent after that, and the dragon went back to eating his tarts one by one.

"Are you the only dragon in these mountains?" she asked at length.

"I am."

"When did the others leave?"

"Many, many centuries ago." His head tipped slightly to the side as he peered down at her once more.

"Why did you stay? If all the rest of your kind was going?" *Why choose perpetual loneliness?*

"This is my home, and where I belong." It was a simple enough response but one Imara felt strike deep within her heart.

"A place to belong," she murmured, softly and contemplatively, more to herself than to the dragon.

"You will find your place." He offered her one of the tarts from off the tip of his nail, and Imara couldn't help but laugh, taking the punctured treat that would have horrified Thyr to see the state of it.

"I hope so." She smiled over at him, then bit into the sweet pastry.

At some point during their afternoon, she had ended up sitting near his snout, which rested on one large paw. The end of his tail was looped around the back of her in an almost protective manner, and he was watching her with something close to fondness. Tentatively, she reached out a hand to gently brush it along his jowls, feeling the warm, stone-like scales beneath her fingertips. The dragon's eyes slid shut, and he seemed to lean a little into the touch, a rumble almost like a happy purr coming from him.

"May I come and visit you again?" she whispered, not wishing to break the spell of whatever this was.

"You may."

Imara felt herself smiling as a newfound happiness settled within her. "What would you like for me to bring?"

The dragon considered her for a moment, then blew a hot breath of air toward her. "I won't turn down an offering of kardemommeboller."

15

RONAR

The horse nudged Ronar between the shoulder blades, but the man didn't move. He only watched as Imara, yet again, emerged from the woods he'd forbidden her to enter. He clucked his tongue, muttering under his breath as he walked to meet her halfway.

Ronar's mood was better than it had been on his last trip. No mages had presented a problem to him, but the land was still dying rapidly, far faster than he'd originally thought. Grass that had still flourished last time was now nothing but dried, infertile dirt. Trees were not only barren but cracked and almost charred looking. How long would it take for the death to spread to the keep, or until everyone below the valley moved on or died? As the guardian of the valley, he knew he had to act now, but selfishly, Ronar wanted to protect his land.

"I'm glad to see you listened yet again." He folded his arms across his chest, eyeing her dryly.

Imara, flushed and somewhat out of breath, smiled warmly. The fact it was the first time she'd greeted him with something less than acid didn't go unnoticed. "I listened, my lord, I just didn't abide by your rule."

"And why not?" He narrowed his eyes and stepped closer to her. Ronar peered down at her, lifting a black brow as he studied her porcelain face. Soft wisps of curls tickled at her temples, and her rosy cheeks brought out the deep blue of her eyes. At once, he loathed the way his heart hammered in his chest and the rising desire to *kiss* those stubborn lips.

"It's a silly rule. The dragon likes me, and I brought him gifts." Imara blinked quickly, glancing away from him.

"Gifts? What did you do, steal some of my fine silver?"

"Silver? You have silver in the keep?" Imara's eyebrows lifted. "Baked goods, my lord. He enjoyed them."

Ronar groaned and lifted a hand to his forehead. Had his entire staff switched fealty in his absence? "If you insist on being foolish, then only enter the woods if the dragon returns your call. Can we agree on that, my bride?"

Silence stretched between them. Imara's full lips pressed into a line.

"Fine," Imara eventually blurted, throwing her hands up in the air.

Ronar chuckled as he turned on his heels. He'd not been absent for more than two days, but he'd missed his routine with her, which consisted of flustering her whenever possible. "I knew better than to expect an embrace, but here I am, still disappointed that I received no warm greeting." He looked at her from the corner of his eyes, but when no retort came, only a lovely shade of crimson painting her cheeks, he sighed.

"Let me tend to the horse first, and then we can head

to the library." The horse snorted as if agreeing that he needed tending. Ronar grabbed the reins and led him into the barn, fully expecting Imara to dash inside the keep. She didn't. Instead, she poured grain for the horse and pumped fresh water into the trough inside the stall.

Ronar paused, regarding her over the tall horse's back. A slight smile curved the corners of his lips as he watched her mill around the barn with ease. "Here are the findings. Be careful with them; some aren't bound as gently as I'd like for them to be." He pulled the bag free from the saddle and handed it over to her before returning to his task at hand. Once Ronar untacked the palfrey and brushed him, he returned him to the stall.

In Imara's palm sat a clump of dirt. She frowned at it, allowing her thumb to roll over the dry earth. "Where was this?"

"That was part of the meadow right at the base of the mountain. I was there recently, and it still thrived. Wildflowers covered the landscape, and now there is very little but that." He pointed at her palm. "Reduced to . . . almost ash." Ronar knew what ash looked like, but this held no nutrients. Nothing that would feed the land, at least nothing that his eyes could see. If Imara could *feel* life inside the soil, perhaps there was hope they could restore the lands.

"What?" Imara whispered.

"I think we'll both need some dragon ale instead of tea this time around," Ronar murmured.

Inside the keep, Ronar momentarily caught Sylvi's gaze, which he held icily. Later on, he'd have a chat with her about where her loyalties lay and who ruled the keep.

He strode briskly down the hallway and stepped to the side to let Imara enter the library first. "I'll grab the ale." Against the wall, near Ronar's desk, sat an intricately carved oak cabinet. He opened it and withdrew two glasses and a bottle before he sat down at the table.

"Pace yourself with this drink. This ale will land a dragon on his ass faster than any arrow could." He poured them each a glass and took a swig, enjoying the fiery burn down his throat. "Now, let's try to see if your hard work has paid off, my darling."

Imara chanced a glance in his direction. She pulled each preserved bundle out of the satchel and laid them out on the table.

A dead limb from a tree. A pile of sandy dirt. Wilted flowers that emitted the stench of rot.

"When you're ready." Ronar motioned to the drink. "You may wish to take a sip." He'd barely spoken the words before Imara took a great gulp of the ale. Ronar winced, knowing the inevitable burn was just around the corner.

He joined her, taking a swig himself, and moments later, fire blazed down his throat all the way to his belly.

Imara gasped for breath. She glared at the glass as if it were a living creature that had assaulted her. "You drink this?" she choked.

"When the spirit moves me. Seeing you emerge from the woods against my will again . . . Well, let's say you've driven me to drink."

Imara huffed, rolling her eyes at him. "Don't blame your bad habits on me."

Ronar's eyebrow arched as he motioned to the items in front of her.

"I know, I know." She sighed and picked up the dead branch. Imara exhaled deeply, closing her eyes as she retreated into herself.

All Ronar could do was watch and hope that she could perform the task. Not only because it was what they'd been working toward for weeks, but it would mean the land was capable of thriving once again.

A leaf abruptly shot out of the trunk of the branch, then another further up. Roots sprouted where the end had been snapped off from the tree, stretching toward the table as if looking for earth to submerge itself into. Ronar watched in complete awe. Imara, *his* Imara, had brought what he couldn't back to life.

"You did it," he whispered. "Again," Ronar instructed, taking the newly formed sapling from her.

Imara laughed, her eyes opening. "I did! It lives again." A smile lit up her eyes and brought a new warmth to her expression. She wasn't done yet, and Ronar was glad to see she wasn't about to celebrate prematurely.

Imara scooped the sandy loam up and stared at it dubiously. She sprinkled grass on it, plucked a few leaves from the new sapling, and laid it on top of the sand. This time, instead of closing her eyes, she concentrated on the pile, whispering words Ronar recalled translating for her recently.

Currents of magic swept through the room, perfuming it with a sweet, earthy scent. Ronar watched in disbelief as the pile of dirt shifted and writhed, rolling in on itself as it grew in size. The leaves and grass withered away, but their death breathed life into the otherwise dead earth. Sprouts of grass jutted upward from the pile, signifying the dirt had healed.

By the time Imara touched the flowers, power surged through her, and the wilted bouquet sprung to life. She dropped the flowers and settled against the chair, breathing heavily.

Time and time again, Imara had proven her affinity for earth magic, but she'd shown the ability to work with water and fire too. Ronar took a healthy swig of his ale and shook his head. How in the Mother's name did the Elders not notice her magic? The more Imara tapped into her ability, the less erratic it became.

Ronar stood from his seat and cupped her cheeks with his hands. "My darling, you did it." He spoke softly, reverently even. His thumb brushed against her high cheek bone, and this time, Imara didn't pull away. He was lost amidst a sea of blue deeper than any gem in his stores. Ronar's heart thrummed wildly in his chest as he felt a pull toward her, and when he realized what he was doing, that he had begun to lean in toward her lips, he pulled away.

Imara, just as flustered as he, leaned back in her chair and cleared her throat. "Lajos," Imara started, twisting to watch him pace. "Take me to the valley. I want to try to heal it. I believe I can—look at what I've done." She flung her hand toward the table and stood.

Ronar shook his head vehemently. He should have known she would ask to go and try. After all, he'd been helping her grow in her knowledge and confidence, and push against the barrier that trapped her magic from freeing itself. However, he didn't want her down in the valley yet. Ronar didn't trust that the mages had ceased their assault on Omdahl. It would be Imara's luck if they suddenly appeared and attacked. The last thing he wanted was for Imara to be hurt. He swiped a hand down his face, cursing in an old tongue. "I do see, and you should know I am pleased." His words sounded cold even to his ears. "But—"

"No. You don't get to say 'but.' I have studied, and I have stayed up into the wee hours of the morning until I thought I'd pass out from exhaustion. I've grown from doubting myself and thinking I'm nothing like *everyone* told me. It was *you* who showed me differently." Imara charged him, and he half turned away until she struck his chest with an open hand. "You showed me I'm not useless, Lajos."

After she half-heartedly assaulted him, Ronar slid his fingers along her wrist. He stroked the tender flesh at her pulse and felt the steady beat beneath the pads of his fingertips. She wasn't afraid—at all. He chuckled; it was a hollow sound that reflected his defeat. She was right, wasn't she? How hypocritical would it be for him to deny her the chance?

"Very well, my darling. Your wish is my command." His fingers slid down the inside of her forearm, and he leaned down close enough that his lips nearly touched her nose. "Whatever you wish to bring, pack it now. We will wait until tomorrow to leave, because I just got home and I'm in dire need of more of that ale. Also, Thyr will roast me if we both skip out on supper." He pulled away from her and stood at the table. Ronar filled his glass to the brim and took a deep drink. He closed his eyes and let the strong brew wash over his senses. The alcohol sank into his marrow, bringing forth a pleasant tingle in his limbs.

Imara sucked in a breath the moment Ronar stepped away. She ran a hand along where his fingers trailed. "Will we travel straight through?"

"No. We will stay the night at the Valley Inn. It's the halfway point, and although I can ride straight through, I'd rather not." The inn was situated not far from the mountain's base, but if they were to spend an entire day out in the meadow, he wanted rest, and Imara would need it too.

Ronar swirled the contents of his glass around. "We will both be exhausted, I'm sure." His words trailed off, but before she could interject, he added, "And Imara, pack trousers instead of dresses."

"Very well. I'll see you at supper." She turned and left without another word or glance in his direction.

When Ronar was certain she was out of hearing range, he slumped against the table. "Dammit all to the depths." His hand raked through his hair as he collapsed into the chair and closed his eyes.

He'd lost that battle, but it was the battle over his feelings he was more concerned with.

In the morning, Thyr had already prepared several days' worth of food. Ronar chuckled as he took the individual bags. "We won't be gone a week, Thyr."

She tutted and patted the air. "You never know. Things happen." Thyr eyed him pointedly.

Ronar squinted at the insinuation that he'd prolong their journey with Imara. As if he had ulterior motives, when having Imara journey to the valley was the last thing he wanted. Neither were certain of what would happen once she homed in on the earth, and what its demands would even do to her.

Sylvi walked in on the exchange, laughing at the tail end of it. "Whatever happens, be safe. I want to see the both of you return—preferably in one piece. Also, I hope I don't have to remind you to be kind and *fair*."

"I am always fair." *Not kind,* he mused. Ronar's gaze followed Sylvi as she approached him, her arms wrapping around his midsection in a tender embrace.

"Just come back to us." She sighed against his chest, clutching on to him a little tighter.

Ronar's arms slid around her to give her a gentle squeeze, then he pushed her away and chuckled. "Don't you worry, little one. The mages haven't been lurking around, and the only threat is the current state of the land —possibly Imara's wrath too . . ."

Sylvi shoved him playfully. "Just do as you're told." Her soft brown eyes held warmth in them, saying what she wouldn't give voice to.

"Have no fear. I can promise we will return." He snapped his fingers and pointed at Sylvi. "When I return, you and I will have a chat about Imara and the dragon."

Sylvi laughed, covering her mouth. "Lucky for me I know the dragon's favorite treats."

"Will you find yourself so lucky when you're without a home or job?"

She sighed dramatically, leaning against the wall. "*You* could never be so lucky."

He grunted in response and headed outside.

Once Ronar was in the stable, he quickly tacked both horses and strapped the food parcel to his saddle. On the back of the saddle, his belongings laid against the seat, light enough not to weigh down the horse or irritate the rider's back. Clucking his tongue, he led the horses from the stable and spotted Imara on the stone steps of the keep. She wore a pair of brown trousers like he'd requested, but he wasn't fond of how they fit her. Not because he was a prude—quite the contrary—but because even fitted loosely, they still showcased the length of her legs and her slender waist. What should have given her a less appealing appearance, per the ideals of everyone else, lent Imara an athletic and daring look, which suited her.

He turned his head, squinting at the ground. "Are you ready?"

She shook her head and strode toward the horses. "No." Her hand ran along the white mare's neck, scratching at it. "But I'm still going."

Imara's words started a slight smile at the corners of his lips. He'd learned in their time together that it was Imara's way of dealing with most things she found difficult. Rather than run from them, she stood her ground or charged headfirst into the situation.

"Off we go then." Ronar turned to help her mount, but

by the time he'd spun to face her, she was already looking down at him from the saddle. Imara lifted her pale brows in response and nudged her mount forward.

Chuckling, he mounted his horse and clucked his tongue. "Well, let's not waste any time then." Ronar urged his horse into a canter.

"Do you think we'll see the dragon in our passing?"

"I don't know. The dragon comes and goes as he pleases. He could be hunting, too."

Imara sighed wistfully. "Lucky," she muttered.

He caught her words on the wind and slowed his horse. "You *can* leave when you want. You're not a prisoner, Imara."

"Does that mean I can venture into the village with Sylvi?"

Ronar's horse slowed to a comfortable trot as they wound through the woods, but when he turned to look over his shoulder, the horse changed pace again and walked. "If Sylvi still has a job when we return."

"What?" Imara shouted, pressing her horse forward to bar Ronar's path.

Ronar erupted in laughter. He leaned forward, swiping a hand down his face. "If you think I would—"

"If I'm to be the lady of the keep, I forbid it."

Ronar's laughter renewed. His horse swung its head as it pressed on through the path. "Let me tell you why I would never *actually* fire Sylvi."

Imara's shoulders didn't relax as she stared him down. "Please do."

It was his fault for not telling her earlier, but most of

their interactions had become focused on research and less on learning about one another.

"While this is her story to tell, I'll let you in on something. Sylvi is like a daughter to me, and when she was a little girl, food was scarce, but the love of her father was even scarcer. His anger at fate was redirected to his daughter, and when I found her bruised and weeping along the roadside, too tired to continue her walk to Vidar, I took her away to the keep. She's been with me since." Ronar's eyes darkened as the memory of Sylvi's condition surfaced, and he was forced to relive the moment. He shook his head, shifting his jaw. "So no, Imara, though I tease her much as I do you, I could never part with her. She is as much a part of the keep as I am."

A long silence stretched between them.

Ronar contemplated breaking away from her, but it was apparent his words were taking their time settling in.

"Thank you," Imara said softly. "For telling me that. I never would have known."

Ronar spurred his horse forward and around Imara's mare. "We all carry scars, but not all of us are keen on talking about them." Without another word, he urged his horse forward. Whether or not Imara wanted to join the pace was up to her. Ronar wanted to leave that memory in the dust where it belonged.

16

RONAR

A few hours into their travels, the Valley Inn came into view. The establishment was a large wooden structure with a wraparound balcony on two levels. It sat high enough in the mountain that it could look over the desolate valley. In the spring, and normally the fall, the meadow's flowers created a moving piece of art.

To one side of the inn, a modest stable was attached. Once Ronar hopped down from his horse, he aided Imara. "Here is some coin to buy our lodging and to cover the horses too. I'll be in shortly." He yanked his bag free from the saddle, then handed it over to her. "There is more than enough to buy a feast, so please do. As much as I enjoy Thyr's biscuits, I need something with substance."

Imara laughed as she took the bag. "Okay. So a whole cow, perhaps a chicken . . . "

"A boar wouldn't hurt either." Ronar grinned at her.

She lifted her brows, then nodded her head. "I will see what I can do." She left for the inn without another word.

Ronar watched as she walked away. Her mare

squealed when a nosey equine neighbor grew too close, forcing Ronar's attention back to them.

Down the row of horses, a young woman dressed in black from head to toe polished her saddle. A piebald horse stuck its head out and nosed at her shoulder. Its white face stood out against the rest of its black coat.

Ronar took note of her apparel. Knee-high boots gave way to black, tight-fitting trousers, and her tunic, which was pulled in by a belt, hid a wool shirt beneath it, save for its sleeves. But it was the crystal which hung from her neck that caught his attention most. A crystal which he'd seen on the necks of other mages.

Ronar turned away, busying himself with wiping down the equipment. He used the moment to reach out toward the woman with his mind, carefully. If he pried too fast with too much energy behind it, she'd feel the intrusion.

"Soon, Gyda. Soon they'll see how invaluable you are. You won't always be an apprentice."

Ronar snorted. "This . . . this here is the difference between human craftsmanship and seidr." He shook his head, lifting up the saddle. "With our hands, we engrave the leather, and they with magic. They believe themselves *so* superior."

Gyda roused in her corner, bristling at the mention of seidrs. She glanced around as if looking to see if the coast was clear. "I know. They believe themselves to be the chosen ones. But we humans deserve to wield magic too. It's our right as much as theirs."

"Of course it is," Ronar encouraged her. "It's time we show them that we humans are here to stay, and that we will fight whatever the cost."

Gyda's cheeks reddened as she grew passionate. "Yes! It's why I'm apprenticing to be a mage . . . We are rallying as many apprentices as possible. We are the true rulers, not the seidrs! We are meant to be the chosen ones." Gyda hopped down from her perch and approached Ronar, her deep brown eyes feverish. She lifted her hand and clutched the dull crystal. "We can amplify magic in our crystals now. The time is nearly upon us—" Gyda clamped her mouth shut as a seidr walked into the barn, her eyes tracking his movement as if he were prey.

Ronar schooled his expression as he drank in this information. Horror washed over him, but he didn't show it. Gyda was only one of how many humans that had joined the mages' efforts? And here he'd thought the mages had given up. No, they were only biding their time.

He quickly took care of his tack and nodded to Gyda before entering the inn. By the time he made it to the counter, Imara was red in the face and flustered.

Ronar attempted to convey his stress to her, trying to catch her eye as he cleared his throat, but she was focused on the floor.

"Hm? What is this about?" He squinted, looking between the innkeeper and Imara. In a blink, Ronar wondered if the woman had offended Imara, which quickly sparked the desire to step in. However, the woman behind the desk reminded him of Thyr: older, stocky, and brimming with warmth, which soothed his irrational thoughts.

"I was just explaining to your wife that there is only one room available," the woman replied.

Some of his tension eased, and he allowed his

shoulders to drop a fraction. "Oh good, we won't have to travel to the outskirts then." Ronar turned his head. A few pieces of his hair tickled his jawline. He watched Imara chew on her bottom lip, and she studiously ignored his eyes. She practically vibrated with anxiety. "Then what is the problem?"

"No problem at all! There is only one bed, which shouldn't be an issue for such a lovely young couple. Your wife was telling me you've traveled for hours, and you must be exhausted!"

Wife, he mused, wondering what Imara had said—or if the woman had merely assumed they were a married couple traveling together. Ronar ran a hand along the nape of his neck, and his lips twitched as he fought the urge to laugh, but instead, he wrapped his arm around Imara's rigid form and squeezed her shoulder. "None at all. We haven't even had a chance since our wedding to really take in the fact we're husband and wife." He winked at the innkeeper, then held his hand out for the key. "Isn't this *grand*, darling?" Ronar peered down at Imara, then back up at the innkeeper. "We will take our lunch in the room."

Once on the stairwell, Imara slipped away from him, uncharacteristically quiet. Did she truly believe *this* would be the place out of all places he'd claim his bride? Ronar shook his head, then slid their bags from his other shoulder.

He needed to speak with her about his findings, but there was a new tension in the air, one that was electric.

Down the hallway, to the left, they both stopped in front of the room's door, and he promptly pushed it open. Imara let loose a strangled noise at the sight of the bed— just one—which wasn't as large as Ronar had been expecting. He scratched at his temple as a slow chuckle slipped out. "This is a suite?" As he stepped inside the room, he spun around to take it in.

"You've been here before. You had to know," Imara whispered. She focused on the floor, avoiding Ronar's gaze.

He snorted, depositing the bags on the dresser before crossing the room to pull the table out from against the wall. "I'm glad to see you've regressed to thinking me vile and without morals, Imara." Against the corner of the wall, a cushioned chair sat, which he assumed would be his bed for the evening. "I have you know I've never once rented a suite here. I have no need when my home isn't far away. Never once have I been so desperate for companionship that I'd resort to renting a room like *this*." His words were clipped as he spoke. "Have no fear. I'll sleep in the chair tonight."

In a quick movement, he grabbed the rickety chair and sat down. One moment he was sitting, and the next, the chair splintered beneath him, breaking apart as he crashed to the floor. Ronar caught himself before his back slammed against the wooden planks, and to his surprise, Imara lurched forward. She visibly warred with laughing and perhaps crying. She reached her hand out to him, which he took and pulled himself upward.

He stood close, *too* close, to Imara. Lifting his hand, he brushed his thumb against her reddened cheek. "I will sleep on the floor if that's what you want." Ronar tilted her head back so he could peer into her eyes. "I want you to know, Imara, I will never take what isn't given to me. I hope you come to understand that. There may be much you don't know about me, but believe me when I say I will respect your wishes."

Imara didn't move away from him. Her body seemed to relax as he spoke. She didn't pull back and she didn't move forward, but when she opened her mouth, with her lips so close to his, he could nearly taste her. Finally, when she spoke, her words surprised Ronar. "We can share the bed. But *please* keep your back to me."

Ronar didn't dare move. Her tone was like ice water dropping onto him, but the notion of sharing a bed with her heated his flesh despite the chill. "If you're certain, then I can accept those terms."

"I didn't . . . I mean, I didn't think . . . " Imara lowered her gaze. Her hands lifted, readying to cover her face, but Ronar stopped her from hiding by tugging on her wrists.

"If I've given you cause to question my motives, then I apologize. As far as I'm concerned, you're not yet my wife. We have time to plan a ceremony if that's something you want to consider. If by then you still cannot stomach having me as your husband, you'll be free to do as you please. Wife in name, but no duties, by which I mean no one will expect you to assume the position as Lady of the Keep."

Ronar had come to the conclusion that Sylvi was right. There was no way Imara could return to Omdahl without being further scorned. She'd be seen as tainted, not only because of her unpredictable magic but because she'd been living with him and partaking in who-knows-what debauchery.

She stared up at him, but not in a way that made him feel as though she were about to scold him, nor was it in disgust. The way Imara looked at him made his heart twist. Ronar could think of a thousand reasons not to kiss her right now, but they all went up in flames as she leaned in closer.

A knock at the door broke the moment. Ronar took a second to glance up at the ceiling and rein himself in.

Imara darted away from him and sat on the bed, looking as flustered as *he* felt.

Ronar answered the door and was met with a full cart of food. The aroma distracted him from the heated moment, and so did the innkeeper's ruddy cheeks.

"Your lunch, as requested by the lady!" The innkeeper beamed.

Ronar stepped aside and motioned to the table.

"Oh my, what is this mess?" the woman inquired, staring down at the destroyed chair.

"Put it on the tab. All I did was sit, and it collapsed."

As if she didn't quite believe him, the innkeeper glanced over at Imara to confirm.

Did the woman believe Ronar would strike Imara? He groaned.

"I won't judge preferences. There is another tray of food in the hall. I'll be right back." She left briefly, then returned with another tray. "If you need anything, just hop down to the desk and let me know." She smiled warmly at the both of them. "Enjoy your stay."

When the woman left, Ronar stared at the door. The sound of Imara's laughter turned his head, and she dissolved into a loud fit. His mouth hung open as if he were to speak, but he didn't want to interrupt Imara's moment.

Selfishly, the sound of her laughter warmed him, and he didn't want it to end.

Finally, Imara composed herself and swiped at her cheeks. "I don't want to know what she thought about us and the chair." Another peel of laughter escaped her.

"I could tell you," he muttered, which only brought another laugh from her.

After a moment, he pushed the table closer to the bed and sat down next to Imara. "Before we eat, I have something to tell you." Ronar frowned, then turned to Imara. "In the stable, there was an apprentice mage . . ."

Imara stilled beside him as he told her of what he'd learned, and by the end of it, she looked as horrified as he'd felt.

"Whether you want to eat or not, make yourself. You're going to need the energy."

After lunch, Ronar ventured back to the stable to prepare his horse. He scanned the aisle for Gyda, but she wasn't there, and neither was her piebald horse. Turning back to his gelding, he finished tacking him up. When he was done, Imara entered the barn, ready to go.

"Just one horse?" Imara asked.

Ronar led the horse out of the barn, then mounted with ease. He extended his hand to Imara with a smile. "Consider this my way of easing you into sleeping next to me." He teased and shook his head. "If something should happen to you, it would be easier to have you riding with me." He grinned widely. "And if something happens to me, just roll my carcass off to the side and find some flowers to sprinkle over my body."

She huffed in response, then grabbed his hand so he could pull her up. The heat of her body passed on to him, and the warmth brought a well of desire. He yearned to brush the hair from her nape and leave a trail of kisses from there to the shell of her pointed ear. But this was no time for that, and as she settled in front of him, he clucked to the horse, and they were off.

As they rode on, it was strange to see the sudden mark of where the blight had spread. The upper meadowlands still thrived; late autumn blossoms danced in the soft breeze, the same breeze that caught Imara's scent and surrounded Ronar. But as they descended further into the meadow, it was clear they were entering tainted land. For the moment, Ronar focused on just the feeling of his arms around Imara, and it was enough to relax him for the time being.

When they were almost there, Imara broke through the silence. "What if it doesn't work?"

"Then I'll search elsewhere. There are more Dragon Masters out there than just myself, and our knowledge runs deep. We are ancient collectors who spend most of our time searching for and hoarding literature, new and old. If I must reach out to other masters, then I will."

"I didn't realize you still spoke to the other masters." Imara turned her head, glancing at him from the corner of her eye.

Ronar chuckled. "Well, my darling, I don't need to divulge every little thing to you now, do I? I never cut ties with the others, and though they're dispersed throughout, we still keep in touch. Just like the other dragons in Brynjar. They do call me Dragon Master for a reason," he offered pointedly.

As much as Ronar longed to jest with her, whatever remark was left on the tip of his tongue withered away the moment they faced the valley in all of its devastation.

Death swallowed life, and the same teasing breeze that had previously blown fresh air against them turned into something stale and putrid. Trees that had stood, clinging on to life just a day ago, were now dead and charred.

Imara sucked in a breath. "No," she whispered.

"Yes, and it's worse than yesterday." Ronar slid from the horse, and Imara did the same. As he knelt down, his fingers dug into the dead earth. "Now, we at least try." His eyes flicked up to Imara, her face paler than usual and full of horror. "I am with you, Imara. If things go awry, I'll sever the connection." In their studies, they'd tried it, and Ronar was able to break the connection by enveloping her in his magic. The bond of the earth shrunk backward, away from the intrusion, and immediately let go.

Imara nodded. Her hands bunched into fists as she strode forward, resolve filtering into her gaze. She knelt down next to Ronar, burying her hands in the soil, then whispered under her breath.

"When you're ready, my darling."

Magic unfurled in the air, the current strong and heady as it pulsed around them. Ronar could taste the sweetness as it flooded into the earth from Imara's essence.

As much as he wanted to focus on the state of the soil beneath her hands, he was more concerned with Imara and her wellbeing. What would a drain like this do to her?

"I feel . . . something, Lajos." Her words came out sluggishly, and the warm glow she initially had slowly faded.

"Imara, are you feeling okay?" Ronar's hand rested against her back. He met a menacing pull on his magic the moment his hand touched her. "Imara," he said with more force. When she didn't answer, he went to pull her away. She rasped against the draw on her magic, but no sounds left her mouth—not even a cry for help.

"You will not fall to whatever this is, not on my watch." Ronar wrapped his hand around her wrist, allowing his magic to flow over her. He felt the tug again, the wish to drain his magic. It was like a slithering snake in search of prey, but when it discovered Ronar wasn't the one it longed for, it pulled away.

Imara collapsed against the ground, still conscious, still alert. But it was as if the earth wanted more of her, yearned for more contact with her. He felt it in the thrum of magic as it coursed between them both.

"Imara!" Ronar bellowed.

IMARA

It began the way it always had, with Imara carefully reaching out to the piece of earth within her grasp, searching for that spark of Jörd always there within it, no matter how slight. Except this time, she had reached, and reached, and reached—sending her magic so deep within the earth she feared that Jörd had abandoned them all. It frightened her, but what frightened her even more was the force she finally connected with.

The force within the depths of the earth was not the pure, life-giving, elemental energy that she was used to connecting with. It was something dark and ravenous. Something with an endless, aching hunger—reaching out and searching, greedily gobbling up everything that it could find.

When she first felt the icy tendrils, like a skeleton hand slipping around her soul, she fought to push back against it. However, there was something familiar about the tendrils, even if they were dark and tainted, and she found it hard to resist. Imara fought against the first tug at her magic, but the ice had already sunk its teeth into her and began to draw from her what it could.

Distantly, she could hear Lajos speaking, but his voice wasn't breaking through, not as she fought against the drain upon herself. Lost to the battle waging on the inside, she barely felt herself drop down to her hip in the ashen soil, her legs no longer able to keep her braced upon them.

A gasp slipped from Imara's lips as something inside of her burst open, a dam broken apart, and a whole new flood of power began to wash through her. With it came the whispered, haunting voices, dark rumbles from the deep echoing inside her mind.

Imara whimpered as the volume of the voices increased, accompanied by memories flashing rapidly through her thoughts. She was five years old and sitting in the midst of the Elders. The four elements surrounded her, and she was meant to be calling out to each, seeing which she connected to. Instead, young Imara had felt a flood of energy surge through her unlike anything she had ever experienced before. It had frightened her, causing her to scream and curl up in a ball, hands over her head as she fought to block herself off from the rush of it.

The icy fingers delved more deeply inside her, and with the floodgates now open to her abilities, whatever lay within the depths of the earth was now using Imara as a siphon. Linked into the very core of the earth's energy, the tendrils drew on the life-giving essence more strongly than ever before. Physically able to feel the life being drained from the world around her, Imara began to fight back, pushing at whatever was in the earth, trying to force it out of herself.

It did not want to leave and fought against every fraction of freedom she regained. In the end, it was too much. She pushed too hard, or the spirits in the depths pulled too much—the world went dark, and Imara fell lifelessly to the ground.

Gradually, Imara left the darkness, becoming aware of the sway of the horse beneath them and her cheek pressed against a firm chest. Too weary to speak, she stirred slightly. It was enough to rouse Lajos from whatever thoughts may have been going on inside his head. His arm tightened about her, and she heard him whisper soothingly above her.

"I've got you, my darling, I've got you." Unable to respond, Imara simply sunk back into the darkness, relieved to know that for the moment, she was safe.

When she woke again, her body was prone upon the bed, and the edge of it dipped beneath the weight of Lajos, who sat at her side. His fingers smoothed back her hair before moving to slip beneath her head, fingertips taking perch at specific areas along her hairline as he began to murmur something ancient over her. In response, she felt a gentle flow of energy filtering into her. It was enough to make the tired, faltering flutter of her heart pick up a steady, healthy pace.

Lajos must have heard the easing of her breath, for he sighed in relief. She had a deep desire to thank him and to let him know that she was going to be just fine. But for the moment, sleep still called to her. Answering the needs of her body, Imara slipped back into the darkness. This time however, it was warm and welcoming.

It was well into the night when her eyes opened at last to a dimly lit room. The candle on the table beside the bed waned low, its wick fighting to maintain every last instance of its bright life. Though it sat across the room, Imara could almost feel the heat of it upon her skin like a soft brush of fingertips over her cheek.

In her ears, a subtle hum sounded out, causing her to rub at the offending lobes. Taking a deep breath, Imara felt the weight of something upon her chest and the dampness of the air drawn into her lungs. It was hard to think clearly as the sensations assailed her all at once.

Gasping, Imara sat up. She held her hand palm-up and thought of water, then watched as her hand filled with droplets pulled from the air in the room. Shuddering with realization, Imara found herself thinking of fire, and the water transformed into steam, billowing up until it was gone.

The hum in her ears was coming from the energy all around her, through the lines of Mother Earth that traveled through every living thing and anything that had come from her depths. Swallowing roughly, Imara took in the space around her, trying to make sense of what was happening. Memories of her elemental ceremony came flooding back once again. She was five years old, scared and uncertain as the strong surge of something *other* rose up inside her, all four elements tugging at her with equal pull.

Could it be? Is it hubris to even think it?

Beside her on the bed, Lajos lay asleep, half propped up on pillows, looking as if he had lost the battle to sit the night through watching over her. His handsome features were pinched slightly with concern, and she could tell that, even in the depths of his own exhaustion, he was still worrying over her. Imara didn't want to wake him, but she knew that he must. She needed to share this revelation with him.

She was reminded of his words earlier in the day, of wishing to finalize their marriage but allowing it to be on her terms. Imara had seen his offer for what it was—an offer of a home in whatever manner she wished for it to be. She wasn't certain what was to become of them, but the day the Elders had come to her, she had vowed to accept this marriage in order to save her family, and that was what Lajos was trying to give her. A lifetime spent with him at Dragon's Keep, surrounded by the devotion of his staff, was not an unappealing offer.

She could be happy there; she *had* been happy there.

"Lajos," she whispered, reaching out a pale hand to rest upon his sun-kissed one that lay on the bed between them. Before his eyes opened, his hand turned over, fingers wrapping gently around her own and offering a subtle squeeze.

His vivid green eyes, which typically sparkled with sarcastic humor, were for the moment soft and showing only concern. He sat up gingerly so as not to jostle her and turned to better look her in the eyes.

"Imara." Her name was soft upon his tongue, and she found it caused a little flutter in her belly hearing it. "How are you feeling? You had me very concerned for your wellbeing, my darling, and I am sorry. I should never have placed you in these circumstances, not so soon after discovering your abilities."

Not wishing for him to continue down this path, Imara lifted her hand to place her fingertips over his lips, silencing him. "Don't," was all she said before slowly sitting up.

Her body was weary, though her spirits were high. Warm fingers gently encircled her wrist and pulled her fingers from his mouth, but there was a touch of a smirk at the corner of his lips now instead of the frown that had been there.

"Don't?"

"Don't pretend as if I didn't have a choice in the matter. I did, and I chose to go to the valley and try. Nor am I sorry. Lajos . . . the barrier has been broken." She rasped the words almost reverently, and wishing to show him what she meant, she lifted her hand. Thinking fire, her fingertips ignited with a bright flame, more than combating the candle on the table.

She could feel it now more than she had ever been able to before: the energy that flowed through every particle of being, in her, through her, around her. Everything was connected to the lines of Jörd's power, from the wooden floorboards that remembered the living trees they once were, to the miniscule droplets of water in the air, and even the solid earth several floors below them. In feeling it, she understood it. The power wasn't something that could be taken from her, because it did not belong to her. Instead, she was a conduit for Jörd's majesty, a being tied so completely to the energy traveling through the earth that there was truly no separating them. Imara was as much a part of the elemental energies as they were a part of her.

"When I connected with whatever was down there," she continued, not giving him a chance to speak, "the beings in the ground forced more power through me than I've ever connected with before, using me to draw the life out of the earth so they could feed on it. It allowed me to see what happened when I was a child . . . during my testing. I believe I put the barrier up to protect myself, out of fear. It was too much for me to bear at such a young age, and I hid from it until I no longer even remembered it was there."

Which felt unbelievable considering how much life was all around her, tied to the essence of everything. How had she denied all of this for so long?

"Gone? Entirely?" he asked, bewilderment in his tone.

"Yes, entirely. At last, I feel as if I understand what has been happening inside of me—how all of this is meant to work." She sighed, feeling the relief of that flow through her. Whatever had been in the depths of the earth was a terrible, endless hunger which needed to be stopped, but her interaction with it had awoken Imara to herself. "Would it be entirely presumptuous of me to say . . . " Could she utter it out loud? The thought that had been whirling about in her mind since she woke up and felt this great flood of energy and awareness all around her.

"To say what?" he asked.

"That I may actually be an Ambient." It felt surreal to say it. "I can feel everything around me," she was quick to add, not wishing for him to think she had lost her mind and was thinking this unfounded. "The air in this room, the wood of the bed posts that were once trees, the flame atop that candle . . . In all of it, I feel the essence of Jörd binding us all together."

It was still overwhelming to be aware of so much around her all at once. She could fully understand how this had been a terrifying experience as a young child, unaware of what was happening to her when her abilities had first woken. Imara took a calming breath, trying to focus on her conversation with Lajos rather than the hum of energy filling the room.

"You're a conduit," Lajos murmured softly, his face studious as he contemplated everything that she was saying. He reached out to smooth a hand gently through her hair, tucking it behind her ear. "You can sense all of the elements now?"

Imara nodded. "And more." Her words were soft, and perhaps a little disbelieving. She wouldn't have thought it possible, but she had read all of Embla's recounting of her own experiences. This simply felt right.

"Those fools. All the while, they had you in their midst."

It was odd that not one of the Elders was taken aback by her reaction during the element ceremony. Imara could vividly remember now her child-self crying out in fear as she coiled in on herself. Had they allowed her to go through life believing she was nothing when they knew otherwise? There was no time to dwell on what had been, not when the valley was rapidly dying and they still had no answers.

"Lajos," she paused after his name, making sure his eyes were meeting hers. "We need to try again."

"Try what, exactly?" he asked slowly.

"We need to go back into the valley tomorrow for me to connect with the earth once more."

"Absolutely not." He shook his head, dark hair spilling into his eyes. With a quick twist of his body, he was off the bed and striding across the room to the table, which held a tray of forgotten food. "It was a mistake to take you down there in the first place. We won't risk it again."

"I have to. We still don't know what I found down there, and until we know what it is, how can we ever hope to stop it?" She watched him silently build a plate of food, his shoulders stiff and resistance in the line of his back. "Lajos, the valley is *dying,* and I don't believe it will stop there!"

His fist hit the top of the table. "I am aware," came his gritted response. "But I will not add you to the death toll."

"I'm not going to die!" she snapped back, but then bit down on her lip, reining in her frustration. Now was not the time to let tempers flare. He was concerned and only trying to protect her, she could see that. "Please," Imara said more softly. "Just have faith in me. I know what happened earlier was frightening, but I believe it happened because I resisted too hard. I just want a chance to delve a little more deeply. I have to . . . I heard voices speaking into my mind when the pull became truly strong. If I connect again, I may be able to learn something of it."

In a show of stamping down his own agitation, Lajos turned to her, the plate of food now in his hands. Carrying it over to the bed, he held it out to her. "Eat. You must be famished."

Imara took the peace offering from him, sitting up a

little straighter. The outcome of her first attempt in the valley had been frightening, but she knew that whatever needed to be done, she could do it so long as she had Lajos there to help her. Carefully, he sat on the edge of the bed once more, watching her.

"What do you think you can now do that you could not before? I watched you collapse after mere minutes of contact." A fire remained lit in his gaze, but Lajos was now approaching this more calmly.

"That was before I was aware of myself. Now that I feel open to it all, I'm able to sense more than I ever could before. This time, I will not resist the pull. I will let whatever is down there draw energy from the earth in hopes that I will be able to understand the voice . . . or voices . . . " Imara sighed. "My only fear is that I still will not be able to make sense of the words. The language felt old."

Lajos sighed, his hand lifting to scrub at his face. "I can aid you in that. I'll listen in."

Imara, pleased he was beginning to cave on the idea, began to smile, only to stop. "What do you mean?"

"I am able to listen in on others' thoughts, Imara."

"What?!" she began, body tensing.

"So if you insist upon this, then I will connect with you throughout the entire ordeal and be another ear," he continued over her.

"Could we go back to the fact that you can listen in on the thoughts of others for just *one* moment please?" she nearly growled, her body filling with rage at the idea of him inside her head, listening to her most intimate thoughts. She felt betrayed.

"Imara, no. While your face tells me you will not believe me, I have not betrayed your confidence and privacy in such a manner," he spoke earnestly.

She wanted to believe him but found it hard to do so when she had no real way of knowing. It took everything not to continue this conversation. Instead, she forced it away for the time being.

"We'll leave at dawn," she murmured. "We'll speak on this again once we've returned home."

The valley surrounded them once more, its ashen desolation fighting to break Imara's spirit. This land had cared for her people for centuries, and now every which way she looked, her eyes found death.

"Are you ready?" Lajos asked, coming to stand beside her.

Was one ever ready for proceedings such as these? "How would be best for us to make the connection?" She tilted her head up to gaze into his eyes.

"Typically, I am capable of listening in simply by reaching out. But for today's matters, I believe a physical connection would be best." He held his hand out to her, and nodding, Imara accepted the offering.

Hands clasped together, both of them dropped to their knees in the lifeless soil. Sinking her one free hand into the earth, Imara took a deep breath. She had promised that she could do this without coming to harm, but she wasn't entirely sure.

"Are you listening now?" she asked him, waiting for the subtle nod of his head before shutting her eyes. Instead of simply reaching into the depths, she began to softly chant the words that had now become second nature to her. Words that called for the spirits and energies of the earth itself, awakening the very lifeforce of the world to her bidding.

Just as before, she had to reach deeper and deeper into the ground before she felt the brush of the force below. This time however, instead of attempting to stem the flow of energy into the spirit in the ground, she opened herself up to it. A shuddered breath left her as a sudden wave of cold hunger wrapped around her, and her mind was filled with the voices from before. Dark, ravening rasps of death echoed through her thoughts in a tongue so ancient it no longer bore even the semblance of current speech.

While Imara could only hope that Lajos was hearing the words and committing them to memory, she dove further into the energy that she was sensing, losing herself for a moment in the seemingly endless hunger. Finally, it washed over her, the definitive sense of five distinct essences in the depths of the ground. Five beings trying to claw their way to the surface where they could devour everything in their wake. Their hunger, as before, slid its phantom hand around her very being, sinking its claws into her core and funneling all the life and essence from the surrounding earth that it could reach.

It was a feeling both foreign and familiar, warring with her but also recognizing her, and it left a tainted shadow of its presence everywhere that it touched—upon her and the earth. The beings wished to latch onto her, to permanently dig their nails into her soul and feed until there was nothing left, and a part of herself recognized their need and almost gave in. Instead, Imara pulled additional energy to her, and with a forceful burst, sent it toward the depths of the ground with thoughts of healing. It was enough of a shock to the spirits below that they retracted their clutch in a moment of surprise. It was just enough for Imara to pull herself back, severing the last of the ties and ending up on her bottom in the dirt, still clutching onto Lajos' hand.

"By the moon and stars . . ." she gasped. "There are spirits in the earth. *Five* spirits."

RONAR

The last thing Ronar wanted was for Imara to return to the valley and try again. The memory of her lifeless body in his arms was too fresh in his mind, while the sensation of her draped there still lingered. But wasn't he a hypocrite if he denied her the chance of returning to at least try to tap into the earth? Perhaps, but the image of her collapsing to the ground was stronger than the guilt.

However, the damnable woman could argue like no other he'd met. Imara navigated debates with expertise and didn't fail to exasperate him. No matter the question or argument Ronar fired at her, she threw his words back at him in retaliation.

His ability to read minds wasn't common knowledge, which Ronar preferred, but it was necessary for him to enlighten Imara, as he wasn't about to tap into her mind without her consent. He could only imagine what hellfire she would rain down on him for doing so. So, amidst the debate, he relented with an exhausted chuckle.

Down in the valley, the scorched land glared at him as the minutes ticked by, and all he could do was listen in as

Imara connected with the earth once more. Ronar could swear a hiss met his ears, then a distinct voice. It echoed in his mind in a foreign tongue, coating his thoughts with a foul fog.

He bared his teeth in a snarl the moment the beings tried to keep Imara, readying for a fight. Ronar's magic ignited in his veins but didn't leach into her yet. His skin prickled in anticipation, waiting for the moment when he could unleash his anger on whatever was beneath the earth.

A deluge of power assaulted his senses, and it stemmed from Imara, bringing forth a rasp from Ronar. He was used to magic, hostile and amiable, but this . . . it wasn't one he was familiar with.

Hissing filled his thoughts, but there were words too, ancient ones. They went around and around, the same phrase over and over, but what it was he couldn't say. Even Ronar had never heard such a language spoken. The hiss turned into a guttural growl, continuing the repetition.

It felt as if he'd just homed in on the words, playing them over in his own mind, when Imara blurted about five beings. Her words sounded garbled and distant to his ears. Ronar scooped her up into his arms, then held her tightly as he stroked her hair lightly. He was half in a trance, focusing on the words, committing them to memory.

"I heard them," Ronar rasped, blinking away the malevolent tendrils swirling in his mind. "I heard them."

Imara sucked in a breath, her hands rising to press against his chest. She lifted her chin, peering into his eyes, her blue pair shining far too bright to be normal. "You heard them." Imara lifted her fingers to her chin, absentmindedly standing up and walking away from Ronar toward their horse. She only paused when he touched her shoulder.

"Imara, take a moment." Ronar studied her expression, the cadence of her breath, and the subtle tension in her posture. Judging by the surge of power, it had been a substantial amount of energy used, and it had frightened whatever those demons were.

"No. We must return to the keep, and quickly. Lajos, that language . . . Do you know of it?"

Ronar nodded, sighing as he glanced up at the sky. "I do—at least, I have the books. I'm not quite that old, thank you." The throaty dialect tickled the back of his mind; it was familiar but just out of reach.

Imara huffed as she gathered the reins of the horse and mounted swiftly. "That is yet to be determined." As color returned to her, so did her wits it seemed.

"Bite your tongue," he grumbled, pulling himself up behind her. Roughly, he wrapped his arms around her body and drew her against his chest. "Or next time, I might do it for you." Ronar barked with laughter as Imara stiffened against him.

"Now isn't the time."

Ronar exhaled loudly for effect. "It appears it never is, my darling wife." The remark earned an elbow to the gut. Chuckling, he clucked his tongue, spurring the horse on. Regrettably, it would take longer than he wished to return to the keep. There was another way, but he was not about to call on it just yet.

Upon the arrival at the inn, Ronar lingered outside the stable, watching the patrons mill around. Most were rail-thin, the consequence of failing crops, which meant inadequate livestock and less food to consume. The rotting land wasn't just about the beautiful flora waning; it was about the villagers suffering, growing sick, and even dying. Water grew scarce deeper in the valley, drying up with the rest of the infertile land.

These people were starving, and only Mother knew how far away from death. It drove him to near madness to consider that an option, to just watch as they withered away and died.

Ronar was so consumed by his thoughts, he didn't hear Imara approach him from the side. Her arm slipped around his, squeezing it, then tugging gently.

"Come inside to eat. I know you, and you haven't eaten as much as you normally do."

She was right, but he didn't feel like eating. Even as he thought about it, Ronar's stomach rebelled, growling loudly. "Very well."

"We will figure it out. We're close, I know it." Imara led the way into the dining area of the inn. She took a seat, crossing her legs at the ankles.

Somehow, it was Ronar whose head still reeled from the valley's events. Imara appeared chipper and more resolute than before. Grunting, Ronar rubbed his face out of frustration. "Not close enough."

A barmaid sidled up to the table, smiling at them. "What a smart couple you make!" Her brown eyes lit with warmth as she placed tankards of cider down. "The drinks are on the house. I'm afraid we aren't able to tap into the well, but the cider is still fresh and flowing."

Imara stared up at the woman with an open mouth, her eyes wide.

"Thank you, I think so too. You'll have to convince my wife of that, I'm afraid." Ronar motioned to Imara, who slowly turned her look of shock into one of annoyance as her gaze settled onto him. "How long has the well been acting up for you?" Curiosity got the better of him, and perhaps he wanted Imara to relax after her ordeal.

The slender woman leaned against the table, her gaze drifting toward the exposed beams in the establishment. "Likely two weeks now. It's worse than it has been, but hasn't the entire area suffered as of late?"

Time was surely running out for the valley. Frowning, Ronar nodded toward the barmaid. "I'll have the roast, and keep the cider flowing."

"The stew sounds delightful, thank you." Imara offered a warm smile, then took up her cider and downed a good portion.

The barmaid bobbed her head and walked away.

Ronar squinted at Imara. "Maybe next time someone compliments us, you can smile and agree that we are a lovely match." He drank some cider, chuckling as Imara's napkin sailed over his head and collided with another patron behind him. "Now you've done it," Ronar muttered as the man turned around with an accusing eye, searching for the one responsible for the attack.

"I am not your wife," Imara hissed.

"Yet," he reminded her, winking. The lack of fire behind Imara's gaze wasn't lost on him, and he wondered if it was because of exhaustion or if he was wearing her down.

"And don't for one moment think you can tell me how I should respond to someone. That is entirely up to *me*."

Ronar reclined in his chair, assessing Imara's flushed cheeks. He smiled without the typical sharpness; it was a warmth that spread from his lips to his eyes, lending him an amiable appearance.

"I shan't forget it, my darling." And he wouldn't, because as long as Imara was a part of his life, he knew she wouldn't allow for it.

This time, when Imara shook her head ruefully, a smile accompanied it.

The next morning, Ronar arrived in the stable before the sun peeked over the horizon. Freshly laid straw tickled his nose as he prepared the horses for the journey home. As much as he wanted to believe there were answers in the library—he was sure there was at least a clue—dread unfurled within.

Not every option had been exhausted yet. There was one wiser than him—older too—who might know more. If

Ronar's library was vast, the one his elder possessed was boundless.

"While we ride, you can explain your telepathy to me." Imara mounted her horse, then turned her gaze to Ronar. She looked down at him expectantly, her chin jutting out with all the pomp of a queen. In this land, she might as well have been.

Ronar patted her upper thigh, chuckling. "I didn't forget." Once mounted, Ronar sped down the street, ready to explain himself for the next few hours.

The sun dipped below the trees by the time the pair reached Dragon's Keep. Ronar's lower back ached in protest, and his legs had long since lost their feeling, but he said nothing as he dismounted and wobbled. Imara did the same, but her body started to sink before Ronar's arm slid around her middle.

"I've never taken you for the swooning sort, my lady," he teased, earning a snort in response. "And speechless. I've exhausted you, haven't I?"

"Thoroughly." Imara shrugged out of his grasp and led her horse to the stable, where they both tended to the animals.

"This is not how I intended to leave you boneless and depleted of energy." One eyebrow raised as he gave her a playful glance.

Flushing, Imara turned her head away to focus on finishing up.

Not even Imara's blushing was enough to stir Ronar further as his energy plummeted, and the trek into the keep seemed a monumental task after the journey from the valley. The first thing he did once inside was hunt down a quill and parchment. Thorne needed to know of the mages' advancements and that the mages were building an army. Omdahl wasn't without defenses entirely, but they weren't warriors. They were a farming people, and to hurl them amidst a war . . . it would be madness. Ronar surmised they could hold their own when it came to magic, but they were not used to battle tactics. He frowned as he signed the letter and sealed it with a glob of wax and a dragon seal.

The crackling of the hearth sounded distant to him as he warred with whether or not to pen another letter. But in the end, he took out a fresh piece of parchment and wrote a quick note. The tip of the quill looped in several ancient glyphs, and once Ronar finished, his shoulders sagged.

Imara quietly approached him, her pale brows furrowed in a silent question.

"King Thorne needs to know. I have faith in the tenacity of Omdahl, but they shouldn't have to battle by themselves. They shouldn't have to battle at all." He shook his head ruefully.

Mikkel emerged from the kitchen with a pastry half in his mouth. His face rumpled in thought as he patted at his chest, then pulled free a letter from his doublet. With his free hand, he withdrew the treat and coughed a mouthful of confectionery sugar out. "My lord, you received a missive from the king."

The rare sight of him looking anything less than composed struck Ronar as amusing. But as he took notice of the letter, Ronar closed the distance between them and broke the seal. In exchange, he handed Mikkel the two sealed missives. "When you're done eating, see to it that the king's letter is sent by pigeon. And as for this one, you know what to do." Ronar turned to Imara, then lifted a hand to lightly run over her head.

"Well, what does it say?" Imara pressed him.

Mikkel bowed his head, taking his cue to leave. When he did, Ronar opened the paper, scanning the king's words. "Only that he wishes us to keep him apprised, and should we need his forces, he will send them immediately. As he put it, *'with shield, steel, and heart, we will meet you, we will guard you.'*" Ronar flicked the paper off to the side, sighing. "What a poet. With this letter I've sent, he'll be sending forces our way. I'd rather have a small band of an army than none at all."

Imara nodded, worrying at her bottom lip. "We will be ready for the mages' next move then."

"One can only hope." Ronar sighed, needing to submerge himself in a boiling tub of water. "I'll meet you in the library, and if I don't show my face, you may have to pry me from the bath." His tone didn't indicate he was jesting; he meant it. Imara's gaze lingered on him, and Ronar felt it even as he turned on his heel, but no playful words came from him as he disappeared upstairs.

After a steaming bath, Ronar dressed in a loose linen shirt with the ties undone to reveal the sculpted chest beneath. It wasn't meant to tease. Rather, he was too lazy and tired to be bound in any fashion. Even his breeches were loose on his form, tied in a loose knot and nearly hanging from his lean hips. He wore no socks, and his hair, which was still wet, curled as it air-dried.

Imara gaped at him from the long table, then busied herself with the notes scribbled in front of her.

Ronar crossed the room and stood in front of the massive bookshelf. He lifted a hand, paused, then called forth a collection of books that settled into his arms.

"We begin here. Again." The pile landed on the table with a thud, and Ronar followed suit by plopping into a chair.

Imara's nose scrunched. "Are you all right?"

"Nothing a week's worth of sleep won't fix, but that will come later." Ronar motioned to the paper in front of her. "Let's begin translating before I start hibernating." The remark earned him a soft laugh. Quill scraped against paper, rustling in the quiet of the library.

Opening a volume on dead languages, Ronar played the words from the valley over in his mind. Focusing on the cadence of the words, he homed in on the oldest tongue of them all: the mother language.

Alarm crept up his spine, which Imara didn't miss. She grew rigid as she leaned across the table, eyes wide with concern. "What is it?"

"Write down these letters as I say them." Ronar's eyes never lifted from the page as he recited the letters, which they then spent the next hour translating.

Hour bled into hour. Soon, they'd repositioned the

translated letters on the page. Ronar's dread only grew when the words formed.

We are hungry, we want more.

Imara jolted upward, a nervous smile on her lips. "We did it. But who are they?"

"Demons, if you ask me."

Gathering the books in her arms, Imara moved to the sofa against the wall. "Let's continue over here. The ride was torture enough, and I've already spent too long in that chair." She curled up in the corner of the cushion and set the books down between them. "They aren't demons, Lajos, they're something else. You didn't feel what I did."

It was true. He had heard them, felt their inky tones caressing and needling his mind, but hadn't felt the energy in the same way Imara clearly had. "Whatever they are, I intend to seal them off from our land forever."

"You don't even know what they are."

Ronar lifted his brows, lazily shrugging his shoulders. "Something that is bent on destroying our land, in turn hurting our people. I don't think it's some bloody saint, Imara."

A sigh from the doorway caught the pair's attention, and both glanced toward the origin.

Sylvi stood with a tray of food. She skated down the stairs and crossed the room, placing the tray down on the table. "I brought you things to nibble on. I know neither one of you eats a full meal when you're consuming books. By the way, I'm glad you have arrived safely. Thanks for letting me know." The last of her words were aimed toward Ronar.

"Thank you, Sylvi, for bringing sustenance along with

your attitude. It was sorely missed," Ronar said, his tone lacking its usual bite.

"Thank you, Sylvi. We had a long ride, and we discovered something. I guess we just lost track of time."

Sylvi tossed her head, twisting her lips to keep from smiling but failing. "I'm only teasing, but I'm glad you are both back. Try not to stay up so late, and for Mother's sake, get some rest." She waved her hand over her shoulder as she left.

"Maybe we ought to." Imara fought off a yawn.

"Soon."

Soon turned into another hour, which became another. Outside, birds started to twitter, signaling the arrival of dawn. Cursing, Ronar started to sit upright, then felt Imara's head shift against his chest. She draped her arm across his torso, cheek against his breast as she slumbered. The sight twisted his gut, rousing an emotion he didn't want to name.

With care, he stood up, sliding his hands beneath her lithe figure and lifting her into his arms. They'd spent far too many hours awake, and judging by how she didn't rouse as he moved her, she was beyond exhausted. He wound his way through the hall, then Ronar pushed her door open with his toe and crept inside.

He lay her prone figure down, then carefully pulled the blankets up to cover her. Soft, creamy curls clung to her temples and forehead. Ronar smiled to himself, watching as she dreamed of Mother only knew what, but she looked as though she were at peace. This wasn't the life she chose, but Ronar hoped in some small way she was growing happier being at the keep. He didn't want to admit it, but *he* was happier with her here.

"Sweetest of dreams, my darling," he whispered, then leaned down and brushed a tender kiss against her forehead. Withdrawing from the bed, he paused in the doorway to watch as she slumbered. He smiled at the memory of feeling her against his body, then turned away to head toward his room.

19

IMARA

Imara pressed a soft kiss to the snout of the dragon, smiling as a sense of peacefulness flooded her. Their world was filled with an endless list of uncertainties, but one thing she could rely on was the acceptance she found here at the foot of the golden dragon in the woods. While his wise, ancient eyes surely saw her as a lesser being, there was no indication of it in their depths.

"Will you return soon?" the creature asked, his head resting on one large, clawed hand. Unable to resist brushing her fingers along his maw, Imara nodded.

"Tomorrow, upon waking. I've asked for a special treat to be made for you," she informed him.

A strange yet wonderful kinship had developed between Imara and the mighty beast here in the woods, and while the library was currently a place of endless frustrations, here in the clearing, she found herself able to lay it all bare. The dragon listened without judgement—offering instead words of encouragement and kindness. She had not imagined she would find a source of happiness in a beast known for its hunger and greed of shiny things, yet that is precisely what had been gifted to her.

"I will happily await you," he rumbled.

Giving him one last stroke upon his nose, Imara turned and found the path that would lead her back to the keep, a path that she had taken every morning over the past five days. Ever since her return from the valley, she'd found a need of escaping their frantic search for answers, and so she took to gathering herself amongst the elements.

Each morning she would awaken early, and before breakfast had even been eaten, Imara disappeared into the forest, calling out to the dragon to make certain he was there. Her time with him in those early hours, as the crisp morning air chilled her cheeks, left her feeling settled. It grounded her. Prepared her mind for pouring through hundreds of books in search of anything that might tell her what was buried beneath the grounds in the valley.

The mornings spent out in the ever-changing forests with the dragon also provided Imara with a chance to commune more with the energies of the earth. The barrier now gone and the floodgates opened, Imara was sensing a whole new world around her—the divine spirit of Jörd herself. The more she connected to her newfound powers, the more she understood of herself and of the world. The monsters in the valley had also begun to make more sense. Imara knew that, somehow, the creatures that were devouring every ounce of life in the valley were connected to Jörd. It was through earth's energies that they were feeding.

Their presence, though tainted nearly beyond recognition, also held a quality of the familiar about it, which, over the last two days, had driven her on an exploration of Lajos' library, searching for any writings of Jörd that she could find.

Nothing. There was nothing to be found within his multitude of bound texts of ancient beings concealed in the depths of the earth—nothing that led her any closer to an answer. Having exhausted all resources available to her, Imara sought out the Dragon Master purposefully.

Coincidentally, he was walking the halls in search of her.

"Imara—"

"Lajos—"

They spoke at the same time, causing a laugh of amusement to slip from Imara. Lajos merely lifted one dark brow over his green eyes, indicating that she should go first.

"I have gone through every book in your possession, and not one of the volumes speaks of the beings buried in the valley. Yet I am positive they are connected to Jörd in some manner. I can feel it in my very being . . ." Her hands were clenched tight at her sides. "I am at a loss."

Lajos closed the distance between them. Taking one of her hands, he gently pressed it open so he could massage the palm. "Then let me light the way. If another library is what you seek, then another library is what you shall get."

Imara gazed up at him in surprise, the warm tingle in her hand helping to ease the tension within her. "You think that we may actually go to these others?"

"Of course I do," he stated, tone cocky and self-assured.

"Where? Whose? When may we go?" she asked in quick succession.

Lajos chuckled, shaking his head at her as he slipped her arm through his, tugging her toward the dining hall. Imara followed along, waiting impatiently for him to explain himself. He so loved lording knowledge over her.

"There is another Dragon Master, older than I," he began, pulling her into the dining hall. "Synda lives on the Isle of Eristyminen, and she is in possession of texts I have not even laid eyes on."

"She would allow us to see them?" Imara questioned, eagerness in her tone.

"For *you* to see them. And yes, she would."

"Me? Why not you?"

"Eristyminen is many leagues away, and it would take far too long to travel by horseback. By the time we returned, the land would already be destroyed beyond hope. I will ask the dragon to take you, and he can only carry one."

Imara gasped and looked up at him in surprise, uncertain she had heard him correctly. "The dragon will take me?"

"If he is willing, yes." He led her up to the long, food-laden table and pulled a seat out for her. Sitting and feeling equal parts shock and awe, Imara, a little dazed, gazed over at Lajos as he took his own seat at the end of the table.

"What is it?" he questioned. "I've never seen you so speechless."

"I simply never believed I would get to ride a dragon."

Lajos chuckled, unfurling his serviette with a swift flick of his wrist. "You are the Dragon Master's bride. Don't you know what that means?"

Imara's pale brows lifted. "What?"

"Dragons shall bow to you." Ronar chuckled, inclining his head toward her.

The trip across the waters to the Isle of Eristyminen was planned in a night. Once the master of the house had made a decision, all others followed suit without hesitation. Imara did find worry in the eyes of Thyr as they discussed what she would take with her to feed upon while she journeyed.

"It's a terrible long way for such a young woman to go all on her own," Thyr commented worriedly as she slathered a piece of bread in warm butter to pass to Imara, as if feeding her now would settle her own nerves.

Imara smiled tenderly at the older woman. "I won't be alone, Thyr. I'm traveling with a dragon. I dare say there is not a safer companion to go with than that."

Mikkel, who happened to be polishing silverware off to the side of the kitchen, snorted softly. While he hadn't said as much, Imara could tell he wasn't exactly approving of her flying off into the unknown on the back of the dragon. Approved by their master or not, Mikkel would have protested had he thought it his place.

The cook tutted in a motherly fashion. "Maybe so, but I would still feel better if the master were going with you."

"He refuses to listen to reason on the matter," Mikkel finally spoke.

Gazing down at the bread in her hand, Imara couldn't help but second Thyr's sentiment. If only Lajos were able to come with her rather than this task falling solely to herself.

"Thank you for the snack, Thyr," she said, rather than voice her feelings out loud.

"Of course, child. Now go, you have plenty more to focus on before you leave. I'll have the bag ready for you at first light tomorrow."

Leaving the kitchens, she met Lajos in the hall, a slight windswept look to his hair that told her he had just come from being outside.

"Has he said yes?"

"He has." He nodded. "At first light, he will meet you outside at the tree line. You are to be the only one present."

She inhaled a shaky breath, feeling equal parts thrill and reservation course through her. She had thought that she would have Lajos standing at her side as she was taken up by the great golden dragon from the woods, not facing him alone as she had so many other things in her life.

"I thought he would allow you to be there . . . " she admitted softly.

Lajos gazed at her tenderly, understanding written on his face even if he would not say it aloud. "Even the Dragon Master is not always desired in the presence of one so ancient and powerful." He looked upon her for a moment longer before adding, "You need not fear, Imara. He will not allow harm to come to you, whether I am there or not. You have my, and his, word on the matter."

Imara recognized his words for truth, yet it did not keep her from wishing that he would be there with her.

She also did not know when having Lajos at her side had begun to give her added courage rather than strife.

"I know," she responded.

"Come." Offering her his arm without hesitation, Lajos turned them in the direction of the library. "We have much to discuss about tomorrow's trip. I must make sure you are prepared for the journey ahead before the night is through."

She didn't feel ready—in truth, she worried what the state of Omdahl would be by the time she had returned. She feared for her family, and the fact that this decision would take her farther from them than she had ever been. Not wishing to set off across the water in the arms of a dragon without having at least sent word, Imara spent her night composing letters to both her parents and Asta, telling them of everything she and Lajos had discovered. Of the Ancients buried in the soil, sapping life and energy from the land. Of the untapping of her abilities, and of her coming journey to the isle to seek answers. Mostly, she encouraged them to warn the others. To tell them the devastation would not stop until the beings in the earth had been contained.

Imara left the letters in the capable hands of Mikkel to see delivered. He understood the haste with which they needed to go, and the importance behind them. Having done what she could to warn her people, Imara joined Lajos in the early morning dawn, with the darkness of the night before still blanketed over the land.

Standing before Lajos in the open landing of Dragon's Keep, dressed in her riding breeches, and with the great open wilds awaiting just beyond the doors, Imara gazed upon him with new eyes. In her short time here, Lajos had transformed from her foe to her companion. He was the first one she wished to share each new discovery of herself with, whether it be a triumph or a failure. While he mocked and tormented her, sometimes beyond endurance, there was a fondness that always lay beneath which she was not entirely blinded to. Imara found herself wishing very strongly that he were accompanying her.

"Try not to argue too much with Sylvi while I am gone . . . " she murmured softly, tugging her cloak more firmly about her, nerves beginning to get the best of her.

"Why are you always setting out to deny me what little enjoyment I can find in a day?"

Imara gave him a sardonic look, shaking her head. "As if you would allow me to deny you whatever it is you may want."

A strange look passed over his features as if he were surprised by her words or perhaps his own thoughts inspired by them. Starting to feel unsure in the moment, Imara opened her lips to say her last farewell before stepping outside, only to find her face clasped very suddenly between his hands. Peering up at him in surprise, Imara found herself at a loss for words.

Lajos was gazing down at her very intently, his green eyes alight with an emotion she could not place but which caused a little shiver to slip through her body, leaving her heart beating faster.

"Imara . . . please be careful, and try not to argue with every creature that crosses your path. Whether you are right or not, generally they will not care and may strike out instead."

Her brows knitted together. Why was he saying such things while holding her so? Did he think she needed to be chastised into behaving while she was gone?

"I'll have you know—" Her words were silenced as his lips descended upon her own. Imara stiffened in shock at the initial feeling of his mouth softly upon hers, pressing just enough to keep her from speaking. But as his lips became firmer and more purposeful, Imara's hands lifted of their own accord to grip at the front of his shirt, and her body leaned toward him as if seeking a new center of gravity.

His fingers were in her hair, slipping along the silken strands that had been woven together in a braid to help contain them, tugging them slightly loose and causing her head to tip back so that she was more accessible to him. Imara felt her body warm, and a tingling sensation spread all the way down to her toes, filling her with an array of new sensations.

He tasted of heat, and power, which made Imara's magic flare to life inside her, seeking out the flames now licking along her veins and engulfing her body. On instinct, her lips fastened around his bottom one, tugging gently, which elicited a rumble from deep within Lajos' chest—it threatened to buckle Imara's knees beneath her.

When he pulled away, they were both breathing quickly, and she felt a little lightheaded.

"Just come back to me in one piece, won't you?" he whispered, his green eyes heated.

Imara merely nodded, licking at lips that felt bruised and wonderful. She should be yelling at him for doing something so improper but found instead her eyes trailing down to his own swollen lips before returning to his eyes. The kiss had left her senses reeling, and while she was too confused to understand what had just happened between them, Imara realized she desired to leave his side even less now.

"Synda will be kind to you. Though she is old, she is fair. Be honest with her about what we need, and whatever aid she can offer, she will do so." His words were in earnest, hands dropping down to curve lightly around the sides of her neck, bracing her jaw so that his thumbs could brush the line of it.

"I know, you said as much last night," she reminded him. A part of her wished to stay here on this landing and never move again. But the first rays of sunlight were beginning to lighten the horizon, and Imara knew that it was time for her to go. "I will go speedily and return with haste, I swear it."

Her hand lifted to gently squeeze his wrist, then she pulled from his embrace, needing to steady herself for what was to come. Their eyes met in the distance between, a shared moment of unspoken words, before Imara opened the large wooden door of Dragon's Keep and stepped out into the cool dawn.

Deciding it was no time to think on what she was

leaving behind, Imara focused instead on the tree line as she made her way down the stone steps of the large manor house and out onto the lawn. The breeze of the late fall morning was crisp and threatening to bring about the first snows of winter. Would those down in the village survive? Had they managed to store away enough to keep them through the long, cold days ahead?

The warm cloud of her breath fanned out before her as Imara came to a halt at the forest. Her eyes strained to peer into the darkness of the trees, searching for a hint of gold, ears primed for the crush of underbrush. Instead, a dark shadow fell over her from above, causing her to lift her arms up to shield her head as she gazed into the air. The great form of the golden dragon descended from the skies, coming to land upon the dewy grass not far from her.

Blowing a puff of smoke from his nostrils, the dragon settled on his large taloned hands and lowered his head so that he could get a better look at her. For the first time, the journey she was about to embark on truly struck Imara in all of its absurdity. Would she really allow this beast to carry her off into the open skies, throwing all caution and self-preservation aside?

"Are you quite ready, little one?" the dragon questioned in his deep, rumbling tones.

Putting on a front far braver than what she felt, Imara nodded. "I am. How . . . should I go about this?"

She looked him over, wondering what way to best climb upon him, or if he would prefer she sit nestled in his hands. He took the decision from her. With one large hand, he reached out to scoop her up, causing a little shout of surprise and mild fear to issue from her mouth. With ease, he deposited her at the base of his neck, just where his shoulder began and above the wide expanse of his wings. Feeling entirely shaken, Imara leaned forward to grasp on to him, her traveling satchel pinned between her body and his scales.

"I'm not so certain about this . . . " she called out.

"Simply hold on and do not let go," the dragon said. His rumbling words were felt by her legs and chest through his body.

Without further warning, the dragon spread his wings and leaped into the air. Clenching her eyes shut and clutching on to his scaly hide with as much strength as she possessed, Imara fought down a scream of pure terror as she felt the dragon lift higher and higher into the air. Each beat of his powerful wings took them farther from the ground and propelled them away from Dragon's Keep.

IMARA

They journeyed relentlessly. The dragon stopped only when he absolutely needed to rest, and Imara would take the chance to stretch aching limbs that had become numb from perching so perilously upon the shoulders of a dragon, soaring hundreds of yards in the air. Over the two days of their journey, Imara had slept mostly when he did—which wasn't often—fearing to fall from her seat should she sleep while in the air. The dragon had only slept a few short hours each night before taking to the air once more. Imara found herself with plenty of time to think while they flew, her mind wandering often to those last moments alone with Lajos before she had left.

What had he meant by that kiss? Was it something frivolous, simply because he had felt like it and the opportunity had presented itself? He had, after all, only mentioned marriage as an option to give her a place to call home. Or had there been something more keenly felt behind those intense green eyes? Angry with herself for dwelling so much on it, Imara fought to push it from her mind and instead focus on the task at hand. Specifically, surviving this trip so that she might, by chance, help save her people from utter devastation.

The dragon brought them to land just as they arrived at the coastline, the early-evening sunlight beginning to fade beyond the horizon. Sliding off him without any sense of grace, Imara stretched her weary limbs and gazed upon the creature in surprise.

"Are we not close? I thought we would finish out the night to arrive at our destination before dawn."

Folding his large wings in against his back, the dragon shook his large, horned head. "Even dragons grow tired, and it is best not to press our luck when there is no safe place to land," he rumbled.

Nodding in understanding, Imara settled herself down upon a rock overlooking the water and rifled through her sack for the last of Thyr's provisions. It was good that they would soon be on the Isle of Eristyminen, or the dragon would have found himself sharing his evening catch. Watching him slip into the water to fish, Imara stretched her legs out and thought of the keep as she bit into a piece of dried herring. Had Lajos continued to do his own research, or was he simply waiting for her to return with word of her findings? Anxiety rose within her, causing her chest to tighten.

What if this journey was all for naught? They were pinning all hopes on her own assumptions, which were based solely on a feeling. But what if she was entirely misguided? Feeling the weight of responsibility and doubt heavily upon her shoulders, Imara lifted a hand to cover her face. Who was she in all of this? With Lajos' aid, she had uncovered her powers, but she was no great Ambient of old, trained to understand and wield her abilities . . . She was but an outcast girl, floundering through things far beyond her experience. What if she failed?

Imara gasped in shock as she was suddenly sprayed with a shower of icy sea water. The dragon, having emerged from the salty depths, was now shaking himself off a short distance from where she sat.

"Wh-why?!" she cried without thinking, half glaring at the beast before her.

A rumble of amusement slipped out of him as he settled back on his haunches and dropped a mouthful of fish upon the ground between them. "You were looking a little too distraught."

Wiping water from her face with the corner of her cloak, Imara grumbled to herself. "I was simply feeling concerned."

"You were doubting your abilities," he corrected.

She gazed at him questioningly, wondering how he would know.

"You will find the answers you need in the libraries of Eristyminen."

"How can you be certain?"

"It isn't in you to give up," was his simple response.

The journey across the sea felt endless but brought them to the small island in the middle of the sea before nightfall.

Landing in the courtyard of a large stone manor, Imara found herself in awe of the castle-like structure. Slipping off the dragon's back with a little more surety than she truly felt, Imara took in the columns and towers of white stone. It was beautiful and seemed to reflect the crystal depths of the powerful sea surrounding it.

Having taken notice of their arrival, a tall, slender woman stepped through the arching columns leading into an inner courtyard and came to greet them. Her hair was a chestnut fall of glorious locks woven with shells and water-buffed stones, trailing over her shoulder and ending below her waist. Her gown of icy blue fell in soft ruffles to the cobblestones beneath them, mimicking the very waves themselves.

"Imara," she said in an unfamiliar accent. "Welcome to Eristyminen. I have been expecting you."

Unsure of how to greet an unfamiliar Dragon Master, Imara offered a little curtsy. "Thank you for agreeing to receive me. My homeland is in dire need, and it is my hope that your archives may offer us some much-needed aid."

Synda nodded in understanding. "Lajos informed me of the circumstances when he sent his request. I have pulled what tomes I could from the shelves in anticipation of your search."

"Truly?" Imara felt her spirits lift in hope. "Can you take me to them?" she requested hurriedly.

Synda lifted her hand. "Soon enough, child. First, let us warm you from your travels and feed you." Her dark, fathomless eyes shifted to the dragon standing above Imara. There was a light of amusement in their depths. "Your dragon can take shelter in the inner courtyard. I've had food and water prepared for him there. I'm afraid he won't fit through the doors to the main house."

Imara gazed back at her traveling companion, hesitating at the thought that she would need to leave him outside.

"I am used to the woods. The courtyard will suffice," he rumbled in reply.

"Splendid." Synda motioned to Imara. "Come, I will show you to your chambers so you can clean up before we dine."

Following the other woman, Imara gave the dragon one final look before slipping into the white-stone castle. Her chamber was even larger than the one she had been given at Dragon's Keep, and decorated in lavish mosaics of stone, shells, and sea-glass depicting images of sea creatures frolicking in the deep waters. It was beautiful, and the flames flickering in the fireplace glistened off the walls, causing the waters to come alive.

Antsy to begin her research despite the exhaustion deep in her bones, Imara changed out of her travel-stained garments and washed up quickly. Dressing in the only other garments she'd brought with her, she re-braided her blond curls and went in search of the dining hall.

The table was heavy with food, far more than either she or the mistress of the house could ever need, but Imara feasted on dishes of roasted fish and waterfowl, delighting in the warm meat she had been several days without. However, it wasn't long before she was turning to Synda, her anxiousness returning.

"Thank you so very much for the wonderful meal, but I must beg of you, please show me to the library."

Synda chuckled softly, her true age showing in her languid movements and lack of haste in anything. "The young . . . always in such a hurry."

Imara felt ire rise within her. While she did not wish to insult her hostess, she did wish that the woman would understand the dire situation they were in. There was no time to sit and enjoy the evening.

"Unfortunately, the state of my homeland requires haste on my part. If I do not return soon with a solution, the land will turn entirely to ash and be lost forever," Imara insisted, a great deal of urgency in her tone.

Synda gazed at her studiously, as if peering into the very heart of her with a question only she knew. At last, the older woman nodded. "Then let's be at it."

Imara had not thought it possible to find a library more impressive than the one Lajos had built for himself at Dragon's Keep, but she was mistaken. Synda's vast archive was situated in the lower levels of the white-stone castle, deep in the earth. Her home was built upon a natural cavern, the stone walls lined in floor-to-ceiling books and scrolls, more than Imara could read in a human lifetime.

Awed by the magnificence around her, she found it hard to concentrate at first, wanting to just spend a few idle hours wandering each different section to naturally discover what lay around each bend. However, time was of the essence, and there was none to waste, so she sat down at the table Synda had prepared for her and began to search. Imara worked well into the late hours of the night, the candles beside her having burnt down to nearly nothing when her gracious host returned to check on her.

"I've found nothing of help," she commented, spotting the Dragon Master as she appeared at the bottom of the stairs.

"I am sad to hear that. However, your dragon is demanding that I pull you from your search and send you off to bed."

Imara huffed, brushing stray curls from her eyes she sat back and closed her current text. "He is not *my* dragon, and typically I would ignore anyone trying to tell me when I need to call it a night. However, I've actually found myself at a stalemate."

"What is the trouble?" Synda questioned, coming forward, a mixture of concern and amusement in her eyes.

"I've already gone through all of the texts that I am able to read. The rest are in a language too old for me to decipher. I haven't a clue of how I am to continue . . . " If only Lajos were here to help her interpret the works.

Synda reflected on this for a moment, then responded, "I can be of assistance with that. I'm capable of reading all the ancient tomes I've collected."

Gazing at her, Imara frowned a little. "Thank you."

"Why do you not seem pleased?" Synda questioned, peering at her creased brows.

"I'm sorry." Imara flushed a little, her face was far too expressive. "I appreciate the offer greatly. It's simply frustrating not to be able to read it all myself so that I miss nothing."

Synda nodded, studying the seidr before her. "I can project into your mind as I read, so that you are present for all of it. Would that help?"

Imara stared at her for a moment, her mind reeling. Was Synda capable of mind reading as Lajos was? If so, did that mean the two of them were of the same breed of magic? In all of the time that they had spent together, Imara realized she had never questioned Lajos on his form of magic or where he had come from. Who were his people?

"That would be most helpful, thank you."

She wished that they could begin that moment, and her eyes drifted to the stack of books she had set aside once she had realized they were in an ancient tongue. Sensing her thoughts—or perhaps reading them—Synda spoke.

"We will begin at first light tomorrow, as I am sure you will awaken early despite your need for rest. However, we will only do so if you retire now."

Knowing she had been beaten, Imara nodded and rose. Sleep would be welcome, and tomorrow, she could pick up where she'd left off. Glancing one last time at the stack of unopened books, she followed her hostess up the stairs.

"They really did kill them over power and position . . . " Imara murmured mostly to herself. Their search had led them to another book on Synda's shelves, a historical recounting of the founding of Brynjar, long before the first kings had come to settle at Ragnhild.

"Yes, which is why you must be cautious of who you expose yourself to, Imara. There are many who would grow jealous and fearful of your abilities once they become known." Synda's long fingers tapped the scrawling print before them. "Ambients couldn't trust each other, let alone the weaker seidrs around them."

Imara nodded thoughtfully, gazing at the foreign words that spoke of a history paramount to who and what she was yet had proven to be of no use to them. If her time were her own, she would have combed over every word, devouring the history there.

"I will allow you to borrow this one when you return home," Synda offered.

"Thank you." The mind-link was turning out to be helpful in more ways than one.

Setting aside the thickly bound book, Imara was just reaching for the next scroll on her periphery when one of Synda's ladies-in-waiting arrived with a tray of supper for the two of them. With no windows in the library cavern, it was impossible to tell the time, and over the last two days, they had begun depending on the few servants Synda possessed to keep them on track.

As bowls of steaming stew were placed before them, along with plates of bread, tarts, and cheese. Imara stood. Needing to stretch her limbs and take a break from sitting, she pilfered a piece of buttered bread from one plate and bit into it as she stretched one arm, and then the next over her head. Wandering aimlessly along the shelves, she allowed her thoughts to drift off for the moment, and simply existed within the hum of energy emitting from the stone walls and ground.

It was an entirely surreal feeling to be here, in the depths of the earth, and feel the crush of water all around them. Energies from both combated and yet balanced each other out. The perfect push and pull of Jörd.

Behind her, Synda was speaking, but Imara didn't pay her any heed as her fingers lifted to brush over the bindings on the shelves, feeling each leather spine as she went along. Thousands of words sharing thousands of tales, so many pieces of history, thoughts, and hopes that others long gone had deemed worth sharing. What was the message they had hoped to convey?

Imara halted suddenly as her fingers brushed against a spine much softer than the rest. It was a book well worn, though not mistreated. Unable to resist, she pulled it off the shelf and found that it was worn because it had been much read. Once upon a time, detailed etchings had been painted along its cover, but these had been nearly rubbed off with age. Only the faintest traces of deep red and gold paints remained.

Opening it, Imara found herself studying lovely sketches of trees crossing fields on bark-covered legs and bending down to trail root-like fingers through soil. Each sketch had a small cluster above it, and with amazement, she recognized the book for what it was: a children's fairytale.

Synda was calling her name, but Imara was engrossed

in what she had found. Each new page showed the progression of these moving tree-beings through forests and valleys, helping where they could but also beginning to leave behind a trail of destruction, until it seemed they were feeding more than they were helping. Until they reached a valley set in the mountains that shockingly looked much like her own, though with mountains much sharper and less rounded from time.

Though she could not read the words, the sketches spoke plainly enough. The creatures faced off with a number of beings whose pointed ears spoke of seidrs. With abilities of wind, earth, water, and fire, the smaller folk, whom she could only assume were Ambients, locked the tree monsters in the earth, sealing them and their devastation away. Feeling a sort of desperation within herself to understand more, Imara flipped back to the beginning of the fairytale.

There the pictures depicted a brightness beginning in the depths of darkness, and out of that brightness emerged the tree-like beings. From their branches sprung up the earth, the waters were called forth, and the sun's rays were pulled toward the ground. Through them, life emerged.

Imara felt breathless. She did not need the words read to her to understand what this fairytale was speaking of. It was a depiction of the formation of the earth's energies, the very powers that she tapped into. These ancient beings had harnessed all of the elements, in many ways *were* the elements. Head spinning, she wondered, could Jörd herself be what was in the ground below Omdahl?

Was the manifestation of energy itself, which had brought forth life in all its glory upon earth, now trapped beneath its surface, locked up in a cage of hunger and greed that had overcome it? The familiar hills . . . the valley . . . It was too much of a coincidence to be merely a child's tale. These ancient beings—Jörd—had been trapped within the earth by Ambients long ago, locking away their destruction. The question was, who had let them out?

RONAR

onar emerged from the depths of the manor to the first floor, his hair askew, wind-blown, and his chest rising as if he'd been running. Barely out of the doorway, the sound of shoes scuffing on the floor echoed in the otherwise quiet home. He didn't wait to see what the commotion was about before he jogged down the corridor.

Down the long, winding hall and toward the great room, he discovered what the excitement was about when Thyr flew into his chest, winded and flushed from her antics.

"Ah, beg your pardon, my lord, I was prepping things for the lady. She's emerging from the woods now. I spied her when I was plucking some mint for a batch of pastries. She must be tired after having been gone for eight days now. Riding a dragon must be exhausting, I'd wager."

His hands steadied Thyr, then Ronar offered her a faint smile. "That stew I smell will do wonders for us both. I imagine she's tired and in need of a bath. Can Sylvi get one prepared?"

Thyr shook her head. "I'll do it before I grab the stew.

Sylvi went to town earlier. She should be back before the sun sets."

Ronar wasn't keen on Sylvi traveling beyond the woods so late in the day. Not since he'd returned from the valley. Although the mages were currently quiet, he hadn't forgotten Gyda's words in the stable, cursing the seidrs, or the fact they were discovering how to amplify their magic with the crystals. If anything happened to Sylvi because of those damnable zealots . . .

Waving his hand, Ronar jerked his chin toward the ceiling. "Off you go then." He twisted his torso, watching the woman scamper off.

Ronar continued down the hall toward the front door. His thoughts tumbled into one another.

"The lady is home."

At the voice, Ronar glanced over to see Mikkel venturing from the direction of the dining hall. It would seem that all of his staff had been keeping an eye out for Imara's return. Perhaps they had missed her as greatly as he'd missed his own daily interactions with her.

"Thank you, Mikkel. I am on my way to greet her now."

He knew what he had to do, what he had to say to Imara when she crossed into the manor. There were so many secrets he'd bound himself—and Dragon's Keep—in, but there were more important things to say. Starting with the kiss they'd parted with. The very kiss that had haunted him day and night.

His hand paused on the door. He could practically see Imara's flushed cheeks, windswept waves, and bright, animated eyes.

When he opened the door, a panting blond stood before him. She smiled, slowly at first, then all at once. It ignited her features into pure beauty.

"Welcome home, my darling bride." He leaned in as if to kiss Imara, but his arm snaked around her waist to tug her into the house instead.

Any romantic notion was tossed aside when she burst into the house and out of his half embrace. She clutched a worn book as if it were a lifeline, and the warm smile vanished from her face, replaced by a feverish look.

"I know what it is. I know what they are and what's happening." Imara lifted the book, shaking it in front of him.

Ronar squinted, momentarily dejected from her brushing off his greeting. He sighed as he stepped forward to look at the cover. A tale of old, taken to be a children's tome, but every religion had their depictions for children to understand too. Illustrations were something every child could understand; when words meant nothing, visuals meant everything. He swallowed and went to take the book, but Imara flipped it open and pointed at it.

He must have looked as skeptical as he felt, because Imara grabbed his arm and sat him down in a nearby chair.

She perched on the arm and flipped to the first page. "It tells the story of the beginning—of Jörd. And here, they must be the Ambients who bound them. But if they're bound, how are they destroying again? Are they loose? If so, what caused them to break free?" Her words tumbled out in a scramble of details. Imara stood, handing the book to Ronar carefully.

Did it have to be anything in particular loosening the

bonds? Magic wore down over time, especially when the caster aged, and worse when they passed on. Ronar pinched the bridge of his nose. Imara's energy was enough to set him on edge. She was pacing back and forth, looking as if she wanted to dart back outside, jump on a horse, and ride down to the valley straightaway.

Ronar swept his fingers across the pages, pausing at the depiction of Jörd trapped beneath the earth. One loose binding wouldn't allow for the land to die so rapidly. His eyebrows pitched inward as he mused.

"You've had a long journey. Why don't you bathe before we dive deeper into this? Thyr drew one up for you, and you look as if you've gone out straight this week." Ronar stood, crossing the distance between them. His knuckles grazed her jawline. "Wash some of that stress away. We can discuss more over a bowl of stew. I'll be waiting for you."

Imara's lips parted as if an argument brewed there. But the moment his knuckles grazed her cheek, she closed her mouth and sighed. "All right. I'll be quick."

Ronar watched as she walked away. He frowned down at the children's book and flipped through the pages again as if hoping to procure additional information from the tale.

Closing the book, he carried it with him to the dining hall.

A quarter of an hour later, Imara arrived in the dining hall. Ronar caught hints of ginger and a floral note he couldn't put his finger on, but he knew Imara would gladly recite the name to him if asked. He didn't.

He sat slumped in his chair, fingers rubbing and pinching at his brows, like the simple act would inspire an answer.

"Are you all right, Lajos?"

He sighed. "Yes. I'm fine. It's just, every time we think we have an answer . . . " Ronar glanced up at Imara, who sat on the bench close to him rather than sitting opposite of him in a chair. A simple gesture, but one that pleased him. Having her this close to him chased away whatever melancholy threatened to eat away at him.

Color rushed into Imara's cheeks, and her hand sought his out to give it a squeeze. "Let's eat, and maybe we can figure it out together."

Ronar nodded. "I am proud of you and your discovery."

The shade of red intensified, spreading even to snake down her neck and up into her pointed ears. "I know."

As she started to pull her hand away, Ronar caught it and lifted it to brush a soft kiss against her knuckles.

They spent the rest of their meal running over the facts, dissecting everything they knew: Jörd was trapped, the mages had lost their minds, and the land was dying steadily. Only one was a recent discovery.

"But who would release them, or what? Why would they?" Imara asked. She locked eyes with Ronar, both staring intently like they could will the knowledge into each other.

The slamming of a door interrupted the quiet in the hall, previously silent except for the flames lapping at logs in the hearth. Shouting immediately came from the front room.

Ronar leaped to his feet, maneuvering around the table in quick strides. He knew that voice, and the panic in it set him on edge. "Sylvi, what is this about?" She wasn't the dramatic sort, so with her outburst, genuine concern grew.

Sylvi rounded the corner, eyes wide, face reddened from running. "Ronar! The mages, oh my goddess. They've broken into the woods—they're coming straight for the keep. There's so many. My goddess, so many of them!" Her words collided into one another, as frantic as the wild look in her eyes. "They've come for you, Ronar. They've come for you."

A sound so dreadful, so loud, erupted from the woods: a distant groaning of trees as they snapped, fell, and collided into their neighbors. The mages were in the woods, destroying his land, threatening his home.

His heartbeat thudded loudly in his ears. This was a nightmare come to fruition. Ronar didn't fear for himself; he feared for everyone he loved. Reflexively, he gripped Sylvi's shoulder, tightening it to reassure her, but it dawned on him in that instant who had released the Ancients, who had wanted their power. When he glanced back at Imara, she blurted the thought at the same time as him.

"The mages!"

That was who was foolish enough to break the seal. Power-hungry, no doubt wanting to be almighty, to rule over everyone. Ronar had slain a good portion of their following, and the fact Ronar ruled the valley must have grated on their nerves.

"Grab Imara, then go find Thyr and Mikkel and head to the hold. It's fortified, and should the walls crumble, there is less chance all of you will be crushed."

Sylvi pressed her face into his chest, her arms embracing him tightly. "Please, please don't do anything foolish. You're all I have." She choked on a sob and withdrew, waiting for Imara off to the side.

Imara approached Ronar, half in a daze. He cupped her chin, and for the second time, he kissed her. This one was desperate, like he would never see her again. He'd meant to tell her everything, open the lid to his secrets, but there was no time.

His lips crushed against hers, no gentleness there as he drew her against him. His fingers wove through her damp hair as he kissed her soft, pillowed lips. She tasted of sunshine, ginger, and that damn flower he still couldn't think of.

Imara didn't protest. In fact, her arms snaked around his neck and pulled him deeper into the kiss. Her mouth parted, allowing for Ronar's tongue to intrude and to taste everything that she offered to him.

The kiss spoke of everything he wanted, everything he promised would come if there were, in fact, a tomorrow for them. Quick, demanding strokes of his tongue, and then as quickly as the kiss started, it had to end.

If he could have, he'd have utilized the table, but there was no time, never enough time.

Withdrawing, he brushed his thumbs over her cheekbones and couldn't help but seal the moment with another quick kiss. "I'll return, and when I do, we can continue."

When Ronar and Imara were finished, they shared a brief, silent look. Then Sylvi looped her arm with Imara's before the two women rushed from the room in search of the other two housemates.

The last thing Ronar wished for was to relinquish his hold on Imara, but it was for the best, the safest thing for everyone.

He collected himself and strode out of the hall, steeling himself for battle against these foolish human degenerates.

Out the front door, he smelled burning pine and wet leaves. Flames rose above the tree line, licking and snapping at the dry wood. Though courageous he might have been, terror still lanced through Ronar. If the mages had penetrated his wards, it meant their magic had doubled. Which meant they really had figured out how to amplify it through the crystals. No one had ever forced their way through the wards, not until now. Were they siphoning magic from the Ancients? Twisting and poisoning it until it was . . .

Black smoke snaked along the ground, writhing like a serpent. Ronar darted into the woods. The same smoke lapped at his arms and face, and it smelled of death.

"Dragon," Ronar whispered.

The earth shuddered, branches snapping as the dragon twisted in rage and emerged from the damaged forest upon the scene of destruction.

Deeper in the woods, the mages sprung loose, circling the golden beast. His neck arched, poised to spray his fire on them, and it worked on a small portion. Flames leaped at them, winding around their shrieking bodies, tearing down their mouths to devour them from the inside. What mages the dragon didn't roast, his tail whipped.

But there always seemed to be *more*. Fear raced through him. The mages were attacking his woods, his home, his family. His figure disappeared amongst the mass of mages, flickering to life behind them, just in time for the dragon to spray fire on them.

Arrows glanced off the dragon's armored scales, his body curling to protect his vulnerable underbelly whenever the assailants thought to strike him. A wall of black smoke curled around the dragon, snuffing out the image of Ronar.

"No!" a feminine voice cried.

The dragon's head lifted, twisting to peer toward the cry's origin.

Imara.

She stood in the clearing, wind tugging her hair free of its braid as she glared toward the mages. "Stop!"

The smoke surrounding Ronar circulated until it formed a cyclone and spun away from him just long enough to leave him prone and open to the surrounding mages' assaults. Amidst the discord, the dragon homed in on Imara. That fraction of a second was all the distraction an attacker needed. A thunderous roar erupted from the dragon, his head swigging downward toward a spear which had found its mark in his underbelly. Blood spilled from the wound, dripping onto the ground in a pool of crimson.

Ronar's body winked out of sight, and the dragon rounded on his attackers once more, shielding Imara from their assailants.

"Lajos?!" she cried as Ronar disappeared, then gasped as the dragon swayed on his clawed feet. "Dragon! No!"

The earth rumbled to life, answering the call of its true mistress. Flames coiled like a living, breathing serpent. Wind created by the inferno and the element itself lent Imara a devastating beauty.

"Cut them down!" the dragon bellowed, shrieking as one of the demons twisted the spear deeper into his chest. Angrily, the dragon ripped it out and grabbed the mage in his clawed hand. He pinned him down, impaling the mage with his own weapon.

A crackle sounded in the air—not flame or tree but lightning.

"Imara—" The dragon choked on her name.

IMARA

How had everything gotten so bad so quickly? Feeling herself gripped by a fear she'd never felt before as Lajos' form disappeared amongst the smoke and flames, Imara was terrified that he was lost to her forever.

Mind reeling over the sudden attack, and puzzling over Sylvi shouting out the name "Ronar" when she had come for Lajos, it had taken Imara a moment to remember that she was no longer helpless. That Lajos was not the only one who possessed great power, and so he should not be facing their fanatical foe alone. Sylvi, bound by her master's orders, had attempted to stop her, but seeing the determination in Imara's eyes, had caved. Promising the other girl that she would be careful, Imara had fled outdoors, discarding her shoes in the process.

She had never fought for her life before.

"Cut them down!" the dragon roared to her in his weakening voice. The words rang in her mind as her bare feet stepped through the flames, which parted instinctively for her, increasing the fear and the fury that raged through her, as did the very essence of the world. Energy

thrummed from her fingertips and filled her to overflowing, causing the very air around her to crackle.

Lajos was nowhere to be found, and the thought of losing him so suddenly and viciously only intensified her draw from the elements surrounding her. If ever her emotions were to unleash a great disaster, now was the time.

"Lajos!" she shouted, desperately searching for him— needing to find him.

Cut them down!

Cut them down!

The mages were advancing, fire spreading deeper into the precious forest around them, greedily eating up the dry underbrush and leaves, climbing tall, ancient trees. The black, poisonous smoke unleashed by the enemy continued on a path of death, killing anything its essence snaked around.

"Contain the dragon!" barked a deep voice from amidst the mages. He was tall, and he was young, only a few years older than Imara herself. "Remember what my father said! If we are to win this war and claim what is rightfully ours, this beast must be done away with!"

"Yes, Captain Hagen!" his troops shouted back, converging on the dragon with more determination.

From behind, several of his men pushed large catapults forward, loading them with barrels of some unknown potion. As the first was released, sending it careening over the tops of the remaining trees to strike somewhere on the grounds of Dragon's Keep, Imara cried out in anger and pain. How dare they come here to this place? How dare they attack this home and its people? She would not allow them to take Dragon's Keep away from her.

With a primal scream, Imara pulled on all the forces, her fingers twining in the air as she wound invisible threads around them. An eerily lyrical chant rose up on the winds, words of power and destruction. She hadn't even realized she'd learned their true meaning, and yet the control was there as the world around her moved to obey. With a ruthless yank, the ground opened up beneath her enemy, a vast crater that began gobbling up falling mages, who screamed in terror and scrambled for any kind of a foothold.

Across the great cavern, Imara locked eyes with the captain of the mages. He did not wear the amulets of the High Mage, but he was still dangerous. It was there, written in the lines of his face and in the command with which he contained himself. In the air, Captain Hagen lifted a fist-sized crystal, one that swam with a murky darkness, weeping black smoke and death from its center. The mage began his own chant, the crystal cupped in his palm glowing as the darkness swirled more viciously around it.

He had brought these men here, attacking at the command of his father. But this land was not theirs to take, and Imara refused to let them have it.

With another tug of her hand, the winds whipped around the area, drawing the fire in to converge on the man-made devices of death and the mages themselves. New screams now joined the others, only drowned out in part by the ravenous fire attacking like a viper, leading any who attempted to escape into the depths of the open earth below.

Imara willed the fire to surround Captain Hagen, forcing him to cease in his own chanting as it struck out at him. Raising his hands in defense, trying to call forth the crystal's magic to protect himself, Imara watched as he was forced back toward the cavern. A primitive urge to protect this land filled her, and with it came a lack of mercy. Somewhere here, Lajos had been swallowed up by the flames. Mikkel, Sylvi, and Thyr, kind and powerless humans, were huddled in the depths of Dragon's Keep. Death at the hands of these heretical mages was not how it was meant to end for them.

The mages lucky enough to be outside the circle of flames were brutalized by winds, clawing at the earth in a desperate effort to save themselves. They gasped for breath as they found the oxygen stolen from their very lips.

There was no time for any of them to try and cast a spear or spell in her direction. The intensity of the flames paired with the strength of the wind had started so suddenly, no one could have prepared. No one had ever seen something of such magnitude come from a single person before.

It should have taken longer. So much destruction and loss should have taken longer. But her fury at losing Lajos in the flames of their greed had left no room for thought or time.

When all who were within Imara's line of sight, including Captain Hagen, had crumpled or fallen into the pit, she swept her hand out before her, killing the flames. In one last act of merciless fury, she drew on the invisible cords, pulling the earth back together, and buried any who had managed to survive the fall.

With a sob of despair and exhaustion, Imara sunk to her knees in the blackened forest, smoke and ash drifting up into the darkening sky. She watched through tears as what remained of the mages fled, leaving behind anything too heavy and running for their lives, no one daring to even look back.

A second ragged sob shook her body as blue eyes took in the battlefield around her, and her death count began to sink in. She'd killed them. *She'd killed them all.*

"Imara—" It was her name, coming from the dragon's lips.

With a gasp of memory, she staggered to her feet, heading to his side, only to halt as his swaying form seemed to shiver and shift. Fearing that she was losing him too, Imara watched as the golden scales softened, his hulking body shrinking and morphing until, to her confusion, it was Lajos standing before her, bleeding profusely from a large wound in his side.

"Wh-what?" she gasped, their eyes locking for a brief moment before Lajos crumpled, unconscious, to the ground.

"Sylvi! *Mikkel!*" Imara shouted, dropping down beside Lajos, her hands moving to stem the flow of blood from his side. "Oh goddess . . . " she whimpered. "How is this possible?"

Shouts rang out from the keep. Realizing that the battle was over, the three hidden in the hold had emerged and were now hurrying across the lawn in their direction.

"Please don't die. Do you hear me? Don't you dare die

on me!" came the rough pleas from her aching throat as trembling hands kept pressing to the wound.

Mikkel was soon bending down beside her, worry etched over his features. Behind him, Thyr cried out, her hands moving to cover her mouth.

"We have to get him inside!" Imara ordered.

Grace under pressure was the nature of the steward of Dragon's Keep. Recognizing the state of everyone around him, he began to bark orders to both Thyr and Sylvi. While Imara continued to press against the wound, they managed to lift his naked form and carry him into the keep. Mikkel led them into the dining hall, the long expanse of the table being the closest surface to stretch him out on.

"If you can get me a needle, thread, hot water, and plenty of rags, I can stitch him up," Imara rushed breathlessly to Mikkel, who nodded.

"You heard her. Sylvi, needles and thread. Thyr, go and boil water. I'll fetch the towels." With his commands crisply uttered, the three of them dispersed.

Still shaking from her own exhaustion and a rush of adrenaline that gratefully still coursed through her, Imara lifted one hand to comb through Lajos' hair, leaving a streak of his blood there. How, just moments ago, had his lips been on hers so desperately she felt that she could feel every unsaid thing between them? And now he lay bleeding out all over their dining hall table?

The other three were back sooner than she had anticipated, the items she requested placed around her.

"Sylvi, thread the needle with plenty of thread," she instructed, not trusting her blood-drenched, trembling hands to do it at the moment. Dunking a towel into the water, she began to clean the wound as quickly and deftly as possible. "If he wakes, you will need to hold him down."

Her eyes locked with Mikkel's, and he nodded. Wiping her hands as best she could on the cloth, Imara accepted the needle from Sylvi and took a deep breath to steady herself. His life depended on her keeping herself together long enough to do this. Clamping down on her bottom lip with her teeth, Imara pierced his flesh with the needle, drawing together one corner of the wound.

Lajos let out a roar of agony and moved to sit up as he came awake at the pain. Mikkel, moving faster than she would have anticipated, swept in to grab at his shoulders, pinning him down.

"You've got to stay down, sir," Mikkel stated simply.

"Get off me, I'm fine," he growled, trying to sit up once more.

"Lajos, stop struggling!" Imara snapped, gritting her teeth as she tried to do the next stitch. "If I don't close this up, you'll bleed to death."

Her angry eyes met his, letting him know that if he didn't listen to her and died, she would find a way to punish him even in the afterlife.

"Dammit," he cursed. "At least get me some of the dragon's ale from my study before you torture me."

Imara nodded to Sylvi, who hurried from the room and down the hall. Pressing the cloth to the wound once again while they waited, Imara lifted her free hand to press the back of it to his forehead. He was burning up, droplets of sweat beading his forehead and dampening his black hair. He couldn't be fighting infection already . . . could he?

Sylvi returned in a breath. Unstopping the jug of ale,

she held it out to Lajos' lips, but he pulled the vessel from her hands and tipped it back, chugging a large amount of it. Swiping at his mouth, his green eyes locked with Imara's, and he nodded.

"No time like the present, darling," he rasped. "And could someone drape a blanket over me? While I don't mind offering a show, one for my entire household seems a bit extreme."

Ever the mother figure, Thyr hurried to do just that, offering her master a little dignity in this moment of vulnerability.

Imara, on the other hand, dipped her head and went back to work, carefully sewing up the gash as best she could and blessing her mother for teaching her a fine, even stitch at a young age. Each wince or hiss of breath from Lajos pierced her heart; she knew the pain she was causing him. But Imara fortified herself and pushed on. She had, after all, committed far worse atrocities this night than a needle pulling through flesh.

When at last it was done, she bent down to use her teeth to snip the thread loose and stepped back. Thyr was instantly there, taking her by the shoulders to lead her toward a chair while Sylvi began the careful task of cleaning up the remainder of the blood.

Slumping weakly into the chair nearest Lajos' head, Imara felt the trembling in her legs and wondered when they had turned to jelly. Her eyes sought out Lajos', but his own were pinched shut as he breathed short, pain-laced breaths in through his nose. His skin was pale, far too pale to be safe, and his hair was drenched with cold sweat. He may no longer have a jagged hole in his side, but he was not out of the woods yet.

Imara felt tears of anger prick at her eyes once more, unable to think of anything but how her people and their plight down in the valley were the entire reason Lajos now lay fighting for his life.

"I'm so sorry," she found herself saying at last.

In surprise, his eyes opened, and he looked over at her. "Sorry?"

"We brought this upon you . . . If only the Elders had sought to fight their own battles, we would not have brought death to your door."

"The mages are hungry for power; death would have come our way eventually. No chance were they leaving the Dragon Master out of their domination, even if this sped things up a little."

At the mention of his title, Imara suddenly remembered watching the beast, her beloved golden-scaled friend, turn into the man lying on the table before her.

"The dragon!" she hissed. "You have a lot of explaining to do."

He let out a chuckle in what was an attempt to brush off the seriousness of her tone but ended up wincing as it tugged roughly on his side.

"I know. I meant to tell you," he said at last, a sigh of resignation on his tongue.

His lips parted to say something else, but instead, his eyes rolled back in his head, and he seemed to lose consciousness once more. Leaping to her feet, Imara motioned to Mikkel.

"Come, we need to get him into his bed and off this table. Thyr, bring me a fresh bucket of water upstairs."

Imara, Mikkel, and Sylvi joined together to lift his body once more and began carrying him out of the dining hall and up to his chambers. He came to enough to begin mumbling incoherently under his breath.

"I'm sorry," she murmured to him, knowing the pain this had to be causing. "You'll be settled soon, and then I'll find you something to help combat the infection." She just didn't understand how it could be happening so quickly.

Again, he muttered something, and Imara found herself leaning down toward his head as they hoisted him up the stairs.

"Lajos, what is it?" she encouraged, but the agony in his face showed the distraction of his thoughts.

RONAR

Pain. That's all that echoed in his mind, throughout his body, deep in his marrow. It threatened to send him tumbling to the floor in a writhing mess of limbs. A hot ache thundered through Ronar's body, begging him to return to his true form and submerge himself in the lake. Maybe then the fire in his veins would cease.

It felt as though tiny ants crawled beneath his skin, but in reality, it was his muscles twitching, quivering even, as poison worked its way through his bloodstream.

Mikkel misunderstood Ronar's feeble gesture of slapping at his arm as telling him to hurry, but in truth, Ronar's side felt as though someone were prying it open and driving a blade into it over and over. It took everything in him to not twist and claw at his side.

Finally, his body met the down-filled mattress, and his hands immediately went to the stitched-up wound.

Ronar's back arched as he clawed at his blanket, fisting the fabric. His jaw clenched too tightly to scream or form an intelligible word. All he could do was groan and hiss.

Mikkel frowned. "Sorry, sir." He had the good grace to

apologize in his softest tone. The following sentence was lost on Ronar, though it sounded something like, *What do you need?*

But no one's eyes were on Mikkel, not as everyone homed in on what Ronar was fussing over. His newly stitched wound seeped black liquid, and around the seam of stitches, dark veins formed.

His eyes rolled into the back of his head, the pain and exhaustion threatening to send him under. Except a wicked feeling stirred in his stomach, and it forced him to roll onto his good side, away from the onlookers and toward the wall.

Immediately, Ronar expelled the sour contents of his stomach; even that had turned the same black as the smoke in the woods. Vile poison. *If I live through this, those zealots will pay,* he thought.

Imara gasped, rushing to his side to help him onto his back. "Oh no," she whispered, eyeing her handiwork on Ronar's side. "He's poisoned."

Their speech faded as his body shuddered, only coming to life when he felt hands at his wound. He caught Imara in a firm grip, half unconscious still.

"Be still. I will not let you die, not when your stubborn ass has too much to explain." Her voice shook with emotion, but it was enough for Ronar. He relaxed his grip and sank into the mattress.

He slipped into darkness once again, only to awaken as Imara poked, prodded, and slid something against his overheated flesh. It felt cold and slimy. She lifted a glass to his mouth.

"Drink it," she commanded. "You have to."

Sleep called to him. Not just sleep, no. An endless slumber pulled at him. "I'm sorry," he mumbled between sips. Was she truly sitting next to him? Staring at him with a furrowed brow and profound worry in her gaze? He was certain he was seeing things. "I meant to tell you. I wanted . . . " he rasped, forcing another gulp of liquid down. "I was going to tell you everything." When he finished the cup, his body sagged against the pillows, and his clear speech became incoherent mumbles again.

Hours later, he supposed, he awakened to more prods at his side. Another cup was offered to him. Ronar didn't want to drink anything, not when his body still felt as if it were being torn asunder.

"You must drink it. It's combatting the poison." Imara sat next to him on the bed, helping him sit in a position that wouldn't tax his bad side. "Lajos, can you talk?"

Ronar's gaze slid toward the cup, then up into Imara's eyes. In his vulnerable state of being, he saw no use in biting his tongue any longer. "When I first saw you," he began, sucking in a labored breath, "I knew why poets wrote pages describing a woman's beauty." He grimaced as another spasm wracked his body. "And then, these past few weeks . . . " Ronar's words weakened, jumbling together despite his strenuous effort in forming them.

Imara's lips pursed, and she tried her best not to smile. "I'm glad to see you're on the mend." She tilted the cup, helping him drink.

He sighed in frustration with himself—and the situation. "No. I saw it in the council hall, but now . . . after your time here . . . you've blossomed into a force to be reckoned with. Someone worthy of the title forced on you."

Ronar chuckled, regretting it instantly. The last images of the battle flickered in his mind: Imara opening the earth, burying most of the mages alive, and sealing the earth again. But death, fury, these weren't things he wanted to think of. He wanted to dwell on her intelligent eyes and the way they sparked with life when she was angry. Or the way her hair always sprang loose around her face to frame it.

"I meant to tell you . . . when you came back. I wanted to tell you everything." His words drifted, sleep pulling at him again, but he wanted so desperately to get this off his chest. "What you mean to me . . . " Ronar blinked hard, trying to fight the urge to sleep. "I care for you deeply, Imara."

Imara took the cup from him, put it down, and helped him get comfortable once again. She pulled a blanket over him, pausing only when Ronar's hand shakily reached out to cup her cheek.

"I adore you. I hope you know," Ronar breathed. His eyes closed as his hand dropped, then his breathing evened as if he were succumbing to the strong pull of sleep. Then suddenly, his eyes opened, and he attempted to sit up, which sent him into another spasm. "Synda." He groaned his friend's name in his last moment of clarity. There was power in a name after all, and Ronar hoped she'd hear him in his time of need. "Synda," Ronar repeated, before his eyes rolled back, and he knew no more.

24

IMARA

All through the night she had stayed with him, wiping his brow with a cool cloth that she chilled with her abilities, helping him to drink the elixir every few hours as was needed, and listening to his feverish ramblings each time he woke long enough to realize that she was there. At some point in the early hours of the morning, Sylvi had shown up, informing her that a bath had been drawn and ordering her to go and make use of it. Imara sought to resist, but Lajos . . . Ronar . . . was now out of danger, and Sylvi promised to remain with him.

She wasted no time in the water, cleaning the blood and grime off her person, though she could not wash away her actions in the woods. There was no explaining her mercilessness beyond feelings of devastation at the thought that Lajos had been consumed by the mages and their flames.

Unable to dwell on her thoughts, Imara dressed herself in a simple shift and overdress, leaving her hair down to dry. She took the time to pen a quick note of warning for her family. Once the ink was dry, Imara handed the note off to Mikkel to send by pigeon. Omdahl needed to know of the mages' attack on Dragon's Keep, lest they be caught unawares themselves and slaughtered by Cuyler Hagen's fury.

With nothing else to keep her, Imara gathered the book on Ambients and seidrs that Synda had leant to her and returned to the master bedroom.

Once Sylvi had left, she reclaimed her place in the chair near the bed and settled in to read. All night long, when her mind wasn't set on trying to keep Lajos—or Ronar, whatever his name *actually* was—alive, her mind was racing with thoughts of the poison, and how the mages had tainted the spears they had used. Eventually, it led her to thoughts of the Ancients—of Jörd—trapped in the earth in the valley, and their own tainted magic. Was there a way to purify them? To cleanse them of the poison within their spirits and restore them to their former glory?

"What are you doing?" came a rough whisper from the bed.

Looking up from her book, Imara found a pair of lucid green eyes staring back at her. Beyond him, the sun was just beginning to rise, first light shining in through the windows. Imara felt a strong sense of relief wash over her. They had made it to dawn, and it looked as if he had truly returned to her.

Narrowing her eyes on him, she spoke. "Good morning, Ronar." She used the name Sylvi had let slip last night during her fear and frenzy.

"So, you did notice that." He had the decency to look abashed, and he moved to sit up. With a huff, Imara set aside her book quickly and moved to his bed. Sitting on the edge, she pulled the blankets down a little as he moved to lean against the headboard, then tucked them in around him.

"Yes, I heard that, along with witnessing many other things last night. For instance, *your* body disappearing into smoke and flame, and then a dragon morphing into the *real* you." Her hand lifted to press to his forehead, then his cheek. She was pleased when she felt no sign of fever.

He caught her wrist, pulling her hand away from his face so that she was forced to meet his gaze once again, but he did not release her hand. Instead, he held it between both of his.

"I know . . . I have much to tell you." He sighed with resignation.

"Yes, you do! I'm not even certain of who you *are* anymore! What should I truly be calling you? Are you the man that I grew to know in the library, or are you the beast that I got to know in the forest?" Angry tears pricked at her eyes. She had allowed herself to care for both of them, and in the end, he had been playing her for the naive fool that she was.

His hand lifted to brush at the dampness in the corner of her eyes, but she turned her head away at the last second, not allowing him the chance. She heard him sigh as his hand fell to the bed beside him.

"Imara . . . I am the man you knew in the library *and* I am the beast in the woods. We are one and the same. I would be lying if I said I never meant to deceive you, but you have to realize that when you first arrived, I had no choice. I've told you of how we were hunted nearly to extinction. Secrecy is our most well-kept form of protection."

She shook her head, wishing to deny everything that he was saying but also knowing in her heart that she understood. It still did not make any of this hurt less, and she hated him for this pain. For once again making her feel like the fool in the situation.

"But you let me befriend him—*you*." She turned angry, hurt eyes on him at last. "You led me to believe that I was speaking with someone entirely different when I bared my heart and soul in the woods. That is just pure deception!"

This time, when his hand came up to cup her cheek, she did not pull away. Instead, she leaned into it, because after witnessing him so close to death for so long, she could not now deny herself his gentle touch.

"I know, I know." He cursed under his breath and reached out with his other hand to brush wayward curls back behind her ear. "But I gave myself to you in the woods as well, and I cherished those moments when you were so lighthearted and looked on me as a friend rather than as a foe."

Filled with conflicting emotions, Imara leaned in to press her face against his chest, eyes shut tight as mind and heart waged war against each other. A part of her simply wanted to lay against him forever and sob with relief that he hadn't died, to pretend that what she had seen outside had been a figment of her imagination. Another part of her wanted to beat at him with her fists until he hurt as badly as she did.

"But when we did become friends, why didn't you tell me who you were then?" She pulled away from him, sitting up as she became invigorated with anger once more. "Why did you allow me to go on believing that the dragon was someone else? Why did you not have the decency to at least tell me your real *name?*"

"Darling, don't you see? There was danger in you knowing, for me and for you. If you were given the knowledge of what I truly was and then you left?" He shook his head. "I couldn't place that knowledge upon your shoulders and expect you to keep it to yourself."

"If I left?" she asked, confusion marring her brow as those words stood out from the rest.

"You were forced here against your will. I've never expected you to want to stay once all of this was settled." There was a yearning deep within his eyes that she felt mirrored inside herself.

"Of course I want to stay," she whispered. "This is my home. I thought . . . you were giving me a place to belong?" Or had she read it all wrong? Had he not told her because he had never meant to keep her? Because he had planned on being rid of her once they solved the issue in the valley? But then, what of his words at the inn, when discussing their marriage plans?

She began to pull away, feeling a sense of nausea coming over her. Oh, goddess of wind and water, perhaps he didn't want her here.

He captured her face in his hands once more, pulling her back toward him and forcing eye contact yet again. "This is your home. For as long as you wish to be here, I want you here. Understood?"

She nodded a little, licking her dry lips.

"Why didn't you tell me your name?" she pressed on in a whisper, not understanding why he would purposefully give her another to refer to him. To go so far as to have all of his servants call him by the false name rather than his true one.

"There is power in a dragon's name, Imara. Just as I could not give you the knowledge of my true form, I could not give you the power to wield my name unless I knew you were going to stay here. Think of it as a spoken enchantment. You may summon me, or in some way bind me. It is no small thing to be given a dragon's name." His own words came out in a soft murmur, as if there was nothing beyond the tiny bubble of conversation they were creating between the two of them.

For a moment, they gazed upon each other, a million things still unsaid as their eyes sought to convey the truth of what lay between them. Her hands rested on his bare chest, feeling the steady thrum of his heart as it slowly began to speed up. Her breath felt shaky as she lost herself to the silent answers within his green depths.

"You let me travel all the way to the Isle on your *back* not realizing it was you!" She gasped, a fresh wave of anger and mortification filling her as this knowledge dawned on her. Smacking her hands on his chest, she sat up and glared at him furiously.

He hissed in pain as she whacked him but had the decency to accept it. "I was going to tell you when we returned, I swear it," he began.

There were so many instances that brought fresh waves of anger. "No! Enough of your excuses! You . . . you stood downstairs by the doorway, wishing me a safe journey, and telling me to be careful . . . Then you—you *kissed* me before ushering me outside to meet the dragon. When all along it was you swooping down out of the sky to take me!" *The pure gall!* "You let me miss you when you were there all along!"

"You missed me?" He gave her a devilish look as a self-satisfied smirk spread over his face.

"Do not even start with me, Ronar," she growled. If he turned this into one of his taunting moments, she would murder him herself.

"Say it again," he rasped, a change having come over him. His hands moved to her waist, gripping her firmly.

Imara felt her heart suddenly become like a frantic bird trying to escape its cage as the look in his eyes sent a shiver through her body, causing sensitive areas to tingle. She swallowed past a throat that was suddenly very dry.

"Ronar." It came out a soft plea. Before she knew it, his hands upon her waist were pulling her in against his chest so that she was half laying on top of him. Catching herself on his chest, her fingers pressed into the firm flesh as Ronar's mouth crushed against hers.

There was a desperate call on his lips that she found her own all too willing to answer, especially as his tongue opened her up to his exploration. Imara released an uncontrollable whimper as new emotions swelled inside of her. She had thought she had lost him this night, inexplicably stolen away in the blink of an eye, yet here he was beneath her. Strong. Healthy. Her hands moved up over his shoulders and into his hair, fisting in the dark tangle of locks as she shifted closer to him, giving herself some elevation to kiss him back just as greedily.

Ronar moaned, a sound that made her gasp and pull back in fear that she had grazed his wound. But there was no pain in his eyes, only hunger as he lifted his head up to follow her lips, capturing them once more. She melted back into the kiss, finding that the need to taste him far outweighed her need for air.

A surprised laugh left her as his hands grasped her waist and drew her into his lap to straddle him, her knees on either side of his hips—only his blanket separated her soft, heated flesh from his rigid length. A shock of primal desire flashed through her at this sudden shift in intimacy, leaving her trembling and staring back at him in innocent wonder and uncertainty. Ronar's hunger softened as he gazed upon her features, hands lifting to brush tenderly through her long, blond curls.

"Imara," he whispered reverently. "Tell me to cease, and I will cease."

Silently, she shook her head. He had almost died last night. Soon, they would face off against the creatures in the valley, with the mages still an uncertain and vicious enemy lurking ever on the horizon. After this last battle, they were sure to only be further enraged. There was a good chance one or both of them could die in the process. Imara did not want to face tomorrow with further regrets.

Finding a courage in herself that she had not known she possessed, Imara grasped the hem of her overdress and shift all in one, gathering them together. Pulling them up and over herself, she cast the garments to the floor as blond hair fell over her bare shoulders, tickling the full swell of her bare breasts. Ronar drank her in, his eyes tracing every curve and valley now on display for him. Beneath her, she felt him stir in response.

"You are a vision I do not deserve," came his throaty response as they found each other once again.

The kiss had a feverish quality to it that their kisses had not possessed before, which only intensified as his hands began to explore her body: the heavy mound of her breast, the soft curve of her stomach, the needy center between her thighs. With each new sensation, Imara moaned or sighed into his mouth, kissing him with a growing hunger as Ronar brought her body to new heights.

Even lost to the heat coursing through her, Imara heard his groan of pain as he shifted their positions, flipping her onto her back and rolling himself above her. Alarmed, her hand came to press against his chest, pushing him away enough that their lips broke contact.

"You're injured . . . What was I thinking? We shouldn't," she protested breathlessly, bare legs entwined with his.

"I don't care if it tears me in two," he growled, then nipped at her lips. This brought forth a happy murmur from Imara, and she lost herself in the taste of him once more. Fire, brimstone, and raw energy.

"But Ronar—"

"Woman, for once, don't argue," he cut her off before she could continue, lips and tongue silencing her with a kiss that left her writhing beneath him, her own hands scraping over his flesh in needy abandon.

When at last they came together, he did so tenderly, pressing soft, reverent kisses along her jaw as her body opened to him. Imara's fingers danced along Ronar's shoulders, then pressed lightly into the flesh of his back as, gently, their bodies began to move together. Discomfort gave way to pleasure, a glorious bonding of body and soul as they drove each other to the peak of pleasure, breathless moans and cries of ecstasy the only words left to say.

In the aftermath, she lay on his good side, head pillowed on his chest and her hand resting just below her chin. His heart, sounding in her ear, still tripped along a little faster than normal as they basked in the warm glow of bliss. Ronar's fingers played absently with her hair, causing her eyes to lower as the weight of her exhaustion threatened to pull her under.

"I assume it is safe to say that I am forgiven?" he murmured, amusement in his tone.

His words drew her back to the moment, and she lifted her head to rest her chin on his chest so that she could look up at his face.

"Yes," she stated, almost begrudgingly. "Though I do have one last question."

He nodded his consent.

"When I came outside to help during the battle, I saw your form on the ground while you were in the air as the dragon." She felt her throat begin to constrict as she remembered that moment, running across the lawn, frantic at the horrors before her. "How?"

"An illusion. No different from the twig of heather I magically healed," he murmured, yawning at the tail end of his words. "It aids in maintaining my secrecy when I must be both dragon and Lajos."

"When your form disappeared, I thought—" Her throat tightened with unsaid emotion.

"Shhh," he whispered softly, combing fingers through her hair soothingly. "I know what it looked like, but I'm here. I am safe and I am not going anywhere."

"But I thought you died." She forced the words past the blockage in her throat, needing to say them out loud. "And then I did . . . terrible things." It filled her with horror to think about it.

Frowning, Ronar shifted so that he could grasp her chin, leaning in a little closer.

"You did exactly what I would have done. What I had planned to do. Do not think for one moment that they did not intend to do the same to us. To Sylvi and Thyr and Mikkel." His voice was soft but firm as he gazed directly into her eyes.

Imara nodded, trying to pair his words with her actions in the woods. He kissed her once more, soft and slow, until the jumbled words of distress in her head became nothing but a blip on the horizon.

When at last they broke apart, Imara let herself be tucked into his side, his arm around her and her head once more pillowed on his chest. Pliant and warm, Imara snuggled closer to his comforting presence as, at last, she let the exhaustion of the night before pull her down into a much needed sleep.

RONAR

Only three days after the attack, and so much had changed.

Ronar woke to the sound of Sylvi shouting in the hall. He couldn't help but be privy to her conversation since her volume increased with each emphasized syllable.

"And if he goes? What then? What if . . . " Sylvi's words trailed off.

It was Mikkel who replied. "Don't. Don't let yourself think that way. The man—dragon—is far too stubborn, and he has a reason to fight with every ounce of his being. Don't you see? You, Thyr, Me, Imara and her family, we are all cause for him to fight if he ever needed one. Have faith in Ronar's abilities, and Imara's. I think that is only fair."

Sylvi huffed in frustration, likely because Mikkel had met her anger with reason. "I can't lose him, Mikkel."

Their voices grew softer, no doubt because Mikkel was herding her away from the hall.

Ronar dragged a hand across his face, frowning over Sylvi's discomfort. It wasn't as if it hadn't occurred to him.

It was plausible that he'd fall in battle, same as Imara, but if he could prevent it at all, he would gladly lay down his neck to appease whatever wicked soul wanted to take her from him. *Just live*, he thought.

With a groan, he rolled to a half sitting position in bed. Imara was still sound asleep next to him, and rightfully so. Between tending to his wound, ensuring the elixir was prepared for him to drink around the clock, and the demands their entanglement put on her, she deserved it.

Ronar watched as she slept, lost in her dream world. She looked at peace, the lines of her face relaxed, lips slightly parted. Something akin to wonder flashed in his gaze. He marveled at her resilience, her determination and heart. In two thousand years, he'd only seen such attributions a handful of times but never had they captured his heart so readily.

He sighed, not wanting to wake her, and certainly not wanting to leave the safe haven of the bed. Ronar would have preferred tugging her into the bath with him again as he had last night, drawing his name from her lips over and over. He didn't think it was possible to tire of hearing it tumble from her, and it made him scold himself for not giving her his true name sooner.

As he leaned over her prone figure, his lips dragged along the pointed shell of her ear, then moved down to her exposed neck.

Imara moved suddenly, accidentally elbowing his sore side, which sent him reeling back against the mattress and pillows. Ronar grimaced, puffing out air and moaning as the pain speared him.

"Oh goddess, I'm sorry!" Imara twisted, her cool fingers settling against the heated skin of his chest.

Gritting his teeth, Ronar glanced at her from the corner of his eyes. "I'm fine, it'll pass."

But Imara crept forward, dipping her head so she could press a kiss right above the offended area.

"Woman, if you continue—" His words were cut off as her lips traversed his abdomen, and that was it. He gripped onto her slender hips and tugged her against him, feeling her slick heat glide against his throbbing member. "Breakfast will wait. I have a few other things in mind."

Imara wiggled on top of him, teasing and inspiring delicious and naughty thoughts in him.

"I'm glad you said that," Imara purred, leaning down to kiss him. It was a drawn-out kiss that muffled his surprise as her hands shifted between them.

One more moment, Ronar thought, *just one more moment with her, and then I can face reality.* But for now, he would bask in her glow, drink in her essence, and be blissfully content with life—this reality—in the master bedroom.

"Ronar," Imara whispered breathily. "Stay here in this moment with me." Her fingers grazed the most sensitive part of his body, eliciting a moan.

"You're making it very hard to be anywhere else, my darling."

Imara pulled the blanket over them, and this time, Ronar allowed her to explore him as boldly or as shyly as she wished.

At the dining table, Ronar stared down at his bowl of stew. A fresh steaming roll sat next to it, but all he wanted to do was push it away. Although his body was healing and the threat of the worst was over, his appetite was considerably lower.

The meal was a quiet one. Not even Sylvi made a peep, although she kept glancing in Imara's direction, hoping she would say something or return the look with something other than shuttered eyes.

When Ronar could bear it no longer, he dropped his spoon into his bowl and sat back. "All right. Have it out, Sylvi! What is bothering you?"

Tears welled up in the girl's eyes, but she fought them off by looking up at the ceiling. "You're leaving soon, aren't you? Both of you. I can hardly stand the idea of losing you, Ronar, but then you, Imara . . . I . . . " She cut herself off.

Ronar's chair slid back as he stood up, scraping the stone floor. He crossed the distance between himself and Sylvi, tugging her up. "Come here you silly girl." He sighed, wrapping his arms around her in a fatherly embrace. "I cannot make you empty promises, I won't do that. You are a remarkably strong woman, my dear, and I want you to remember that. I have no doubt that is why the two of you hit it off so well. Iron sharpens iron, does it not?" He pulled back, glancing down at the tear-streaked face.

Something strange flickered in Sylvi's gaze, then she

laughed despite herself. "But you . . . you finally just took her to bed!" Frustration laced her tone, and she sighed, her body sagging against his. "I just want you to be happy, and you finally seem to be. Now this . . ."

Ronar barked in laughter, squeezing Sylvi a little tighter as he glanced over her head at Imara, who was approaching but found her steps halted by the statement.

"Oh yes, that. More of a reason to live another day." He winked at Imara, then turned his attention to the girl before him. "My dear, if the world wishes to keep me, then it will. I can't dispute what the forces want, but I will give it my all. I can promise you that."

"I, too, can promise you that much, Sylvi. I will do everything I can to make sure Ronar survives," Imara added.

"We survive," he corrected her.

Sylvi twisted, turning to embrace Imara next. "Have you decided when you leave?"

They hadn't spoken on the matter, but the truth was, they should have left the same day he nearly died. There was no telling what the remaining mages were doing now that their attack on Dragon's Keep had failed. But there was no way he would have been fit to fight then. He needed to wait for the elixir to drive the poison out of his system, and the wound to heal. Remarkably, his body had stitched itself together rather quickly, but the dull ache was still there, and should someone assault the area, the new tissue wouldn't hold up for long.

"We probably shouldn't dally here too long." His gaze flicked to Imara, and she nodded in confirmation.

Sylvi tightened her hold on Imara, then turned to pull

Ronar in. "Let me have a moment like this with both of you. Just for a minute."

If he could have promised she'd have more moments of squabbling with him and complaining to Imara, he would have.

When the moment passed, and the adrenaline of what was to come kicked in, Ronar pulled away and headed toward the hall. "You can have a minute longer, but we really ought to leave as soon as possible." He nodded and left the women to it.

By the lake, Ronar knelt, touching the surface of the water. The images reflected in the body of water, the evergreens and mountaintops, were worthy of a portrait. His touch disturbed the glass surface, and in a blink, a dragon took the man's place.

Days had gone by since he had flexed and felt his true body. He stretched his wings wide, lifting on his hind legs to beat them.

A beloved scent wafted his way. His neck curved, and a reptilian green eye focused on Imara. "Are you ready?" Tipping his head down, Ronar let his nose rest against her side. A rumble like a purr resounded in his chest.

"No, but will I ever be?" Her hand swept beneath his chin in a tender stroke.

"No, I'm afraid not." Flattening himself to the ground

as best as he could, Ronar turned a clawed hand over, waiting for Imara to step in. He admired her for a moment, raking his marbled eyes over her lithe figure. Now he knew every curve that hid beneath her tunic and breeches.

A smoky laugh erupted from him. "Wise choice with the breeches, my darling."

"You'd choose now to discuss my wardrobe choices?" She fought a smile, dipping her head to hide it.

When Imara situated herself in his palm, Ronar raised her to his neck and let her become comfortable before he stood.

Ronar's wings unfolded, beating the air as he lifted himself toward the sky. It was only a stretch, and perhaps a little mischief on his end. "Whatever you do, don't fall." He chuckled, then pushed off his haunches, flapping his leathery wings to lift them into the air.

Quickly, he ascended, taking them far above the trees. Out of morbid curiosity, he wanted to survey the damage from the assault on the keep—on himself. Swooping over the area, the smell of ash tickled his nose, but it was the loss of trees that bothered him most.

His companion shifted, leaning to survey the damage. "Goddess . . . it's in ruins. A graveyard."

Ronar rumbled in protest. "They're one with the land now and will nourish the new growth as time passes. A fitting and complete life cycle for the ones who sought to destroy our home."

She didn't need to say a word; he could feel her body sink against him. Ronar knew her thoughts were on those she'd slain and the lives they'd never live.

"Come now, don't make me say something that'll ruin

this morning's efforts . . . I'd rather go into battle with the notion you actually like me."

She groaned. "Of course I do!"

"Then think no more of those wretched souls." Ronar beat his wings a little harder as he soared above the land. Devastation spread far and wide beneath them, and it wasn't from the mages burning it. Oddly, there were no deer running, no birds chirping. How could there be when their food sources were so diminished?

Instead of flying lower to the ground, he lifted himself against the sun's rays, drawing on his magic to render him invisible to eyes from the ground. But as high as he was, his keen eyesight still spied a cluster of individuals in the valley. Dread filled him at once.

"They've started already. The mages, they're exactly where we were when you connected with the Ancients."

"What!?" Imara shouted, clutching her legs tighter around him. "Then we must hurry! They must be seeking to break them free of the bond trapping them in the earth."

Ronar dipped down, bringing them lower, and as he swooped in for a closer look, he and Imara shared the same curse.

Where the mages stood, in the center of their circle, the devastated ground had split open. Branch-like fingers ran along the edge, but the earth wasn't ready to part for them entirely.

Tendrils of light escaped the seam of the ground, shifting every time the grasping fingers blindly searched beyond the crevice.

With a new urgency spurring him on, Ronar drew his body in, streamlining himself as he soared across the valley and toward the village. When he landed, it wasn't as inconspicuous as he would have liked. With his wings folded against his sides, Imara slid from his neck, then Ronar shifted into his other form, using magic to dress himself once more.

He wore black leather breeches and a thickly padded doublet—not that it would stop an arrow or blade from impaling him, but it would take some doing.

It dawned on Ronar that the last time he had been in Omdahl was when he first met Imara, and somehow what was only two months ago felt like years. Dragging his hand over his mouth, he knew that, before anything else, the Elders needed to be assembled and the villagers prepared for the inevitable war.

All Ronar could do was pray and hope Thorne had sent an army. "Synda, I truly hope you heard my call," he murmured.

Ronar opened his mouth to speak to Imara, but the sound of a man's voice and then a woman's gasp silenced him. The couple rushed to Imara, embracing her, and it didn't take long for him to know exactly who they were: her parents.

"We received your letters and my goddess, Imara! A dragon?" Dagny glanced toward Ronar, uncertainty in her gaze. "You really have embraced your position as the Dragon Mistress." Dagny fussed over her daughter, cupping her cheek. "How are you?"

"I am fine, Mother. I swear it." There was a fondness in her eyes as she withstood her mother's coddling.

"We warned the Elders, telling them everything that the two of you have discovered. Yet they have done nothing." Dagny shook her head and gripped her daughter's forearms.

"And my letter of the attack on the keep? Did you receive it? Did you tell them?"

"The fools. The Elders would not listen and said it was nothing but a feeble attempt on your part at wheedling your way back into the village," Erlend spoke at last, a deep frown creasing his brow.

Ronar watched as Imara's face went from shining with happiness at the reunion to crestfallen at the news. He turned away from them, running a hand over his mouth to silence a rumbling curse. "Did they now?"

"Oh, my lord, thank you for bringing her. My apologies, we were excited to see our girl." Dagny bowed her head, forcing her husband to do the same.

Erlend bowed at the waist, narrowing his eyes in Ronar's direction. "But you're here now, which means . . . ?"

Ronar sighed. "I wish we were here for a visit, but we are heading to see the Elders. They've ignored a problem for far too long, and now action is required. I suggest you warn every abled man and woman to get ready for battle. Gather those with the strongest magic in their element because we will need them, and those who are willing to fight, we will use them too. Mothers and children are exempt." Ronar's lips pressed into a grim line. He walked away from them, seething over what the foolish Elders had done. Their prejudice and idiocy had cost them all very precious time.

Ronar visited each council member's home, bellowing for them or pounding on their doors. If they weren't home, he hunted them down rather quickly. At last, they were all gathered in the council hall.

Imara sat in a newly carved throne beside Ronar's, but he wasn't sitting. Rather, he was pacing back and forth like a predator readying to pounce on prey.

"I am disappointed in all of you, but that will come later. Let it be known a reckoning is coming to this village, and there are consequences to actions, or lack thereof. However, we are gathered here to assemble a militia against the mages. You've forced my hand," he said, motioning to the Elders. "You will listen to what you are told, and you will do it. As your Dragon Master, I order it. If you oppose, we can sort that out later." His words rumbled in his chest. As much as he may want to bite into them now, this wasn't the time.

He lifted a hand, motioning for Imara to continue what he started. It was important to him that they listen to her too, as she was an equal leader and would be fighting alongside him and her people.

She stood from the throne, addressing her Elders and the villagers. "The mages attacked us days ago, and now they're in the valley trying to extract a power they have no right to. They're tainting it, and with it, they will conquer every land they can. We need everyone to work together and fight." She glanced at Ronar, nodding. "I know you are not soldiers trained for battle, but Lajos and I will do our part, and we need you to do yours."

Ronar folded his arms across his chest and glared down at the pinched face of the head Elder.

"And what is that?" Fridolf dared to ask.

Thankfully, Imara answered, because Ronar wanted to

throw him into the circle of mages and let him fend for himself.

She quickly summarized the entire tale of who was trapped beneath the earth, why they were there, and what had to be done. "And so, I must purify them."

A puzzled expression wrinkled the head Elder's brow. "You . . . are to purify them?"

Imara didn't answer him. Ronar felt giddy over the very notion that she was superior to the dolt because she was and always had been.

"Ah, so curious about how what you deemed useless is, in fact, going to save your despicable ass." Ronar bared a toothy smile that was more threatening than a show of humor. "Everyone who is about to fight, you may remain. Those who aren't, you may leave."

RONAR

Those who weren't joining the battle fled the meeting hall, but the Elders and the villagers willing to fight, as requested, stayed behind. Ronar sneered, believing the Elders didn't deserve the respect of knowing what the plan was. It was, however, in his best interest they did. If he fell in battle, or he and Imara didn't make it, they had to know what to do—if they could manage it. Without a plan in place, none of them stood a chance.

Ronar had to remind himself that the Elders were ignorant, especially when it came to the mages and what they were capable of. They didn't know because they couldn't, unless they'd been studying them unbeknownst to everyone. However, judging by the apparent shock on their faces coupled with clear doubt, they didn't know a damn thing.

"There are far more intricacies to this than you know, but to spare us all a day-long lecture we cannot afford, I'll be to the point." Ronar loosed a breath before continuing. "I'm sure you've noticed the land has been dying, but it was slow to begin with. As the mages grew in number, so did their greed for power. We believe them to be responsible for cracking the barrier holding the Ancients trapped in the earth, all so they could fill their crystals with a dark energy. The more they have siphoned this power, the more the barrier has opened, and the Ancients have been able to feed off the land. Unless we stop them, they will not cease until all that remains is dead."

Questions rang out, as Ronar suspected they would. Panic filled the hall, creating a tension so thick he could nearly cut it.

"Enough. Settle so we can quickly discuss this!" he bellowed.

As Ronar's frustration mounted, he opted to sit on the throne at last. He glowered from the dais, toward Fridolf specifically. "I'll be plain with you. I don't like you one bit. But I'll tell you what Imara and I are going to do and what we need from all of you." He leaned forward, the planes of his face hardening. "The mages gathered in the valley need to be forced back as best as you can manage. This will allow for Imara to remain unscathed and tethered to the earth. She needs the connection to purify it. As it stands, these beings are tainted."

"How is *she* going to purify them?" The question was innocent enough, but the inflection in Fridolf's tone wasn't. Fridolf's doubt-filled gaze flicked toward Imara, and his sour face said what he did not.

Ronar reeled himself in, or tried to, worn thin from days of being ill and the stress of an upcoming battle. He was close to throwing the seidr out and chasing him away, if not worse. While he might have been partial in his feelings toward Imara, it didn't matter. She was his bride and the Dragon Mistress. The title alone demanded respect, and to not give it was a direct insult to *him*.

As much as he wanted to thrash the man's head into the wall, Ronar's eyes glowed a deep green, and his words came out sharply. "That's beyond your comprehension." Ronar offered a toothy smile, which was more threatening than not. "While Imara reaches the Ancients, I'll fend off most of the mages and their lackeys."

"Just you?" Jorunn asked, incredulous.

Imara cleared her throat to cover a laugh.

Ronar, glancing back at Imara, grinned. "Mostly. With the aid of the fellow villagers, we stand a fair chance." When he read each face of the council, he realized half of them either weren't taking him seriously or didn't believe that Imara was quite capable.

It was his hope, foolish or not, that Synda had heard his cry for help, and that Thorne had received his letter in time. But they were not yet present, and the villagers needed a leader as well as a battle plan.

"How are we to do this? Our village has no army. Our men and women are farmers and shop owners. We have lived peacefully in this valley for centuries and have never had to use our abilities for harm." This was Ranell, his features pinched with disbelief.

"That changes today." Ronar waved his hand and sighed. "Let us begin our plan of attack, shall we?" He didn't leave room for an interjection, instead launching into his battle tactics. Imara needed protection at all costs and cover whenever possible. Ronar would do his best to remain by her side, but if the field called him forward, he needed villagers willing to surround her too.

Most of the inhabitants in the hall agreed with his plan, nodding as it sunk in, but Fridolf stammered his disagreement. Ronar bristled, his jaw clenching so tightly he thought his teeth would snap.

"Enough discussion," Imara cut in. She descended the stairs toward the aisle. Gone was the brow-beaten expression she had once worn in this hall. Instead, she looked every bit the part of his bride and the mistress of the land. "Time is being wasted. Our people are strong, and they will adapt as is needed. Relay the message to the designated leaders, and we will meet you there."

Ronar nodded. He followed Imara as she exited the hall, close on her heels.

Outside, the villagers' energy filled the air. He could almost taste their adrenaline as they ran back and forth, collecting whatever could be used as a weapon or locating brethren.

It was the sound of war, and as Imara had predicted, they were adapting.

Children shrieked as one or both of their parents gave them perhaps their last farewell. Shouts rang out, accompanied by the hurried footsteps of Elders moving at last to do what had been demanded of them. The people were ready and willing to go to war, to at last end the suffering that had been plaguing them for months. It was good; they would need every able-bodied individual fighting with them.

"Ronar, let's go." Imara tugged on his arm, pulling him away from the gathering army and toward the valley.

Dust kicked up as they ran, but the scent of death and something distinctly other met his nose too. As they dipped down a hill, Ronar's arm caught Imara from furthering her descent.

At the bottom of the hill, gnarled branches twisted, snapping into place to form legs, arms, and even a head. It was just one, and Imara had said there were five. The being, however, stunk of death, and the scent wafted toward them. A sick, rotting scent that threatened to choke Ronar.

Black sludge dripped from it, pooling at its feet as it slowly lumbered toward the hill.

"Goddess," Imara breathed. "We're too late."

Assessing the area, Ronar spun around and saw the mages advancing, moving to surround High Mage Cuyler Hagen at the center near the split earth. Luckily, the small militia of villagers peeked around the corner from where he and Imara had come from.

"Or just in time. You see, darling, the mages spared us having to figure out how to pry them from the ground. Besides, most of them are still trapped." Ronar offered a smile that wasn't returned. Perhaps it wasn't the time for good humor. Quickly, he glanced around, noting a collection of boulders on the hillside. As he approached it, he nodded. "Here, ground yourself there, it'll block you from most of the attacks. I'll do what I can to hold them back." There was a small nook created by the collection of stone. It'd make a grand shield from physical attacks, and no one would be able to see her from afar. He wasn't planning on allowing them to get close enough to see her, either.

Moving to the boulders, Imara stood against them, placing her hand against the surface. She gazed across the field, no doubt calculating their odds, which weren't in their favor to begin with.

Ronar reached out, his hand grazing her cheek then sliding beneath her chin to turn her head to him. "I will give it my all." He leaned in, kissing her forehead tenderly. "If something separates us, call to me." Ronar placed a lingering, soft kiss to her lips, then pulled away. His hands spread out as he conjured a shield above Imara. He could only hope it would hold during the battle. He wished to stay by her, but the seidrs were vulnerable and inexperienced; they needed someone to lead them, to instruct, at least until instinct hopefully took over.

A soft breeze ruffled his raven-colored hair, tickling it at the nape of his neck. Ronar didn't wear battle armor, nor did he wield a weapon like those he stood in front of.

"I don't have any fanciful words for you. Do your best to hold them back because if they reach the bottom of that hill, we're done for." Ronar turned his head as a wet groaning snap sounded.

Curses rang out amongst the seidrs as the full situation dawned on them, their eyes finally drinking in the sight of the Ancient clawing at the hill.

That noise, a low, crackling moan, it wasn't simply the creature moving. Had another started its climb from the depths? He couldn't chance a distraction by looking down or calling out to Imara.

Ronar cursed. "Drive the mages back as best as you can. Magic, weapons, whatever means you are capable of."

The throng of men and women nodded grimly.

"Fight because this world depends on you." Ronar stepped out of the way, motioning for them to move forward while he hung back. When he looked to the side, Imara was already barefoot with her hands and feet plastered against the earth.

Magic coursed thickly through the air, and he felt it flex against him, pulling, tugging, and calling him to aid. But Imara knew what to do, and he trusted her and her abilities.

Black flames ripped across the ground, sending smoke he knew all too well snaking through the militia. Steeling himself, Ronar outstretched his arms, pulling on the strands of his magic. The well within was deep, allowing him to call on a grand portion of it. As his hands swept downward, a shockwave of magic met the assault of flames, suffocating them and slamming into the wielders.

So the dance started.

Seidrs charged ahead, spearing their opponents with weapons, fighting with wind, earth, and fire of their own. Humans joined the fray with the mages, ending in a swift and ugly fate for a cause that was not just.

"They're moving to the side! We need more force to the left!" a voice cried.

"We will lose the ground if we can't block them!"

The left. The left was several hundred yards away from Imara. Too far from where Ronar wanted to be.

Lightning crackled across the sky, striking the dry land and eating it up as though it were only kindling. Fire leaped from dry wood to grass, spread in a matter of seconds. Walls of flame formed, coalescing with the black flames until they grew as tall as the keep, if not taller.

He gawked for a moment. Even a dragon was sorely outmatched against the mages. Reinforcements had arrived, and it was clear that it was an army ready to take what they wanted. The addition of powerless humans to the mage forces aided in their numbers and brute strength but would fortunately be of little help where seidr magic was concerned.

The earth shook beneath his feet, but it wasn't from the Ancients, nor was it from the seidrs sinking their magic into the ground and calling forth quakes. No, it was something in the distance, a rolling hum.

Ronar's gaze homed in on a mass in the sky at the same moment he realized what it was. "Catapults!" He extended his arms, fingers flexing as he threw up a shield, blocking the massive boulder from landing on a group of fighting seidrs.

Damn. Double damn! Dropping the shield, Ronar tore across the ground, running as fast as he could toward where the catapults were set up. His side protested, the familiar ache reminding him to favor the recovering wound. "Damn you, all of you. Set fire to those trebuchets!" Within him, tension grew and grew.

Flakes of snow caught in Ronar's lashes, melting seconds later. The field was about to become slick and muddy, which would add to the misery felt by all.

Beyond the line the seidrs held, a voice bellowed above the shrieks and guttural growls of the fighters.

The seidrs couldn't advance on the catapults; they were overwhelmed by the press of the humans and mages. What they needed was a dragon. Ronar readied to shift, but then a voice rang out above the din of battle.

"Dragon, you will pay for what was taken from me, and you will suffer as I have suffered. My son was amongst those you killed, and that is something I won't forgive," Hagen shouted at him, raising his hands as he called to the tainted magic.

The ground shook, cracking open by Ronar's feet, which sent him tumbling to the side.

"Your son attacked *me*. My home, my loved ones," Ronar roared back, willing Imara's shield to stay in place. He picked up a discarded sword and charged an approaching human.

Steel met steel, but Ronar wasn't human, and his strength wasn't confined to the laws of nature. When his blade parried the other, he pinned it down and struck his attacker in the side with a thunderous punch. The sound of bones cracking beneath the blow resounded, followed by groans of pain and wet rasping breaths.

"You should have chosen a different side," Ronar muttered.

The crack in the ground widened, forcing Ronar to leap over it, which offset his balance. As he centered himself again, a spear crashed through his guard and narrowly missed his face. Ronar stared for a moment, then glanced upward at the covered face of his opponent. He swung his blade upward, knocking the other man backward. As his foe recovered, Ronar walked in a circle until the man's back faced the gaping hole in the earth.

With sword in hand, Ronar parried the spear as the other drove it forward. This forced the human to twist and stumble in place, but Ronar didn't ease up. He forced the other backward until his feet no longer touched the earth, and he was falling.

The other man clung onto the edge, dangling

precariously over a wide, gaping mouth. He didn't cry for help or curse Ronar. Instead, he relinquished his hold and let himself fall into the depths.

Out of the corner of his eye, Ronar saw a billowing black cape and knew at once who it was: Cuyler Hagen.

"Your magic is nothing compared to ours, unadulterated and siphoned from the earth."

Ronar scoffed. "I don't steal or borrow magic from beings. *I am* magic." Instead of lashing out with his own brand of flame, he pulled on the strands offered to him from the crystal-wielding mages. These were humans who learned to *steal* abilities from the earth, who took and took until the well ran dry.

Outstretching his hand, Ronar pulled in the strands of magic one by one until he felt as though they would snap. Then, in one push, he repelled the magic away from him, sending a rushing blast of air toward the mage and his followers.

It was enough to hold them back, just a little.

Ronar's eyes widened as dread wound around his heart. A burst in the air brought his attention back to where Imara hid. An assault on the shield tested his strength, which was already being pulled in several directions. He couldn't race to Imara's side, not when seidrs fell around him. All he could do was hope—pray— that the villagers surrounding her could ward off attackers until he could run to her.

IMARA

All around her waged a war, and as if feeling the need to denote its displeasure, the skies opened up further. The snow transformed into freezing rain, pelting down upon their heads. Her bare hands and feet felt like ice where they clutched the cold, ashen earth, digging into what was once rich soil.

Each quick draw of breath brought the cool winter air into her lungs, like shards of glass to her throat and chest. Imara shut her eyes, desperately seeking to block out the violence around her and focus instead on the task at hand. Nothing that anyone did today would matter if the poisonous creatures continued to crawl from the earth, spewing their venom and siphoning off all the energy there was to feed on.

She could feel it, the ravenous draw upon the earth's energy as they sought to scavenge everything within reach upon their release. Steeling herself for the feel of those cloying hands once more, Imara threw herself into the midst of the feeding, opening herself up to them as she had before. Her connection was a beacon; instantly, they gravitated to her, using her control of the natural flow of the earth's energies to feed more readily.

The ground trembled beneath her as a large explosion rumbled. Somewhere beyond, there was the sound of stone crumbling and crashing to the earth. The mages had come out in full force, bringing with them all their weapons—magical and man-made. Desperately, she lifted her head to peer around her, searching for her family. Were her parents safe? Asta? Already there were bodies strewn in tragic heaps over the valley, littering it in further death. These were the people she had grown up with, her neighbors and her parents' friends. Breath stuttering out of her in white clouds, she searched frantically for Ronar's form, catching sight of him now several hundred feet away, battling heroically with a broadsword.

Goddess, what if I fail them? Imara felt the wind tearing at her clothes and hair, biting her pale cheeks, and freezing the tips of her ears as the sense of inevitability settled over her. No matter what happened, she had to try. There had to be a reason that she had been gifted with these abilities. That after all these centuries, an Ambient had been born. Shutting her eyes to the world around her once more, Imara pressed on, opening herself entirely to the Ancients and their endless hunger, sliding deeper into the void that resided within them, searching for the faintest glimmer of hope.

Until the moment she and Ronar had stepped onto the field, she hadn't been certain how she would go about purifying them. It was at the sight of the ashen earth blowing in the cold winds that she had recalled the sample of dead earth Ronar had brought her. That little handful she'd managed to bring back to life once she'd found the life left buried in it.

Once upon a time, the Ancients had been pure beings who tended to this world rather than seeking to destroy it. She simply had to find that part of them—wherever it remained.

There were keen eyes watching her from the depths, knowing and displeased. A shiver turned her blood cold, freezing in a way not even the winds buffeting her could manage. Imara pushed against the resistance, seeking life in the pit of darkness, wading through the cloying feel of death and rot, of hunger so ravenous it had become toxic.

It was a wave of poison coursing over her spirit, drinking her essence and threatening to pull her down with them. There was nothing but greed and despair no matter where she searched. With rage and desperation of her own, Imara let loose a scream and sent with it a blast of her own magic, shooting it into the depths of that hungry maw.

She sensed it then, a faint flicker of something else: life. Joy sparked through her, and Imara pressed on, fueling everything into that one area of light.

The impact on her body was sudden and shocking. All of the air rushed out of her lungs as her body flew through the air and landed hard upon the ground. Gasping for breath, and ears ringing, Imara opened her eyes to flames and earth raining from the sky. One of the catapults was aimed directly at her, and in the distance, a furious mage bellowed demands. From out of the flames, a body emerged, face contorted with anger and a crystal shining with stolen energy held aloft.

They had found her.

Stumbling to her feet, center of gravity still entirely off, Imara brought her hands up before her, coughing out the smoke that hovered around them from the flaming ball of fire that had knocked her to the ground. Ears still ringing, Imara watched the mage before her mouth words she could not hear, the crystal shining more brightly. Beside her, the large stones Ronar had hid her behind began to pull from the earth, levitating in the air. She could see in the eyes of the mage that he intended to crush her beneath the weight of them.

The largest boulder followed the quick slash of the man's arm through the air. Imara raised a shield of wind up before her just in time to block the attack, groaning at the press of the boulder against the resistance she was putting up. With great effort, she forced the boulder out of reach of the mage's magic, sending it flying through the air to land a hundred feet away. However, the mage was not alone, and Imara was knocked down as a body tackled her to the ash.

Head reeling once more, she brought her hands up to push at the attacker, a human whose fingers were now firmly around her throat. Fighting for air, Imara panicked. Forgetting her abilities, she clawed at the hands choking her and causing her vision to swim, heels digging into the earth as she fought to knock him off.

It was the cold of the winter winds around them that broke through her panic, reminding her that she was not helpless, and she would not die like this. Her hand stretching out into the air, Imara reached for the fire in the clouds and called down a lightning bolt. It impacted with the body atop her and sent her attacker flying backward.

Coughing and gasping for breath, she held a crackling hand out toward the mage who had initially bombarded her.

"Run," she growled in a broken voice, eyes narrowed upon him. "Don't make me kill you."

She could tell that he was thinking about it. What he'd witnessed with the lightning had clearly startled him, but it wasn't enough to drive him back. He shouted a spell, and this time, as the crystal in his hand glowed, Imara felt an invisible fist connect with her chest. Crying out in pain, she stumbled back, hands grasping at her torso just as another invisible fist hit her in the side, causing her to double over. *Why has it come to this?* Kill or be killed.

The next hit forced her to her knees, and by that point, she'd had enough of the quick assault raining down on her. Hands sinking into the earth, Imara screamed her fury, and the ground cracked open before her, racing toward her aggressor. He stumbled into the shallow crack she had formed. With a swift movement, fingers tangling in the lines of energy around them, Imara forced the wind to drive him forward so that he had no choice but to release his crystal and grab at the ground to prevent himself from falling headfirst. Once he was in position, Imara pulled the earth closed, trapping his hands and feet in the ground, which she then hardened to stone around him.

Panting from pain and exertion, Imara climbed to her feet, scraping damp strands of hair out of her eyes. Moving to the trapped mage, she bent down to pick up his crystal.

"You do not deserve these powers if you use them for ill-gotten gain," she hissed at him. Feeling the tainted energy swirling within the crystal, Imara willed it to expand until the crystal shattered. Pouring the shards off her palm before the mage, she dusted her hands off. "Should you survive this, make better choices."

Turning from him, Imara cast her eyes around her, searching for the all-too-familiar form in the disarray surrounding her. "Ronar!" she shouted, knowing that she could not do this if she did not have him beside her.

She could not protect herself and also put all her focus into what was needed to cleanse the Ancients. Knowing that he would come to her, Imara faced the creatures continuing to climb free of the earth. Giant, tree-like monsters who reeked of death, stretching their limbs up into the air and casting a shadow of despair over them all.

Gleaming eyes in the depths of tangled features stared at her from across the expanse of the field. They were aware of Imara and her position on this battlefield; they knew what she was trying to do. Those freed began a slow but terrifying trek in her direction, sweeping long limbs along the ground to bat at anyone in their way, mage, human, or seidr.

At her sides, Imara's fingers sparked with flame. She would not be able to cleanse the Ancients if they were upon her, but she could not ignore the path they were taking directly for her.

Two figures raced toward the Ancients, the ground rising up around them to catch at their feet while the rain was transformed into spears of ice.

"No! Stay back!" Imara shouted, recognizing both her parents wading into the fray.

They were joined by several others from the village,

attacking the Ancients from all sides, doing whatever they could to keep them at bay.

As bodies went flying, beat out of the way by a branch-like hand, Imara had to turn away. She had to trust that her parents would be okay and remind herself that no one would be safe until she managed to stop the Ancients for good.

"Ronar!" she cried once more, putting all the force into his name that she could, begging him to hear her call.

Dropping to her knees once more, Imara sunk her toes and fingers into the ground, reaching out toward the creatures now towering over the field. In the back of her mind, she sensed when Ronar appeared over her, and with determination, she let herself go. Sinking back down into the depths of their hunger, she sought for that small flicker of light.

Gritting her teeth, Imara pushed everything she was, every ounce of energy she could tap into, toward that spark, forcing it to begin spreading through its hosts. They fought it, a scream of rage sounding out from the creatures as the poison within them resisted. Gasping for a breath, Imara pushed on, her body beginning to shake.

There just weren't enough energy lines to draw on, not with how much the Ancients had feasted on them, and she was but one Ambient, not several.

"Ronar," she gasped. "Help me."

Imara's eyes flew open as she felt the presence above her, old and pure, something beautifully other. Her dragon.

RONAR

Pain crept up Ronar's side, forcing him to hunch over. His body wasn't entirely ready for battle, not after three days of fending off poison, and especially not in his current form. It drained precious energy and stole away a portion of his magic's strength. But how vulnerable would he be in dragon form? Instead of a smaller target, he'd be one lumbering mass and easier to strike.

Staggering to the side, his hand hovered over the dull ache. A grimace spread across his face, and his damp hair clung to the sharp angles of his face.

The High Mage called to his blind followers, shouting orders to push against the shield with their magic and shatter it.

Ronar brushed off the help of a young male seidr, who frowned at the Dragon Master but stood by him.

"We weren't ready, not for something like this . . . "

Ronar grimaced. His hand landed on the boy's shoulder, and he squeezed it. "I know, but we have no choice but to rise to the occasion. So we'll give them everything we have and a little more."

"But what if it isn't enough?" the boy asked.

"It'll have to be."

If the shield he had in place shattered, Imara wouldn't be safe.

Ronar blinked. *Imara.*

He knew he'd been pushed away from Imara, but it hadn't dawned on him until that moment how far.

His gaze swept along the muddied field in search of her, where he'd left her. Lightning crackled, and the wind carried the distinct scent of ozone toward Ronar. Frantically, he searched for Imara, his body already in motion until a figure collided into his. He fell to the ground hard, landing on a cluster of rocks which knocked the wind from him and tore whatever tender flesh and muscle had healed. The scent of blood struck his nose, but he ignored it, grabbed ahold of his assailant's shoulders, and rolled with him.

"You cannot win this!" The crystal hung around the young mage's neck, glowing purple as he murmured quickly beneath his breath.

"Oh no you don't." Ronar grasped for purchase on one of the nearby rocks as the mage chanted and his eyes rolled back to reveal the whites. The earth beneath them rumbled, but Ronar was quick to lash out, the rock connecting with the man's head. Immediately, he went limp, but the earth still gave way beneath them.

Ronar cried out as he planted his hands on the ground, pulling himself out of the gaping hole. As his gaze lifted, he saw Imara crush a crystal in her grasp.

Again, hot, blazing shards of pain screamed at him in

protest. If he fell victim to the battlefield, so be it. As long as Imara was safe.

"You won't," a familiar voice came from above. The beat of leathery wings filled the area with a strong gust of wind. A bronze dragon landed, curling her wings against her figure. "Go on, you fool. Go to her. We have you." Synda's yellow eye flicked toward the sky, toward Omro, the dragon he'd written to. Relief swept through him. Not that he doubted Mikkel's ability to deliver the missive, but seeing his friend fly above bolstered his confidence in winning this battle.

"Dragons! There are dragons! Watch the sky!" a mage howled, which abruptly ended as Synda's spiked tail lashed out at her. The woman's figure flew into a nearby tree with an audible snap. It was unclear whether it was tree or bone. Her body crumpled to the ground, bent in an unnatural way. Omro circled the sky, his great neck extending as he rained fire on the trebuchets. The nearby humans weren't able to escape before the fire leaped to them, lapping at their flesh and bones greedily.

Ronar.

"Thank you," he shouted above the disarray.

The sound of his name echoed in his mind as a whisper, then louder. He knew who spoke his name at once, and anxiety filled his chest.

With three dragons on the battlefield, and the catapults rendered useless, hope blossomed in his chest. He wasn't nearly as vulnerable now, not when they offered him cover.

The ground rumbled as Ronar's transformation took over him, the image of the man rippling as he turned into a plated gold dragon. His clawed hands flexed as he leaped at a cluster of humans who sought to charge him. He squashed them, ending their feeble efforts to bar his path from Imara. Very little could keep him away from her, especially as she called to him again.

"He's . . . a dragon?!" a collective question rang out in a shout.

The seidrs were far less surprised than the humans because they knew and had heard of the dragon in the woods. But until now, Ronar had purposely kept his truth a secret from even the loyal seidrs.

Now, they needed him and his truth.

Ronar. Help me.

Swinging his tail, he knocked into several humans readying to converge on him. With a rumbling growl, he bounded across the ground, hovering over Imara to protect her.

"I'm just . . . I need more," Imara panted. Exhaustion tugged at the skin beneath her eyes and drew her shoulders downward. But even amidst her trial and fatigue, she didn't miss the blood dripping from his belly. With horror etched on her face, she stumbled to her feet and pressed her dirty hand against his soft scales. "You're bleeding!"

"I will live. I am here now, Imara. Take what you need, and I'll fend the rest off. Synda has come to offer aid, and so has an old friend, Omro." Ronar took a moment to move his head, one green eye focusing on her long enough so he could wink.

"Just . . . live," Imara blurted, then pulled away and took but a moment to collect herself, to focus on the power circulating within her, then sunk to the ground.

He felt Imara the moment she clung to his magic. The familiar stroke of her ability against his, and the greedy draw on it as she pulled his strength toward her.

Imara was strong enough to succeed in purifying the Ancients, Ronar knew that. She just needed a little more substance behind her.

In a quick reflex, he lowered his head toward a throng of individuals, spraying fire at them. Flames licked at their robes, devouring the fabric down to their flesh. The scent of scorched skin filled the air, and so Ronar's new lethal dance started.

"Don't let them push us back. Drive them toward their starting point, whatever it takes!" Ronar called to the minds of the seidrs, encouraging them and barking orders. *"Omro, aid the seidrs battling the Ancients. They mustn't reach Imara and me before she's managed to finish this."* There was only so much he could do as he shielded Imara, but his task was an important one: protecting her so she could finish this, once and for all.

The plan had been for the seidrs to battle while Ronar and Imara dealt with the Ancients; it was never the plan to battle alongside them.

"T'would be my pleasure!" Omro responded jovially. The red-scaled dragon beat his heavy wings and dove over the heads of the toxic monsters. A long blast of fire fell upon them, causing the Ancients to leave their smaller attackers be while swinging at the dragon above.

The fire wasn't enough to slay them, but it was enough to stop them in their tracks—for now.

A spear sailed through the air, striking Ronar's scales.

It clattered to the slush-covered ground, snagging his attention rather quickly.

His lips peeled back, revealing sharp, dagger-like teeth. Ronar rumbled in annoyance, sounding more like a groaning tree than a snarling predator.

Ronar hunkered down lower, still shielding Imara.

"Well, don't just stand there. Use your magic, you dolts," Ronar bellowed to the minds of the seidrs nearby, his eyes searching for the High Mage once again.

Cuyler Hagen needed to die. If he fell, then his men would lose their fight. But where had he gone?

Ronar lifted his head, searching the field with a narrowed eye. The arrogant bastard wasn't amongst those fighting; why would he be? With the catapults burned to the ground, they'd lost their long-range advantage.

"Synda, do you see Hagen?" Ronar sent an image to the elder dragon's mind, and she sniffed in response.

"I don't. But I feel a growing surge of power. It comes from beyond the catapults. I'll investigate." She lifted into the sky, vanishing into the cover of clouds and smoke. What seemed like ages was truly only a minute or so, then a smoky laugh resounded in Ronar's head. *"Your salvation has arrived. It seems Cuyler Hagen is preoccupied with the king's army."*

The king's army? Ronar's wings beat against the air in sheer glee. They had a chance in this battle then. All of them. *"Do they need aid?"*

"It would seem the High Mage has turned tail and run. He's disappeared again, but the calvary is riding toward the field. Have heart."

Amidst his display of excitement, an arrow sunk into

his belly, but it was a minor inconvenience compared to the tear of muscle and tissue on his other side. With a clawed hand, he pulled it out, and crimson droplets fell to the ground, melding with the muddy slush beneath him.

"We will prevail, my darling. We will," Ronar crooned softly.

IMARA

With the broad wingspan concealing her from the humans as well as the pelting icy snow, Imara felt distraction melt away from her. Ronar had come, and while the battle raged furiously around them, she could now lose herself in the task at hand. Beneath her hands, the ground shook as the creatures continued to crawl their way out of the cavern splitting the earth, their attention now focused on Imara and her surge of power. They could feel that she was not only siphoning magic into their hungry maws but digging into the essence of them.

Thankfully, they were also being deterred in their fight toward her by dragon fire falling from above: Omro doing his part to hold the freed ones back.

Everything around her was tied in some manner to the earth, including the Ancients who sought to destroy it. Yet, as Ronar's magic flooded into her, instinctively responding to her call and bonding with her own as it had on so many occasions in the keep, she could feel the difference of it. Could see in her mind's eye the draw of his magic from somewhere beyond their realm. His was not something that the Ancients could feed on, thus it was the perfect storehouse to fuel her own abilities.

Close by, another rumbling explosion sounded as the High Mage opened the earth to create crevices in a desperate attempt to separate the king's army from him and his followers.

The mages had been mad to think that they could ever hope to control the creatures they were in the midst of setting free. While the tainted energies flowing from the Ancients were surely filling their crystals near to bursting, Imara could sense their anger and resentment, the sheer force of the strength inside. Within them was the power of creation, and also destruction—Jörd. The spirit of Mother Earth, tainted or not, could not be controlled by any crystal known to man. Imara wasn't certain they could be controlled by any power that she possessed either.

As she delved deeper within the hungry essence of the Ancients, a chill ran through her body that was not from the cold winds whipping about her. The aura of dark, toxic energy flowing through her from the core of the putrid, tree-like beings made Imara balk. Even with that subtle spark of light she'd encouraged to life earlier, what could she possibly do against such overpowering death?

Imara trembled, poisonous claws curling around her mind as a lifetime of doubt-filled memories were pulled to the forefront.

She was twelve years old once more, and everyone in the Omdahl schoolhouse was watching her complete inability to perform the simple task of filling an orb with light. An endeavor that required only basic magic, orbs responded to the presence of elemental energy itself, and would spark to life, creating enough light to fill a room.

Laughter filled her mind's ear with its mocking nature.

She was fifteen, and the boy she had begun to develop feelings for had spurned her without hesitation, quickly reminding her that no one would become involved with a seidr who lacked even the smallest hint of elemental ability. Imara remembered that bitterly cold day, wrapping her shawl around her slender shoulders as she left the schoolhouse at the noonday break. There was no one to eat with, and she couldn't bear to burden Asta with her woes, not when her younger sister had so many friends around her.

The laughter quickly morphed into judgmental eyes and cold shoulders. The townsfolk turning away from her, keeping their distance as if she might taint them should their hands touch or the hem of her dress brush against their own. They never outright spoke of their disdain for her, but it was always present: in every clipped response, with every step backward, and all through the years of witnessing the greeting smiles Asta would receive, which then changed to blank looks of apprehension as they glanced to her.

So many years of living on the sidelines of her own village, never truly one of them because she *wasn't* one of them. She was empty. Crippled. Useless.

Useless. Useless. *Useless.*

Everything she had accomplished over the past couple of months had happened because of Ronar's presence at her side—because Ronar managed to pull from her whatever magic resided within. What if she was unable to do this because she was diving into the depths on her own? Why had she thought that she could do this? Doubt and shame became a large, billowing monster inside her head, tearing through the confidence she had built with tooth and claw.

"*Imara.*"

This task was beyond her. Doubt and desolation were a heavy weight upon her soul, bearing down at a punishing rate. She could not do this.

"*Imara!*"

With a gasp, Imara jolted back to herself, eyes opening quickly as the painful memories faded away, and once more, she was aware of the biting cold winds and the half-frozen ash beneath her fingertips. All around her, the battle continued to rage on while she fought the dark shadow inside herself.

"Ronar?" she whispered, recognizing the voice in her mind at last.

"*Fight them, darling. Show them the indomitable spirit that burns bright inside you. You do not back down to anyone, even monstrous Ancients from the world's depths.*"

His words filled her with a newfound warmth, yet the doubt still slithered at the back of her mind. Had she learned enough yet? Practiced enough? "I don't know if I'm strong enough."

The fairytale had depicted several Ambients sealing the Ancients into the ground. How was she to do this on her own?

"*Of course you are. You turned sticks into trees. Found life within death.*" He spoke directly to her mind while above her, his great tail whipped out at an impending threat, sending the body soaring through the air. *"What are these but giant sticks that need life returned to them? Imara, you know what to do. I know you can do it."*

Through the psychic link between them, Imara could feel his confidence in her. There wasn't even a hint of doubt or waver in it—Ronar believed that she could do this.

Taking a deep, steadying breath, Imara glanced up at the golden dragon above her. She had been given to him as a sacrifice, unwilling and unwanted. Yet, despite it all, Ronar had become her one true source of encouragement. She reached out with a hand to run fingers reverently over the clawed foot closest to her. He saw into her and did not turn away. Saw everything that she was and did not balk. Ronar had possessed faith in her when she had been unable to have it for herself. That thought renewed her.

"I will," she responded determinedly.

Gathering Ronar's freely offered magic into herself and digging her fingers deep into the earth below her once more, Imara threw herself down into the depths of the Ancients, diving through murky, cloying darkness and tainted power until she felt around her the true essence of the beings themselves. It reminded her of the barren soil Ronar had brought her from here in the valley: empty and lifeless, but with all the ingredients it took to create life, if only the power were there to force growth.

Her chest filled with a ragged draw of breath, and her form glowed faintly with a golden light. Her mind dug into that empty essence until it surrounded her, and once Imara had planted herself firmly in the center, she began to release all the lifegiving light and energy that she could muster. Drawing on the lifeforce of the people around her and from Ronar's well of power—siphoning it from somewhere deep and beyond the world itself.

At first, there was nothing but her struggle. Imara gritting her teeth, and the darkness swallowing up the life she was spilling into it as fast as she could force it out. Rather than give up, she persisted, and with great joy, she saw that spark from before light into a small blaze, burning away the murky poison and leaving space for life to bloom. As the first sprout of green took root within the core, a shrill scream rang in both her mind and her ears.

The Ancients were not pleased.

Imara gasped raggedly at what felt like the rake of claws through her mind and soul, leaving her panting for breath as her physical body reacted to the force of the resistance from the Ancients. Faintly, she could hear Ronar calling out her name in concern, but she dared not break her concentration to respond—her foothold at the core of the tainted beings was too precarious. Instead, she began to chant, words of growth and purification pouring off her tongue like song.

The mental claws struck again, latching on to whatever they could reach and making her whimper, but she pressed on. Forcing a yell through tightly clenched teeth, Imara pushed forward with all the strength she could muster, drawing on Ronar's magic even more. Like oil hitting flame, the poison within the Ancients hissed and fumed, flaring up, wild and noxious, before disappearing to leave barren space for growth.

"*No!*" started the shrill screams, while other moans echoed their sentiments, speaking at last in a language she could understand

"You cannot doooo this! Leeaaave ussssss beeeeee!"

Now fighting for breath, Imara braced herself for the additional onslaught being waged upon her as the Ancients fought with force against what was happening inside of them. The cleansing was not an easy process, and through the connection she'd established, she could feel their agony as her magic burned the tainted essence out of them.

This time, their resistance was more than a fist or claws; it was a force so staggering that her body shook, and she felt herself retching what remained in her stomach upon the ground before her. Sheer determination kept her up on her hands and knees rather than collapsing into the sodden earth.

Ronar was shouting to her once more, and she knew that, had he been free in human form to peel her away from the soil and force her consciousness back to the forefront of her mind, he would have done it. But he was not, for still the mages warred against them, firing what balls of flame and stone they could.

Through her own pain, Imara pushed on, murmuring the words of ancient magic Ronar had taught her, breathing life into emptiness, even as a hailstorm of rage and agony rained down upon her mind and spirit. Even as her essence was broken apart piece by piece, shredded by the resistance within the five spirits of Jörd.

"Leeeeave usssss!" The wailing increased until it was all she could hear and understand. Until every sense was taken up with the howls of pain and rebellion.

When it had become almost too unbearable to withstand any longer, Imara felt the wall of resistance break, and positive energy began to rush back into her—a bubbling well of life bursting at the seams. Her own body still shaking from the force of the Ancients' assault, Imara sobbed in relief. The healing was not complete, but there was now enough pure life inside the beings that she could feel the true nature of what they had once been. As she continued to cleanse them, Imara sensed the Ancients adding to her magic and beginning to heal themselves.

"*Bind us,*" came a far gentler whisper.

No, Imara thought. Trapping them within the earth once more was not what she had come down here to do.

"*Bind us, lest it happen again.*" The first voice was joined by another, and then another, until the same request rang out from all of the beings who had escaped their imprisonment in the earth.

She wanted to refuse but understood the truth of what they were seeking. It was not an outside poison that had tainted them but a poison within themselves. Imara's eyes opened so that she could tip her head back and gaze up at the towering beings. As her healing magic continued to course through them, breathing life into what had once been death, she saw their tree-like forms slowly shifting in the snow-speckled skies above.

With more energy than she'd thought she still had, Imara scrambled to her feet beneath Ronar's overshadowing form, icy mud clinging to her damp breeches.

"Stop the attack!" Imara shouted over the field to those surrounding the Ancients. Ronar must have seconded her call, for the red dragon in the skies stopped his assault and flew to another area of the battle where he could be of use.

Wiping her hands off on what dry spots she could find, Imara then wove her arms in the air, gathering to her those natural lines of elemental magics that wound themselves through every living thing. Taking a deep breath to steady herself, Imara wound her magic around each of the Ancients and, gathering all her strength to her, she gave a great shout and pulled, forcing all of the beings together. Their branch-like arms swayed in the air as they reached outward in protest at the movement, feet built from giant roots scraping at the ground, digging in where they could.

When at last all five were standing together, Imara lifted her hands above her head. Wind tickled at her fingertips and lifted the ends of her hair as it swept past her and began winding its way around the Ancients in a swirling tornado that trapped them in place. Increasing the pressure upon them, Imara forced them more tightly together, the winds rushing until their arms twisted and interlocked.

Toes digging into the earth, Imara sought to ground herself. Humming softly beneath her breath, she pictured in her mind's eye a large, beautiful tree towering above them all, with branches stretching up toward the sunshine and roots growing deep in the earth.

A great sigh sounded from amidst the tornado as the Ancients felt themselves slowly being bound within the form of an enormous tree. Legs fused together as white, paper-like bark grew over them, binding their bodies together. Above, their arms melded into actual branches, while fingertips started to sprout leaves.

Just before their deep, eternal gaze was covered over by the new skin of their binding, Imara saw the gratefulness and peace. Tears of relief filled her own eyes as she forced the last of her energy into driving their roots deep into the soil so that this life-giving tree would stand long, without wavering. From their branches bloomed glistening purple fruit that shimmered with energy.

Finding her task at last complete, Imara sunk to her knees in the sleet and mud, a cry of fury rising up from the ranks of the mages as Cuyler Hagen realized his source of untold dark power had just been taken from him.

30

RONAR

The metal tips of spears glanced off his scales, and each time an offender grew too close, Ronar would lunge toward them with his mouth, clawed hand, or tail. The dull scrape of a weapon slid over his forearm toward his vulnerable underbelly, but in a lightning quick moment, he snapped at the offender. His teeth clamped around the man's bottom half, and in one wet crunch, he went still.

Ronar flung the corpse into a swarm of approaching individuals. Irritation melded with desperation. He couldn't leave Imara, not now when she needed him as a shield, and certainly not as the Ancients sought to poison her mind.

"Omro, ensure none grow too close!" Ronar called out to the dragon, twisting his long neck so he could face the swarm of men racing toward him with crystals aglow and weapons raised. A mob launched at him, but Ronar dipped low, his lips curling to reveal his bloodied teeth. With a deep inhale, he opened his maw, then exhaled a heavy blast of fire.

Many humans fell, but those bearing crystals didn't

stop. Instead, they used their stolen magic to control the flame. Black wisps burst forth from the crystals, fusing with the fire. Ronar knew all too well what they were about to do, and he had nowhere to go. But the mages were too occupied with the twisting of magic; they didn't notice the seidrs flanking to their side.

The villagers converged, focusing their efforts on the attackers. Pure magic pulsed in the air, bursting vibrantly in the form of a lightning bolt striking the remaining mages.

"Now, turn your efforts across the field. Take down the High Mage's guards and create a window for the others," Ronar shouted into their minds, then stumbled at the sudden intense draw on his magic. It was like a noose around his neck, pulling him down, harnessing him in place as Imara siphoned what she needed from him. *"Create a bridge with the earth for the army! The king has offered us aid."*

As instructed, the seidrs nearest to the crevice concentrated their efforts on restoring the earth. Their ability wove it together no differently than a seamstress pulling together two pieces of cloth. When a section as large as a bridge had formed, the cavalry closest to it converged and poured over it, shouting as they rode into battle, each wielding a sword or an axe.

Freezing rain pelted his heated scales, running off in numerous rivulets, but it did nothing to quench the fire blazing across the field of death.

In the next moment, the Ancients writhed in fury, their limbs moved against their will, and they screamed, a high-pitched keening that buzzed in Ronar's mind. But even as they moved, their bodies lining up in a row of five, their wails grew softer until it became the sound of them pleading.

Ronar looked from the twining of the Ancients to Cuyler Hagen across the field. The mage stood with his arms outstretched and his face toward the sky. A deluge of black wisps emanated from his chest and snaked forward as if they were about to constrict the nearest seidr, but to Hagen's horror, the magic ceased moving forward and writhed around him as his anger surged.

Cries of fear rang out from the human forces and the mages alike, and Ronar suddenly realized why. The crystals they clung to or that swung from their necks were as dull as a stone on the ground. No pulse of life thrummed, no magic swept around them. They were without power, unable to wield magic in this moment.

With no time to recharge their crystals with another source, the mages and humans were overwhelmed by the other forces. Several hordes knelt in submission as the scale tipped in the seidrs' favor.

A thunderous groan echoed nearby Ronar and Imara. He crouched low, curling around her even more. But it wasn't a threat. It was a massive, healthy tree where the Ancients had once stood.

Ronar's heart thrummed wildly in his chest. Imara had done it! The pull on his magic ceased. With the draw on his power gone, a weight lifted from him, allowing him to stand upright once again.

A purr-like noise rumbled in his chest; it was time to end this. With care, he stepped to the side, his clawed hands scooping up Imara's spent figure.

"Ah, my darling, you've done your part. Now let me do mine, and we can finish this." He gently deposited Imara beneath the beautiful tree.

A noise escaped Imara, her hand clutching onto his before Ronar could pull away. He dipped his head low, exhaling through his nostrils to fluff her hair.

"Come back," Imara whispered, letting her hand drop into her lap. Painted beneath her eyes were signs of exhaustion, and her skin lacked its usual vibrance.

An ache formed in his chest at the sight. He knew Imara didn't have much left to give, fatigued beyond her limits. It was his time to do his part.

"*I will do my best.*" Without another word, he launched into the air, wings flapping quickly to gain as much height as he could. The smoke from the fire created cover, but Ronar tapped into his magic, conjuring an illusion that hid his form in the smoke and clouds.

"*Stop them from escaping, but don't press them. You're all going to want to stand back.*" Ronar's words ended abruptly as he tucked his wings against his side and streamlined his body. Like an arrow, he cut through the air, pulling up at the last moment before his body collided with the ground. His mouth opened, and he rained fire down on the useless mages nearest the High Mage.

Without his crystals, Hagen was nothing. There was no source left to draw power from, but the man still stuttered with empty confidence. With arms held out wide, he walked toward Ronar. "You foolish beast. Those Ancients . . . the sheer power they held, and now what? It's gone and wasted."

Ronar's head cocked. "You meddle with a magic you

don't comprehend. You twist and contort something pure into something vile." A deep, gravelly rumble resonated in his chest. "You are an infant toying with a force you know nothing about, and you are balancing on the tip of a blade."

Cuyler Hagen's tanned face contorted. Rage, desperation, grief—it all flashed in his gaze. "You have no idea what you've done. You don't know the source of—"

Ronar didn't wait for him to finish. Instead, he lunged forward, mouth gaping wide, and snapped down on the man with a satisfying crunch. He didn't spit him out or thrash his lifeless body around. Ronar swallowed him in one gulp, then spun around to face the remaining assembly.

Weapons dropped immediately, and those who were left battling soon realized it was futile.

"Round up the survivors, bind them, and let the king's army do the rest. They are useless without their crystals, and King Thorne will have fun doling out punishments for them all." Ronar snarled, eyeing a nearby human before he took flight again. This time, he landed next to the newly formed tree. It was nearly as tall as him in dragon form, its limbs and branches stretching far and wide to form an umbrella above Imara.

In a burst of air, Ronar transformed back into his human form, his body worn and tired from the drain on his magic. Cold, sticky blood trickled down his side, but for the most part, it kept his layers of clothing glued to him. His lips pressed into a thin line, devoid of his usual humor. Weariness had sapped that from him, at least for the moment.

Ronar's legs buckled, so he knelt before Imara and the

tree. Leaning forward, he pressed his forehead against hers and inhaled the soft fragrance that was wholly Imara. "It is done," he whispered, cupping her face gently. "It is done." With a grunt, he twisted and leaned against the trunk of the tree.

Laughter spilled from Imara, softly, then melded into a quiet sob. Her lips placed soft kisses on his cheek, then temple. Ronar wrapped an arm around her shoulder, pulling her into his lap so he could embrace her and hold her against his chest.

"We did it. We actually did it." Disbelief clung to her words.

"My darling, I'd like to say on record, for an unwanted pariah, you sure managed to pull off a miracle." He chuckled, brushing a kiss against the tip of her ear. "If I may ask one thing of you . . . don't ever let them forget that fact. Always remind them that it was you who came to the rescue. You who saved them and their land."

Imara rustled and twisted so she could peer up at him. "And you."

"I am their Dragon Master. They'd never doubted me, but you . . . They owe you a great many apologies and countless praises. That aside, I did little when it came down to it. Imara, you are the one who did it." Ronar's hand swept through the dried dirt at the tree's base, noticing the consistency differed from that of the field. He frowned in thought, lifting it. Instead of dust, it held moisture, and in the moisture, there was life. A small sprout of grass stuck up, dancing in the whipping wind.

Imara's eyes focused on the clump of dirt, and she scrambled to sit upright, legs straddling Ronar as she cupped his hand. "It's . . . it's life. It's alive again." A strangled laugh escaped her, then her hands lifted to rest against the bark by Ronar's head. Her eyes grew feverish, filling with light again, and when she glanced down at him, she captured his lips in a tender kiss.

Gladly, he returned it, but she pulled away abruptly, hands patting at the bark, then gliding over it.

Upstaged by a piece of wood? Ronar internally complained.

"To think," he murmured. "No roof to ruin, no pot to shatter, and regrettably . . . no heather in sight." His eyes lingered on the sight in front of him, hand dropping the clump of dirt as he stared directly at her breasts. He was far too tired, too weary to the bone, to act on anything, but he'd admire the view in front of him just the same.

"No heather," Imara echoed, sighing as she lowered her gaze. "Ronar." His name rolled off her tongue sternly.

It was enough to jerk his attention upward, his shoulders bunching by his ears. "What?" The distant sound of weapons clattering into a pile ricocheted off the rocks. Sobs blended in with the growls of demands, and it sobered him from their private moment. "As much as I'd prefer to remain here, exactly like this, we have a lot to do yet. I want nothing more than to obliterate the entire mass of survivors, but I can be sensible." Although every fiber in his being cried for him to do away with the wretched humans.

"We will find a suitable punishment." Imara nodded. Slowly, she climbed to her feet, using her hand against the tree to steady herself. Her brow furrowed in concentration as she looked at it. "This tree will serve a purpose, a new one that will sustain us all."

Ronar, far less fluid than usual, stood too. His gaze followed the trunk up to the expansion of the umbrella of branches, and to the purple engorged fruit that hung from it. He didn't know whether it was edible or not. Even if the Ancients were purified, what if their poison lurked inside the juicy flesh?

Skepticism wrinkled his brow.

"Ronar," Imara repeated his name as sternly as before. "The tree . . ."

"What?" His skin prickled, not in fear but in anticipation and readiness to shift back.

Small branches curled toward them, but when they couldn't reach any longer, broader limbs stretched toward them instead. Ronar growled in warning, his arm reaching out to Imara, but she sidestepped him and smiled at the leafy green vine of ivy that wound itself around her wrist. Another strand stroked the dirt covering Imara's cheek.

Ronar's muscles tensed. If he moved quickly enough, he could tear the strands in half and pull them away.

Imara glanced his way. She must have seen the calculating look in his eyes because she extended her free hand, as if he were a wild animal on the verge of attacking. In truth, he was.

He wanted to trust Imara and whatever connection she had with the tree, but with leafy appendages stretching out toward them and branches groaning, it was difficult. There was also the fact these had been murderous beings not moments ago.

Ronar would singe them, reduce them to ash if they—

"Ronar!" Imara cut through his thoughts, snapping at him. "You will do no such thing."

Had he said that out loud?

Imara motioned for him to place his hand against the bark, so he did.

At first, nothing. But then another vine extended from the branches, blooming with soft, fragrant flowers. It tickled along the back of Ronar's neck, snaked against his ear, and several more vines extended, only adding to his mounting trepidation.

"Tell me why I won't," he ground out.

IMARA

"They asked to be bound," she murmured as the vines reached out to wrap around Ronar in a tender embrace, just as they had wound around her. "There is no need to fear them any longer."

Despite the tenderness of the branches now twining over his form, Ronar still did not seem convinced.

"In the final stages, as I was binding them, I saw an image of this giant tree with branches heavy-laden with fruit. There is a purpose for all of it: so that the earth can be restored, and their corruption will not return."

As she spoke, something began to tickle at Imara's mind, like the faint whispers of fingertips brushing lightly over skin. Before she had a chance to ask Ronar if he was feeling something too, the vines of the tree tightened about her and pulled her in toward the trunk, the bark opening to draw her inside and curling out and over her form. There was no time to fight; images were already flashing through her mind, ceasing any resistance.

The images were indeed memories from a time long ago, when the world did not exist as it did now, and the Ancients were lonely beings searching for a home. Imara saw them eventually combine their powers to form the earth, a creation that could siphon the energies of the universe through itself in a manner that the five of them could then feed from more readily.

It was a symbiotic relationship that saw the world flourish as the Ancients nurtured it in return for the constant flow of the universe's magic. As the world blossomed and expanded, other living creatures took form upon its surface, which only increased the amount of energy lines there were to draw on. It also increased the amount the Ancients had to feed on, overburdening them with an excess that was far more than they ever needed.

Imara saw the birth of the dragons from the essence of the universe itself, created as guardians, meant to watch over and protect the earth. Then came the seidrs, tapping into the elemental magics of the earth itself, and the Ancients found themselves sharing the energy they had so long fed off of. With this, the first seeds of greed were planted.

The taint was a gradual growth, but once it had started, greed and an endless thirst twisted their minds until there was nothing but hunger left. Gone was the nurturing nature of the world's life-givers, and in its place was death.

Then came the long centuries bound in the earth, trapped away and starving, longing for the taste of the universe once more. Trapped—until the High Mage had begun to crack a hole in the shield the Ambients had placed around them.

Gasping for breath, and her head spinning from the rapid imagery that had flashed through her mind, Imara stumbled forward as the bark propelled her to freedom.

Feeling dazed, her hand reached out to rest against the tree again, using it to brace herself.

"The fruit," she rasped breathlessly. "It's filled with energy." Her eyes lifted to take in the wonderful offering from the Ancients, which was also a safeguard for themselves. "It's safe," she assured him, already anticipating Ronar's hesitation. "Access to too much energy is what soured them long ago. Now, what they don't need will go into the fruit to feed our people."

There was awe in her eyes as she gazed upon the tree that was both her creation and a great sacrifice from Jörd herself. This tree: filled with the life-giving essence of the world, ever a memory of what had been but also a promise for a brighter future.

Glancing to Ronar, she found him at her side, his arm slipping around her waist to draw her in toward him. Grateful for his steadying frame, Imara leaned against him, letting her head rest on his shoulder.

"We have much still to do, don't we?" she whispered.

"We do," was his simple response.

They were surrounded by the sounds and movements of cleanup, as the dead and wounded were gathered and carted into Omdahl to be dealt with accordingly. Imara wished to stay right here beneath Jörd's tree and simply be with Ronar. His fingers were in her hair, fingertips gently brushing at her scalp, making her eyes close as pleasant tingles traveled down her spine.

"Perhaps we can just . . . not?" Opening her eyes and tipping her head up, Imara caught his eye with her own.

Ronar smiled down at her, offering a little shake of his

head. "As much as I would like to slip away into hiding, I don't believe we have that option."

Imara sighed wearily, and Ronar dipped his head to capture it from her lips, giving her something else to sigh about—the wonderful, newly familiar taste and feel of him. It was something Imara didn't think would ever stop making her knees feel like jelly and her belly somersault.

A frown pinched at both of their features as someone cleared their throat nearby. Pulling apart, they glanced at the unwanted intruder to find Erlend Hjelmstad standing before them, dirty, bloody, and exhausted, but very much still alive. Stepping away from Ronar, Imara quickly hurled herself into her father's awaiting arms, letting out a sob of relief.

"Papa! Oh, thank the moon and stars, you're all right!"

His hold upon her was just as fierce, if not more so, as he pulled her tight into him, pressing a kiss atop her wayward blond curls. Imara silently thanked whatever force had kept him safe on the battlefield.

"As are you," he murmured, his words like a prayer of thanks.

"Mother? Asta?" Imara looked up into his face, searching his eyes for an answer, and was relieved at his nod.

"They're helping retrieve the injured and get them into town," he supplied, his large, work-roughened hand lifting to smooth back her curls as he peered proudly down at her. "You amaze me."

Imara blinked as tears suddenly skimmed her eyes. Clearing her throat, she shook her head, chasing away the emotions swelling up inside her. "I had help."

Her father's keen eyes silently told her to simply accept his words. "Imara, I saw what you did out here." For a moment, his blue gaze shifted to the tree towering over them before it returned to her face. "Most importantly, they all saw."

Imara bit her lip, unable to find words to express what she was feeling in this moment. Instead, she nodded, acknowledging her father's words.

Erlend's focus shifted as Ronar appeared at their side. "Imara, we need to head to the council hall." The two men shared a nod of greeting before looking back to Imara.

Taking a deep breath, Imara took a step back from her father and dug deep for whatever strength remained within her. There would be enough time later to speak with her family, and to rest. Finally, there was all the time in the world.

"Very well, let's go." Reaching out, Imara took Ronar's hand, coiling her fingers through his as they started across the field.

The king's soldiers were busy binding up what remained of the mages, most having already been rounded up. Imara tried her best not to dwell too much on the bodies lying strewn in the mud but knew the sight would forever be with her. This was not something she or her people would ever be able to forget. Nor should they.

At the edge of the field, Synda and Omro were waiting for them, looking a little scuffed up but no worse for wear. Dragons, the both of them.

"Thank you, so very much," Imara was quick to say, reaching out for the tall woman's hand. "You have already done so much for us; this was more than I could have hoped for."

"We did naught but answer the call of a friend," Synda stated, her ancient eyes peering back into Imara's.

"Perhaps, but still, you have our thanks." She looked to Omro, a large, burly man with a thick bristle of red beard covering his chin.

"It's been a might too long since dragons last took to the skies and unleashed their hellfire on those below. It was our pleasure to help," Omro added, a jovial twinkle in his eye.

Imara took an instant liking to him. While a little gruff, there was something very likable about the newest dragon to make her acquaintance.

"I can only second Imara's thanks with that of my own." Ronar stepped forward, clasping forearms with first Synda, and then with Omro. "While Imara and I are still needed here, you should both head to Dragon's Keep. My people will see to it you have rooms and are well fed. They would appreciate hearing that all is well, and that we've succeeded."

"If you are certain?" Omro questioned, looking around the field as if he mightn't enjoy another skirmish or two.

"Absolutely. You've done your part. Go, eat, rest. We'll join you once we've dealt with the last of the situation here," Ronar reaffirmed.

Imara found herself gazing into the eyes of Synda, who studied her in that silent, knowledgeable way she had on Eristyminen.

"I suppose I should not be as surprised as I am to learn that you, too, are a dragon."

The ancient woman chuckled softly and gave a little shake of her head. "You did not yet know the man at your side was a dragon; you weren't meant to see the truth of me either."

It made so much sense though. And now that she knew the truth, Imara wasn't sure how she hadn't pieced it together once Ronar's secret had come to light.

The council hall was not as crowded as it would typically have been for such an important meeting, not with all of the bodies left to be dealt with on top of their large group of prisoners. But each head of family was present, along with the Elders. They sat—or stood—in a semi-circle around the dais, looking haggard and battle-worn. No one had been prepared for the fight the mages had brought to their doorstep.

Once more, Imara found herself seated in the wooden throne the council had placed beside Ronar's, a carved piece that had been meant for the bride of the Dragon Master, but which had now become the seat of their Ambient. Imara could see the change in their faces as the townspeople gazed upon her. Where once scorn had filled their glances, their eyes now held shock and awe.

They had all doubted her, even with Ronar so vehemently supporting her. None of them had believed that she was capable of stopping the Ancients crawling out of the earth. Gazing upon the Elders from her throne, Imara wondered if they had completely missed her overwhelming influx of magic when she'd had her elemental test all those years ago. Or had they feared what they sensed in her and allowed her to block herself off from it entirely?

Had they allowed her to believe herself broken and to become reviled by all simply because they couldn't handle the rising strength of her magic when it had surfaced? Because they felt their own power slipping away and wished to greedily hold onto it as long as they could? Branding a young, innocent child an invalid to keep it for themselves . . . Letting her bear the brunt of the town's disdain, as well as the scars she bore from each hurtful word, each time someone stepped back in haste, each time a parent had stopped their child from playing with her . . .

A shudder of anger coursed through her, fueling Imara with a sudden flash of energy she had not possessed before. Even if each one of them had been blinded to her rising powers and had not sensed the flash of it at her testing as Ronar had with one simple touch, they had still branded her the town outcast.

It was not only her newfound powers that made her unable to simply accept the years of misery any longer, but the knowledge that at Dragon's Keep, she had found acceptance and love. No one in Ronar's household had cared whether she possessed abilities or not. They had taken her at face value, seeing the worth in her person and character rather than her command over an element.

Hands gripping tightly onto the armrests of her throne, Imara remained silent, allowing her anger to seethe inside her. There were words to be had, long awaited words, but instead of spewing them incoherently now, she would sit on them. Let them stew for the moment and leave the council nervously wondering.

"You were correct about the mages," Elder Fridolf began, his hands buried inside the sleeve of the opposite arm, giving the sage appearance Imara knew he was striving for. "We apologize for not adhering to your warning at first, but in our defense—" A loud snort from Ronar interrupted him.

Elder Ylva looked affronted at this behavior, and her mouth opened to reprimand him for the rudeness but quickly snapped shut once more. They had all been witness to the final death of the High Mage Cuyler Hagen, and it was not a sight any of them were bound to forget any time soon. The truth of the Dragon Master had been exposed, and now the council understood for the first time just what they were dealing with when it came to Ronar.

"You have no defense, and to be honest, I grow tired of the excuses. You're nothing but idiots." The Elders all visibly stiffened at these words. Unfazed, Ronar continued. "Stuck in your old ways is no defense either. I have centuries on all of you, and yet I'm capable of changing views."

The room grew quiet enough that, should a pin have dropped, it would have echoed.

32

RONAR

Ronar's fingers swept along his brows in an attempt to smooth out the angry lines. Tired didn't even begin to describe how Ronar felt, but he was furious too. If the Elders had heeded the warning, they would have been ready. But here they were: several empty seats in the hall, the sound of wailing from now broken families and wounded men as well as women sitting before them. Death hung in the air, both foe and allied. So much of it could have been prevented.

On top of it all, Ronar's energy had been sapped away on the battlefield. The strength it took to stay in this form weighed him down, and his movements lacked their typical finesse. His patience thinned, and the last things he wanted to hear were wretched excuses and half-hearted apologies from the very beings who had sought to banish Imara from her home—like she was expendable.

The pariah was now their savior. He assumed that would be hard to swallow for them, and that another excuse lurked around the corner.

Ronar's previous declaration had visibly rankled the Elders and even a few of the villagers. The pinched expression on Ylva's face amused him. *Good*, he thought, *be offended*. The council stood before them, ruffled from his words, and all Ronar could think of was how familiar this felt. But instead of Imara bowing her head to him, she was by his side, and these damnable fools would bow to her.

If they didn't, he would force them to.

The engraved throne beneath Ronar begged for him to remain reclined, and although the thought of towering over Fridolf tickled him, he couldn't bring himself to stand. But the Elder's very demeanor aggravated Ronar to the core. He knew they'd disregarded Imara's warnings and that they hadn't prepared for the mages' arrival. They now grasped at sparse straws, attempting to cover up their mistakes.

Whatever slivers of humor Ronar had possessed moments ago vanished. The lines of his face grew harsher, further furrowing his brows, creasing the corners of his mouth.

"What have I just said?" Ronar raised his voice. "Apologize, but don't for one moment try and excuse your behavior with a 'but.' I can assure you that it won't end well. Not when you were warned by letter, and certainly not beforehand when you gave one of your own up in the trade of, what?" Ronar pushed himself from the chair, his anger fueling each brisk step. "Prior to gifting me a bride, you had several chances to come to me and put an end to the mages. We could have cut them off before things got out of hand, but I'm assuming you didn't want a war. I didn't require a bride as my tithe, but it was so convenient for you to unload Imara off onto me."

"My lord, that isn't fair," Ylva spoke up. Color rushed into her weathered cheeks, irritation roughening her tone. "We didn't know it would escalate so quickly."

"Do not cry to me and tell me what is fair!" No one could have known, but ignoring the threat of the mages had done nothing but allow for it to worsen—rapidly. Ronar's fists clenched in frustration.

If Ronar chanced sneaking a glance at Imara, he might have felt the need to reel himself in. If she sent a warning glare to the back of his head, he didn't feel it, but he also didn't look at her to confirm it, didn't even allow his mind to reach out toward hers to question if he should calm down. She could have screamed his name in her mind to snap him out of it—but she didn't.

"Fridolf, kneel." Ronar swept a hand at the platform. Thinly controlled anger caused his words to sharpen.

The seidr stepped forward with a clenched jaw and knelt on the platform, hands folded in his lap.

Ronar squatted beside Fridolf, squeezing his chin firmly to force his gaze upward. "An apology from your lips could never quell the amount of disgust you fill me with. So, not only have I decided this, but I can think of no better way to punish all of you." A deep, rumbling laugh erupted from Ronar, but he kept his vice-like grip on Fridolf's face. "Greet your new head Elder: Imara." He released the man's face, turning to watch not only the council's reaction but the other villagers' as well.

Most nodded in agreement, but there was a murmur rapidly spreading like wildfire amongst them.

"Imara? Erlend's oldest?"

"Did you see her on the field?"

"She is what we need."

"Such a sweet girl."

"That one? Why her?"

Ronar's eyes settled on Fridolf's face again. "Before you raise your eyebrows at me and attempt to argue, let me say I'll hear none of it. I say this while taking note of the reaction of your villagers. Do you think they're keen on you after that knowledge has come to light? Do you think they trust you? Perhaps we should ask." Jerking his chin toward the front row of seats, Ronar motioned for a young male to stand and speak.

The youth looked to be around Imara's age. Dark red hair hung in several braids over his shoulders, and his pale face boasted several bruises and specks of dried blood. "How could you withhold such valuable information from us? Had we known, we could have turned our efforts toward preparing!"

A low murmur spread through the hall until voices raised above others, resulting in yelling.

Pandemonium wasn't what Ronar wanted. He longed for order, but he also wanted the Elders to see the result of their failures.

"Ronar," a soft voice cut through the mounting hysteria.

He twisted, facing Imara as she sat perched on the edge of her chair. No amusement shone in her bright eyes but rather a reprimand. Without probing her mind, he sighed, knowing this wasn't what she wanted. A shaming, a lashing, that was what they deserved, but an explosion of chaos wasn't what either of them wanted.

If a mob formed, converging on the Elders and tearing

them to shreds, it would be a just punishment in Ronar's mind. However, Imara likely didn't agree with that, and this was her decision.

"Enough," Ronar spat. His long legs carried him to his throne, where he plopped himself down unceremoniously. "There has been more than enough fighting and bloodshed for one day. It is time for your councilwoman to speak. Let me remind you, Elders, your fate lies in her hands." He dragged his gaze from one end of the line of them to the other. "I hope you planted goodness, for you're about to reap what you have sown."

Fridolf's face blanched. Panic crept into his features, drawing his lips downward and loaning his eyes a bulbous appearance.

"But let it be known, after this meeting is concluded, you must find another place to lodge, Fridolf." Ronar was too tired to fly himself and Imara home. They'd need a place to rest, and he wasn't above displacing the sour man.

He had never been inside of the home, but it was elegant, built from logs and stone instead of sitting inside a hill. Ronar knew it was beside the lake too, but Fridolf, head of the council, had never once extended hospitality to the Dragon Master. Not that he would've accepted the offer, for he found the man equally as detestable as the Elder found him.

Fridolf's eyes widened on Imara, but he averted his gaze quickly and shoved his clenched fists to his eyes. "You cannot mean . . . the lodge is my home. Where am I to go?"

Ronar waved his hand in the air. "Who can say? I'm sure one of your family members or friends will take you in until a more permanent home is built. This is all for the *good* of your people." This still wasn't payment enough for what they'd done to Imara. Humiliated her in front of the village, cast her off onto another as Ronar's problem . . .

He looked to Imara, offering her a wink. "As your leader, Imara has the right to select a new council, unless she sees you fit." He cocked his head to the side, giving her the slightest nod to let her know it was her turn.

Imara's blue gaze brightened. Whatever color she'd lost from the battle had returned slowly, enough so that her cheeks were rosy. "I do not." She stood, clasping her hands in front of her. Whether it was to steady quaking hands or to appear at ease, she didn't convey.

"I gather very few of you would dispute what your Dragon Master has said. All of it is truth, but I'm not here to trudge up old grudges. I'm here to judge each of you on the council for your actions. The question is, are you fit to lead? To which I say, no." As Imara spoke, she descended the stairs and stood before Ylva.

"You have a hard heart and deaf ears. Never once have you truly listened to a villager's plight. For that, you are deemed unfit, and you will take a seat amongst your kin."

Warmth spread through Ronar as Imara settled into her newfound confidence. In a short amount of time, he'd watched as she blossomed and stood out above all the others in her village. What had once set her apart as a pariah now set her apart as a superior, and that, above all, brought him joy.

A foreign feeling tugged at the deepest part of him. Ronar knew love—Sylvi was much like a daughter to him— but this was different. This love tore through him, just as the fire Imara had set in his wounds had. It consumed him, devoured every corner of his being, and still demanded more.

As he relaxed into the chair, his fingers fidgeted with the ends of his hair. It wasn't lost on him how quiet the room had become once again, or that the villagers watched on with deep interest.

Imara didn't flinch as she made her way down the line, listing the Elders' wrongs one by one. When she reached Ranell, the last councilman, Imara instructed him to sit as well.

"You have all failed your people, blinded by your prejudice and unwilling to see the truth from a different standpoint. We need Elders who will see not from their own point of view but from all of our views. As a whole, what is for the greater good?" Imara pointed at each Elder, frustration furrowing her brow. "Not hiding from what you fear, and certainly not ignoring it."

Imara took a deep breath. She proceeded to take a step back onto the platform, taking her time surveying the room. "I have a truth I must share with all of you. One that sets me apart from you and one that by natural law indicates that I am your true leader." She paused, loosing a breath before continuing. "I am an Ambient."

Most of the inhabitants in the hall hadn't a clue what it meant. When it came down to it, even Ronar had barely recalled what an Ambient was, and he expected these fools to recall what they were? No. But much to his annoyance, Fridolf did not look surprised. Neither did Ranell. It was as if they knew what Imara had been all along, which only added to Ronar's disgust. If they knew and chose to stamp down her abilities, they chose to make her a pariah when she was first tested.

As much as Ronar wanted to reduce them to sniveling and cowering infants as they knelt before him, Imara's degradation of them was enough for her. It would have to be enough for him as well.

Imara deserved her moment, and as she gauged the reaction of the villagers, she eased into her new role naturally, at least to Ronar's watchful gaze.

33

IMARA

er heart hammered wildly in her chest as Imara gazed out over the council hall at the villagers gathered before her. Never once, in all her years growing up in Omdahl, did she expect to find herself in the position she now did. Yet, things had changed—*she* had changed. While she no longer resented being sent off to be the Dragon Master's wife, as it had led to the truth about herself, and to Ronar, what she did resent were the years of exclusion that led up to that moment. The years of being kept on the outside because of how powerless she had seemed, and their need to do away with her so that she was no longer a blight upon their village.

"I know that many of you may be asking what an Ambient is. I, too, did not understand, as it is something that has been wiped from our history." Her eyes scanned over each person assembled before her, making certain that she had their attention before continuing. "In the beginning, there were those born with the ability to control all four elements, and through this, tap into the very energy lines running through the earth. Because of this power, they were given the role of ruling over their villages, acting as heads of their councils."

Soft murmurs rang out through the group as they began to comprehend just a little.

"Ambients have all but disappeared from our race due to those who were power-hungry and refused accession of the position to the next born. Greed drove Ambients to slay each other to maintain their positions. Others were slaughtered by seidrs too fearful and mistrusting of their abilities. In the end, this eradicated them from existence. There hasn't been an Ambient in so long, even our Elders have forgotten." Her eyes fell to those who had formed the council, looking into their eyes as they either met her own or shied away.

There was a look upon Fridolf and Ranell's faces that spoke of something other than surprise. They did not look confused; they did not look as if they had forgotten.

This caused Imara to pause, an understanding dawning in her that was fierce enough to steal away her breath. Her head swam as the anger surged, and it took all of her inner strength to calm the storm enough to speak.

"Elders Fridolf and Ranell . . . You hadn't forgotten, had you?"

The two men remained silent, but the looks on their faces was all the answer she required.

"You knew what I was." Her words came out as a whisper. "At my elemental ceremony, you knew . . . and yet you acted as if I were broken."

Their eyes remained on the stone floor as voices murmured around them.

"Answer me," she demanded coldly. Her fury had turned to ice in her veins.

"Yes," Fridolf answered at last, lifting his head to meet her gaze—unrepentant.

"You knew that I would take your place."

"Yes."

The gasps carried throughout the council hall as this truth sounded for all to hear.

Imara had to turn away, pinching her eyes shut against the tide of anger now threatening to sweep her away. All those years of self-doubt and shame, feeling unworthy of being a member of this village, all while they had known. Instead of supporting her, teaching her, and taking her into their guidance, they had shunned her.

She had to hold out a hand to stop Ronar from getting to his feet. She could tell he was ready to bring the whole place to the ground, but she was not done.

Inhaling deeply, Imara spun back to the Elders before her, blue eyes cold. "You will never again hold the fate of a child in your hands. You have proven to us all that your judgement cannot be trusted. You knew what had come into your presence, and yet, out of a sense of selfishness for your own position, you branded a child an outcast."

Imara smoothed a hand over the tangled strands of her hair, seeking for a calm she did not feel. In the end, she threaded her fingers together to hide the way they trembled with emotion.

Turning her attention away from the Elders, Imara focused once more on the villagers before her.

"I believe Jörd brought this ability back to us because she knew we would have need of it. It was a group of

Ambients who locked the Ancients in the earth the first time, and only an Ambient would have been able to cure them now." Imara took a steadying breath, her heart still beating wildly—exhaustion and nerves warring with the anger inside of her.

Imara's head turned slightly, giving her a moment to look at Ronar. She caught sight of a deep pride gleaming within his gaze. He believed in her. In truth, he always had. Even in the days when she saw no need to believe in herself, Ronar had known that she would find herself in her magic. Smiling softly, feeling the weight of his pride like a shield around her, Imara turned back to the gathering.

"Why did you not display any abilities until now?" someone called out from the crowd.

"During my trials, I felt the surge of power in myself rise up and, frightened by it and too young to understand what I was feeling, I blocked myself off from it. In so doing, I forgot all of it entirely. Instead, in my innocence, I believed the lies the Elders painted about my lack of ability. It wasn't until my magic was unlocked that my memories returned."

"What did you create out there?" asked another.

"Yes! That giant tree! How do we know that those creatures won't return and finish what they began?" a young mother asked, her infant child cradled in her arms.

Imara could see the fear written in all of their faces and knew that none of them had reason to believe that the threat was entirely over or to trust that she had trapped them away for good. Not when all of this was so new to them, and they had been led to believe all her life that she was of no use. Fed lies that had turned her into an outcast as reviled as the magicless humans outside their village.

"You have no need to fear them. The Ancients were cleansed as they came from the ground, and they asked to be bound once more in their healthy forms. They were the creators of this earth long ago and wish only to see it prosper as was intended. If you go to the tree, you will see heavy fruit hanging from its branches. These fruits contain the excess energy the Ancients feed upon and will insure they do not become clouded with greed and hunger once more, causing the taint to return. Instead . . . " She looked over their faces, wanting only what was best for all of them. "We will be able to eat this fruit and be sustained and rejuvenated. It is also my belief we will see many magical cures and remedies come from the fruit as well."

A soft murmur fell over the villagers as they discussed this amongst themselves. As they spoke, Imara looked to the former council once more. She would do better than they had—she had to. Because she knew what it was like to be on the outside.

"You say you are an Ambient . . . but why should we believe you that it makes you our new leader? How do we know you simply don't find yourself filled with self-importance and are trying to become a queen?" This was Tavvetti, the blacksmith. A gruff, surly man on his best days. He looked at Imara with suspicion but not without reason.

"I have no desire to be your queen. We still owe our allegiance to King Thorne and Queen Kelda, but I *am* the head of this village." Imara squared her shoulders and held her chin high. She refused to be brought down by their disfavor any longer. "I can bring you the source laws if you so desire, Tavvetti, or you can square off against me outside, should you decide you can do better." One blond brow lifted in question, and the older seidr shook his head and reclaimed his seat, not speaking another word.

Behind her, she could have sworn Ronar chuckled softly, but it quickly became a slight cough instead.

"Our council has not been entirely wrong in all their decisions, and in many ways, they have done the best that they could. However, it is also a council that has been built on prejudice. They sought only to build up those who they deemed worthy to be considered members of our society, and the rest were left outside looking in."

Imara began to pace, feeling her emotions well up deep inside of her, wishing to spill over. It caused the magic within to crackle, and in turn, the room surged with enough energy for all inside to feel it. Slight gasps rang out as the swell registered with the villagers, and all eyes were locked upon her pacing form.

"I speak not just of myself but also of the humans . . . the mages." She looked to Ronar once more, who was giving her a questioning glance, before she walked too far past and looked to the villagers instead. "We've kept ourselves separated from them simply because they do not possess the magic that we do, looking down on them as if they were something inferior. Is it any surprise that they would seek to obtain any magic that they could, tainted or not, and then turn it against us?" A hand lifted to tuck a stray piece of hair behind her ear. "What did we expect would happen with such strained relations between us and them?"

Voices of argument rose up, but Imara swept her hand out before her, sending a rush of wind to sweep over them like a gentle but stern warning. The protests quieted.

"If we had been more accepting of them, open to easier trade, and worked on forming a friendship with them rather than antagonizing them with our disdain, we may have never found ourselves in this situation to begin with."

Imara looked at Elders Ranell and Fridolf. Why had they thought themselves so above everyone else?

"Because of this, we will aid in treatment of all the wounded mages and humans. Any of the humans that the king's men release will be returned home, which we will allow. Once they do, we will send a delegation to address any food shortages in their village." The voices rose again, but a hand lifted in the air from her was enough to soften the roar to a murmur. "We *will* bridge this gap between our people. Better to befriend our foe than to further the divide. We will no longer be the ones looking down on others with disdain but a people who seek to help and improve life for all."

She would not allow others to live the life that she had lived, to feel less-than simply for their differences.

"The fruit from the Great Tree will help to sustain us, and once a tally of our own cellars has been made, any shortages that are found will be supplemented with supplies from the stores at Dragon's Keep. Lord Lajos and I will not see any of you starve this winter, that I vow. And when spring arrives, all will have enough to plant for the fall harvest."

If it were possible, the air within the council hall

shifted more than ever, the atmosphere becoming lighter as relief passed through many.

"I know this year has been one of struggle and loss as we've watched our lands and waters dry up, leaving us with barely enough to survive on. But I will not leave you to flounder on your own." She had ceased her pacing and come to stand in the center of the dais, her hands clasped before her. "I want to form a new council, one that recognizes, accepts, and believes in what I have spoken. A council that will uphold my desire for peace and will aid relations with the humans, as well as help to care for this village and its people. I do not want to choose this new council on my own. I wish to hear your voices. Who do you, as the citizens of Omdahl, wish to help govern you?"

They hadn't been expecting this, of that she was certain. Perhaps they had thought she would be a tyrannical leader and only insert people she wished. At first, there was hesitation. But soon enough, a number of names had been called out, and Imara brought the chosen to stand before her. She was pleased to see her father amongst the ones who had been suggested. Moving to stand before them, she spoke quickly to each one, allowing a few who were disinterested in the position to reclaim their seats, leaving only the ones who wished to reside on the council to remain.

Imara smiled a little at Taavetti, both amused and pleased to see the gruff blacksmith before her. Though he could be rough, she had always known him to be fair with his customers and willing to help those who had need of it when they found hard times falling upon themselves.

"I fully expect you to keep us all on our toes," she

murmured to him, then moved to stand before another man. "Melker." Their eyes met, and before she had spoken, she knew that he expected what she was about to say. "You may sit down as well. A man who would beat his apprentice for failing to learn when his own teaching methods are to blame is no man I want helping to guide this village."

She looked to the villagers and pointed to one of the senior women, Tuva. A kind but stern lady who had helped to guide many of the children of the village into the world. There was a wisdom that resided within her eyes that Imara had always respected.

"Will you accept a position on the council?" Imara asked her.

"I would be honored."

Imara waited for the woman to move from her seat and down the stairs to stand before the dais along with the others.

"I welcome you to the Council of Elders. It is a position which I hope each of you will accept with both pride and responsibility. Remember, we are the voice of this village, and also its example." Taking a deep breath, she studied them for a moment, once again wondering who she was to be making these decisions. Yet, she felt the gentle hum of Jörd all around her, a welcoming and also reassuring sensation. "Erlend Hjelmstad, you will oversee the food stores. I want thorough stock taken of what every home has, what the human village has, and what will be needed to see everyone through the winter."

Her father nodded, his eyes shining with pride at her

while his features held a solemnity for the new responsibilities placed upon him.

"Tuva Njall, I want you to see to the care of all those who were injured in the battle, seidr or human. See that their wounds are tended to. Taavetti Herulf and Yver Varanger, you will help repair the homes and barns that were damaged in the initial attacks from the mages. I expect all of you to choose those who will best aid in quick action for all of this. The snows have already begun, and we haven't much time to see it all taken care of. Taavetti, you will also be my voice in the village and relay all activity and proceedings to me as needed."

The man nodded in understanding and acceptance.

"I know that all of you are tired and worn, but we must see everyone out of the cold, and the bodies of those lost must be collected and dealt with." She nodded to the council.

"We'll see it done, Lady Imara," Taavetti grunted, then turned to begin barking orders.

Imara found her father before her, his hands upon her arms as he beamed at her with love and pride. "Imara." His voice cracked, and his words paused for a moment. "You have become all and more than I always knew you were, and I will not fail you in this, I vow it."

"Oh, Father," she rasped, voice husky with emotion. Leaning in, she wrapped her arms around him, sighing in relief at it finally being over. Knowing that at last her family was safe and their lives no longer hung over her.

Pulling away, she found Ronar there at their side, satisfaction written all over his face.

"Dragon Master—" her father began.

"Lajos will suffice."

Erlend reached out to grasp Ronar's forearm firmly but respectfully. "Lajos, thank you. The day they offered Imara up to you, I almost drove off with her in the wagon, bent on hiding her away from everyone. But you have brought to her a new life I could not even dream for her. So, thank you, for seeing what no one else could."

Ronar smiled gently. "It was my pleasure."

Erlend nodded to him, then turned back to Imara. "I must be off to aid in whatever way I can." He leaned in and pressed a kiss to her cheek before turning to head off with the others.

Imara watched him go—watched all of the council go—for but a moment, then turned to Ronar.

"It was only your pleasure because you enjoyed tormenting me beyond endurance each day until I snapped." Her eyes narrowed on him.

With a soft chuckle, Ronar's arms reached out to pull her into his chest, and she went willingly, melting into his form in relief as the full weight of her exhaustion returned.

Finally, it was over.

Finally, they could simply just be.

RONAR

The hall erupted in excitement, but all Ronar wanted was a moment with Imara. He gingerly touched his side, wincing as the fabric shifted and peeled away from his body. When he turned his hand over, his fingers were coated in crimson. Ronar frowned, wishing he could will the hall empty. Instead, villagers rushed forward, bowing before her. A few grasped on to her wrist, squeezing it, nearly sobbing as they thanked Imara for what she'd done.

Ronar knew she was as tired as he, if not more so. He frowned as more individuals approached, but when he extended his arm, it halted them from coming any farther. "We are taxed far more than you know. Tomorrow is another day, and you can continue your jubilation then. For now, the lady and I need rest." His brows slanted inward at the same time his lips formed a thin line. Accompanied by the tone which brooked no room for an argument, none opened their mouths to protest.

With an incline of the head, Ronar led Imara from the hall and out into the icy air. To him, it was refreshing and much needed against his skin, which almost felt feverish.

"Well, darling, after all of our work . . . It is over." He stopped in his tracks, inclining his head to glance down at her, carefully watching her expression in an attempt to pick apart her thoughts.

After months of research, of clashing opinions and frustration, it was all over. The notion vexed him. Mostly because, now that the fight was finished and the village's struggles would lessen as the weeks went on, Imara was free to decide if she wanted to remain with him at the keep or stay behind in Omdahl to oversee them.

Imara looped her arm through his. She smiled tiredly and shook her head. "I know. It's difficult to believe. After months of working on a solution . . . It's resolved." She paused, popping her lips. "Perhaps not as peacefully as I would have liked."

"There was no peace with them. Greed cannot coincide with peace. They were no different than the tainted Ancients. Once the greed bled into them, that was it." Ronar caught a dark look in Imara's eyes. Regret? Guilt? He sighed, lifting his hand to capture her chin. "Darling, we did what we had to."

She nodded. "I know, but it doesn't make it any easier."

"I know." Ronar leaned forward, brushing a kiss against her forehead. "Let's go to the lodge. You're filthy and in dire need of a bath." His gaze raked up and down her figure, grinning as his words sparked her ire.

"Coming from a man who looks as if he's been dragged across the muddy field." Imara pulled her arm back, readying to swat his chest, but obviously recalled that he'd been wounded during battle. "What of your wounds? I should tend to those before anything else."

"I'll live. Whatever was on the mend no longer is, and one of those devils fired an arrow at me." He rubbed the lesser of his injuries, his rib opposite of where the major wound was. "If you'd like to fuss over me . . ."

Imara huffed, carefully looping her arm through his again. "I'll mend you and have words with you too."

"Now, now. Save that energy for later."

"Oh, you!" Imara groaned.

He couldn't help himself. Teasing Imara had become one of his greatest joys in life, mostly because she bristled and rose to the occasion. Her clever mind worked quickly, formulating the best verbal counterattack.

Ronar cherished that.

As they walked down the dirt road, his playfulness diminished. Several families wailed in misery as their loved ones were hauled into their homes. It sobered Ronar, and from the grim expression on Imara's face, it did the same for her too.

Ten minutes down the road, the lodge came into view: a massive log building with a body of water running through the center. Long ago, the seidrs had built the home around it, and even incorporated the trees into it. Not that Ronar knew this from the inside—he'd never been invited in—but outside, it was clear to see.

Ronar approached the rounded front door, then opened it, bowing to Imara. "Mistress," he murmured.

She bobbed a curtsy to him, then entered the lodge. Imara gasped once she stepped past the threshold, then spun around, drinking in the vaulted ceilings.

Ronar followed her gaze, admiring the craftsmanship. The keep had been his home for centuries, longer than this structure had been around. However, the lodge was not only on par with his but in some ways was even better.

Whole trees supported the ceiling, and stone walls served as accents against the granite slab stairs. The building was truly a work of art, but it rankled Ronar to know such a useless individual had lived in luxury while the others suffered.

"That bastard!" Ronar spat, motioning to the house. "He lived like a king."

Imara sighed. She approached him, grasping his hands in hers, and tugged him farther into the room. "Forget him. He's not worth a corner of your mind. Let us move on, build a better society for our people, and truly make a difference."

Ronar couldn't help the way her words tugged a smile from his lips. He lifted a hand, then stroked strands of blond curls back. "Our people?" Such simple words, yet they made his heart feel as if it were going to burst.

"Yes. *Our* people," Imara confirmed vehemently.

"For you, Imara, I'll do my best." He pulled his gaze away, wrinkling his nose. The moment was too close to his heart, and if he continued to stare into her eyes, continued to tease and press her about what she wanted, he knew he'd only end up a babbling mess. Turning away from her, he lifted his hand and shoved it through his unruly dark hair. "Where the hell is the bathing room?" Ronar stalked off in search of it.

The ground floor didn't have a bathing room, but the second floor, where all the rooms were, had an elaborate suite. In front of a large window, a bathtub sat, overlooking the lake behind it. Although the water only trickled now,

Ronar assumed that when normal levels returned, it'd be a remarkable view.

"Imara!" Ronar bellowed, striding toward the tub. Without fussing with the knob, he waved his hand, and with a *whoosh,* the tub filled with steaming water. "Where did she go off to?" he murmured, rummaging around a shelf near the tub. The glass bottles clinked against one another, and a few fell over. Cursing under his breath, Ronar selected one and pulled the stopper out. Soft floral notes tickled his nose.

"What is it?" Imara's breathless words died off fairly quickly. "Oh! You found a tub." She stepped into the room, carrying a small finding of her own beneath her arm.

"Mm-hmm." Ronar tipped the glass container and watched the clear liquid drizzle across the top of the water.

"Take off your shirt," Imara instructed, coming over to him.

"Excuse me?" Ronar offered her a heated look, which brought a flush of bashfulness to her cheeks.

"Your wounds, I must tend to them. Before you begin to leave a trail of blood behind you." The basket, which she had carried in under her arm and was now set on the rim of the tub, turned out to be a sewing kit. Offering him but a single warning look not to argue, she went about threading a needle.

Too weary to fight it, Ronar began stripping off layers until he stood in nothing but his breeches. Half sitting on the tub, he watched Imara dampen a cloth and then move purposefully toward him. It pleased him to see the way her eyes traveled over his torso in a way that was not entirely detached.

Spreading his feet wide so that she could settle between his thighs, Ronar watched the subtle shift of emotions over her features. First, she carefully washed his wounds. Then, for the second time in only three days, she pierced his flesh with a sewing needle.

He hissed, cursing beneath his breath. "I think a part of you takes pleasure in hurting me so," he jested around a sharp inhale of breath. His flesh was on fire as each pass of the thread through him set his teeth on edge.

"No man or woman could blame me," Imara muttered. Lifting her eyes from her work momentarily, she leaned in to press a soft kiss to his lips. "I am almost done."

True to her word, she made quick work of stitching up the small arrow hole and resealing the tear in his side. When it was done, a newfound weariness had settled into his bones. Had they not both been covered in muck from head to foot, he would have considered pulling her straight into the awaiting bed.

Imara moved away, cleaning her hands on the cloth and setting aside the sewing basket.

"Now may we bathe?" he asked, turning to test that the water had not lost its heat.

"Yes, now we may bathe."

Movement from the corner of his eye stole his attention, and what he saw sent his heart into a gallop.

Imara stripped the sullied clothing off of her body, revealing milk-white skin. Her fingers nimbly released her hair from the braid it was in, letting it tumble down her shoulders and back.

Ronar groaned as she approached him, his hand reaching up to cup her cheek. "As much as it pains me to say this, I'll behave. Or rather, I *must* behave. If I don't, I'm afraid I'll make a spectacle of myself."

Imara nodded. "I don't see how that is any different than usual, but very well," she murmured, rising onto her tiptoes to kiss him. "I don't think either of us are in the mood."

"Don't challenge me," he grumbled, then scooped her up into his arms and placed her in the tub. It was less about the mood and more about the state the pair of them were in. Ronar knew that Imara wouldn't entertain the idea outside of his teasing. He couldn't blame her, not after what she'd endured.

"Ronar!" she gasped. "Your wounds!"

"They are fine. I am fine," he consoled her, raising his arms to showcase he was alive and well.

"If you reopen that one more time . . ."

"I'll find another seamstress." He winked and then made quick work of his remaining clothes, discarding them on the floor in a careless heap before he joined her. Nestling behind her, he reached for a clean cloth and started to cleanse the aftermath of the battle from her.

She sighed, leaning into his gentle caresses.

Ronar took his time, lightly scrubbing away her stress and hopefully coaxing her into the mindset of comfort. When he was finished, Imara returned the favor with equal tenderness. In that moment, they didn't need to speak or tease, because there was a silent, unspoken emotion coursing between them.

After they were both clean, Ronar pulled Imara out of the tub and wrapped her in an awaiting robe. He smiled lazily, then pressed a kiss to her temple. The bed across the room called to him, begging him to rest his head and tired limbs. "Let us begin healing together," he whispered, leading her to it.

Imara crawled on top of the downy bed, peeling back the covers for them both. She scooted underneath them and turned toward Ronar. When he lowered himself onto the mattress, he reached out for her, pulling her flush against his chest. If things were to change come morning, he at least wanted this moment.

He brushed soft kisses along her nape, hoping to erase a fraction of the terror she'd witnessed. He ran his fingers over her shoulder in a feather-light touch, repeating the motion until her breathing slowed.

And as he slipped into slumber, he thought—or hoped—Imara had uttered the words he longed to hear.

Unfortunately, prior to falling asleep, Ronar hadn't thought to close the curtains. So, when the sun decided to peek through the trees and shine through the window, it was directly on his face. He cursed, slipping his hand over the mattress to feel for Imara, only to discover she wasn't there. The absence was enough to startle him into sitting up in bed.

As he glanced around the room, he still didn't find her. His brows furrowed in question, and it prompted him to hop from the bed. Snagging a spare robe, he wrapped it around his body and quickly left the room.

The lodge was silent save for the soft crackling of the main hearth. Fresh logs filled the space, and healthy, hungry flames lapped at the wood greedily. In front of it, an oversized chair sat with a blanket tossed over the side. Snatching it up, he didn't feel any lingering heat save for what came from the fireplace.

Where has she gone off to? he wondered. Perhaps she'd left already to help the villagers tend to their business, though while he thought this, he felt it was not so. Ronar's chest ached enough that he felt the need to rub at it. It felt similar to a summoning when someone used his name but sharper.

Curiously, he pressed on and ventured outside the lodge. Instead of venturing down the road, Ronar took the path toward the lake. To his surprise, Imara stood in the crisp morning air with nothing but a robe on.

"I don't suggest leaping in. For one, the water is terribly low, and you'll only end up covered in mud. Two . . . Ah, nevermind. I lost my train of thought picturing you covered in mud."

Imara laughed. It was strained, as if she were trying not to give in.

"Imara?" Ronar stepped forward, halting when she spun around to face him. Tears spilled onto her cheeks, leaving red streaks behind. "Imara! Mother . . . What is wrong?" He studied her pinched expression, and it twisted his heart. What had he done? They hadn't spoken after the bath last night, and Ronar hadn't awakened in the middle of the night to speak to her. How could he have muddled things up in his sleep? It was possible, he supposed.

Imara sucked in a ragged breath. "While you slept last night, I lay awake all night thinking over and over again." She lifted her hands, pressing her fingers against her eyes. "'What now, Imara?' I asked myself repeatedly. I was sent to you for the promise of aid, and you gave it. But you never said you wanted a wife. You've never said you wanted this. So I kept wondering what was to come of me. How easy would it be to deposit me in this . . . *Stupid* lodge and leave me behind?"

Ronar didn't budge. He remained frozen, but not impassive, as she unloaded her worries.

"And there is no way I can just continue where I left off. Not when I'm not the same, things aren't the same as they were. Amidst all of our trials, somewhere, somehow, I fell in love with you, and to think of us parting ways . . . "

"Oh, darling, no." Ronar stepped forward, his arms enfolding her. "You don't know how difficult it would be for me to leave you behind?" He pulled back and slid his hands beneath her jaw, his fingers threading through her hair. "Allow me to apologize then, for I've been an imbecile for not making it clear." A gentle smile formed on his lips, belying the beast that lay hidden beneath the surface. "It would be impossible. I could no more leave you behind anywhere than I could leave my dragon-self behind. You've woven your very essence into me, and I am a fool for you. Whether it was intended or not, I fell for you. By the sun, I've tumbled headfirst. I love you." His thumbs brushed against her cheek to wipe the tears away. "If you wanted my heart, Imara, I'd gladly give it to you."

Imara's teary eyes widened at his words. "You would?" she whispered.

"I'm many things, but not a liar." His eyebrows slanted inward, lending him a severe expression.

"No, I know. You said as much at the keep during your fever . . . But I thought it was the poison. I didn't think you wished to have me after all." Imara sniffed and looked away from him.

Ronar drew her gaze back to him. "I said what?" He rolled his eyes toward the heavens, sighing. "Then you are a foolish woman for not listening."

"You weren't coherent!"

"I meant what I said!" He laughed.

Flushing, she pulled away from his hold and hid behind one of her hands. "I didn't know. It isn't as if you were clear in your actions prior, and we haven't had time."

"But now we do. Imara, I love you, and I want nothing more than for you to be my bride. It would be a shame if your heather wasn't put to use." Ronar drew Imara's hand away from her face and tilted her head back. "We belong together."

Imara smiled, closing the distance between their lips. "For a lifetime."

"And after that. I'll find a way to you." Ronar chuckled against her mouth, drawing her against his chest as he claimed her lips once more.

EPILOGUE

The morning had dawned serene, with a faint fog rolling in off the mountaintop to cover the land in a cotton blanket. The trees of the forest seemed more tranquil than ever before, until the dusting of clouds was broken by the large form of a golden dragon lifting up from below. The great beast soared high in the air, circling the beacon that was Dragon's Keep. Below, the forest began to waken, birds chirping and small critters adventuring from their burrows as the sun's warm rays melted away the fog.

Inside the keep, life was more than astir; it was a happy frenzy of preparation as final flourishes were made to flowers, and the kitchen buzzed with activity, steam rising from bubbling pots, oven stoked with a heated fire, and the quick chopping of vegetables ringing out. Thyr was in her element, delegating duties to the hired girls from the village as they set about preparing a feast worthy of an entire kingdom rather than just a handful of intimate guests.

Upstairs in the living quarters, the lady of the house was freshly bathed and in the early stages of dressing. Beside Imara, her younger sister worked happily on massaging ointment into her arms and hands. Behind them, their mother hummed contentedly as she pinned wayward blond locks up into an ornate cascade of curls with a spray of purple heather tucked into the top.

"You're going to make a beautiful bride, Imara," Dagny whispered with pride, love shining in her eyes.

"Thank you, Mother." Their eyes met in the mirror as mother and daughter shared a private moment of unspoken words.

"I have to say, I will delight in watching Master Lajos find himself at a loss for words at the first sight of you," Sylvi declared from across the chamber, fussing with the braid that dangled over her shoulder.

"He is rarely without something to say," Imara responded, smiling fondly.

Through the reflection of the mirror, she studied Sylvi. In her time at Dragon's Keep they had become dear friends, which was a gift in its own right. Everything had changed for Imara once Ronar brought her to live at his mountain home, and now she knew such happiness that it felt as if it may overflow inside her. She had never deemed herself a sappy person. However, Imara now wanted nothing more than to see all her loved ones experience the joy she now felt.

It had not escaped Imara's attention that, in the months since the attack on Omdahl, Sylvi had been stealing glances at Mikkel, which pleased Imara to no end. If Mikkel was the one to catch Sylvi's eye, she could think of no better man suited to her.

"Well, don't look at me like that, it's far too scrutinizing for my taste," Sylvi blurted, sounding more like Ronar than anything else and shifting beneath Imara's knowing gaze.

Imara pinched her cheeks as her eyes returned to her own reflection in the mirror. "Oh, dear one, I am thinking of nothing but the wedding ceremony in a few hours. Besides, today it's all about me and—" As Imara turned around to look at Sylvi, she saw the hulking mass of a dragon soar by the window.

"Lajos . . . " Imara rolled her eyes, then laughed, which prompted the rest of the room to follow suit.

The ceremony took place outside on the vast lawns of Dragon's Keep. Those invited from the village had been ushered through a particularly safe portion of the forest. They met and gathered on seats formed by vines the bride had summoned from the earth. Besides the bride's family and the groom's household staff, the newly appointed council and their spouses, those families who had stepped up the most during the days following the battle, and a few carefully selected members of the human village made up the guest list.

When at last the bride made her way over the grassy lawn toward her lord, Sylvi's eyes were far too misted to be able to tell whether her master was speechless or not. Though deep emotions swirled in the depths of his own eyes, he did find his words as he took her hands and led her up to stand before Synda.

"So, you did not change your mind." Ronar's lips tilted upward, amusement dancing within his eyes.

"Never about this."

"My sentiments exactly." He brought her hand to his lips, kissing the knuckles tenderly.

Their attention was captured by the ancient dragon before them as she began to speak, addressing those gathered as well as the couple before her.

In truth, as the elder dragon spoke, neither the bride nor groom seemed to focus on the words.

Synda spoke of the strength and bond of a union, of the trials faced and more to come, but it was the final words that brought focus back to Imara and Ronar. "Now, repeat these words," Synda prompted, coiling three swaths of cloth around their joined hands with every word she spoke. "By destiny we are aligned, our love true and eternal. We will face challenges together and find strength in our union. By the sun, moon, and stars, our union is blessed."

In unison, Ronar and Imara echoed the vow, their eyes locked on one another's.

"By the forces that be, you are now wed." Synda bowed her head, hiding a small smile as she motioned to the cloth.

At the same time, Ronar and Imara pulled their hands away. The cloths unraveled, but as the fabric grew taut, it was clear they were bound in the middle, representing their union.

Synda stepped in, removing the cloth and holding it up to those present.

Ronar didn't need any further prompting. As he stepped forward, he curled an arm around Imara's waist and tugged her to him. He dipped his head, teasing her lips with his, then kissed her soundly. Lifting her up, he spun them around and faced the guests.

"And now, we feast because, as if winning Imara's heart wasn't a feat in of itself, she has also agreed to become the Dragon Mistress. That is cause for celebration if I do say so." He winked, then peered down at his bride, who rolled her eyes at him.

"A feat."

"Tell me it wasn't."

Inside the keep, guests raised their goblets in toast to the newlywed couple, cheering and encouraging them to kiss. A grand chaos erupted in the home, but it was a welcome one. Ronar pried himself away from Imara long enough to fill his goblet, but his gaze settled on an approaching figure. Long, braided auburn hair swung past his shoulders, and the furs he wore only added to his bulk.

Ronar drank deeply and shook his head. "Now there is a face I wasn't expecting to see. Knute," he murmured, arching a dark eyebrow. The steward of the crown wasn't a figure Ronar had anticipated being in attendance. For one, he hadn't invited him; for another, it had been a long time since they'd last spoken.

Knute approached, then bowed. "Congratulations. You've tricked a beauty into wedding you."

"Other way around, I think. But I don't recall inviting you . . . " Ronar's gaze slid from the man, then searched for Imara.

Knute laughed. "A steward hardly needs one. Besides, I'm not the only one who came without invitation."

Confusion wrinkled Ronar's brow. "Who else would think to crash my wedding day?" Knute's fair eyebrows lifted as he raised his goblet. A light touch at Ronar's elbow brought his attention to his side. Imara looked up at him in a silent question.

"I think you know." Knute bowed his head. "My lady, my deepest condolences that you're bound to this man." Knute cracked a grin.

Imara laughed, inclining her head toward him. "Thank you. It is a burden I must bear alone."

Ronar cleared his throat. "My darling, where are my manners," he interjected. "This is Knute, Lord Steward. I suggest someone guard the ale because he'll be deep in his cups before long."

"I don't think he'll be the only one." Imara eyed Ronar, then the goblet in his grasp. "That aside, who do you mean is here?"

Knute motioned toward the hall. "All bow to His Majesty and Her Majesty."

"What?" Imara whispered, clutching onto Ronar's arm. "Truly?" She turned to him with wide eyes.

"I helped him when he was a boy. It turns out he fancies us friends or something of the sort." His eyes narrowed as he lifted his finger and pointed at the approaching couple. "But if he dares to kiss you . . . " Ronar's words trailed as he bowed to the king.

Instead of the old grizzly man Imara had expected, the king was young, as was his queen. No more than thirty years of age, and his face was as smooth as marble. Keen hazel eyes raked the newlywed couple up and down. Unlike his steward, he was lean and muscled. The sides of his scalp were shaved down to skin, but the top was where his ash-blond hair was pulled back into a shoulder-length braid.

"Old friend, I'm a little put off you didn't invite us. Nonetheless, let me offer my blessings to you and your new bride." The king bowed, and his wife followed suit. "Go about being merry, the lot of you." He waved his hand toward the guests and then stepped closer to Ronar. "I have a proposition for the two of you . . . "

Ronar and Imara shared a glance with one another, then in unison, they replied, "We're listening."

King Thorne closed the gap between the two of them, lowering his voice so only they could hear. "We're in need of a new Order. After these events, it's become clear that our kingdom needs a force able to fend off magic, or others. I'd like to—"

A thunderous crash in the hall ended the king's proposal, but more than that, the entirety of the keep's celebration.

"I'm okay!" Omro's voice called out, and his body slithered along the stone floor, clumsily picking up shattered pieces of glass. He was clearly drunk, because he missed the same piece several times over.

"Blast it, you fool, leave it be!" Ronar dragged a hand

along his face and sighed. "Do continue," he prompted Thorne.

The young king looked between the newlyweds and the fallen man on the floor. He chuckled, reaching out to clap Ronar on the shoulder. "What am I thinking? No. It is your day of union. Go on, be merry. Come find me when you're ready to continue this conversation."

Ronar bowed his head, smiling. "Of course, Your Majesty. Enjoy all of what the keep has to offer you."

Imara glanced up at him. "What help does he think we can give him in this?"

He grinned down at his wife, lightly taking hold of her shoulders. "Our minds, my darling, and what we can accomplish together." He winked, then leaned down, capturing her mouth with his own. Ronar tasted the honey mead on her lips and caught the sweet fragrance that was wholly her own.

The dragon and his bride. What couldn't they accomplish together?

ACKNOWLEDGMENTS

First of all, we want to thank you for reading our story! We sincerely hope you loved it as much as we did. But did you know this book all started with a proposal? It did. Elle propositioned Christis with an offer she couldn't refuse and here we are!

Behind every successful book is a village and we want to thank our village from the bottom of our hearts.

Candace, Lou and Jenny, thank you so much for beta reading for us, and helping to shape this story into what it is. We can't thank you enough!

Meg, thank you x3000 for editing this baby for us. We may have written it, but you were the artist who polished this piece to perfection.

A special shoutout to Jacque H. for helping us proof this novel! You were an amazing help to us. Your feedback and live reactions honestly made our days brighter. Thank you, thank you, thank you!

A heartfelt thank you to all of our ARC readers. Donna, Melanie, and everyone else. You guys are amazing. We appreciate each and every one of you who took the time to read and review the Dragon's Bride!

To all of the amazing authors at Midnight Tide

Publishing, thank you for all of your support and amazing work. We are a team, never forget that!

THE OFFICIAL PLAYLIST

Want to listen along while you read and immerse yourself into the world of The Dragon's Bride? Listen to the playlist below!

1. Czerwone Jabluszko by Kapela ze Wsi Warszawa
2. The Trail by Marcin Przybylowicz
3. I Am Not Nothing by Beth Crowley
4. Sweet Little Lies by J2 ft. Midian
5. Brave Enough by Lindsey Stirling ft. Christina Perri
6. Time After Time by Joseph William Morgan
7. Far Across The Land by Eurielle
8. Strange Young Land by Hidden Citizens
9. Where The Hills Are Green by Peter Roe
10. The Song of The Stones by Trobor de Morte

ABOUT ELLE BEAUMONT

Elle Beaumont loves creating vivid and fantastical worlds. She lives in Southeastern Massachusetts with her husband and two children. When not writing or chasing around her children, she enjoys making candles. More than once she has proclaimed that coffee is the lifeblood and it is how she refrains from becoming a zombie.

Stay up to date and receive some free books by signing up for her newsletter! ellebeaumontbooks.com/newsletter

Join Elle's Facebook group and hang out with her facebook.com/groups/ElleBeaumontStreetTeam

For more information visit
www.ellebeaumontbooks.com
Follow Elle on social media!

facebook.com/ellebeaumontbooks

instagram.com/ellebeaumontbooks

ABOUT CHRISTIS CHRISTIE

Christis Christie lives on the east coast of Canada, in Nova Scotia. She gets most excited about diving into a new fantasy world while writing, but also loves a good supernatural plot. Tiss, as she is affectionately called by her friends, enjoys being creative in any way she can, so if she's not writing then she's crocheting or she's embroidering. Her favorite animal is the sloth, and her favorite retellings are anything Beauty and the Beast related.

Follow Christis on social media!

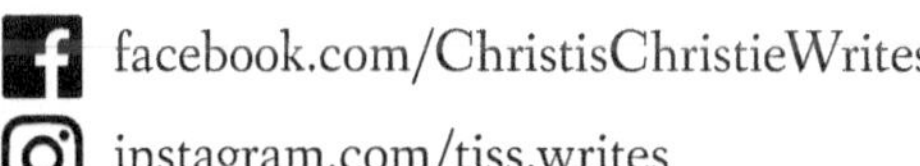

facebook.com/ChristisChristieWrites

instagram.com/tiss.writes

Immortal Realms Trilogy

Seeds of Sorrow

Tides of Torment

Wages of War

The Hunter Series

Hunter's Truce

Royal's Vow

Assassin's Gambit

Queen's Edge

Secrets of Galathea

Brotherhood

Bindings

Voice

King

Demons of Frosteria

Slaying the Frost King

Frost Mate

Frost Claim

MORE FROM CHRISTIS

Immortal Realms Trilogy

Seeds of Sorrow

Tides of Torment

Wages of War

Sanctuary of the Lost

Of Loyalties & Wreckage

Of Love & Ruin

Of Hope & Blight

Standalones

Ephesus

Spun Gold

Anthologies

Emporium of Superstition

SNEAK PEAK!

Continue reading for the first chapter of Seeds of Sorrow by Christis Christie & Elle Beaumont!

Prologue

Draven

The smells of blood and brimstone mingled on the breeze, followed by dark clouds of smoke billowing overhead as the village burned down around the three kings. Draven kicked roughly at the back of a monster feasting on the body of a young woman. When it fell onto its back, he thrust his sword into the beast's chest and slit it fully down the middle of its body. The creature's innards spilled out onto the ground, and Draven took a step back to protect his sandals from the sludge.

The moment of distraction was all that it took for another beast to catch him unawares. The sharp prick of claws digging into his back was the only warning he had before the full impact of the creature sent him staggering to the side.

The force of hitting the ground knocked the breath from his lungs, and with a harsh grunt, Draven rolled away from his attacker. The sharp drag of claws over his back seared his body with pain and shredded the red fabric of his tunic. He didn't have time to compose himself, however. Feeling the heat of the beast's breath at his nape,

Draven rolled once more and swung toward it with his sword.

The beast roared in fury as the blade sliced through the corner of its jaw, sending a hunk of flesh and bone flying through the air. Lying on his back, Draven called on his powers and turned himself invisible. Rising up onto his knees, he used the beast's confusion over where its prey had disappeared to his advantage and brought his sword down on its neck. The monstrous head thudded to the ground, spinning away from him over bloodstained grass, and the beast's body crumpled.

Panting, Draven staggered to his feet, the muscles of his back protesting every movement. Behind him, his brothers Travion and Zryan were in the midst of dispatching their own monsters. Large fur and scale-covered bodies dropping to the ground with heavy thuds. Draven looked around him quickly, noting that the last of the beasts seemed to have been put down, and any that could be had been driven back through the Veil into the dark realm they'd crawled out of.

Swiping his brow with the back of his hand, Draven smeared a patch of black blood over his forehead. He turned to his siblings and noted that the fine linen of Travion's green tunic hung in tatters; the only thing keeping it from falling to the ground was the belt around his waist. His dark auburn hair lay plastered to his head with sweat and blood—some of which appeared to be his own. However, the sparkle of victory in his blue eyes let Draven know he was okay.

Zryan, on the other hand, stood naked as the day he

was born. Running a hand through his dark brown locks, Draven's youngest brother shot him a proud smirk.

"Where are your clothes?" Draven asked, staring at him blandly.

"I shifted into a griffin. It seemed more efficient than a sword."

"Of course." In Draven's opinion, Zryan was always looking for a reason to end up naked, no matter what he was doing. Looking away from his brothers, Draven watched the humans, who were frantically trying to contain the fires as best they could. Their pitiful buckets of water did little to quell the blaze. "We should do something about that."

Travion turned to face the village. "Allow me," he grunted. Lifting his hands, Travion pulled storm clouds into the beautiful blue sky and brought a torrent of rain down on the inferno.

At first, the fire merely sputtered in agitation, continuing to lap at straw rooftops. But Travion persisted, and finally it succumbed to the intensity of his rainfall. Once it was out and nothing but lightly smoking embers remained, Travion released the clouds, and the blue sky returned. A cheer rang out from the villagers followed by many cries of thanks mixed with Travion's name.

"Of course. I bring the aid to drive back the beasts, and it's Travion who receives all the praise for a little cloud play." Zryan had come up to Draven's side, his arms crossed over his chest.

"Where credit lies is hardly of importance right now. The more important thing is what is to be done about the Veil," Draven said, eyeing Zryan.

"I'd also like to make mention that I was correct about that as well." Zryan's smirk had only grown.

"Correct about what?" Travion asked, returning to their small huddle.

"That Midniva was being overrun with creatures from Andhera. And no one wanted to believe me!"

"How were we to know? Nothing is meant to be alive in the dark realm," Travion countered.

Draven's eyes fell to the final beast he had slain. Its eyes were clouded and staring lifelessly into the distance. It was a monstrosity of a thing: a humanoid face with razor fangs hanging down over its bottom lip, all surrounded by a red mane, a muscular lion body, taloned paws, and a hard-shelled scorpion tail. Draven had never seen anything like it before, and a deep fear of what exactly was happening in the dark realm coursed through him.

"That was true in the beginning days," he began, waiting until he knew he had both Travion and Zryan's attention before continuing. "But there are rumors that Ludari banished all of his enemies to Andhera. There is a chance the lost souls unfortunate enough to have made their way into the dark realm now find themselves twisted beyond recognition." He pointed down at the beast. "I think this thing used to be a person."

His brothers froze, all eyes now on the monster.

"By the sun," Travion rasped.

"This has to be contained," Zryan followed. "Before the body count rises higher and it grows entirely out of our control." His shoulders had stiffened, and a dark frown now creased his brow. "There have been too many accounts of attacks on the humans living here. People bloodied, torn apart . . . *feasted* on."

Draven found the almost tangible unease coursing its way through his youngest brother an unnatural sight for one typically brimming with arrogance. His own features pinched together. He had seen some of the bodies himself during his trips here to the middle realm. The mortals were terrified. Fearful of moving anywhere in the dark lest they be attacked, and now it seemed even the daylight was not safe.

"And what are you suggesting?" Travion asked, looking between his brothers.

"Andhera needs a warden . . . "someone we can trust to abide by our rule and keep the monsters there in check."

Contemplating Zryan's words, Draven let his eyes fall to the hand still curled around the hilt of his sword. It was coated in dark blood and grime. Currently the hand of a warrior. His hands had been used to dole out punishment for as long as he could remember. Not always because he wanted them to but because that was what was demanded of him.

"A warden? Zryan, who could we trust with such a task? Would we not be setting up our own future aggressor? With such power behind them—" Travion began.

"What choice do we have?" Zryan growled, confidence fueling his vehemence. "If it is not Andhera rising against us later, it will be Midniva rising in rebellion *now* at our inaction to protect them."

Zryan does speak true, Draven reflected. Shifting the grip on his hilt, he considered what he was about to say, taking that extra moment to ensure he was certain before he spoke.

"I will go."

Both Zryan and Travion stilled instantly, their eyes leaving each other to focus on Draven instead, shock and rejection mingling in their gaze. He stared back at them, an eerie calmness settling over him.

"Draven—" Travion hissed, and dread rumpled his brow.

"You cannot honestly be—" said Zryan at the same time.

Draven held up his hand to silence them both. "I will go. Better a king than a warden."

Travion only sputtered, but it was Zryan, now eyeing him with contemplation, who spoke.

"You realize we do not know what will happen to you if you go? We have no understanding of the dark realm or what is happening there. Should you choose to live in the dark realm . . . "it may twist you in unimaginable ways." It was his turn to gesture at the dead beast at their feet. "You may no longer be fae, Draven, but something *other*. Something that Andhera chooses for you." Zryan paused, and their eyes locked. "There may be no coming back."

"I realize." There was only calmness and finality in Draven's voice.

"No!" Travion growled deeply, his pale, freckled face reddening. He reached forward to wrap his fingers around Draven's wrist. A motion that had been repeated hundreds of times throughout Travion's childhood, his thumb at Draven's pulse. "This is absurd, Draven." Travion's eyes looked deeply back into his, and Draven heard the unspoken words of his brother. Travion understood what he was trying to do, and he would not stand for it. "No one is saying it needs to be one of us, and no one is asking this of you. Zryan, do not encourage him in this insanity." He shot Zryan an imploring glance.

Zryan did not reply, simply continued to study Draven's features.

"If Andhera is left unchecked, then the inhabitants there will continue to plague the mortal realm until there is nothing left. Who better to claim the dark realm but one of our own? Who better to build a kingdom and enforce the laws that we would see fit?" Draven said, catching Travion's eyes once more and accepting the love and concern he found there but only letting it fuel his resolve rather than convince him to change his mind. Draven knew what he could be sacrificing, and he also knew he couldn't allow either of his brothers to take up the burden. Better he should suffer through hell than either of them. "I am aware of what may very well happen once I go, and I can accept that."

Travion moved to protest once more, but Zryan pressed a hand to his chest, silencing him before he could begin.

"Now, the only question left to settle is, when do I leave?"

SEEDS OF SORROW BY CHRISTIS CHRISTIE & ELLE BEAUMONT

If you loved the prologue, you can snag it at books2read.com/seedsofsorrow

Available in ebook and paperback

MORE BOOKS YOU'LL LOVE

If you enjoyed this story, please consider leaving a review!

Then check out more books from Midnight Tide Publishing!

**Of Flames & Curses by Whitney L.
Spradling**

Do fairies exist?

This is the question Lainey asks herself after her sister's brutal murder in Central Park. Armed with her sister's diary and the mysterious entries within, Lainey's quest for answers leads her to Phoenix, a surly but handsome fae.

The answer to Lainey's question reveals a truth that will change everything she thought she knew about herself and the world she lives in. A sacrifice must be made to break a curse that locked the gate between the human and faerie realms.

Leaving the only world she has known, Lainey finds herself surrounded by evil queens, curses, and magical creatures. Together, Lainey and Phoenix must find a way to break the curse that doesn't result in Lainey's death—like her sister's.

Available Now

Bound Island by G.D. Roman

◆Until the Knots of Avalon break.◆

Brye, Lenna, and Tara have lived their entire lives on an island surrounded by mists and protected by magical bonds. Nothing could be more perfect. Until one night, when magic begins to fray at the seams, and their lives change forever.

The Healer – Brye's healing abilities are her pride, making her the best match of the season. If only someone were interesting enough for her. Until she catches the eye of Prince Gareth, the least interesting one of all.

The Mist Maiden – Lenna has lived her life in the shadow of her sisters. Until Beltane, when her magic explodes. Now, she has been chosen to be a Mist Maiden, protector of Avalon. A role she was never destined to play.

The Warrior – Tara knows that she is meant to be more than being someone's mate. A warrior through and through, Tara strives for the extraordinary. No matter the cost. Even if that means she might have to sacrifice her growing feelings for Aiden.

As Avalon slowly becomes an island lost in the mists, will the sisters strengthen their bonds and save their home, or will they break apart forever?

Available Now

The Songs That Beckon by M.A. Brown

Their grief binds them
The Song calls them
The Darkness wants to claim them

As winter wraps Areth in its frozen embrace, nightmarish beasts descend upon the Hastings household kidnapping Mr. and Mrs. Hastings and leaving behind their daughter, Bianca, as sole witness. In the wake of their abduction her quiet world is turned upside down and shaken revealing the secrets and lies her parents have buried.

As truths unravel it binds her to those who have similarly lost. Together they must wade through the thorny tangles of growing love and grief to find those that they hold dear before the looming threat of darkness is unleashed to destroy them all.

Travel worlds in this dark, dreamy and romantic debut filled with dusty books and pining looks.

Available Now